Alison Kervin is an award-winning freelance writer and journalist who has worked as the Chief Sports Feature Writer of *The Times* newspaper and Chief Sports Interviewer of the *Daily Telegraph* newspaper.

Alison has written nine highly-acclaimed books including three previous novels, *The Wag's Diary*, *A Wag Abroad* and *Celebrity Bride*

Praise for Alison Kervin and *Wags at the World Cup*:

'Very, very funny. I loved it! Kelly Brook

'The essential summer beach read' *Glamour*

'Brilliant! Now we can all be voyeurs into the ritzy and ridiculous world of the WAG' *Daily Mail*

'This rags-to-riches-to-rags tale cannot fail to amuse everyone' *Mirror*

'Hilarious page-turner' *LOOK Magazine*

'A hilarious tale' *Closer*

'It's the sort of book you just devour. Just great. Hysterical' *Daily Mail*

'Girls, leave space in the Miu Miu beach bag for this deliciously dark cautionary tale of what happens when dreams come true' Shari Low

'One of the most eagerly anticipated books of this year . . . Fabulously funny. A very cool book' *Trashionista*

Also by Alison Kervin:

The Wag's Diary
A Wag Abroad
Celebrity Bride

WAGs

AT THE
WORLD CUP

Alison Kervin

13 5 7 9 10 8 6 4 2

Published in 2010 by Ebury Press, an imprint of Ebury Publishing
A Random House Group Company

The Random House Group Limited Reg. No. 954009

Addresses for companies within the Random House Group can be found at
www.randomhouse.co.uk

A CIP catalogue record for this book is available from the British Library

The Random House Group Limited supports The Forest Stewardship Council
(FSC), the leading international forest certification organisation. All our titles
that are printed on Greenpeace approved FSC certified paper carry the FSC
logo. Our paper procurement policy can be found at
www.rbooks.co.uk/environment

Mixed Sources
Product group from well-managed
forests and other controlled sources
www.fsc.org Cert no. TT-COC-2139
© 1996 Forest Stewardship Council
FSC

Printed in the UK by CPI Cox & Wyman, Reading RG1 8EX

ISBN 9780091932121

To buy books by your favourite authors and register for offers visit
www.rbooks.co.uk

Acknowledgements

Many thanks to everyone at Ebury, especially Gillian Green who helped me to deal with a series of increasingly tight deadlines with serenity and calmness! Thanks also to Hannah Robinson and Louise McKee for their help with the promotion of the book.

Thanks to my family and friends, particularly Charlie Bronks and Tammy Perry who made sure that I was dragged out for the occasional cup of coffee or glass of wine between chapters! Also Daniel Evans, Carmel Southons and Abi Bunney. Enormous thanks to my brother - Gareth Kervin - for being the best and most terrifying lawyer in the whole wide world. I'm so glad we're on the same side!

Thanks also to the magnificent book launch organizers – Sue Dorrington, Amie Daniels, Sarah Escott & Victoria Bower, and thanks to the WWs (wonder wags – you'll understand these terms when you've read the book) for consistently bouncing into the headlines and presenting me with such colourful theatre.

Finally thanks so much to everyone who buys the book – I hope it makes you smile!

For George Kervin-Evans
and all his little friends

England

Chapter One

9 a.m., Monday 3rd May 2010: leaping gaily around my house in Oxshott
(which is three roads along from Cheryl's house and two away from The Terrys... I keep telling Dean to get me a telescope, but he won't... he says it's pervy!).

The sun bursts through the kitchen windows and bounces across the gorgeous all-white work surfaces like Jordan on a trampoline. Honestly, it's so bright in here that you could get snow blindness. My husband Dean won't come near the place without his sunglasses on.

Not that it bothers me that much; I only come in to get Bacardi Breezers out of the fridge, and nothing – not snow blindness or a terror attack or a nuclear explosion – could ever get in the way of that. I'm usually wearing sunglasses anyway; my lovely Wag ones that cover my face completely. My daughter Paskia-Rose says they make me look like an unnaturally large and rather terrifying beetle. She's probably got a point. To be honest I sometimes scare myself when I see my bug-eyed reflection in shop windows as I pass, but my lovely Pask is missing the point. These glasses are *Wag* glasses. Coleen Rooney has been seen wearing them, Abbey Clancy owns a pair, and Alex Gerrard had them tucked into her pocket when she did that *Vogue* shoot. I tell you, if they're good enough for the queens of the Wags, they're good enough for me.

'Tell me again,' says Shiraz, appearing at the kitchen door without sunglasses, then leaping back and clutching her watering eyes in pain, 'what's Dean going to be?'

'OK, listen carefully and I'll tell you.' I fill my arms with Bacardi Breezer bottles from the fridge and follow her back into the sitting room. I wish she'd wear those great sunglasses I gave her but she won't. She doesn't wear any of the shiny pink accessories I gave her either, not even the sparkly pompom musical earrings. She's got such weird taste and yet she's a very attractive girl with perfect, peachy glowing skin and thick dark hair cut into a non-descript short style that she pushes back behind her ears. She's got a lovely figure, albeit one that is hidden behind baggy clothing most of the time, and she has these amazing big brown eyes that remind me of a dog (in the nicest way).

'He's going to be the deputy assistant, second-in-command, to the assistant defence coach in the England team,' I say. The pride is rippling off me as I speak. I still can't believe what's happened.

'Is that good?' she asks earnestly. 'Because I'll be honest, Trace, it doesn't sound all that special. It sounds like he's quite a way down the pecking order.'

'Shiraz, Shiraz, Shiraz. What are you talking about? Is it *good*? My dear, we need a whole new word for good. My husband has been chosen as a coach for the England team!! In a few weeks time I'm going to be getting on an airplane with all the other Wags and going to South Africa for the World Cup!! Don't you understand the full magnitude of this? I'm not going to be just a "Wag" any more . . . I'm going to be an "England Wag"!! "Good" doesn't begin to cover it.'

Shiraz wears an uncomfortable look of bemusement and quiet contemplation as she sits down on the sofa. My poor assistant has no idea how much this all means to me, bless her. She's been working for me for a week and she's struggling to grasp how much I love being a footballer's wife. I loved it when Dean was a player at Luton, I love it now he's a coach at Chelsea and I'm damn sure I'm going to love it when he's an England coach and I finally get the opportunity to mix with Abs'n'Col'n'Alex'n'all. (Except not Cheryl. I'm heartbroken that she won't be there. Heartbroken.)

You see, I was made to be a Wag. It means so much to me. When I first met Dean he was a junior Arsenal player scrabbling to get a place in the youth team and I was struggling to make sense of feather cuts, shags and post-shags (I was a hairdresser at the time, just in case you were wondering!). I met him, believed in him and stuck with him when he was transferred to Luton, demoted through the ranks at Luton and eventually told that his only future in football lay as a coach or a spectator. It was a tough time, but we got through it, together.

We travelled to Los Angeles when Dean landed a coaching position there, and I continued to back my husband all the way. There have been ups and lots of downs but I've always been there by his side – as consistent in my support for him as the sport has been inconsistent in its treatment of him.

Whatever happened on the pitch he could always be sure

that I would be there off the pitch – a sparkling blonde vision in pink, wearing the best hair accessories and sporting the most orange tan on all the terraces in all the world. And now, finally, Dean is on the brink of greatness and I will be there for him once again, with my gorgeous daughter Paskia firmly by my side.

I stagger towards the sofa, which is set in the middle of the sitting room in my mock-Tudor mansion. I'm wearing six-inch candy-floss pink, Marabou fringed mules and a terrifyingly short silk négligée so staggering it's as good as it gets. I plonk myself down next to my lovely, but desperately naive assistant who's dressed, as always, in a plain and unadorned tracksuit of dubious origin, and I take a large gulp. I wish Shiraz would consider getting highlights in her plain hair. She's got glossy chocolate brown hair; it would look lovely with highlights, lowlights, extensions and styling products.

'So you're quite excited then?' she says.

Er . . . yes.

Dean knew how excited I'd be. He came rushing in a couple of days ago and as soon as I heard his shiny, new Gucci shoes bounding up the stairs, I knew he had good news to impart. I just had no idea how good the news would be. He burst into my dressing room, a smile sweeping across his stubbly face and the tattoos on his biceps jumping with excitement.

I was squinting out across the Oxshott sky in the direction of the Coles' house through a pair of rather large bird-watching binoculars that I'd bought from a wildlife catalogue and had been hiding in my lingerie drawer when he burst in. I must stress that I'm not being nosy or borderline stalker-ish in any way – really, I'm not! I'm not trying to find out what's going on between her and Ashley. That's their own business. I want to know the important stuff – like whether Cheryl wears Spanx (She must, surely – no one has a waist and hips that smooth). Thankfully Dean was so excited about his news that he didn't even notice the binoculars. He just dropped to the floor next to my collection of cowboy boots (I have a lot of cowboy boots . . . way more than the average cowboy), and announced that he was in the England World Cup set-up.

'Fabio Capello called me,' Dean blurted out by way of a greeting. I have to confess that I had no idea who this Capello chap was at the time, but I could sense that he was someone important by the way in which Dean looked heavenward when he mentioned his name.

'Just repeat that again, would you?' I said, wanting to be quite clear about all this.

'I'm in the England World Cup squad,' he said proudly, thumping his chest patriotically before remembering the whole tattoo/skin graft/scar situation and retracting his hand with the speed of light while wincing in pain

'As the captain?' I asked, wide-eyed, dropping the binoculars and only just missing his head. I turned to look at him with renewed love and respect.

'No, love, not as the captain,' he replied, a look of miserable disconsolation on his face. 'Of course not as the bloody captain.'

'Oh. As a player? With Becks'n'Ash'n'Joe'n'Wayne'n' Frank? And Crouchy? And Theo? And JT? Is it? Is it?! As a player? That's brilliant. It doesn't matter that you're not the captain.'

'No, love. Oh – you're completely spoiling this for me. I wanted this to be the best news ever . Of course it's not as a player. You know I retired from playing years ago. Why would I suddenly become a player again? I'm too old . . .'

'I know!' I said, brightening, and dropping down next to my husband so we were both sitting there surrounded by cowboy boots. 'Are you the new England coach?'

'Well, kind of . . . I'm the deputy assistant, second-in-command, to the assistant defence coach' he said proudly.

'Oh. Well, that's practically like being the England coach, isn't it?' I replied supportively.

'Practically,' he agreed, as he shuffled around to get comfortable between the fine collection of milky-white and pale-pink boots. I love the pink and white cowboy boots – they remind me of marshmallows. 'But I'm not exactly the main coach, just one of the coaches.'

'Well, I'm proud of you all the same,' I told him, and that's the absolute truth. I'm always immensely proud of Dean – I think he's the most amazing, talented and lovely, decent man I've ever met, and there's not a day that goes by when I don't thank my lucky stars that he's mine. I can't begin to tell you how much I love him. He's everything to me, and I'd do anything for him. And I mean that sincerely – no sarcasm – which is rare for me.

'You're an amazing man,' I said, and I watched as his chest puffed out with pride. 'You're my hero, Dean Martin, and I can see why this Capillaries bloke has chosen you for one of the most important coaching roles in the England team.'

'Thanks love. His name's Capello actually, but don't worry about that. Are you really proud?'

'I've never been more proud of anyone or anything,' I

said. 'I just wish your nan was here now to celebrate with us. She'd have been very proud of you too.'

I casually smooth the skin on my thighs, loving the way they glow the colour of over-ripe pumpkins. The spray tanners have done me up a treat this time. An absolute treat. To the uninitiated I might look like I've been tangoed – but for a Wag they're perfect. When I first came out of the tanning place I had orange teeth, orange eyelashes and orange ears. I looked like a bloody Oompa-Loompa, I did. But after Paskia had taken to me with a scrubbing brush, a loofah, salt-scrub and then a whole can of Vim, I'm now orange in all the right places. Bless her. I can always rely on my daughter to come through for me on the things that really matter.

Anyway, back to Shiraz. 'Love, to say I'm "quite excited" might be the understatement of the century!'

'So where's Dean now?' she asks.

'He's gone off to see that Fabio bloke,' I explain. 'The man who's in charge of the team. He's called all the coaches to a meeting. I wish Dean would bloody hurry up and come back. I'm dying to hear what the plans are.' I lift my bottle of Bacardi Breezer to my shiny, glittery, unnaturally plump and surprisingly youthful cherry red lips and take a large gulp.

'I'm going to have to do a whole ton of shopping,' I tell her. 'A whole bloody ton of it and I could do with knowing when the shopping needs to be done by so I don't leave it all too late. I'm going to have to *really* shop Shiraz, *really shop*.'

'You always do,' she retorts, but she has no idea of the level of shopping I'm talking about here . . . extreme shopping skills will be required. I'm going to need at least twenty-five pairs of new, ludicrously high Gucci shoes, several pink miniskirts (about eighteen should do it), silly, wafty, impractical kaftans (thirty-two), microshorts (nineteen pairs in a range of eye-meltingly bright colours, plus nine pairs of skin-tight white ones), more cowboy boots (all colours), dozens of gloriously colourful crop tops, bikinis, dresses, Ugg boots, bags, bangles, earrings and a pile of huge sunglasses.

When I'm in that stand in South Africa I want to be more blonde, more tanned and more heavily made-up than any other Wag on the continent. I want to be wearing so much make-up that it takes three people to carry my head. I want earrings that are so heavy I get whiplash if I turn round too quickly. And I need to be properly Wag thin. 'Don't let me eat anything between now and the World Cup,' I say to Shiraz. 'Not *anything*. Understand?'

'Sure,' she says nervously. 'Shall I put that in the pink file?'

'Yes,' I say with confidence. 'Put a note in the pink file.'

I've adopted a new filing system to help Shiraz understand life as a Wag. I leave her notes every so often that outline the key attributes of, and greatest demands upon, a Wag. She keeps the notes in these pink files that I proudly presented her with. I told her that I would test her every Friday on what she'd learnt in the previous week. Last Friday, in her first test, she let herself down badly when she was unable to name three different brands of self-tanning cream. She knows how bitterly disappointed I was in her and she has vowed to do better this week, so she's taken to writing everything down.

'TRACIE MUST NOT EAT' I see her write in capital letters on the top of the page.

'Add a couple of exclamation marks,' I say.

'How many?'

Oh, for God's sake. 'Three,' I suggest, watching how she laboriously strokes her pen down the page and adds the little dot. She has her tongue out as she does so, as if performing a highly complex task.

Being thin is so important to me that I'd do anything to stay skinny. I have to be thin. I rarely eat solid foods . . . I get all the nutritional value I need from vodka, Bacardi and champagne.

When I hear stories about people like Cher having their ribs removed in order to get a tiny waist, I just think 'good on you girl!' All power to you. I know I shouldn't, and I understand why most people would think the woman was stark, staring mad, but between you and me, I totally understand why she would do that. I don't think a woman can ever be too thin or too heavily made-up.

It's been three days since Dean told me about his ascendancy to the England team and I'm not sure I've been sober since. It's been non-stop celebration. I really don't think any human being on earth has ever drunk more. We clambered out of my shoe and boot collection, with Dean remarking, as he always does, on how ridiculous it is that I have more shoes in my dressing room than there are legs in west London, while I mounted a hopelessly feeble defence – as I always do – of my indefensibly large shoe collection, before hurriedly changing the conversation back to his great news.

'You're going to be an England football coach. Yeah, let's tell everyone straight away!' I exclaimed.

'Oh, love, I forgot to say . . . you can't tell anyone yet. This is our secret. Just for the next few days, until after the weekend. The coaching team is being revealed to the public on Monday. Is that all right?'

All right? Of course it wasn't bloody all right. I'd been sworn to secrecy. Secrecy! Me? What was the point in that? I mean, what was the point in me knowing a good bit of juicy gossip if I couldn't tell anyone about it? It's pointless knowing gossip you can't share. It's like saying 'Oh, Tracie, here you are love: have a brand new Chloé handbag, a gorgeous pair of Missoni hot pants and some Marc Jacobs platforms. Oh, but you can't use them.' Eh? A fabulous piece of news that you can't share is like a skin-tight, glittery next season Matthew Williamson dress that you can't wear. Bloody pointless.

'So, can I just get this straight? Is it true that I can tell people on Monday?' I asked. I write this monthly column all about life behind the scenes as a Wag for a new magazine called *Metropolis* and I knew that my next article was due to appear in Monday's magazine. I also knew it was beyond me to write the article without mentioning my glorious news.

'You can tell a few people. We can tell Paskia now, and then tell close friends on Monday, but Tracie – don't tell everyone. The guys at the FA are really keen for the media to focus on the football this time out. They don't want the wrong sort of publicity and they don't want the Wags all over the papers all the time. There's already been a lot of football scandal hitting the newspapers recently. So keep it low key, awright love?'

The problem is I have no concept of what 'low key' means. Everything about me from my wardrobe choices to my alcohol consumption is the very opposite of low key. Dean didn't marry me because I'm low key. But I didn't want to frighten Dean, so I told him that I would just tell a few people, and I have more or less been true to that.

Now here we are on Monday, and I've told those closest to me, as promised. Dean told Paskia and I told the butcher, the pizza delivery guy and the bloke who valet parks the cars at the Queens Hotel in Chelsea (we went to dinner there, where I drank my body weight in vodka Red Bull . . . you know how it is). I've also mentioned it to every single one of my friends (including those I haven't seen for 20 years. It was quite a battle to track some of them down – thank God for Friends Reunited, Facebook and Twitter!). I've told my friends' mums, our neighbours, our old neighbours from Luton, and the bloke on directory enquiries. Then there's the baker, the milkman, the guy in Waitrose who collects the trolleys, our bank, building society, bin men . . . I also might have mentioned it to the guy who came to read the gas meter. Obviously I told the postman, Maria, our housekeeper, and her brother Marco who fled over here from Serbia after some sort of incident involving the police, three guns and a man dressed as a horse (he does our gardening now). Oh, and there was the facialist with the lovely salon at the end of the High Street. But no one else. Well, only my lovely readers who'll hear all about it when they read my column in *Metropolis* magazine this morning. Talking of which, Shiraz said I had an email from the editor.

'Where's that note from *Metropolis*, Shiraz?' I ask.

She puts down the pink file and hands me the email that she's printed out in what I'm coming to realise is her usual efficient way:

To: Tracie.Martin@wags.com
From: Barry.Claughton@metropolisgroupinc.com
Dear Tracie,
Thank you very much for your weekly 'Soccer'n'Stilettos: Wags Eye-view' article for *Metropolis* magazine. As you know, I'm a huge fan of your columns but – once again – I'm forced to write to you on the small matter of accuracy.

I understand how excited you must all be that Dean has been selected as a member of the England coaching team for the 2010 World Cup in South Africa, but it is important that we ensure that all the facts are correct even when writing about such a joyous and uplifting event. While you stated last week that Dean was 'practically the coach of the England football team', we understand from the news this morning that he has been appointed deputy assistant, second-in-command, to the assistant defence coach. Is this correct? If so, I feel we may need to offer clarification of this in your next article. Please remember, Tracie, that accuracy is the cornerstone of good journalism.

Kindest regards, and please convey our congratulations to your husband on his appointment to work with the national team, and I look forward to seeing you this week for the filming of *Soccer'n'Stilettos on TV*.
Barry Claughton
Editor-in-Chief
Metropolis Magazine Group Inc.

11 a.m.

For Christ's sake, how long is this meeting with Capello going to go on for? Dean thought he'd be there for half an hour, then he was going to pop into Chelsea's training camp just down the road from our house, and be back home by about 11am. I've called him dozens of times on his mobile, hoping to find out when he'll be home so we can have another little celebratory drink, but there's no response. None at all! All I have had from him is a text, sent about five minutes ago, to tell me that he's still with the England guys, and isn't sure when he'll be back. I tried to call him again, the minute I got the text, but his mobile was off. Off! Dean never turns his phone off. What's going on? He even leaves his phone on during the final of *X Factor*, when he's in the bath and when we're making love. (Like he says, hardly worth switching it off for a couple of minutes, is it?). He must be taking this England coaching thing very seriously if he's switched his phone off.

Without Dean being here I have no drinking buddy. Shiraz drinks nothing but strange teas, wheatgrass juice and liquidised air. Anyway, she's gone now: I've sent her off to track down some football-shaped earrings that I saw in the 'What Are They Wearing?' column of this week's *Heat*. I *have* to have them.

I hear Maria hoovering and whistling away to herself as she goes merrily through her chores. I bet Maria was a bit of a drinker in her day. She is from Serbia where all they do is drink vodka, I think. And eat sauerkraut and those bizarre little rolls stuffed with mixed minced meat. Maria made them for my daughter once and they were unbelievably disgusting. You know how when you drink some of that terrible Greek wine called Retsina it makes you gasp like a dog when it hits the back of your throat? Well, those ridiculous rolls were the same. Even Paskia, who loves eating foreign food, had to rush off to the bathroom while waving her arms around in distress.

Still, beggars can't be choosers, and any drinking buddy is better than no drinking buddy. 'Maria, Maria!' I shout, fighting to make myself heard above the combined racket of the Hoover and a Serbian folk song being whistled loudly and out of tune. It's no good, she can't hear me, so I go clip-clopping my way out into our lovely entrance hall with its highly polished, gleaming surface (all down to Maria, of course. What that woman lacks in whistling ability, she makes up for with her thoroughly professional approach to polishing of all woods). As I hit the shiny hallway in my highly impractical but terribly beautiful and rather sexy shoes, my footwear gets the better of me and I go flying into the side table, which goes scooting across the floor, ending up just a millimetre from Maria. At least it's caught her attention. She looks at the side table like it's arrived from the heavens, and even bows her head in a small prayer before spotting me in a heap on the floor.

'Switch it off!' I shout, while scrabbling to my feet and pointing at the Hoover. Maria continues to stare at me with a look that's a mix of confusion and concern. 'The Hoover! Off!' I try again.

'Hoover gone,' she says, making her way over to me in her big sturdy shoes that look as if they were designed for going down salt mines. She really is a very large woman. She's barrel-shaped, like those Russian dolls you can get with a tiny doll inside and increasingly larger dolls on the outside until you get to one large outer doll. That large, outer doll is what Maria looks like.

'What would you like to drink?' I ask her, as she helps me to my feet.

'Tea with much sugar,' she says. I know that already. My sugar bill has gone up by around a hundred pounds a week since she arrived.

'No, I mean alcoholic drinks. What alcohol would you like? We're going to have a party, Maria. A big party for the two of us so you need to tell me what you want to drink. I have every drink you could possibly want. Just say the word, and I will provide it.'

'Would be nice to have plum brandy,' she says, her little brown eyes all alight with excitement in a large round face that looks as if it's made of uncooked dough.

'Plum brandy?' I reply. Whoever heard of plum brandy? I can do Cosmopolitans, Sex on the Beach, a Comfortable Screw Against the Wall, anything with Malibu, Amaretto, Baileys, whiskey, sherry, every type of lager known to man, every type of Bacardi-based drink known to woman, Ginger Wine, Advocaat, Brandy even. Just not plum brandy. What even is plum brandy? I've heard of plum jam, but plum brandy . . . er . . . no! Anyway, I avoid alcoholic drinks with fruit in the title because they count as food and as you might remember I'm not eating food any more.

'Is there something else you like to drink?' I ask. 'Anything besides plum brandy? I have lots of choice here.'

'Maybe some grape brandy?'

Is she taking the piss?

'Would you like any sort of drink that is not a fruit-flavoured brandy?'

'Maybe vodka,' she says.

Now we're talking. I tell her to follow me, and we walk through my gorgeous sitting room and head towards the magnificent bar in the corner.

'Vodka coming up,' I tell her.

'Yes. Plum vodka?' she says.

'No, not plum vodka.'

'OK. Grape Vodka?'

'Certainly,' I reply, tipping half a pint of vodka into a glass, squeezing a handful of Paskia's grapes over the top, adding a multicoloured cocktail umbrella and handing it over to her.

She looks at me sympathetically. 'Very not usual way of making,' she says, raising her eyebrows like thick, black moustaches. To her credit, she downs the enormous drink in one almighty gulp and smiles at me. 'Lovely drink. Different. I finish hoover and polish now.'

I look into the glass and even the shattered skins from the grapes I pulped manually have been consumed. I'm filled with an overwhelming respect for my chunky housekeeper, and a huge respect for all things Serbian. I've clearly not found myself a suitable drinking buddy for the morning though, since the whistling has started up again, this time in Dean's football trophy room (there's not much to polish in there, to be honest, so it won't take her too long). I grab my mobile and decide to invite my gorgeous friends Michele (known as Mich) and Susie (known as Suse) over for the morning. They're fellow Wags (sort of) so they're definitely up for all-morning drinking. I also decide to give Maria another glass of my home-made grape vodka, just for the sheer thrill of seeing the speed at which she downs it. I summon her across the slippery floor to me, to save me having to make the treacherous journey to the trophy room myself, and place the glass into a large hand that has never troubled a manicurist. She downs it straight away. It's official: she is one of the most talented women I've ever met. She is completely wasted as a housekeeper; she should be in the circus.

11.15 a.m. *(These girls don't mess around – you invite them for a booze-up on Monday morning and they're with you before you can find a cocktail shaker.)*

The bell rings and I stand back and wait for Maria to answer the door.

'Welcome to home of Dean, Tracie and Paskia-Rose Martin,' she says. 'Mrs Martin would like to inform you that her husband will be one of the most important England coaches during the World Cup. Please to come in.'

Marvellous. Maria is a star. The woman's on the wrong side of a pint of vodka but she hasn't put a foot wrong in her delivery of our new welcome message. This is in stark contrast to Mich and Suse who don't put a foot right as they come flying across the lovely polished hallway and skidding into the kitchen like speed skaters. 'Tracccciiiieeeeee!!!!' they both squeal, hurling their arms around me. 'Come on, tell us all about it,' says Suse, reaching over and displaying inch-long nails painted in a terrifying fuchsia colour that immediately puts my teeth on edge. She grabs herself a couple of bottles, passes a couple to Mich, who's looking beyond-gorgeous in a white hot pants and white blazer combo that sets off her blindingly orange-coloured tan a treat. She's gorgeous, is Mich. She used to have thick, bouncy auburn hair but now it's full of yellow streaks and looks much better. She has a pretty oval face and lovely green cat-like eyes that are proudly bearing three pairs of false eyelashes and spadefuls of eyeshadow. We then stagger into the sitting room and sit ourselves down. When Mich takes a pew on the white sofa, her outfit matches the upholstery perfectly, making it look like the sofa's grown orange limbs. You can't see where the sofa ends and her outfit starts. It's a lovely look, to be fair.

Our sitting room is all white, much like the kitchen. I've ordered a rug with a big red rose in the middle but it's not here yet, so for now it's more like an England training kit than the playing kit. I've draped a couple of leopard-skin rugs across the floor under the 134-inch 3D flat-screen TV on the far wall because Dean was complaining that having white everywhere was starting to send him mad.

'You need to tell us everything about Dean's new job with England. I mean everything!' says Suse with an enormous smile. Suse is lovely, and far too gorgeous for that animal she's going out with. Her marriage to an ex-team mate of Dean's broke up around two years ago because of an awful three-in-a-bed betrayal. Imagine the upset and devastation you'd feel if you caught your loved one writhing around on the bed with two hot, sexy bodies? There was real heart-break to deal with, I tell you. Happily, the heartbreak wasn't Suse's because she was the one having the threesome. Surprised? I was! Usually you expect it to be the footballer, not the Wag who indulges in such disgraceful behaviour, don't you? Well, our Suse was having a ball on that hot summer's afternoon, as the light flickered through the blinds and highlighted the sweaty, writhing bodies of Pierre (B team central defender) and Didi (reserve goalkeeper). They'd come over because her husband was at a training camp. How was Suse to know he'd come back early because he missed her so much?

Anyway, the marriage broke up, Suse got custody of her wardrobe and a small dog the size of a hamster and the two of them went their separate ways. She saw Didi for a while and relished the fact that she was still with a footballer, and was full of hope that he might be able to take her back to the world of large modern housing, wall-to-wall cream carpets and walk-in wardrobes to which she'd become accustomed, but he didn't last long. Turned out he couldn't 'perform' without Pierre in the room. Now she's going out with a guy called Clive who's the hairiest man in the world. He's got a chest like a chimp. He can hardly speak, and kind of barks orders instead of talking. If he were here now, he'd say 'beer' to Suse, then she'd have to say to me, 'Trace, would you mind if Clivey had a beer?' and I always have to fight back the urge to say 'only if he asks nicely' like you do when you're talking to a four-year-old. I know that what Suse really wants is a premiership footballer whose salary exceeds the health budget of an African nation. Not sure what Clive actually does but he earns about £100 a day and he loses most of that in the pub, the betting shop and the chip shop so it would be fair to say that she has compromised a little from her image of the ideal man, though she still dresses the part of a Wag in the continuing hope of one day finding the footballer of her dreams.

The stress of the whole thing has led to Suse putting on a bit of weight, which isn't very good. Oh, sure, she looks healthier but she's perilously close to being a size 10, so she really needs to take herself in hand. She's naturally very, very pretty, with this mane of thick blonde hair and a round, soft, baby face with a snub nose, big blue eyes and the loveliest smile ever. Men adore her – I'm not sure whether it's because she looks all vulnerable and childlike or because she wears skin-tight PVC a lot of the time and has massive boobs.

Mich is gorgeous too. She's going out with a footballer, which is great, but he's a muppet who plays in some god-forsaken, inconsequential third division so we try not to mention him in polite company. I know she could do a lot better if she put her mind to it and got longer hair extensions and shorter crop tops.

'So Dean's gonna be an England coach,' I say as casually as I can, as if it's something you can just throw into a con-versation. The girls recognise the importance of the news though, and scream their appreciation. There's such a noise that Maria comes to investigate and is persuaded to indulge in another half pint of vodka. Once again, she impresses with her flawless performance. The others are stunned too, and they cheer even louder than they did for my 'Dean's gonna be an England coach' announcement.

'Let's get back to Dean, shall we?' I say, ushering the large Serbian from the room and fighting to take centre stage again.

I start to tell them about Dean's glorious role with the

team. I don't lie to them or embellish anything. These are my mates and we always talk straight to one another.

'I'm not saying that he was first choice for the highly esteemed position of deputy assistant, second-in-command, to the assistant defence coach,' I explain. 'There was this guy Andy Mackenzie who was given the job to start with. He was an assistant defence coach for Milan or something.'

'What happened to him then?' asks Suse, all bright eyed. 'Is he still involved? Is he single?'

'Neither,' I explain, and I tell them how he disappeared quite suddenly so a replacement had to be found. Dean said it was something to do with a betting scam that Andy was involved with: the guy was apparently taking money in return for making sure that certain things happened on the pitch. Apparently it was all over the papers but not in the showbiz gossip or fashion pages so I missed it. Anyway, the result was that Andy Mackenzie was out before he could unpack his kit bag and my lovely Dean was in and I couldn't be more thrilled for him. I also couldn't be more thrilled for me because I now get to go skipping through Cape Town with the Wags, all of us wearing identical lurid green and pink printed tunic tops, white shorts and cowboys boots (I have enough pairs for all of us so not to worry if one of the other Wags forget theirs).

I picture us arm in arm, singing 'Ingerland, Ingerland, Ingerland' like a bunch of navvies on the whisky. It's the stuff that dreams are made of – well, my dreams anyway. I mean, the truth is that I've been fantasising *forever* about spending sunshine-filled days chatting to Abbey Clancy about her modelling career and trading make-up tips as we while away the hours in the beauty salon wearing large pink rollers in our blonde hair extensions.

I've also had so many fantasies about going out on the town with Cheryl at night wearing two and a half pounds of deep tan-coloured make-up, and sporting lipstick in an unhealthy neon colour but I guess that's not going to happen now if the papers are to be believed. But no matter what happens with her and Ashley, no matter if Cheryl never dates another footballer, she'll still be my all-time-favourite Wag. She is the patron saint of Wagdom. I dream of being like Cheryl in so many ways. I used to love Victoria Beckham and I still do, deep down. You never forget your first love, do you? But Cheryl is my latest crush, and you know why? Because she advertises products that give you 'natural looking effects', then there has to be a note on the screen to mention all the unnatural things they've had to do to get Cheryl looking like that. I LOVE her for that.

It's like the ad she does for shampoo and conditioner in which she declares 'My hair feels stronger, full of life, replenished with a healthy shine' while tucked away in the bottom right hand corner of the screen is the statement 'styled with some natural extensions'. I love it. It brings joy and harmony to my life. It's like the advert in which Penelope Cruz states that a simple mascara will give you naturally luscious lashes that can 'reach for the stars'. Wow! You look at Penelope batting her unbelievably, crazily thick and glossy lashes, and think, really? Is it really a tube of inexpensive mascara that has created these astonishing lashes that make her look as if she has grown wings on her eyelids? Then you let your eyes drift down to the bottom of the screen and feel your heart lift with joy when you see the line which indicates that

Penelope's eyelashes are no more natural than Jordan's breasts or Anne Robinson's face. Or Cheryl's hair. Yes, I love Cheryl Cole for lots of reasons, but none more than those lines at the bottom of the screen declaring her dedication to the unnatural. And who wants natural beauty in any case? I think Cheryl Cole should be prime minister.

So, when Dean mentioned that he was in the England coaching set-up, I thought 'well done, love, I'm thrilled for you' and then began fantasising about the possible and phenomenal Wag-related consequences. I slipped into my own dream world in which I'd make Coleen my new best friend. And in my dream Abbey would be staggering down the street, clutching on to Posh and Alex as they fought to steady one another on six-inch heels after twelve and a half pints of Bacardi, eighteen bottles of champagne, fourteen vodka Red Bulls and a couple of cheeky Sambucas. I thought of *Hello!* and *OK!* magazines. I thought of the clothes I'd get to buy and the drinks I'd get to drink. I thought of the make-up, the nails, the hair extensions and the platform shoes associated with the occasion. I thought of Coleen's baby and all the fun she would have dressing it up in daft, designer outfits. I thought of orange skin, yellow hair, bags that weigh more than the average family car and shoes that cost more than the average family house. I didn't really, if I'm honest, think about Dean and his football at all after a while . . .

3 p.m.

Blimey, I'm feeling quite drunk now. My life at the moment is about varying degrees of drunkenness without a moment's sobriety linking them. That can't be good, can it? Oh, well, at least I'm not downing half pints of vodka with crushed grapes in them every ten minutes. I can't work out whether Maria really likes my efforts at grape vodka, or whether she is just being kind because I'm the boss. Certainly, she seems more than happy to drink them. The woman's been back in clutching a cloth, and preparing to polish, about five times so far today when I know what she's really after is another drink. 'Here you go, love,' I say every time, and sure enough the great lady downs the half pint and impresses us all. I dread to think what her cleaning is like today. Or her liver, for that matter. I mean, I love a drink (as you have no doubt come to realise by now) and I'm much happier being drunk than I ever am being sober (though I do try not to drink too much when Paskia's in the house), it's just that I never saw Maria as being someone who had a secret drinking ability. Big respect.

The phone rings and I dive across to answer it before Maria comes waddling in. 'Tracie Martin, wife of the England coach,' I say, winking at Suse as she claps her hands together in joy and chews on the pink pompoms that hang from her pink Juicy Couture tracksuit top. She looks adorable today, she really does. The tracksuit top, the PVC miniskirt and the long PVC boots. You can't fault Suse when it comes to Wag dressing. It's so sad that she's no longer a proper Wag.

Mich is excited too, but she doesn't have pompoms on, so she deals with her excitement by downing her bottle and looking around for some more. She doesn't have to look far – I've dragged the big cardboard box full of Bacardi Breezers in from the kitchen, and it's sitting right by her feet. There's a whole stack of WKD vodka blueberry in the corner as well, before we get started on the ever-diminishing bottles of vodka at the bar, so we should be all right for drinks for while yet. And I've got a new cocktail shaker too. Well, technically it's one of those vibrating power plate exercise machines. I ordered one when I heard that Danni Minogue swears by them for losing weight, but standing there while it shook me about was hellishly dull; I couldn't even concentrate on *Heat*. So now I just use it for shaking cocktails, and it works a treat!

'Trace, it's me, Dean,' says my husband. He doesn't sound happy.

'Hi, sweetheart. How are you? Are you all right?' I ask. 'You sound stressed.' I make a sad face expression to the girls to illustrate that there's bad news on the line, and they make sad faces back.

'The reason I'm stressed, sweetheart, is because Fabio told me to keep the fact that I'm in the coaching set-up quiet for now. He wants to announce who the coaches are at the same time as he announces the players next week.'

'But you told me I could tell people from today.'

'Yes, love, but I meant you could tell Suse and Mich, not write about it in your column and tell everyone you've ever met.'

'Oh, sorry,' I say. 'I didn't mean to cause any trouble.'

'No, I know you didn't, babe, but they are hyper-sensitive here because of what happened last time in Baden-Baden when the Wags got more publicity than the players. They want to clamp down on the Wags this year, I told you that. The England communications guy wants to come and talk to you about all this, is that OK? He says it's crucial that you understand how important it is that the Wags fall in line, and help the England team. He seems to think because you're a veteran Wag you might be able to influence the others.'

'The Football Association want to see me? They think I can help the England team?' I say, my voice rising with every syllable. I'm not sure about the 'veteran Wag' description, that just makes me sound old, but 'help the England team', yes, I'm liking that. The girls have perked up on the sofa. Suse is busy shortening her skirt by wrapping over the waistband much like we used to do when we were 14-year-old schoolgirls (little about our hopes and dreams for ourselves, our wardrobes or our general air of responsibility have changed since we were schoolgirls, to be honest).

'Yes, Tracie. He wants to see you to talk to you about what you need to do to help the England team.'

Oh. My. God.

'Suse, Mich,' I announce. 'We're gonna have to hide all this booze and make like we're proper, serious people with real lives,' I say, standing up dramatically and puffing out my not inconsiderable chest. 'My country needs me.'

Ten minutes later . . .

I hear a noise at the front door and go galloping out of the sitting room to let the England team management into our lovely home. How exciting! And more pertinently, how the hell have they got here so quickly? Perhaps they have a time machine, or a rocket, or perhaps they were holding their meeting in my garage or something? Who knows what goes on at this level of elite sport?

But before I can get anywhere near the hallway, I hear Paskia-Rose's voice bursting through the house.

'I'm home, mum,' she says.

'Oh, it's you sweetheart. I was expecting the England football team coaches and communications officers,' I say. Paskia looks at me like I might be a little mad. I notice out of the corner of my eye that Maria is piling dusters on top of her head and singing a Serbian song to the mop. Oh, dear, a vodka or seven too far.

'I didn't think you'd be back until much later, love,' I say. Paskia's been on a field trip with the school. I wasn't expecting her back until this evening. I might not have drunk quite so much if I thought she'd be home this morning. 'Come and say hi to Mich and Suse.'

I see Paskia's pretty, freckly face fall at the prospect, but she's a decent kid and so she puts her rucksack down and dutifully follows me into the sitting room. There she sees the heart-warming sight of my two closest friends, layering so much gloopy, scarlet gloss on to their unnaturally plump lips that it's starting to drip off, and is running down from their mouths in much the same way as blood might run from a vampire's lips. The look is far from attractive, and makes me think that, despite all my previously held views on make-up application, it may be that you can wear too much lip gloss.

The contrast between my daughter and my friends has never been starker. Paskia has never once worn lipstick (well, she did that time I pinned her down, sat on her and made her wear it, but that doesn't really count). She's not interested in anything to do with beauty and fashion. She has dark blonde hair that is usually in a ponytail or a plait, pale skin, freckles and a gorgeous little snub nose that's a bit like Suse's except Paskia was born with hers. While she stands there, staring at my friends, they are busy rubbing extra fake tan into their already luminous thighs in preparation for the arrival of the England football team coaching staff. I notice that Suse's G-string is now completely on show where she's hitched her skirt up so much. It's very pretty; I make a mental note to ask her where she got it from. Paskia, in direct contrast to my fabulously well-dressed friends, is wearing these daft cargo pants, trainers and a T-shirt. I love my daughter but sometimes she looks like a boy who wants to join the army.

The thing about Paskia is that she is a mathematical and linguistic genius. Her teachers appear to be stunned by her natural brilliance on a daily basis, whereas my friends Mich and Suse – well, let's be honest here – they're not geniuses of any kind. In fact, they struggle to work out how to open bottles of Bacardi Breezer unaided. Suse is twisting, biting and shaking the bottles with a look of complete bafflement on her heavily made-up face, while Pask looks on in amazement. My daughter's arms are usually full of books, and her head is full of thoughts about the Industrial Revolution and First World War poetry. She's as bright as a camera flash on a Wag's pearly white teeth. She could easily open a bottle of Bacardi Breezer unaided; she's a very practical girl is Pask. The great unfair irony is that she'd never want to do so. Life's cruel sometimes.

Pask looks at Mich as my dear friend tries a new strategy, and starts to roll the bottle vigorously between her tango-coloured thighs in a desperate attempt to warm the thing up in the hope that that will allow her to open it more easily.

'I'd better be off, I've got loads to do ... unpacking and stuff.' says Paskia, backing out of the door. 'Nice to see you again, ladies. See you soon.' We settle ourselves back down, and the conversation quickly moves on to a discussion about British foreign policy, and the continuing problems in the Middle East. Only joking! We start talking about boob jobs and, in our semi-drunken state, the three of us get our breasts out to compare size, shape and scarring. I'm delighted to reveal that it is unanimously judged that my scarring is better than Mich and Suse's and the shape of them is thought to be infinitely more 'boob-like' than the giant footballs on Suse's chest.

I've just put them away, and am still basking in the warm glow brought about by victory when the doorbell goes. The sound of the national anthem bursts through the house again (I got our doorbell ring changed from the Pussycat Dolls' 'Don't Cha' to the national anthem when Dean told me that he would be involved with the England team).

I hear Maria drop her mop, cease her interminable singing and begin padding towards the door, shrieking with laughter as she goes. Oh, God, no, the fine gentlemen of the Football Association can't be greeted by a drunk and disorderly Serbian. I almost break my neck to get to the door before she does, leaping across the sitting room and beginning to sprint towards the door with a speed more commonly associated with Usain Bolt. One of the many differences between me and Usain Bolt, though, is our footwear. I bet he never tried to run at speed in 6-inch heels across newly polished floors (well, not that he's ever admitted to publicly, as far as I'm aware). The difficulties inherent in speeding across a shiny surface in high-heeled shoes are difficulties that cannot be easily overcome. I do a short and rather inelegant dance on the spot as my legs try to move in unnatural and opposing directions, much like a baby giraffe trying to stand up for the first time, then I collapse in a heap with my legs in the air. Paskia hears the commotion and runs downstairs, past me and to the front door, which she swings open to greet the blazered communications officer of the Football Association.

'Hello. Do come in,' she says, ever so politely, and I feel a rush of pride and gratitude towards my desperately sensible and sophisticated daughter.

'Hello, love. Good to have you home,' says Dean, introducing Paskia to the officials standing beside him. But when he turns to look at them, he realises that their attention is focused elsewhere: at me, lying on the floor, legs in the air, clip-in hair extensions scattered everywhere and my sexy shoes to either side of the hallway. Their stares move from me to Maria, who has stuck the mop bucket over her head, and is running around in ever decreasing circles shouting, 'I'm a Dalek, I'm a Dalek.' This is not the way I would have planned introducing them to my home.

I'm beginning the process of attempting to stand up when a young, rather bookish man rushes over to help. 'Goodness, you OK there?' he asks, in the world's poshest accent. He flings off his jacket gallantly and lays it over my legs, presumably to protect a modesty that he wrongly assumes I have.

'I'm fine, please don't worry,' I say, staggering to my feet with the same level of grace and flexibility that led to me collapsing in the first place. I finally make it back upright, assisted all the way by this lovely young man with the ever-so slightly buck teeth and the brain-meltingly posh accent. 'I'm Oliver, by the way,' he says. 'It's an absolute pleasure to meet you.'

I shake his hand, and Paskia comes to join us. Paskia looks at Oliver and I swear I see her swoon. Meanwhile Oliver starts staring at Paskia, his eyes wide beneath his hideous and enormous 80s-style glasses. They are gawping at each other through the glaze of their respective spectacles and I swear I can see small love hearts dancing through the sky around them, as they hold each other's gaze like a couple of lovers in a 1950s movie. They stand there for what seems like an interminable amount of time. Oh, God . . . not this . . . not raging teenage hormones to deal with on top of everything else. It's been a hell of a morning, what with the drunk and delirious twenty-stone housekeeper, two highly excitable impossibly glamorous friends wearing terrifying amounts of lip gloss, and the fact that I have shown my G-string to some of the most important guys at the Football Association. Surely, my daughter is not going to fall for a guy who wears thick and unsightly glasses and has teeth like Austin Powers. Surely not.

'It's lovely to meet you,' says Oliver, taking my daughter's hand gently.

'You too,' she says with a bashful smile. 'Are you with the Football Association?'

'Yes,' he says. 'I'm helping them out. I'm at uni. How about you?'

'I'm at St Paul's. I'm in the Lower Sixth.'

'How marvellous,' says Oliver.

'Come in, please,' I instruct the men poised in the

doorway, hurrying them through, past love's young dream and into the sitting room. 'Please follow me. Don't mind her,' I say, pointing to Maria who is now dizzy, as well as drunk, and staggering into the walls.

We walk into the sitting room, where Mich and Suse have moved on from comparing breast enlargements to comparing bikini waxes. 'Or, indeed, them,' I say, as my two dear friends cover themselves up rather too late to avoid giving the surly looking communications director an eyeful of immaculately waxed flesh. 'This is Mark Gower,' says Dean, introducing me to the older chap, who is in a horrible nylon blazer that struggles to wrap itself around his rather sturdy girth. We shake hands.

'I want to have a little chat to you about what we're expecting from the wives and girlfriends this summer,' he says. 'Do you mind if I sit down?'

'Of course not,' I say. 'I'm not used to holding business meetings in my house, but as far as I'm concerned, if some-one is invited in to my home, they're more than welcome to help themselves to a seat.'

'We thought that if we spoke to you about our concern, then you might be able to help us,' Mark continues, while Mich and Suse pout at him in what even I can see is an off-putting manner. 'If you can see your way to helping us, you will be in turn helping the football team to achieve glory in the World Cup.'

I feel like saluting. Suddenly I've gone from feeding half pints of alcohol to my housekeeper, and chatting away to my girlfriends about boob jobs, to being the only person in the world who can help England win the World Cup.

'OK,' I say. 'Well, of course I'll do my best. Just explain what you need, and I'll try and help. I don't know much about football, so if you want me on the pitch, you'd probably be better off putting me in goal where I can't make too many mistakes.'

'No, Tracie, that's not what we mean. We don't need you to be on the pitch, or involved with the team in any way. In fact, the reverse is true. What we need more than anything from the Wags during this World Cup is for them to take as low a profile as possible.' He pauses. 'Now Tracie, we know you've been one of the leading Wags in the past with your column and your book. The other Wags look up to you and you're one of the women in the group who most understands how important the Wags are to the national team. I for one love your weekly columns in *Metropolis*. The trouble is that Fabio is very keen to make sure that the Wags are not all over the papers all of the time. We want to focus on the football.'

'Doesn't he enjoy my columns?' I ask. 'Lots of people do enjoy them.'

'Oh, I'm sure he does,' replies the smarmy, blazered man. 'I'm sure he enjoys them immensely, and I should emphasise to you that neither the England coach, nor indeed any of the England coaches, are being critical of you in any way. It's just that when we saw your piece in *Metropolis* this morning, it did make us worry a teeny little bit about what you planned to write in your columns leading up to, and during, the tournament, and thought it might be worth coming along today for a little chat about it. I suppose that all I'm saying is that we would prefer it if you could just run past us anything that you are thinking of writing before you send it into the magazine in the run up to the World Cup. Does that sound OK?'

'OK,' I say. 'Is that all?'

'Almost all,' says Mark. 'There's also the issue of what other sort of media work you want to do. Do you have any plans for further columns, TV work or for newspaper interviews?'

'No,' I say. 'Well, I don't think so. I hadn't really thought about it. Is it going to be a problem?' Shit. I had planned to be on every newspaper gossip page, and every magazine cover that'd have me by the end of the tournament . . . not for me, of course, but in order to help raise my lovely husband's profile.

'What about that TV thing you're doing,' says Mich, much to my horror. I think she can see the anguish written on my face because she withdraws her ill-advised comment as fast as she makes it. 'Nothing,' she says quickly. 'Just ignore me.'

'No, do carry on,' says Mark. 'Are you planning to go on to one of the TV shows or something, Tracie? Not another season of *Wags Boutique* or *Wags In South Africa*, is it?'

'What's this?' asks Dean.

Fuck.

'It's nothing, honestly,' I say, trying to reassure them. 'It's not *Wags Boutique* or that other one, it's just that *Metropolis* is planning to set up a TV station in October, and they are putting together a few pilots to show to backers what they're capable of in order to try and get funding for it. I offered to make a show for them about my life, just to help them out. But it's never going to be shown on TV, so there's really nothing to worry about.'

'Right,' says Mark. 'Well, that seems harmless enough, but all the same I'd much prefer it if you didn't do the show, just in case. Fabio would be much happier if you just kept away from any TV work for the time being. Is that OK?'

'Sure,' I say because Dean is staring at me and I don't feel I can possibly say anything else, but I am worried about letting *Metropolis* down at such short notice. They must have asked me whether I'll come in and do it about twenty times, and I keep reassuring them that yes, I definitely will do it. They have my word, and I never go back on my word. Shit. This is quite a difficult position.

'Well, that all seems to be sorted then. Tracie won't be doing any newspaper or magazine columns without letting us see them first, and she'll cancel this television pilot just to be completely on the safe side. That sounds perfect, Tracie.' Mark nods enthusiastically as he speaks, as does Dean, presumably feeling relieved that things appear to be sorted out. 'I know it might seem like we're being petty and controlling, but one thing that those of us who have worked in elite-level sport for a long time realise is that every little detail counts. It does matter what impression is given of the team, whether that be from the players themselves, the coaches or their loved ones. Everything matters at this level – what hotel you're staying in, how much fitness and altitude preparation work you do, what you eat, and the support you get from your loved ones. The last thing we want in this World Cup is for what happened last time,' he says. 'Baden-Baden was a complete mess up as far as the Wags are concerned.'

'Excuse me?' I say. He's completely lost me now. For me, and for other wise and worldly Wags, Baden-Baden was the very height of greatness. It was, to the Wags, what 1966 was to the players. Mark saying that he doesn't want a repeat of Baden-Baden is like me telling the players that I do not want to see a repeat of 1966. It is totally insulting to Wags everywhere. How dare he?

'Sir,' I say, rising to my feet, while Dean looks on, quite petrified. 'How can you possibly say that Baden-Baden was anything other than a triumph of unprecedented, super-human proportions? The Wags came into their very own on that wonderful adventure. They spent more on sunglasses in an afternoon than Donald Trump spends on hair dye in a lifetime. They bought more pairs of skin-tight hot pants than you have hairs on your chest.' I'm on a roll now. 'They were astonishing. Magnificent. Peerless. They were the stars of the tournament. To be honest with you, I can't under-stand why the Wags didn't have a float through the centre of London when they returned from that trip. Why was there not a gathering of hundreds of thousands in Leicester Square to see them arrive home? Why was there no reception at Buckingham Palace and no invitation to tea with the prime minister?' I pause for emphasis. 'I'll tell you why . . . because the men let them down. The Wags could have done no more – if they'd drunk a drop more alcohol they would have ended up in hospital. Yet, while they were playing a blinder, what were the footballers doing? Playing like blind men, that's what.'

'Very amusing,' says Mark. 'But I think you'll find plenty of people who will say that the Wags had a very negative impact on the players at the last World Cup. Some might say that the wives were to blame for England's early departure.'

'What?? How can you say that? The Wags spent the

2006 World Cup parading through the streets of Baden-Baden in ludicrously short skirts and unfeasibly high shoes. Their minds were focused on the purchase of glittery hair accessories. They weren't responsible for the national team's defensive strategies, nor were they working on ball skills. That was your job. They were too busy spray-tanning themselves to a ludicrous shade of orange and drinking frightening amounts of Bacardi to contemplate playing formations. That was your job. In Baden-Baden the Wags drank more Cristal than should reasonably be drunk in a lifetime. That's what they did and, if I may say, they did it very well. You, on the other hand, did not do your job well. Do not ever tell me that the tournament was anything other than a tremendous success for the Wags. The Wags did brilliantly, and should be applauded. It was the players who let them down. Is that clear?'

There is a rather deathly silence, and a considerable amount of confusion flickering across the faces of those in my rather pathetic audience. Mark, in particular, looks dazzled by the force of my logic. Fuck him ... I'm going to do that TV show on Wednesday whether he likes it or not. I can't pull out on them now just because some bigwig in a blazer has got his Y-fronts in a twist.

6 p.m.

'Mum, have you got a minute?' asks Paskia, bounding into my office and sitting down on the St George's Cross bean-bag next to my 'Wags hair and weights' wall-chart (I like to keep a track of everything that the other Wags are up to. It's not stalking – it's 'research').

'Sure,' I say.

'Can you do me a massive favour?'

'Anything darling, anything at all,' I reply.

'Well, I just wondered whether you could try really hard not to make a big thing about Daddy's England coaching job. I think the guys at the FA are serious about it all. They really don't want the Wags to get loads of publicity.'

'OK, sweetheart,' I say. 'But why are *you* so bothered about it?'

'I just think it would make life easier for Daddy if we all kept ourselves out of the papers and magazines as much as possible. And by "we", I mean you.'

'I told the guys from the FA today, I'll make sure that anything I write goes through their communications department first so they have the chance to check things and make sure they're happy. I can't do any more than that.'

'No, I know. That would be great. I just think we should do our best to get on with these guys from the FA because Daddy would really like that and it will make things easier for all of us when we get out to South Africa,' she responds.

'True,' I say, 'but would this sudden interest in doing all we can to get on with the FA be because of a certain Oliver?' I notice how my lovely, freshly scrubbed daughter turns the colour of strawberry lip gloss at the mention of his name.

'No, I'm just trying to help,' she says. 'Although Oliver is nice, isn't he? We had a nice chat while you were talking to the FA men. He's going to be in South Africa you know ... based with the players. We'll probably bump into him when we go to the matches.'

'I'm sure we will,' I say, while Paskia continues to smile and blush.

Dean had filled me in on Oliver and it turns out he's the son of Richard Kenton-Smythe, the Chief Executive of the Football Association. He is studying at Oxford University, and is doing a work placement with the communications department thanks to some interference from his dad. Paskia, who loves football as much as Dean, thinks the combination of a leading university and the Football Association is about as exciting as it gets.

'I think that Oliver will do very well, don't you?' she says. 'He really seems to know what he's talking about, and he comes over as being very professional for someone who has only just finished his first year at university.'

When she talks about him, it is with a voice that sounds nothing like hers. She is gone all Marilyn Monroe on me. How peculiar.

'He's studying maths, you know,' she says, giggling a little and smiling a lot. To her, a guy studying maths at Oxford is a real turn-on. When I was her age I looked for a guy with a car, a leather jacket and a nice arse. Sometimes, I don't know where I went wrong with Paskia.

'You know that's what I want to do, don't you?' she says. 'Studying maths at Oxford would be an absolute dream. It's amazing that Oliver is doing just that . . . I don't know anyone else who wants to study maths – most of my friends want to do media studies, American studies or poncey things like that. You know he was really impressed when I told him that I was at St Paul's Girls' School.'

'I bet he was, love,' I say, while I'm thinking: what happened to the days when a guy would be impressed by a girl's legs or boob size?

'Do you think I'll end up getting to see him before we go to South Africa?' she asks.

'Of course you'll see him, you're bound to. I'm sure there'll be lots of social functions before the team leaves, and your father will no doubt invite you to anything organised at the FA.'

'Yes,' she says, all dreamily. I've not seen her this excited since she's was invited to that lecture on Pythagoras' Theorem. She's still standing there, it is most unlike her; she usually comes in, says what she has to say, and then rushes off somewhere to read something or learn something else.

'Is that all you wanted, love? So you want me to make sure that I don't get myself into the papers and magazines. If that's all you're worried about, then you can stop worrying right now.'

'Thanks, Mum,' she says and I swear she skips out of the room like a four-year-old going to her best friend's birthday party. My tomboy daughter with a passion for all things academic has fallen in love. Who'd have predicted it?

To: Tracie.Martin@wags.com
From: Barry.Claughton@metropolisgroupinc.com
Dear Tracie,
I understand that you have just spoken to Alex Butts, our creative director, about coming in on Wednesday to film *Soccer'n'Stilettos on TV*. If you have any queries about this, please let me know.

We are very excited about our move into local broadcasting and are all extremely grateful to you for offering to do this. As you know, this is a pilot show so it is a chance for us to experiment, and to have fun thinking of different ways in which we can potentially bring the regular features of the magazine to a wider audience via television.

There is no need to get dressed up for the show, just come along as you are. Be yourself and everything will work out fine. Thanks again for agreeing to be part of the future of the magazine.

Kindest regards,

Barry Claughton

Editor-in-Chief

Metropolis Magazine Group Inc.

Chapter Two

Following a day spent getting over the most ferocious hangover since the Wags invaded Baden-Baden, I'm now in my office, preparing to spend the day helping someone out by filming a TV show that will never be aired. How ridiculous is that? More ridiculous still, I'm doing it secretly as it's against the wishes of my family and the entire staff of the FA and the England football team. It's hard to see how this can end well . . .

Before doing anything else, I should probably tell you a little bit about my office. I say office because that's what Paskia and Dean call it but I like to think of it as my underground Cabinet Wag Room. I didn't want to tell you too much about it before in case you thought I was a crazy, mad stalker or something like that. You have to realise that I'm not at all. I admit that I look through binoculars towards Cheryl Cole's house every night, and I did see them putting in a new swimming pool one time, but that doesn't make me a stalker. In fact I've never seen Cheryl in her house (or in her swimming pool for that matter). The only time I've ever seen her away from Chelsea, where Dean is one of the assistant defence coaches and where Ashley is a player, was that time I followed her back from a match and went a bit too close to her car. It wasn't so much that I crashed into her as lost concentration for a second. Either way, I got to spend some quality one-on-one time with her while we exchanged insurance details.

So, anyway, my lovely underground Cabinet Wag Room . . . it is the business! It really is a magnificent place, situated beneath the house so that if we ever got bombed, it would survive. In fact, if we did get bombed, and we all rushed down there for safety, we would all be absolutely fine for weeks because I've got a great big cabinet full of booze down there. It's named the Cabinet Wag Room partially out of respect for the Cabinet that actually contains the booze, but there's also another reason. Have you ever heard of a guy called Winston Churchill? Well, I didn't really know who he was until I watched this film about him (Dean insisted. When he became one of the Chelsea coaches the power went straight to his head and he started researching all the country's great leaders to see what he could learn from them – Churchill was one such leader).

He was prime minister during the war, and he had this underground Cabinet War Room, and as I was watching the programme I developed this ache inside, this yearning to have an underground operations room just like his, so I had my Wag room built underground, just like Churchill's.

I have copied a few things from this guy actually. I loved the way that he had a map of Europe and put plastic soldiers, aeroplanes and boats on it to indicate where all his troops and enemy troops were stationed. Then he had a collection of officers in sharp uniforms moving the troops about to reflect real troop movements around the world.

It was awesome; he knew at a glance where all his soldiers were.

Well, I've done the same with a map of England, on to which I've put England's finest clothes shops, and I update things when the new shoes, handbags and clothing are being delivered. I then know where the latest Chloé handbag can be found and where those hard to find sequined, bobble hats with fairies on the side are.

As well as the Wag room being a valuable collection point for useful information about the world of fashion and beauty, it is also designed for the studying of Wags. Let me run through what we have here. I have little dolls representing the Wags on a second map. The little Wag dolls sit happily next to little Subbuteo men who represent their footballer husbands. I've had to do a certain amount of swapping the Wags around with the footballers recently, as you can imagine. It's been hellishly busy in the Oxshott area of the map.

The walls are dedicated to Wags, with four Wags featured on each wall (the walls are divided into quarters for this purpose). Look in any quarter wall space and you will everything you need to know about that particular Wag.

For example, want to know what Abbey Clancy's waist size is? Look at the huge Abbey Clancy quarter and you will see that according to my in-depth research (whatever I have been able to discover from the glossy magazines and tabloids) my best estimate is that she delights in a twenty-inch waist. Wonder when Coleen last got her hair done? Wonder no more. Look at the Coleen wall, and there you will see a rough diary of her beauty and fashion movements based on the spotted column in *Heat* magazine, what Mich has managed to glean from her best friend Donna, who lives near the Rooneys, and what it says in the *Sun*.

Keeping this up to date with all Wag movements, and Wag information, is a full-time job. And it was for that reason that I employed the very lovely but very un-Wag-like Shiraz. She's the daughter of Phil, this guy who once played with Dean. Apparently Phil spoke to Dean about whether we knew of any jobs going because Shiraz had been made redundant from her office job. Dean asked me if I needed anyone to help out around the house and I said 'hell yes!' I love staff. The more the better.

She arrived at the beginning of last week and she's a delight. A lovely girl. The only thing that's a bit odd about her is that she's madly into exercise classes like yoga and Pilates and rubbish like that. I keep saying to her, 'You're never going to meet a footballer of your own in bloody ashtanga and wangtanga and all the rest of them,' but she doesn't seem to be that bothered about finding a footballer. All she wants to do is go to fitness classes, so I give her an hour and a half off at lunch time so she can go and put her toes up her nose or whatever the hell it is they do in those classes, then she comes back and keeps the Cabinet Wag Room up-to-date.

'All right, Shiraz?' I say, as she comes in to collect her deep pink file.

'Yes, I'm great. Thanks, Trace,' she replies.

Good girl. She smells divine today and I know instantly why. She's wearing Wag-scent, a perfume I created myself by mixing the scents of Alex Gerrard, Coleen Rooney and the Beckhams all together. Mmmmm . . . it's delicious.

Dean says it smells like a particularly sugary and unpleasant air-freshener but he's a man so what does he know? And he's missing the point – the primary reason for my new Wag-tastic scent is not its cloying artificial smell but its links to all the country's leading Wags.

I look at Shiraz sitting there and realise that she's covered in so much of my homemade perfume that she is practically wet.

'I'm off now, but good luck with the computer,' I say. I've asked her to create a spreadsheet of Wag weight fluctuations during the week while I'm out. Every time I try to do it myself I run into little technical hitches (i.e. I've broken three computers).

'See you later,' I say, and she smiles warmly.

I'm mindful of the advice from the TV guys that there's really no need to get dressed up today, but all the same I am more dressed up than most people are on their wedding day. I have my lovely bright pink and black zebra print dress on, with matching bright pink boots and these great, shocking pink earrings that I designed for the great accessories shop Glitzy Girlz soon after Dean joined Chelsea. Glitzy Girlz decided to do a range of Wag-related jewellery and I was the only one willing to do it for practically nothing, so I did the designing which, even though I do say so myself, was an absolute triumph. Coleen may have Argos sewn up but I've got the cheaper end of the market to myself. I tried to capture the heart of Waggishness in my designs, so I kept everything pink and fluffy, but reflected the brashness of the Wags in the gaudy design and sheer size. For example, if you take the earrings I'm wearing today, you might say that if they were a little smaller (like six inches smaller) they would be the sort of earrings that any woman might wear. But given their huge, shoulder-touching size, and the fact that they are moulded out of plastic, you'd have to admit that it is only hard-core Wags – and blind people – who would ever think about wearing them.

I arrive at the studio bang on time, with Mich and Suse in tow. We've had to get a taxi, because Mich was too drunk to drive. She turned up at 11 a.m, having picked up Suse on route, and the two of them fell into the house in a terrible state, scaring poor Shiraz half to death. I was the only one fit to drive, but there was no way I could drive in these enormous platform boots so we called a cab. Mich and Suse were dead impressed with my professionalism. Even now, they still can't believe that it's nearly midday and I haven't had a drink yet. They cannot work out what is driving me to behave in this unusual manner.

'I just thought it would be better all round if I didn't go on the television drunk,' I say, and I can see the confusion written across both of their faces. Perhaps I am being a little strange; I *am* a bit nervous. I lean over and help myself to a swig of Suse's vodka. The sharp taste hits the back of my throat, and I feel instantly more alert, confident and articulate. I take a couple more swigs before getting out of the taxi.

'Morning, Tracie. Thank you so much for coming,' says some guy called Matt who meets us at the entrance to the TV studios. 'You look amazing,' he says, regarding my back-combed hair that's like a luxurious mane around my painted face with nothing short of wonder and delight. 'I

didn't know they'd asked you to ham it up. That's just perfect. Wonderful in fact. You're like a living Barbie doll. Wow!'

'No problem,' I say, turning to shrug at Mich and Suse. Who's hamming what up?

Suse is dancing around a little on the spot, which can only mean one of two things. Either she is desperate to go to the toilet, or she's wearing that uncomfortable G-string again: the one that disappears into unmentionable places all the time.

'Follow me,' says Matt, as he leads me into a dusty old TV studio that has camera cables rolled across the floor and in piles all over the place. They look like yellow snakes. I step over them as carefully as I can, making sure I don't catch the heel of my boot around one of them. As I step gingerly, there is an enormous racket from behind, followed by an inordinate amount of giggling. Mich and Suse have tangled themselves up and fallen in a heap.

'Oh, heavens,' says Matt, rushing to help them.

'I'm Alex,' says another guy, who's much older than Matt. He looks like a mad artist or something, in a brown smock over white three-quarter-length trousers. His hair is gelled back and he's wearing a cravat around his neck. When he shakes hands, he reveals an astonishingly weak and weedy handshake.

'I am the creative director,' he says, waving his hands around as he speaks. Is this guy for real? I've done a bit of TV before, and all the people I've met have been quite normal and down-to-earth. I've been on the lovely Lorraine Kelly's show, for God's sake, and you don't get much more professional than that. I never saw one cravat and I certainly never saw a tunic top when I was on *LK Today*. Not on a man anyway. And all the male crew members knew how to shake hands properly as well.

'Before we start, Tracie, I wonder whether you'd mind improvising a little, so I get a sense of the mood and creative direction.'

'Eh?'

'Perhaps you could tell us, to start with, how you first met Dean.'

'Oh, right,' I say. I'm starting to wonder whether this was such a good idea. I thought it would be a fun day out but Mich and Suse are having their wounds treated while I'm being asked to improvise creatively by some nonce who thinks he's Van Gogh. Still, I'm always one to rise to a challenge, so I give it a go.

'I met Dean when he came into my hairdressing salon,' I explain, adding rather unnecessarily. 'I was a hairdresser back then.'

I tell the camera that Dean was a teenage Arsenal player who was a real man about town, and everyone fancied him. I was just this budding hairdresser with nothing to offer but my sweet personality and natural – well, Dean thought so – good looks. Looking back, it was a match made in heaven. I had everything a footballer could ever want, and he earned a fortune and didn't have to work very much so could spend loads of time buying me things. What could be more perfect than that?

I look up, and Alex is nodding in a way that makes me feel that he wants me to continue. He's clearly not going to ask me any questions – he just looks at me as if he's looking straight through me and into my soul as I sit there, fiddling with the ring I designed for my Glitzy Girlz range, until it falls apart in my hand. Shit.

'Our first date was good, shall I tell you about that?' I ask. Alex nods and bows like a Chinese man.

'Well, our first date ended up being at the zoo,' I explain. 'You know, the place where they have lots of animals in cages and stuff.'

Alex nods and urges me to continue.

'I'm only explaining what I mean by "zoo" because when Dean called me and said, "hey, babes. How about we go on a date to the zoo?" I immediately thought he meant " The Zoo", as in London's trendiest nightclub.

'I had visions of being in the VIP area with lots of footballers, a bunch of scantily clad soap stars and a magnum of champagne, and he clearly had visions of us going to see a bunch of animals waddling around and glaring at us through the bars of their cages. If I'd realised what sort of day he was planning to take me on, I'd probably never have gone. So it's good sometimes that these misunderstandings take place.

'Anyway, my Dean told me that he would pick me up at three o'clock in the afternoon. Looking back, that's when my concern should have registered. I think you'll agree with me when I say that three o'clock on a Sunday afternoon is not when most people go to celebrity hang-out-type nightclubs to drink Cristal with footballers, soap stars and some of the blokes who've been mildly successful on *X Factor*.

'The thing is though, and in my defence, I was used to going to a great club called The Church in Clapham on a Sunday afternoon. Me and the girls would turn up there midday on Sunday, dressed like Barbie dolls and scouring the room for footballers. We'd be hammered by three o'clock, snogging all manner of inappropriate men (who were usually pretending to be footballers in order to get the snogs in the first place) by six o'clock, and we would be on the bus home clutching kebabs and chips by half past seven. So I suppose that when Dean started talking about a nightclub in the afternoon, it didn't strike me as that completely barking mad.

'I got ready like I always get ready, taking approximately three hours to slip myself into a tiny weenie little pink Lycra dress and matching thigh-length boots, before fanning my hair out so that it stood out from my head and covering my face in so much make-up that you couldn't see what I actually look like. Finally, I put on earrings that were so large that my ears in danger of being stretched to my shoulders.

'I'd say that I'd pretty much managed to nail a look that would be perfect in a lively nightclub with a young Arsenal footballer on my arm. It was an image, however, that looked utterly absurd for walking round a zoo in the afternoon.

'Dean, bless him, never even commented when he saw me standing at the door, dressed like a Page Three Girl on the pull. "Jump in the motor," he said, failing to realise that jumping was something I was significantly unable to do in the tiny weenie dress and the long, long marshmallow-coloured boots. Other things I was significantly unable to do were walking, standing, sitting down without showing my bottom, and bending over at all. These were all things that one needed to do if one was to fully enjoy a day at the zoo.

'Dean has always been the most patient and kind man in the world, and I don't think he's ever criticised me for the way I've dressed, but even he – on that auspicious afternoon in Regent's Park – squealed like a girl who's smudged her nail varnish when he saw me bend over to read the sign about the animals.

"'Knickers!' he announced, which rather confused me, I have to say, because I wasn't wearing any.

"'I'll make sure I don't bend down any more," I promised, and Dean gave me a big hug. The thing was, I was only bending over the sign to try and work out what animals were there. They all look the same to me, whether they're otters or weasels or badgers or stoats or whatever. How the hell does Dean know the difference between a chipmunk and a weasel?

"'I've no idea which animal is which," I told him. "How do people know? Like, what's that?"

"'What do you mean 'what's that'?", he asked me. "Tracie, you know what that is, surely. Everyone knows what penguins look like."

"'Oh, are they penguins? I didn't know that, Dean. Why have they got some penguins over here, but they keep the fat penguins over there."

"'No, love, all the penguins are here," he said.

'I grabbed his arm, making him follow me as I clomped back over to the other side of the zoo, where I had seen fat penguins playing together earlier. I didn't want Dean to think I was stupid; I needed to show him the fat penguins.

"'There you are," I said proudly, when we'd reached the fat penguin enclosure. "Look at them. If they're not fat penguins, then what on earth are they?"

"'God, Trace, are you being serious? Are you telling me that you think they're fat penguins?"

'"Yes," I said swiftly, refusing to be put off. "What else could they possibly be?"

'"They're koala bears, love," he said, looking at me like I was ever so slightly nuts. "They're koala bears. Please tell me that you've heard of koala bears."

'"I have now," I said.'

I look over at Alex, who has clearly been struck dumb by my story.

'You're a very good talker,' he says. 'Have you done TV before?'

I tell him that I've done a few pieces, including *LK Today*, which was clearly the highlight.

'I think you could be a huge TV star . . . huge . . . really massive,' he says, more to himself than to anyone else.

I look over at Mich and Suse, expecting them to be as thrilled and excited as I am by the news that I'm a natural television star but they just look up at me from their position on the floor. 'You thought koalas were fat penguins?' says Suse. 'Christ, I don't feel so bad about getting cows and ducks muddled up now.'

Alex is looking through his notes and chewing his pen. 'Is there any chance that you could come back tomorrow, Tracie, and do another show for us? I really think I could make you into a little TV star.'

'I can't be a TV star. You said none of this would be broadcast,' I say. 'You see, I promised the England football team I wouldn't be on TV.'

'I understand that,' says Alex. 'I meant just as material for our pilot. The better the material we have, the greater our chances of getting backing for the channel. Please, Tracie, can you help us? I beg of you. *Please*.'

'OK,' I say, thinking how nice it is to be wanted – even by a man in a smock. 'That should be fine. Dean is busy altitude training with the other coaches tomorrow anyway.'

'Altitude training?' says Alex. Matt stands by his side, looking equally puzzled.

'Yes,' I explain. 'The team is going to be playing at altitude when they get to South Africa, so the coaches are going along tomorrow to meet some altitude training experts. Then they're off to Austria for a week before the World Cup starts, living in a mountain resort in the Alps where the altitude's major or something.'

'Right, altitude training . . . interesting,' says Alex . 'Do you know what that will involve?'

'Cycling on a bicycle in a sauna with an oxygen mask on, from what Dean's told me.' I say.

It looks like Alex and Matt have died and gone to heaven. 'That's fascinating,' says Alex. 'Absolutely fascinating. Listen, is there any chance you could come back here at ten o'clock tomorrow morning?'

'Yes, of course,' I say. 'Mich and Suse, is that OK for you?'

'Of course,' they chorus, sounding incredibly drunk now. 'Fine for us.'

That evening I head up to my bedroom, alone. Dean has had to go to a Chelsea Football Club end of season coaches' dinner. 'It's a boys' night,' he says. If I were married to any other footballing man in the world, I'd be worried that 'boys' night' meant wild sex with untamed strippers, cocaine, lap dancing and lurid newspaper headlines all week, but not Dean. He's one of the good guys. I trust him with my life.

He's my heart and soul and I know more than I know anything else in this world, that he'd never let me down. Not ever!

I walk up to my bed, and I see a heart-shaped, pink, Post-it note on the bedpost. It says: *Tracie, I love you more than words can say. Dean xx.* I feel tears pricking at the backs of my eyes. God, I'm lucky to have found that man.

Chapter Three

To: Shiraz@yogalovers.com
From: Tracie.Martin@wags.com
Dear Shiraz,
I'm going to be out again this morning doing some more
pilot TV shows (don't tell Paskia). While I'm away, please
study this list carefully, learn off by heart and put it in your
pink file for safe-keeping. It's important that we step up
your Wag education before we all go to Cape Town.
Hopefully it will help you to understand a little more
about my way of life. It's really not that complicated, but
PLEASE concentrate hard. Try and stop thinking about
the lotus position and focus on this.
1. *Wonder-Wags* – this is the name given to Wags whose
husbands play for the England team. They are usually
known by their first names alone, and develop public
images of their own (often bigger than their partners),
e.g. Alex, Abbey, Coleen, Cheryl and Victoria. (Note:
Cheryl may be on her way to achieving international
superstardom but it is her Wag achievements that are
important!).
2. *Waggery* – the process of being like a Wag. So, if I say
that something was done with 'good Waggery', it means it

was done in a manner that we Wags would approve of (i.e. done while drunk, and wearing pink, most likely).

3. *WIW* – Wags in waiting, i.e. girls who wish to be Wags and therefore trawl nightclubs in search of footballers. Their only criterion is that the guy must play football. It doesn't matter what he looks like, sounds like, behaves like, dresses like, as long as he plays football.

4. *SWAG* – single wife or girlfriend. This is a difficult term to grasp, but it means someone who's obviously destined to be a Wag but right now is between footballers. Slightly different to a WIW who is way more desperate and predatory.

5. *MAG* – Mother and girlfriend of a footballer.

6. *SAD* – sons and daughters of a footballer.

7. *SHAG* – a girl who isn't a Wag and doesn't have proper relationships with footballers, but makes herself available to footballers for the price of a couple of glasses of champagne and a lift home.

8. *BRAG* – what the Shag will threaten to do in the papers the next day unless the footballer pays her £1 million.

9. *GAG* – the restraining order that the footballer will end up having to get in order to keep the bragging shag gagged.

Also, while I'm away today, could you forward the following email to Carla at Glitzy Girlz (<u>Carla_Cresta@GlitzyGirlz.com</u>) for me from my email account? Keep sending it every few hours until she says 'yes'. Carla's the head of the Celebrity Product ranges.

Hi Carla, it's Tracie Martin here. I wondered whether you'd had the chance to think about my jewellery range, and whether you would like me to design some more jewellery for you. You may remember that when we started, I just designed a couple of pieces, but now I wonder whether you would like me to design some more, since the range I designed was clearly lovely. Please let me know.

With lots of love,

Tracie Martin *(wife of Dean Martin, the England team's deputy assistant, second-in-command, to the assistant defence coach).*

PS We'll be heading off to South Africa this summer where I'll be spending lots of time with the other Wags.

I decide to drive to the film studio this morning and am flattered to see that Alex and Matt are both there to greet us. We feel like celebrities arriving at the stage door.

'Listen, Tracie, we have a bit of a favour to ask you?' says Matt as soon as we stumble out of the car.

'You look lovely today, by the way,' chips in Alex. 'Really ... all of you .... very lovely.'

The girls giggle appreciatively, and Matt continues to outline the favour he's after.

'We thought that it might be fun to look at the whole issue of altitude training,' he says. 'You know, as the players are going to be doing it, it might make a fun thing if we had the Wags doing it. If you know what I mean ...'

'Right.'

Actually, I don't know what he means. What on earth is the point in all this? I really don't know anything about altitude training. Only what Dean told me, which isn't very much. He just said that the players will have to do altitude training when they get to South Africa, because they're playing at sea level or not at sea level. I don't even know what that means.

'I think it would be better if I did something else because I don't know about altitude training,' I say.

'But you mentioned yesterday that the players would probably have to do things like cycling in a sauna, is that right?'

'Yes, they'll definitely have to do that, but that's all I know. My specialist subject is not the detailed training programmes required for elite footballers embarking on a World Cup campaign. Sorry, but it's not.'

'We've got some exercise bikes here for you to use,' says Matt, appealingly. 'We thought it would be fun if we did an interview with you while you are sitting on the bikes, and we would slowly fill the room with steam, so it's like a sauna. I just think that would be great fun. If you don't mind.'

'I don't think this is a very good idea,' I say, thinking of the vast amount that I drank last night, and the sneaky glass of champagne with breakfast.

'Oh, but we could have a go, couldn't we?' says Mich, batting her eyelids at Matt so much that I think she's going to take flight. 'You never know, it might be fun!'

Oh, for God's sake, woman. I don't know why I bring her. Well she can say what she wants. I'm not doing it. No way.

Twenty minutes and a glass of champagne later . . .

So, it turns out that it's pretty damn difficult to cycle on a stationary bicycle while twelve kettles pump out steam all around you. I'm dressed in the brightest pink Lycra catsuit ever seen. Honestly, it's so tight the words 'camel toe' don't even begin to cover the problems I'm having right now.

The aim is to get me, Mich and Suse cycling for twenty minutes to see how we fare. 'It's only for fun,' says Matt. Interesting observation from someone who remains fully dressed on the sidelines, and has made not one effort to either dress in Lycra or mount one of these bikes.

When they first presented us with the pink Lycra catsuits, pale-pink leg warmers and headbands, pink socks and trainers, I thought the outfit was adorable! I loved that all three of us would be wearing the same thing. That really appeals to me. I just think it's so sweet when you've got friends all dressed up the same, looking like triplet toddlers going to the park on Christmas day. I know that a lot of women would hate to be pictured next to girls wearing the same outfit as their friend, and it might provoke a return home to get changed, but in Wag-world, we love identical dressing.

Anyway, we've all got different footwear on, because we all refuse to wear the trainers presented to us. Mich is in stilettos, Suse is in wedges, and I've opted to stay with my favourite platform-heeled boots.

'Do you want to tell us a few things about your life?' asks Alex, with his now familiar line in non-interviewing. 'For example, do the three of you all enjoy being Wags?'

I was dreading a question like this because I'm the only real Wag here. I don't want to show the others up in front of the TV guys by questioning their Wag-status because having your Wag status questioned is, as we all realise, the most devastating thing that can happen to a woman, so I prevaricate.

'I can hardly breathe, let alone talk,' I say.

'Perhaps you need a drink?' Matt suggests, wisely. Perhaps I've underestimated him; a drink might be just the thing I need. I ask Matt to pass me my handbag and I reach inside to pull out the vodka bottle, taking a huge slug before passing it to Mich who passes it to Suse who passes it back down the line to me.

'I didn't mean an alcoholic drink,' says Matt. 'I thought you might be dehydrated, and in need of some water. I don't think that alcohol is the best idea when you're exercising like this.'

'No, it's fine. Everything is fine. Please, Matt, move away from the ladies on the bikes. Let them drink all they want.'

Matt backs away and I hear Alex tell him that their job is to make good television. 'What will make better television than three drunk Wags on stationary bikes pedalling away in a steam-filled room dressed like Olivia Newton-John circa nineteen-eighty?' he asks. To be fair, he's got a point.

'I'm worried about their health, though,' says Matt. 'I don't want them to injure themselves or anything.'

'They'll be fine. This is all fine. This is just perfect. It's just altitude training. This is what elite performers do when they are altitude training.'

Suddenly Alex is a biomechanic with specialist know-ledge of altitude training, is he? It's enough to drive you to drink. Talking of which . . . 'Pass the bottle down, love,' I shout to Suse. She looks over at me, her damp face and half-closed eyes indicating that the training is starting to get to her. I take a huge slug of vodka once it reaches me and feel instantly better. 'Wh-hey . . . do these things do wheelies?' I ask, smiling broadly and pedalling faster.

'No, they don't do wheelies,' says Matt, rushing to my side. 'I really think you need to sit down properly in the saddle. You might fall off the bike and hurt yourself.'

To be quite honest with you, those were the last words I heard. Then there was just a scream from Mich, a cry from Matt, and the bizarre sound of clicking as the kettles were being switched off. After that there was just complete silence.

Later that evening . . .

Down in the Cabinet Wag Room, things are getting serious tonight as Shiraz prepares to measure me in our weekly sizing session to see how closely my figure now resembles the bodies of my favourite Wags. I'm desperate to look like Cheryl and Abbey more than anyone else. I mean, I'm not saying that Alex Gerrard has a bad figure or anything – it's just that these twenty-somethings who've never had babies are much more inspirational as far as I'm concerned. The trouble is, while I'm very thin (because I never eat) I'm nowhere near as naturally narrow as some of the newer girls on the scene now. I lie awake at night trying to work out how to be as thin as them. When I last went to a Chelsea game I saw one of the younger Wags with shoulder blades that sit about two inches apart and with the hips of a toddler. All a girl like that has to do to keep the weight off is not eat. That's so easy.

To have a figure like hers I'd have to have my whole

skeleton broken up and put back together again in a much more compact fashion. Not so easy. I want to be as thin as I can possibly be, but I just don't think that the hospitals would allow me to go in for an operation like that. Doctors would get all weird on me and just say crap things like, 'You should learn to love the body you were born with.' Yeah right. Whatever. Some doctors need to work harder at understanding the demands on a Wag instead of just spouting off this rubbish.

I do all I can to help myself by monitoring my diet with religious fervour. I started off by giving up fat, then decided carbs would have to go, then realised that protein was lying between me and extreme thinness so gave up that too. Now it's getting altogether too difficult to know what to eat that doesn't fall into those categories so I've pretty much given up eating altogether.

Shiraz takes the measurements, and I feel her pulling the tape measure so tight that I can't breathe. 'If you do that you'll get an artificially low figure,' I say.

'Er, yes, that's why I'm doing it,' she says.

'No, let's take a proper measurement. Let's see what my waist measurement really is, so I know how far I have to go with my diet,' I insist

She looks worried but wraps the tape measure around my waist all the same, and I brace myself for the result. As long as it's less than 20 inches I don't mind. I'll be just about able to deal with it if it's 20.5 inches or something vile like that. I'll just have to tap into my inner resources and find a way to come to terms with my solidity. But any more than that and I'm down that liposuction place before you can say pasta.

'Well?' Shiraz has gone very quiet since she did the measurements.

'Well, um . . . it seems to be 22.5 inches.'

'Twenty-fucking-what-point-what? I mean, what? Is something wrong with you? Is this a bad joke, or have you gone blind and can't see the tape measure properly?'

'No, I'm just saying what it says,' she mutters, sounding nervous and worried.

'Well, pull the fucking thing tighter then,' I say, urging her to do exactly what she was doing before I stopped her.

'Ah, there we are. It's 20 inches now.'

'Twenty inches now? What, now that you've pulled the damn thing so tight I can't breathe?'

'Er . . . yes,' she says.

Bloody hell. That's it. No more! All fruit is being taken out of cocktails before I drink them. This descent into obesity has to stop.

'This is terrifying,' I say to Shiraz, and I can see from the look on her face that she thinks it's pretty terrifying too.

'You could try coming to one of my classes with me,' she says, but I know that it's too late for that. I have a vision of the future in which they'll have to wheel me out of here on a reinforced trolley, and take me away in a reinforced ambulance to some home for the morbidly overweight, where some poor bastard in a white uniform will have to clean the festering mould from between the folds of fat on my stomach and assist me as I gently walk three steps a day as part of my fitness routine.

It's 8 p.m. when Paskia-Rose comes to my room and sits on the bed, looking at me while I remove my jewellery. I'm still wholly distracted by the news that I'm clinically obese. I put the jewellery back into its special box. I wonder whether I'm the first ever obese Wag. I could well be.

'Is everything OK, Mum?' she asks.

'Sure. Everything is fine. Why?' I ask her, while inside I'm thinking, Is everything OK? Is everything OK? Er . . . no. Everything is *not* OK. I'm the size of Vanessa Feltz and the two fat ladies moulded together. Things are *far* from OK.

'Well, it's just that Dad asked me to come up and check that you were OK, because he said that you arrived back dressed like Sinitta used to in the eighties, all sweaty and dishevelled in headband and leg warmers, and you weren't really sure where you'd been. Also, the car is not outside, and he wondered where it was.'

Oh, that. I'd completely forgotten about the car. 'Everything's fine, sweetheart,' I say. 'I just went along to help these guys out today – you know, the ones who wanted me to do the filming for them for the programme that will never be on air, but will help them get backing.' That filming session seems a long time ago – back in the days when I was living life freely, not knowing that I was the Wag world's answer to Big Daddy.

'Wooah, wooah, wooah, wooah, wooah,' exclaims Paskia, 'I thought you weren't going to do that. I mean, didn't Oliver and the big fat guy in a blazer tell you not to do it? Don't you remember, you're not supposed to do any media and publicity work without clearing it with the FA first? They especially asked you not to do this filming.'

'Oh, don't worry about them,' I reply. 'Everything will be fine because no one in the world is ever going to see the footage anyway. It was all just for their internal use.'

'Can I call Oliver anyway though?' asks my daughter. 'I just think we should be honest and fair with the people from the FA at all times. Then, whatever happens, we're not to blame. I'll tell them that you didn't say anything silly, or behave madly. I'll tell them you decided to go ahead and do the TV thing because you promised that you would, and you hate to let people down at the last minute. There, that sounds good, doesn't it? So, shall I call him? Can I, Mum?' She's wide-eyed with excitement as she looks at me pleadingly. I know what this is all about: she wants an excuse to ring the geeky boy. I knew she fancied him. I just knew it.

'Look,' I tell her. 'I don't want you to mention this to the FA. Everything will be fine. There will be lots of opportunities for you to call the Football Association and speak to Oliver over the next few weeks. If we tell them I did the filming, they'll just get cross, and that might have an impact on your father. I'd rather just leave it. But I promise you that when I write this week's column, you can be the one to show the FA, and check that Oliver is happy with it before we proceed. But please don't worry about the filming I did today. It really was just to help these guys out, none of it will ever appear in the public domain so it's not like I was on a TV show at all. You can be like my official spokesperson when it comes to dealing with the FA, so you'd better start preparing yourself for lots of in-depth conversations with Oliver.'

'Yes, I'll be the spokesperson,' she says, enthusiastically. 'Thanks very much, Mum.' She gives me a big squeeze and heads out of my room. As she gets to the door, she stops in the door frame and turns round, 'Mum, where's the car? I need my history book and it's in the back of it.'

'The car? It's outside the film studios. We ended up leaving it there.'

'We? Who's "we"? Did Dad go with you?'

'Mich and Suse came with me and joined in on the filming, which made it all much more fun.'

'Mich and Suse?' asks Paskia, with unease. 'And what did they "join in" on? I thought you were just doing an interview.'

'No, what they did in the end was they decided to take a look at altitude training, and wanted us to illustrate what the players might do. They did the interview with me as part of that.'

'Oh,' says Paskia, now looking quite impressed. 'That's interesting, Mum. I didn't know you knew anything about football training at altitude. Has Dad been talking to you about it? What did you do?'

I can see the renewed respect in her eyes. 'Well, they got us all dressed up in pink Lycra, and put us on to stationary bikes and asked us to start pedalling away. Then they filled the room with steam to make it look like we were cycling in a sauna, just like the players will do before going to South Africa. All they did then was filmed us chatting and drinking vodka until we got so drunk that we fell off our bikes. They splashed us with cold water to cool us down and sober us up, and then they put us in a taxi home.'

'Oh, shit!' says Paskia, now clinging to the door frame. I've never heard her swear before. This is serious. 'Oh, God.'

'Don't worry, angel, everything will be fine,' I say. 'It was just a bit of fun to give these guys a light-hearted look at the world of the Wags. No one will ever see the footage, and the bonus is that Mich, Suse and I got to have a little drink, a bit of exercise and a nice chat about which of the footballers we think would be best in bed, and at the end of it all we got to keep the luminous pink bodysuits, which was a complete bonus.'

'Oh, God, no more. Please, no more,' says Paskia, slumping down in the doorway until she's sitting on the floor like a rag doll. 'No more, Mum.'

Chapter Three

To: Shiraz@yogalovers.com
From: Tracie.Martin@wags.com
Dear Shiraz,

It's Friday and you know what that means . . . no, it doesn't mean that it's time to focus on a weekend of mad exercise-related classes; it means it's time for your weekly Wag test. Please answer these questions to the best of your ability and leave your answers next to the life-size cardboard cut-out of Coleen Rooney at the back of the Cabinet Wag Room (by the Wag hairstyles board) for me to mark over the weekend.

1. Which of these tastes would most appeal to a Wag: chips, chocolate, meat pie, Bacardi?

2. If three Wags in high heels, two Wags in flat shoes and four Wags in a taxi arrive at Mahiki, how many Wags will there be in total?

(I'm really hoping that she's studied properly and remembers that Wags NEVER wear flat shoes so those in flats are imposters and not real Wags)

3. Name three of the country's leading Wags.

4. What do most Wags model themselves on: brave and fearless female politicians, Oscar-winning film stars, great, bold and colourful historical figures or little plastic Barbie dolls?

5. What percentage of a Wag's daily nutritional intake should come from alcohol: 1%, 5%, 10% or 99.66%?

Chapter Four

Saturday 8th May

Hi ho, hi ho, my hair can never grow because it's bleached and plastic (but looks fantastic), Hi ho, hi ho–hi ho–hi ho . . .

At last – a day without a filming session. Thank goodness I've got the day to myself. The thrill of being a major TV star was starting wear off a little. I wonder whether Kate Winslet would feel the same if she had to endure sitting on a stationary bike in a steam-filled room with a nonce called Alex who couldn't interview someone if his life depended on it? I don't know how people in showbiz cope with the pressure, I really don't. And they actually have people watching them in their movies! Imagine that? At least I'm an undercover movie star. I'm a silent movie star. I'm the Charlie Chaplin of the Wag world.

Anyway, today I can put all that behind me and focus on more important things . . . like getting some extreme shopping under my belt. I've got so bloody much to do to prepare myself for South Africa that I really need to get started. We leave on the twenty-third of May when the players go to their altitude camp and we'll be based in Cape Town, in the most luxurious accommodation you can ever imagine. The players will have to move around, depending on which team they are playing, but we get to stay put. It suits me down to the ground. Much as I love Dean, I've got no particular desire to spend quality time with him in Cape Town. It's Abbey and the girls who I want to get to know.

Like the players, though, I know I need to be properly prepared for the tournament if I am to have any chance of making a success of it. Can you imagine if I was seen in South Africa carrying the same bag on more than one occasion? It would be bloody awful. Dean would probably lose his job and the national team would be sent home from the tournament in disgrace.

I bet that, for all Fabio Capello's jibberish about keeping the wives away from the paparazzi and not letting their shopping habits become the major story of the summer, if it came down to it, he'd rather his Wags had handbags to match their earrings, shoes, knickers and bangles than madly mismatching accessories. He's Italian, for God's sake. If he doesn't know about properly coordinating accessories, then no one does.

So, with thoughts of the national team's reputation in mind, and feeling very clear about the important role I have to play, I have decided to head up to Pitch – this great new Wagalicious shop in Liverpool – to buy just about every bloody thing they have in there. For the flight alone I'll need at least five outfit changes so it's going to be a long day.

Mich called this morning to ask me how I am planning to get up there. (Needless to say, I never went to get the car yesterday and when I sent Shiraz up there this morning after her underwater yoga class, it had been taken to the pound. Again!!! This happened to me before. The year before we went to live in LA, my car spent most of its time in the pound because I was too busy/drunk/unbothered to collect it. Dean wasn't very happy, so I must remember to go and get it this time). Anyway, the reason I'm saying all this is that not having my car means that I can't drive to Pitch.

'It doesn't matter, I'll drive,' Mich says with a wink. She's got eyes exactly like a cat; it's actually quite unnerving sometimes. The wink doesn't fool me, though – this decision to drive has disaster written all over it. Like me, Mich can't go anywhere without having a drink. Whenever either one of us takes the car anywhere, we end up having to leave it and get a cab back because the lure of Bacardi is always so much greater than any sense of responsibility that either of us may feel. This doesn't matter, of course. But what Mich obviously hasn't properly thought through is just how bloody far away Liverpool is, meaning that if she leaves her car there, getting it back down to London will be a feat of astronomical proportions that will be, inevitably, beyond us both. I have no hesitation in predicting that if Mich drives today she will never, ever see her car again.

'No, mate,' she says, when I explain my theory to her. 'I'll be fine, honestly. I won't drink much.'

Won't what? Has she gone completely mad? I fear she might have.

'But I'll be drinking,' I remind her. 'There's no way that I can go there and back in the car without having a little drink at some point. You'll have to sit there with the smell of Bacardi wafting through the car, and not drink any. How are you going to do that? No human being can do that. It's impossible! Please don't pretend that you can do it.'

'I *can*,' she insists, with a surprising amount of conviction. 'Watch me. I'll drive us there and drive us back. It's important that you have all the time you need to get the right clothes for your trip to South Africa, so neither of us wants to be worrying about where we're going to get a cab home from. We certainly can't get the train, because you will have far too many bags for that. It's really the only solution and I want to do it because you're always so kind to everyone else, Tracie. Now I want to help you and drive you there today so you can have an extra special time getting the clothes you want for the World Cup.'

It's a lovely speech, and the sentiment of it is very much appreciated, but it doesn't change my view and I remain convinced that there is NO WAY on God's earth that Mich will be sober enough to drive me home.

'Thanks,' I say, pushing my reservations to the back of my mind. 'That's very kind of you.'

'I'll be there in a couple of hours then,' she says. 'That should be enough time for us to do our make-up, shouldn't it?'

It's going to be tight, I tell her, but I'll do my best.

Three hours later ...

'I *knew* I hadn't given us quite enough time for make-up,' Mich apologises, 'I don't know what I was thinking suggesting I'd be here in a couple of hours.'

Before we leave, I insist that she comes in to measure me. I haven't been able to sleep since the shock of Shiraz's measuring yesterday. The truth is that I simply refuse to believe that the measurements she took were correct. I mean, I don't think she's lying or anything, I just think they need to be done again by someone else.

'OK, measure me,' I instruct Mich. I'm wearing my shocking pink, sky high, wedge-heeled stilettos and a basque that is three sizes too small. I think it was designed with six-year-olds in mind so I'm hopeful of a good result in the waistline test. Mich begins to wrap the tape measure around my waist.

'What on earth are you doing?' I shriek.

'I'm measuring you,' she says. 'Just like you asked me to.'

'Yeah, I asked you to measure me but you need to say "go" when you're about to do it so I know when to suck everything in.'

'Oh, OK, well, "go!"' she says, and I squeeze my stomach in and upwards, and try to force it up somewhere behind my rib cage to give me the tiniest waist imaginable. In my head, and certainly in my heart, I have a waist of about eighteen inches.

'OK, done. You're twenty-three inches.'

'I'm fucking *what*?' I ask, staring challengingly at my dear friend. 'Are you fucking mad? My waist size cannot have gone up since last night. What is going on here? Is your tape measure right? It just can't be. There's definitely something wrong. This is making no sense at all.'

'I can't help it,' says Mich. 'All I can do is read what it says.'

'Perhaps that's the problem!' I say, suddenly realising what's going on here. 'Were you any good at numbers in school? You used to be dyslexic, didn't you? Perhaps you've got the numbers jumbled? Perhaps you should measure me again, and show me that point on the tape measure and I can have a look at what number it says.'

'OK,' says Mich, looking miserable, presumably because

I'd reminded her about the awful time she used to have at school. They called her 'cat-face' and used to make meow noises whenever she walked into the room. Then suddenly she gives a sarcastic smile. 'But that would make you thirty-two inches if I'm being dyslexic.'

'I AM NOT THIRTY-TWO INCHES!' I practically shriek through gritted teeth. 'Or twenty-three for that matter. Now, let's make sure we do this properly this time, shall we?'

'I did it properly last time, you cheeky mare,' she says. 'Anyway, seen any fat penguins recently?'

'Fuck off,' I reply. 'Milked any ducks?'

We troop out to the car in silence, both of us stinging from the impact of the harsh words of the other. Luckily, in our world, these moments of introspection and hurt don't last very long and I know that by the time we've made the short walk to the car, we'll be best buddies again.

'OK, baby, let's roll,' I say, as Mich pushes her sunglasses down on to her elegant nose (it took three operations but now I think Mich has the nicest nose of any of us). Mich looks into the mirror and throws the car into reverse by mistake, almost hurling it backwards into the pillars alongside our impressive gateway. This, ladies and gentlemen, is before she's had a drink.

'Forward would be good,' I say lightly. 'Maybe go for first gear just to get us on our way, if you don't mind ...'

She drives through the gates, up and over the kerb, narrowly missing a handful of pedestrians, and stalls it twice before she gets to the end of my road. Lord knows what trouble awaits us.

I'm dressed in a remarkably sober-looking black skirt and

black crop top today. Both items earn Wag status because of their respective lengths. The skirt is little more than a hem on the bottom of my knickers, while the crop top fights valiantly to cover my breasts, but loses quite dramatically every time I raise my arm. I've further Tracied up the garments by adding leopard-skin print ankle boots and fishnet stockings. My hair is in bunches on the side of my head. I've got big leopard-skin coloured earrings on which the word 'Wag' is spelled out, leaving no one in any doubt as to what my background is.

Mich is dressed beautifully too. She's gone for white today in the form of a simple white dress that skims her knickers without showing any bum cheek and so is perfectly elegant and ladylike (unlike mine, which exposes my magnificent butt cheeks to the world). She's teamed this with fuchsia-coloured leg warmers, candyfloss-pink shoes and all manner of candyfloss-pink glittery hair accessories dotted through her newly blonde mane of hair (she's naturally very dark and it's taken me a long time to persuade her to come over to the light side).

We're singing along to 'Fight For This Love' as we chug up the motorway. I'm swigging Bacardi from the bottle as we go, and giving her the very occasional sip (to deny her entirely would be cruel in the extreme, and probably strictly illegal. I don't think Wags are allowed to be within six feet of Bacardi or vodka without consuming any of it).

One of the things about Pitch that I love already is that you can phone up and say, 'Hi, it's Tracie Martin, wife of Dean Martin, Chelsea coach and recently chosen as one of the coaches to go to South Africa with the World Cup squad and I'd really like to come up for the day to buy a

load of clothes' and they listen patiently to your require-
ments, then put aside anything they think will be
particularly appropriate.

'Just ask at the till point when you arrive,' said the lady,
'and all your garments will be waiting for you.'

How cool is that?

Obviously, when I get to Pitch I discover that there are
many, many other things in the shop that I fancy as well,
but that was always going to happen. I'm the sort of girl
who fancies things when she gets into shops. I always think
that females fall into two categories when they shop – there
are those who shop reluctantly, getting buyer's guilt with
every penny that leaves their tightly closed purse. They try
on things in about eight million shops, then end up going
back to the first shop to buy the first thing they tried on,
then the next day they take it back. These people have the
WRONG approach to shopping. I don't mean to be
dictatorial, and I know that using 'right' and 'wrong' is very
judgemental but there are times when someone needs to
take a stand and make a judgement call.

It's wrong to hurt children, it's wrong to have pale skin,
tweed is wrong, corduroy is very wrong and waterproof
is wrong (except in the case of mascara). Pink is right,
lycra is right, short, frilly, white and orange are right.
Unnatural is right and loud is right. Sober is wrong and
drunk is right. Sorry, you got me off on a rant then, all I'm
saying is that there is a RIGHT way to go shopping, and
that's with great pride and eagerness. Some people can't
walk past a shop without spending money in it. These
people are right because, for them, there is a direct link
between money spent on clothes and complete happiness

in life. Theirs is a wholly healthy and admirably positive view. I'm not suggesting that everyone throws themselves headlong and recklessly into debt (well, I suppose I am, really, if the truth be known), but I suggest that if you're going to spend it, enjoy spending it, do it with love, lust and passion, and with a huge smile on your shiny and inflated lips.

I'm one of the shoppers who spends all the money she has in the first shop, then it's on to credit cards and hastily arranged store cards, overdrafts and loans signed up at exorbitant interest rates for the rest of the trip. The thing is that once I get the shopping bug (and, I'll be straight with you here: I have the shopping bug pretty much 24/7), I can't stop spending. I become possessed by something bigger than myself when I'm within sight of a shop, and I become convinced that the certain route to happiness, and to unbridled joy, is to buy everything I see.

Now I know this isn't the way you're supposed to behave these days, what with the recession and everything, but I figure that my spending on clothes is OK because I never waste a penny on food. It's people who buy bread *and* shoes – they're the ones who really ought to cut back.

As soon as I stagger through the door of Pitch, I feel warmth and love radiating from the hundreds of pairs of earrings, brightly coloured Juicy tracksuits, swirly-patterned maxi dresses and sparkly tights hung elegantly along the back wall. It's like an art gallery in here, it really is. I don't think it's possible to go to Pitch and not fall hopelessly in love. Happily, today it is not too busy, so I don't end up in any of the fist fights I usually find myself involved in. I wander around, picking things up, squealing at their sheer bloody marvellousness, and throwing them over my arm until a kindly assistant takes them off me and puts them a changing room.

I don't know whether there's some sort of drug in the air in lovely clothes shops but it seems to me that the time I spend in them is time spent in another dimension. I have no real recollection, no real control. I salivate wildly, my pupils dilate, and I develop a mild fever as I rush around hungrily collecting garments with lightning speed. If I could adopt such speed when it came to other issues, I'd be prime minister by now.

In Pitch, as well as buying everything that sparkles, gleams or screams out in a lurid lime green, I am also attempting to establish whether Alex, Abbey or Coleen have been in to buy clothes for South Africa. It's important that I don't look wildly different from them. I want to look like I belong. The lady in the shop though seems unwilling to give me any information on which of them have been in, and what they've bought. She remains particularly tight lipped on the subject of what size clothing they buy (yes, I asked!). She won't even tell me what size shoe Abbey wears. 'She's practically my best friend,' I hear myself yell, as much to my surprise as everyone else's.

'Well, if she's your best friend, you can ask yourself then, can't you?' says the lady with annoying logic.

'I'll just try these on,' I say haughtily, handing over a pile that consists of most of the clothes in the shop to another, much younger, lady.

She struggles beneath the weight of it all as she leads me through to a small cubicle. 'Just call if you need anything, won't you?' she says.

'Certainly,' I reply. 'I just had to pick out a few things for my trip to South Africa. I don't know whether I mentioned that my husband Dean has been selected as one of the coaches for the England team at the World Cup.'

'Yes, you did mention that,' she says politely.

'Sorry,' I shout after her. 'If I keep mentioning that my husband is in the England squad, it's just because I'm so proud. I'm so excited to be going to South Africa with the Wags this summer. I'm not trying to name drop or impress you when I keep chatting on about Abbey'n'Cheryl'n' Mel'n'Coleen'n'Alex and the rest of my girls.'

'No, that's fine,' she says. 'We've had a lot of the England team's wives and girlfriends in already over the past few weeks, picking out outfits to take with them.'

'Have you? Really?'

Oooo ... she's much nicer than that other woman.

'Who's been in? What did they buy? Please, you must tell me what they've bought. I don't want to be completely the odd one out. What sort of clothes did they get? Did they just buy summer clothes or did they buy wintry clothes in case it's freezing at night-time? Na, they won't have bought cold weather clothing. It's an unwritten rule – Wags don't worry about the cold. Even though it'll be Autumn in South Africa when we get there, that won't bother me. I'd happily wear boob tubes in England in December. I bet Cheryl would too – she's from Newcastle. I don't think tops in Newcastle come with sleeves on them, do they?'

'No, quite. Well, I can't tell you exactly what they bought, because we have to be discreet in a shop like this where we get lots of famous ladies coming in. I will tell you though that you don't have to worry – the items you've got here are not the same as the ones picked out by any of the other Wags.'

With that she turns and walks out of the dressing room. How ridiculous! She's *completely* missed the point. I WANT to look like the other Wags; I would even go so far as to say that trying to look like the other Wags is something that keeps me awake at night. There's really nothing in this world I want more than to look like Abbey Clancy's sister or Posh's favourite blonde cousin.

Why would I have an underground Cabinet Wag Room in which I spend hours analysing the movements, beauty regimes and sartorial decisions of the country's leading Wags if I didn't want to look exactly like them? Why would I bother spending hours every day in an effort to find out where Cheryl buys her shoes if I didn't want to look like her? It's insane! Doesn't everybody want to look like the Wags?

Once she's left the changing room I start trying on the clothes, squeezing into, wriggling out of, sighing, laughing and thinking to myself that I don't know how I got so far in life without a pink, sparkly, cutaway jumpsuit. 'I'll take them all,' I say to the assistant.

She looks amazed. 'Is there anything else?' she asks.

'Yes, there is actually,' I say, and I show her the beautiful picture of Cheryl on the beach in a high-cut swimming costume and a cowboy hat that I cut out of *Hello!*. 'I want to buy both of these but I can't find them,' I say. She comes back with a cowboy hat but has less luck finding me a swimming costume cut so high that it fails to cover my belly button. Where does Cheryl buy those things from? Once again, the value of me having a telescope trained on her bedroom raises its ugly head.

'Here we go,' says the assistant, eventually handing me a swimming costume that consists of little more than a couple of bandages and a gusset. How on earth can I wear this and be decent?

'I think it's the very one that Cheryl tried on here,' says the lady.

'I'll take it.'

I'm back outside and into the car within four hours. It's a shopping record. I sit down, smile at Mich, and glance at all the bags on the back seat. I've got all sorts of gorgeous clothes in there . . . the sort of clothes that will make me look a million dollars in South Africa.

We are just about to hit the motorway on our mammoth journey back down south, when my phone goes. It's Dean and he is so excited he can barely talk.

'Love,' I can just about make out him saying, 'can you hear me, love?'

'Yes,' I say, and pause to take a swig out of the bottle of Bacardi. 'You keep breaking up though. What is it?'

'I've been promoted,' he says, and I feel the world tilt a little on its shiny axis. This might be the greatest moment of my life. I'm here in the car, with a shedload of carrier bags from Pitch, swigging Bacardi while my husband tells me he's been promoted up the ranks of the England coaching set-up, with the World Cup just a few weeks away.

'What's happened?' I ask, and he tells me that the assistant to the second-in-command to the assistant defence coach, some guy called Kieran Harrison, and the second-in-command to the assistant defence coach – Chris Barnes –

have both also been implicated in the betting scam, so have been dismissed. 'Don't tell anyone love, will you?' he says. 'Grimaldi Palladino, the assistant manager, was fighting like mad for them to keep their jobs. It's really angered him, and those in his "camp", that Fabio has kicked them out and promoted me. Keep quiet about it, OK?'

Here we go again: juicy gossip but I'm not allowed to tell anyone. 'So what are you now then?' I ask, and he tells me the triumphant news that he's now second-in-command to the assistant defence coach. 'They're bringing in two coaches below me. I'll have management and leadership responsibility over them,' he says. 'Imagine that?'

No, frankly, I can't imagine that at all. I love Dean more than I love earrings, but I can't imagine him in a serious leadership role because I don't want to imagine him in a serious leadership role.

'I'm going to do this,' he says, in a wild and quasi-presidential moment. 'The defensive strategy of this team will be the greatest the sports world has ever seen.'

I do get a little bit scared when Dean starts taking his coaching responsibilities too seriously. It reminds me of when we went to LA and Dean was coach of a team there. He threw himself heart and soul into the team, taking them to victory after victory until they won every bloody league in America, and Dean was headhunted to become the assistant defence coach at Chelsea. Those weeks of him working long evenings and early mornings, and returning home to study piles of books on management strategy and leadership technique have left a scar. I married a footballer, not a businessman. I wanted a man who would wear inappropriately tight shiny grey trousers, have over-gelled hair and an annoying habit of winking at waitresses; I hadn't expected him to become some super smart, briefcase-wielding professional with his sights set on world domination. When we got back to England, Dean eventually slipped back into the role of gum-chewing, snorting, donkey-jacket-wearing football coach. But I've never quite erased the memory of him as entrepreneur.

I share my concerns with him while Mich nods, and uses my temporary lack of attention to snatch the Bacardi bottle from between my sticky orange, fishnet encased thighs, and takes a huge gulp. I snatch it back while Dean continues to reassure me that he won't become a sensible person, and will always have more gold in his ears than Bet Lynch.

'Thanks, love,' I say, and I reassure myself that although he has had a massive promotion up through the ranks to the dizzying heights of second-in-command to the assistant defence coach, he's still pretty lowly; he's still my Dean.

'The only other thing I need to mention,' he continues, 'is that Oliver popped round today after he heard the news about my promotion and he said that I had to be even more careful now. He emphasised that anything you write has to be overseen by him or the others in the communications team or I'll land myself in trouble.'

'It's going to be just fine. I'll make sure they see everything I write. Paskia's going to act as go-between and pass everything on to them for approval first,' I say playfully. 'I don't have a column going in this week anyway so tell them to take a chill pill. Everything's going to be ok.'

'Thanks, Trace, it's really important. Hey, guess what? There's some other really exciting news . . .'

'Ooooo, let me think,' I say. What other great news? 'Um . . . all the wives get clothing allowances and free shoes?'

'No, silly,' he says.

'All the wives get free champagne?'.

'No. The great news is that Dio is going to be in the World Cup squad. He's the one I've been backing. Isn't that great?'

'Dio?' I say thinking that this is the dullest news I've ever heard. 'Am I supposed to even know who he is?'

'Yes,' says Dean. 'You know Dio. I pointed him out when he was in the clubhouse. He plays for Arsenal. We saw him being interviewed on *Match of the Day*. Oh, love, you know him; he's a great footballer and you said he looked cute, like he should be in JLS or something. He's got the swagger and strut, and "star potential" written all over him. He's going to be huge, love. *Huge.*'

'Does he have a girlfriend?' I ask, trying to remember who Dean means.

'I imagine so,' says Dean. 'He's a young, up-and-coming football star so he'll have had enough offers. And it's not like he could be gay, is it? He's a footballer.'

Dean has a rather traditional view of footballers, and is wholly convinced that there is no way on earth that a gay man has ever played football in England. All the startling statistics, facts, and concrete evidence that run in the face of this are just blithely ignored by him. There was a gay footballer at Luton one time, and Dean was convinced he was gay because of an earlier hamstring injury that put him out of the team and into a spiral of depression, which there- fore resulted in homosexuality. 'He caught it from the injury,' Dean said once but, to be fair to him, I think even he realised, as the peculiar words left his mouth, that it was unlikely that 'gayness' could be caught from a run-of-the-mill football injury.

'I've got to go love. Just don't tell anyone that I've been promoted, will you?' Dean says, but his timing is as atrocious as Cheryl Cole's lip synching. I've just put him on the loudspeaker. Mich hears the word 'promoted' and squeals with delight. 'No, I mean it Tracie,' says Dean. 'I don't want a big scene with the guys from the FA so just be careful, OK? We really need to start keeping things quiet until the formal announcements, and we need to listen to what the FA said and try and keep a low profile. Is that OK, Trace? Only now I've got this promotion, it's more import-ant than ever.'

'Sure,' I say. I don't want to do any harm at all to Dean or to his career; I love him more than anything in the world. Any profile I get or ever have got has always been in my efforts to be the perfect Wag, the perfect wife and mother. I have no desire to be the main celebrity in this relationship at all. Honest!

'Mich,' I say, watching my friend as she takes a sneaky gulp of Bacardi when she thinks I'm not looking.

'Yep. Just smelling the bottle,' she says.

'I was just thinking . . . you don't think anyone will ever find out about that TV interview we did when I got drunk and I fell off that bike, do you?'

'It's not going on TV, is it?' she says. 'You said they were only interested in us doing an interview for them so they would have some material to use in order to try and get funding.'

'Yes, that's what they said,' I reply, and Mich shrugs.

'Well then, of course it's not going to end up on TV. How could it?'

'Yes, good point,' I agree, feeling mightily relieved. Of course there's no way that the film is going to end up being broadcast. I'm worrying about nothing.

'Shall we go for a sneaky drink?' she says. 'I'm a bit bored of driving. Let's get a cab back and I'll pick the car up in the morning.'

Lots of booze and one cab ride later . . .

Hi Tracie, Hope you had a good time at Pitch and managed to buy some clothes you like. These emails came in today. It's not looking good on the Glitzy Girlz front, to be honest. See you tomorrow. S x

To: Carla_Cresta@GlitzyGirlz.com
From: Tracie.Martin@wags.com
Hi Carla,
It's actually Shiraz, Tracie Martin's assistant, here again. Sorry to keep pestering you with emails but I have some very exciting news for you: Trace's lovely husband Dean has been promoted and is now one of the senior England coaches for the World Cup squad. It means that Tracie's profile will be raised, and she will probably end up in the newspapers every day. So I wondered whether you thought it would be a good time for her to do a new range of Tracie Martin jewellery (as suggested in our many previous emails).

Please let me know if you would like her to come in and discuss this further.
Yours,
Shiraz (on behalf of Tracie)

To: All PR, Tracie.Martin@wags.com
From: Carla_Cresta@GlitzyGirlz.com
Subject: Tracie Martin
Dear all,
I thought I should forward this email that I received today from Tracie Martin's PA regarding her husband's selection for the England World Cup squad, and how she now wants to design a new range of jewellery for us. In case she contacts anyone else, I just want to make it clear that this is never going to happen.

To bring you all up to speed with the situation with regards to Mrs Martin, the only reason that we asked her to design a range of jewellery for us was in order to try and get our products promoted by the Chelsea Wags. As you know, her range was pitiful, didn't sell, and has been abandoned in most shops. Annoyingly, our efforts to befriend other Chelsea Wags also failed, so the process is regarded as being a bit of a dismal failure. I suggest that we ignore any future requests from Tracie Martin to have further jewellery ranges, or to extend the one currently failing in shops around the country.
Kind regards.
Yours,
Carla

To: Tracie.Martin@wags.com
From: Carla_Cresta@GlitzyGirlz.com
Subject: Tracie Martin
Carla Cresta would like to recall the message, "Tracie Martin"

To: Tracie.Martin@wags.com
From: Carla_Cresta@GlitzyGirlz.com
Subject: Previous email.
Please ignore. This email was sent to you in error.

Later that day, as evening descends and my mind drifts away from thoughts of Bacardi Breezer and towards thoughts of cocktails with lurid, sexually explicit names, Dean comes in to talk to me. He looks tired, dishevelled and slightly stubbly which, I admit, I find quite a turn-on, but Dean's not in the mood for love. Despite me lying back on the sofa and pushing my chest out so far that it's astonishing my pink boob tube doesn't explode under the pressure, all he wants to talk about is football.

'Dio being in the squad is amazing, isn't it?' he says. 'It makes my vision of an impenetrable defence even more valid. I mean, with a striker like Dio up front it's more important than ever that we close down all the opposition's attacking options—' He stops when he sees the look of confusion on my face. 'Sorry love, I didn't mean to talk about football. I just get so excited by it all. I know I can be a great coach. I just wish I was higher up the coaching ladder so I could have more influence. I wish I didn't have to report to the Grim bloody Reaper – that's what we call Grimaldi Palladino. He's the assistant coach and his plans for the team's defences are ludicrous.'

I'd love to be able to discuss defensive formations with Dean but what's the point? The only defensive strategies I know are keeping your legs crossed on a first date and never getting into unlicensed minicabs. I've watched football most weeks for all of my adult life and I don't have a bloody clue what's going on out there.

'I do have a special request,' he says, and I smile up at him as alluringly as possible and lick my lips seductively.

'Anything you want,' I say. 'Anything...'

'Will you keep a look out for Dio's girlfriend when she gets to South Africa? She might find the whole scene a bit frightening at first and I need Dio focused on the football and not worrying about her.'

'Of course, darling,' I say, I'm disappointed that his special request doesn't involve us getting naked, but am thrilled to have such heady responsibility. Delighted to be able to help. Despite what people may think of me, that's all I want.

Chapter Five

4 p.m., Sunday 9th May

When I wake up and stumble out of bed – a vision of tangled hair extensions and smudged mascara, I look out of the bedroom window, trying to will Cheryl Cole into view. I try to think positively Cheryl-esque thoughts in the hope of tempting her into my line of vision.

'Come on, Cheryl. You know you want to show me where you got the lovely hooded body suit that you were wearing on the Brits.'

Nope. I can't see anything. It's ridiculous. Dean is going to have to get me a telescope . . . one of those ones where you can see the stars.

I put down the binoculars and turn my attention to the mountain of carrier bags filling the dressing room. Christ, I always have a field day when I go up to Pitch, but yesterday's excursion does mark a new, alarming high in terms of quantity of garments purchased. I just love clothes shopping. And the thing is Dean doesn't mind it at all, and he always encourages me to enjoy life and do those things that will make me happy. 'We've got the money. I want you to have it,' he always says, which is kind of him if not just a little bit reckless. However, I think that even he might feel moved to complain, perhaps even shriek very loudly, if he saw the colossal amount of clothing that I bought yesterday. Thank God we've got a dressing room so I was able to hide it overnight.

My job now, in common with every woman who spends too much when she goes shopping, is to tuck it all away in my wardrobe (or, in my case, my fabulous walk-in wardrobe . . . I'll make no bones about it, that's the reason we bought this house) so Dean never sees it. At some stage in the future he'll look in to my wardrobe and say, 'My God, Trace, you have a lot of clothes' with a look of bemusement on his face, and I'll say, 'Deany, I've had all these clothes for years' and he'll never be any the wiser.

'Maria,' I call, and I hear her softly padded feet as they come up the stairs towards my bedroom door. Good, she's wearing slippers today instead of those chunky salt-mine shoes she sometimes crashes around in. She knocks gently, and asks whether she can come in. 'Of course, of course,' I say. 'Come in, Maria.'

'Vodka?' she asks. I must admit that she has taken to saying this every time she sees me over the past few days. When I call her, her eyes light up, and she thinks she might be in for another drinking session.

'Not today,' I say, as if life isn't one big long drinking session in this house. 'Today we have to put all my new clothes into the wardrobe.'

'Goodness,' she says, clasping her hands around her face. 'Where all these come from?'

'Never mind that,' I say. 'Your job is to make sure they all get put away. Can you do that?'

'Of course,' she says. 'I do now?'

'Yes, please, Maria.'

Dean is at Chelsea today for their last game of the season. It's lovely that even though he's hyper-excited about being second-in-command to the assistant defence coach of the England team for the World Cup (will I ever tire of saying that?), he still retains all his former excitement for the club game, and desperately wants Chelsea to do well in this last match. They're playing Wigan today, and Dean seems confident that Chelsea will win.

'But it's not just about winning,' he says.

Oh, I thought it was. God, this game can be confusing at times.

'It's about *how* we win sweetheart, or, more accurately, how we don't lose.'

Eh?

Dean explains that his main concern is what the Chelsea defence is like today. If the team doesn't concede any goals and puts into practice some of the clever set pieces he's been working on, Dean will be chuffed and will know that his plans for world defence domination are proceeding well. If they don't, he'll come home, open the first of many beers, and moan constantly all evening.

I was going to go along to the match today, but there aren't many of the other girls going – and Cheryl clearly won't be there – so there's just no point in me bothering. It's not as if I go to watch the bloody football!

As Maria empties carrier bags, and lays gorgeous skimpy clothes across the bed, the phone rings downstairs. I love watching Maria's face when she is busy doing one task, and another task suddenly appears. She has no idea what to do: should she leave the job she is doing, or stay with it? She looks at me for answers, and I tell her that I'll get the phone.

'Tracie Martin speaking.'

'What have you done?'

It's Dean. He's clearly found out that I bought half the clothes in Pitch when I went there yesterday. I never expected him to be this cross.

'Sorry, love,' I say. 'It was just a couple of bits and pieces to take with me to the World Cup. I had to get a swimming costume like Cheryl Cole's and a collection of little dresses like Alex wears. You're not really cross, are you?'

'What?' he says. 'What are you talking about? Bits and pieces for the World Cup? Alex's dresses? What have they got to do with anything?'

'From Pitch. Isn't that why you're angry?'

'No, love. Have you not seen any of the football news today?'

Er . . . no. Of course I haven't.

'No, love. Why? Didn't Chelsea win?'

'Chelsea won 4–0. They did brilliantly. Their defence was impassable. I've never seen my team play so well. Capello came to watch and shook my hand afterwards. But do you know what questions were being asked at the press conference? Do you?'

'Did they ask, "Dean Martin, how did you get your defence so good"?'

'No, love. They wanted a quote on how I was feeling after the video of my wife cycling in a room full of steam, drinking vodka, and telling her friends that she thought Frank Lampard was probably the best hung of all the players in the squad, became a YouTube hit.'

'Holy. Fucking. God,' I reply. 'Fuck, fuck, fuck, fuck, fuuuuuuuuuuck.'

'Yep,' says Dean. 'That's what I thought. Unfortunately I didn't know anything about it, so I looked a complete fool and the journalist from the *Daily Mail* kindly showed me the video on his laptop, in front of the whole press conference.'

'Bollocks.'

'Indeed,' he replies sharply. 'Bollocks is exactly the way I'd describe it. Tracie, what on earth possessed you to go and do this when the guys from the FA had specifically asked you not to?'

'I thought it would be OK,' I say. 'I thought that the film was for them to use internally to get financing. I never imagined for one minute that it would get out, and end up on YouTube.'

'Oh, grow up, love. They saw the perfect chance to get loads of publicity. Of course they put it on YouTube. You've been used. Paskia's talking to the guys from the FA now, so we can make some sort of plan about how we deal with this. Be careful when you answer your phone . . . the press all want to talk to you.'

Fuck it.

'Maria,' I say, and I watch her large face contort with confusion as she mentally weighs up whether to stop what she is doing or carry on with it and attempt to talk at the same time. 'Put the bags down,' I instruct, saving her from any complicated decision-making. 'Come with me now.'

I lead her into the sitting room, pour her a large vodka, and myself an even larger one, and decide to deal with this disaster as I have dealt with so many in my life, by drinking heavily.

'No grape?' she says.

'No,' I reply. 'No grapes today Maria. Just alcohol.'

7 p.m.

'You're drunk!' Paskia looks horrified. 'I don't believe it. How can you possibly drink at a time like this? When the whole world is talking about you and that nasty video, and trying to get interviews with you and causing absolute chaos for Oliver and the other guys at the FA. They are running around trying to sort it all out, and you're just at home drinking vodka. I don't understand you sometimes, Mum, I really don't.'

Maria goes running out of the room. She's drunker than I am, and is twit-twooing like an unfeasibly large owl as she goes. I turn to my daughter.

'It's irrelevant whether I'm drunk or sober,' I say defensively, trying to mask my sadness while trying equally hard not to slur my words, because I know that will only make everything so much worse if she realises just how much I've drunk.

'You couldn't have, just this once, done what everyone begged you to do and cancelled the filming, could you? I don't understand why you have to be out on a limb all the time, Mum.'

'I'm not out anywhere. I'm here trying to cope.'

She seems to think I'm drinking because I don't care. The truth, of course, is that I'm drinking because I care desperately that I have upset my husband and my daughter, and getting drunk is my default response to all things of an even slightly stressful or upsetting nature. I feel a lone tear escape and slide down my face, leaving a greasy track in my make-up.

'Mum, I love you so much. Don't cry. I'm only getting

cross because I'm worried about what people will think about you, and what this will do for Dad's reputation, that's all.' She gives me a big hug and I feel instantly better. The girl's only sixteen but she's more responsible now than I've ever been and I'm disappointed that I seem to have let her down.

A few years ago, I would have been thrilled at all the attention that this YouTube video has clearly caused, and seen it as a positive endorsement of who I am and what I am. But I'm a different person now . . . since I shut my mother out of my life I've grown massively in confidence, and don't need the same level of reassurance every five seconds that I once needed. I'll tell you more about Mum later; it's too depressing to go into it now.

I sit back down and look at my fingernails in my lap.

'Don't worry, Mum,' says Paskia. 'I'm sure it'll all blow over. I'm sorry if I seemed cross earlier – I'm just worried about you. Whatever happens I love you and Dad loves you, and nothing else matters.'

'But what should I do? Do I have to keep myself locked away indoors for the rest of time?'

'No, of course not,' she replies, attempting to stroke my hair but almost giving herself an electric shock from the static build-up around the extensions. 'I had a long chat to Oliver earlier, and he eventually agreed with me that this could end up being nothing more than a blip, and if we react too much to it and take it too seriously, we could make a bigger deal out of it.

'I spoke to Mark Gower too, and he said that because it's not in the newspapers, which is still where most people get their news, it's not such a major problem. It's just on the Internet, and there are more things appearing on the Internet every minute so he really doesn't think your YouTube clip will be top of the news agenda tomorrow. In fact, he said he thought it would die a death overnight.'

'Yes,' I respond. 'That's exactly right. It will die a death overnight and tomorrow we'll be wondering what on earth we were worried about.'

Chapter Six

Monday 10th May

Oh my God. OH MY FUCKING GOD. It turns out that Mark and Oliver were very wrong. Having a video that's a huge hit on YouTube is something that doesn't just disappear overnight. Do they know nothing? What they and everyone else have failed to recognise is that a day in the world of the Internet is twenty-four hours long. There is no overnight. While we've been sleeping, half the world has been awake and – so it seems – calling up the YouTube clip and having a good old laugh at three drunk women in pink falling off exercise bikes while cycling in a cloud of steam.

I am now, officially, a 'YouTube sensation'. Imagine that! In different circumstances I'd be delighted and pathetically flattered. But right now I think I'll stick with feeling horrified and terrified. I woke up this morning to one hundred and forty requests for interviews on my mobile from journalists on newspapers and magazines as far afield as New Zealand and Mexico. I seem to be a huge star in towns and countries I've never even heard of. Paskia tells me that Dean's agent has had fifty calls and there have been so many calls into the club asking for me that they've put the work experience girl permanently on 'Tracie duty', logging the calls and notifying Paskia. Most annoyingly of all, Alex and Matt appear to be making the absolute most of their time in the headlines, and are all over the newspapers this morning talking about how they got their coup.

By lunchtime, I've had to switch the phone off because I'm getting so many calls from media outlets around the world that I can't keep up. A guy from a Japanese daily newspaper has rung about eight times . . . unless there are eight different Japanese newspapers? I don't know. TV and radio stations are calling too, as I'm slowly moving up the news agenda. It seems that the fact that they've got a video to show alongside their story is making this an even more popular news item than it would be otherwise.

Meanwhile, with every minute that passes, the YouTube video gets a greater and greater number of hits. The more hits it gets, the more publicity it gets, which in turn generates hits. This would be a dream scenario if I wanted anyone to see the damn video. Since I don't, you could quite truthfully describe this as a total fucking nightmare scenario.

I haven't had the guts to go and watch the video myself, mainly because I'm terrified I'll look fat in it. The video was shot before I realised that I didn't have the teeny-weeny waist of my imagination. Apparently, on one of the news channels they have helpfully put together a sequence of the bike-fall in slow motion, so you can see my completely inelegant tumble towards the floor in the greatest of detail. How nice is that? What people appear to be finding most amusing is the fact that I hit the floor and promptly fall straight to sleep. Reluctantly, even I can see that that's really very funny. Paskia can't see the humour in it all, neither can Oliver nor, I doubt, many of the others at the Football Association, but I guarantee that if it was anyone else in the video I'd be giggling along too.

Mich calls me and tells me that she cannot get out of her house because of the number of photographers hanging around outside. I tell her it's her own fault; she has given about ten interviews already so the press think that she is the most likely one of us to talk. She says it's not her fault; her boyfriend told her it would be a really good idea to do the interview. Her boyfriend Trevor, I should point out, is a small-time, third division football player from a little club that plays near Guildford (he's the one we never mention in polite company – third division??). He's rubbish. He's also the most boring man in the world, and I've never under-stood what Mich sees in him. Whenever I ask her why she is going out with such a deathly dull guy, she retorts simply 'he's a footballer!', which is fair enough, but she could have worked a little harder and found herself a footballer with the power of speech, and maybe half a personality.

Dean went to watch Trevor play once when there was no Chelsea game on, and reported back that the guy was hopeless. I mean, *really* bad. Dean's professional summary of Trevor's playing skills was to suggest that he could get me up to that standard with a couple of training sessions. Bearing all that in mind, I can see why he is urging his girlfriend to do interviews with the national press and to mention him in them (and according to Paskia, Mich was wearing his club shirt with a large white belt and white hot pants on the local news. White belt: yes; white hot pants: double yes; her dodgy boyfriend's club shirt: no, no, *no*!).

When I'm brave enough to turn my mobile on again later, I see Shiraz has texted me to say, 'you're all over the news while drunk and dressed in pink!!!! Hoorah!!', which leads me to believe that despite her getting a very good score in Friday's test, we have some way to go in her 'understanding the world of the Wags' training. I reply that pink is good, drunk is good, but disgracing your husband and the whole international team just weeks before the World Cup kicks off is not so good.

6 p.m.

I decide that I'd better watch the news to see what is going on, and am greeted by the fact that my YouTube video has now got more international hits than the inauguration of President Obama, and is behind only Susan Boyle's audition in terms of its rating in the YouTube charts. Mich is featured on the news too, which is weird for me to watch; I've never seen her on TV before. She has her boyfriend beside her, in his Godalming Rangers football shirt but, needless to say, he doesn't utter a word, but just stands there looking like the dope that he is, next to the lovely Mich.

10 p.m.

By now the news is reporting that my YouTube video has more hits than any other YouTube video ever. I went sailing past Susan Boyle around an hour ago, and the YouTube network collapsed temporarily under the pressure of the hits. I have to confess that I see this as some sort of triumph, though I'd never tell anyone else that. I couldn't bear to be stuck below Susan Boyle in terms of popularity. I know she's a great singer and all that, but I was wearing a pink catsuit in my video . . . surely that counts for something!

Dean comes back from one of the many emergency meetings he's been attending at the Football Association and I brace myself for what he might say. It matters so much to me that Dean doesn't think badly of me. I know he's upset, but I just hope with all my heart that he believes me when I say that I never meant to hurt him. Happily, he says straight away that he is standing beside me, that he loves me, and that I'm not to worry about this. Everything will be OK in the end.

I know he's been having a horrendous time at the Football Association and his face is a picture of absolute horror and fear as he updates me on new developments. Reluctantly I tell him that my video is now the biggest YouTube hit of all-time.

'Perhaps you should have released a statement this morning,' Dean says. 'Perhaps that would have killed the interest off a little bit. Maybe everyone is going on to the YouTube site to have a look at the video because they've heard about it, and you haven't said anything publicly, so they're intrigued.'

Ah, bless him. I think the truth is that people are going on to YouTube to see a ridiculous bunch of semi-famous women in catsuits making fools of themselves. I also think the fact that we all said that we'd like to sleep with David Beckham and loudly speculated on who in the England team had the smallest penis might have something to do with the interest generated by the video. I don't think it's got anything to do with whether or not I released a statement.

'You know that I don't really want to sleep with David Beckham, don't you?' I tell him, crossing my fingers behind my back. I realise that I would have been wiser not to have shared my lust for Mr Beckham with the world, given that my husband should have been one of his coaches. (Another tragedy!) But I'm only human.

'Yeah,' he says, though he sounds unconvinced.

'Good. I love you, sweetheart, and I always will. Always. You know that, don't you?'

'Yeah,' he says again. 'I love you too, Trace. We're in this together, OK? Whatever happens, we're in this together.'

'Thanks, love,' I say. 'I love you so much. And I'm really sorry that I said on video that I called you "snuggly sex bomb". I only said it because I'm so proud of our relationship, and what we mean to one another. I wasn't trying to embarrass you, snuggles. You know I'd never do that, don't you?'

'Yeah,' he says again. 'I know, and perhaps the players will stop ribbing me about it one day. Now let me just give these guys at the FA a quick ring to check everything is OK, and I'll come back and we'll have a little glass of something. OK?'

'Big OK.'

11 p.m.

Dean is back from his chat with the FA guys. They are about to go into what they are calling 'a highest order of emergency meeting of the Association'. For God's sake, they do have a way of making everything sound even more dramatic than it is. Dean is due to talk to them later when they have formulated a plan of action.

All that's left for us to do in the meantime is to snuggle up on the sofa, drinking champagne and trying to talk about everything but YouTube videos and the international embarrassment they can cause. I get a text from Mich while we're sitting there, locked in each other's arms, in which she says that she has dumped her boyfriend because she felt as if she was being used by him. She says that when Trevor suggested that she should contact *Celebrity Wife Swap* and get them on there 'to earn some dosh and get every ounce of publicity out of this' she realised the truth.

'Trevor's gone,' I say to Dean, and he smiles broadly. You see, every cloud does have a silver lining. If it weren't for the YouTube video, Mich would never have worked out what a tosser Trevor is and she wouldn't have dumped him.

'Hooray!' we clink our glasses together in celebration.

'Life's weird, isn't it?' I say. 'I mean, who'd have thought that me talking about altitude training would cause all these problems.'

'Life's very weird, love,' Dean replies, adding, 'Do you actually know anything about altitude training? Only, I can't work out why they ever thought it would be a good idea to get three women who know nothing about altitude to simulate it in a TV studio. Why would they ever have thought that would be a good idea?'

'I mentioned altitude on my first filming session because I was just chatting on about the sort of work that you do with the players. As soon as I said it, this guy Alex got all excited and started talking about wanting to feature it in the pilot show they were doing. It always seemed like it would be a pretty silly idea to me, but I assumed that they knew what they were doing.'

'What do you mean "on my first filming session"? Did you do more than one filming session?'

'Um ... yes, I did.'

I feel a familiar clawing through my stomach when I think about the first video ... me talking about not knowing the difference between penguins and koala bears. Bollocks.

'Did you talk about football in that one?' he asks.

'No,' I reply truthfully, and I can see him relax.

'Would you like me to tell you a bit about the altitude training we will be doing with the players?' asks Dean, reaching for his file on the coffee table. I can't think of anything that would interest me less. In any case, I'm too distracted now with trying to remember what I might have said in that first filming session that could come back to bite me on the arse in the next few days.

'It's quite interesting,' he tries, and I see the look of enthusiasm on his face and decide that it would be good to let him talk about football. I know how much he loves the sport.

'Sure,' I say, and he flicks open the folder. How funny would it be if in his file he has pictures of the entire England team cycling like mad on stationary bicycles, dressed in luminous pink catsuits and drinking vodka while chatting away about the sexual prowess of the most high-profile of the Wags?

Nope. Not a pink catsuit or a drop of vodka in sight. The file is full of rather technical notes about the impact of altitude on the body and its detrimental effect on the players' fitness.

'Here, look. This explains it all nice and simply,' says Dean, pointing to something neither nice nor simple. It's a chart of the players possibly going to South Africa, and it shows the results from the work they did back in March to prepare themselves. It outlines that their first match against the USA will be played at almost five thousand feet above sea level, and goes through the altitude training they're going to be doing at some godforsaken training camp in Austria to prepare for it.

'One of the problems we're facing is that only two of the regular squad members have played at altitude in South Africa before, so for everyone else it's going to be a new experience and they don't know what to expect. We need to make sure that they're prepared for that first game. After that, we're playing at sea level, so we should be OK, but then we will be back at altitude after that.'

Oh, God, let the world end. This has to be the most boring conversation that my husband and I have ever had.

'The training camp in Irdning in Austria is going to really help us because that's two thousand, two hundred feet above sea level. But even that is only half as high as Rustenburg. Now as you know, the other thing we've been doing is having the players sleeping in hypoxic tents and taking iron and carbohydrate supplements. Tracie? Tracie? Are you asleep, Tracie?'

'No, I'm still awake,' I say, but only just.

'The whole subject is a bit of a minefield,' he continues. 'You can't train them too hard at altitude to begin with, so you have to make sure that you start the altitude training early. This means you can reduce the intensity for the first few sessions, then build it up as the tournament approaches so they're doing full training sessions at altitude by the time the World Cup arrives.'

'Interesting. Now then, tell me again about the hotel that the Wags are going to be staying in. It sounds gorgeous. I can't wait to go there.'

'Let me just run through this altitude training a bit more – I really think you'll find it fascinating. Do you know what happens to players if they start playing at altitude without acclimatising beforehand?'

He hands me a brochure. 'You want to read this?

'No, Dean, I can't. I'd rather eat my hair than read it.'

'Come on, Tracie. If you concentrated you'd genuinely find it all very interesting. Do you know what else is amazing about altitude during this World Cup?'

Oh, God . . . I really am losing the will to live now.

'It's the different flight of the new World Cup ball at altitude and at sea level. Can you imagine the impact that is going to have? Some people say it will fly around five per cent more quickly, and with less bend, in Johannesburg than it will in Port Elizabeth. Isn't that amazing? Apparently lower air resistance at altitude changes the flight path of the ball. That will take some getting used to once you get to altitude and your body and your mind gets used to that different flight path. But then to go immediately to sea level where the flight pattern is back to where it was originally? Honestly, Trace, it's been a hell of a job to sort out this altitude situation. It's all been very different from when I used to coach at Luton.'

Dean's mobile rings and he sees that it's Mark Gower, so apologises and leaves the room to take the call. I feel a wave of love for Mark Gower. Finally something has made my husband stop talking about bloody altitude.

A few minutes later, Dean pops his head round the door, and tells me he's going to be a while. 'Have a look through the file, and I'll answer any questions you have when I get back,' he says.

'Sure,' I reply. 'I'll have a look through . . .' when hell freezes over. He leaves the room and I pick up a copy of *Heat* magazine instead, flicking absently through the pages until I come across the most amazing, lovely, perfect thing I've ever seen: thigh-length, silver, sparkly Louboutin boots. I stop in my tracks, starring at the page. They're unbelievable. I have to have them. I can feel the excitement rising within me. I haven't lusted after boots like this for ages. Oh, God, I want them now. I have to have them. Have to . . .

Midnight

'Trace, can I have a word with you?' says Dean. He comes into the room, accompanied by Oliver and Mark Gower. When did they arrive? I had no idea they were here. Blimey, they must've been sneaked into the house through the back door to avoid the photographers hanging around our gates at the front. I'm horrified to see that Mark is still wearing his blazer. It's midnight for Christ's sake – what is the fool doing wearing a brass-buttoned blazer at midnight?

I stand up to greet them. 'Hello. I didn't hear you arrive.'

'We sneaked in,' says Oliver. 'Quietly. Lots of paparazzi at the front.'

'Tell me about it,' I reply.

'Are you OK?' asks Oliver. 'You look very, very pale.'

I'm touched by his concern, but I fear that the change in my pallor is more to do with the fact that I haven't trowelled on my usual eight inches of make-up. In fact, come to think of it, it's been hours since I put any on. Imagine that? It shows just how stressed I've been feeling; I've never, ever been seen without copious amounts of make-up before. Now I am sitting here with a simple, normal face. Right this minute, Oliver is probably seeing me closer to my natural state than anyone outside my own family has ever seen me. No wonder he thinks I'm fucking ill.

'Thank you, I'm fine,' I say coyly, hoping that the fact that I look ill will play into my hands a little, and persuade them to be more gentle with me that they might otherwise be.

'Why don't you take a seat,' says Mark. 'You really do look unwell.'

OK, OK. I get the message: I'm too pale! I'm booked in for a double spray tan in the morning, but there's no need for everyone to keep going on about how bloody ill I look.

I take a seat, and the other three sit down next to me.

'This story isn't going to die down any time soon,' says Oliver, in direct contrast to his boss's prediction yesterday that the story would disappear completely overnight. Not for the first time, I'm doubting the validity of the whole world of PR and communications. They just don't seem to know anything.

'I thought you said yesterday that everything would be OK,' I respond.

'Ah, but this is the trouble with things when they get on

the Internet . . . they go global, and can really take off. It's much easier to contain stories when they're in British newspapers,' he says, without flinching a muscle. Does he think I don't remember that Mark said last night that things on the Internet were fine?

'Sweetheart, the long and short of it is that we think you should head out to South Africa straight away,' says Dean. 'This story is obviously huge in England, and has become big in America, but in South Africa there are very few English journalists and the story hasn't exploded there. Grimaldi Palladino's wife, Jane, is already out there, so you'd have someone there with you, and obviously Paskia and Shiraz can go with you, and Mich and Suse if you want. Though I think it might be nice if Paskia came to see me, later on in the tournament – she'd love to be around the players and talking about football.'

'You really need to go out there soon, much sooner than we planned,' chips in Oliver. 'With the England squad due to be announced a week today, and all the build-up to the team leaving on the Sunday after that, it will be too hard and much too distracting for all of us to try and control press coverage during that time. I mean . . . it's completely up to you, Tracie, and obviously if you really don't want to go, you don't have to, but we think that will be the easiest way of dealing with the story in the short term. I have a feeling that it will make life much easier for Dean.'

It's that last sentence that gets me, as I'm sure they knew it would. I have no desire to be out in South Africa while my husband is here, but if it's going to make life easier for him to have me over there then that's what I should do. It'll mean taking Paskia out of school early but she's in the lower sixth – she can study in South Africa.

'OK,' I say. 'When do you think I should go?'

'As soon as possible,' says Mark. 'How about tomorrow evening?'

Shit.

South Africa

Chapter Seven

Saturday 15th May

The early morning sun is shining when we touch down in Cape Town. It glints off the tarmac and bursts through the large glass walls as we trundle along with our copious amounts of hand luggage (thirteen suitcases, four handbags, eight vanity cases and a small hamper full of large drag-queen-style fake eyelashes and sparkly lip gloss. Best to be prepared for anything as far as I'm concerned).

I'm glad the sun's out because I'm simply not the sort of girl who can dress for cold weather. I don't do freezing temperatures with any sort of dignity at all. My approach to bad weather is much like my approach to red traffic lights: I ignore them and keep going. I pretend the cold weather isn't happening and I persist with the tiny miniskirts, high heels and fake tans as if it were midsummer in the Mediterranean. I don't approve of coats; they just hide your outfit. Any fool knows that coats and Wags don't mix – it's not natural.

Picture a Wag in your head for a moment … any Wag … it doesn't matter who it is. Now, tell me … is she wearing a coat? Is she bollocks. Wags exist in their own mental microclimate in which it's always summertime and always appropriate to wear floaty kaftans and microshorts with strappy sandals revealing perfectly manicured pink toe-nails ... even in the cold ... and the rain ... and the snow.

Anyway, here we are in South Africa. It's Autumn here but it's madly hot, happily, and makes me want to forget the hassles of the last few days. Mark from the FA may have wanted us to leave as soon as possible but it took me a few days to pack, so it was Friday before we headed off. Even so, there was another challenge in getting to the airport without being seen by the paparazzi who were still gathered around my house in such numbers that you'd think they were waiting for a rock concert to start. But I now feel relaxed and happy.

I'm going to miss Dean over the next week, and I hope he's OK back in England with just Maria to look after him, and I really hope that Maria manages to stay off the vodka for just a couple of hours a day to cook for him and iron his tracksuits. (He hates it if his tracksuits don't have an ironed-in crease down the centre of them). It's OK for me ... I'll be fine because I'll be able to get through the days with the help of my great friends, my daughter and my PA and with the assistance of copious amounts of alcohol and daily beauty treatments. It's Dean I'm worried about.

We collect eighteen trolleys, which will be nowhere near enough for the baggage we have but will at least get us started, and we head to the mad conveyor belt thing where people always make a grab for the wrong suitcase and nearly beat each other up over who owns it. I lost a whole load of luggage when I was travelling out to LA one time. It ended up in Guatemala or somewhere, and because I never got round to collecting it, I was told it was eventually distributed amongst the city's poorest people. It still brings

joy to my heart that in the slums of South America somewhere there are ladies begging for money while dressed in
pink, fringed miniskirts, gold lame maxi dresses and skin-
tight lilac hot pants.

'This way,' says Paskia, who is taking quite a Scout-leader
approach to this trip, insisting on holding passports and
tickets at all times, and frequently stopping to count heads
and bags to make sure everything and everyone we came
with is still with us. She leads us now, with confidence and
surety. We all follow dutifully, happy in the knowledge that
someone else is taking control and taking full responsibility
for leading us through the right customs channel. I'm
always terrified I'll go through the red one by mistake, and
have to endure an intimate body search or whatever it is
that they do to you in that channel. Our group sails past
the angry-looking customs people, and as we approach the
entrance to the main airport concourse, we hear hundreds
of raised voices, shouting 'Spacey'.

'I think Kevin Spacey must be coming through here. I
didn't see him on the flight, though. Did you?' asks Mich.

I definitely didn't see him either, but the chanting of his
name makes it clear that he is due to appear any time soon.
'Spacey, Spacey, Spacey!' they shout. We continue to walk,
passing through into the terminal building where the
volume of the shouting rises to fever pitch. As we appear,
the whole place erupts into screaming and shouting. There
are hundreds, maybe thousands, of people gathered. They
push forward, screaming out.

'Oh, God – they're shouting "Tracie" not "Spacey",' says
Paskia. 'This is unreal.'

Unreal? Christ, unreal doesn't even begin to cover it.

Many of the people, now screaming and pushing forward, are carrying huge placards that declare things like: GOD AGAINST TRACIE MARTIN. TRACIE MARTIN PROMOTES ALCOHOL. ALCOHOL KILLS. WE WANT TRACIE MARTIN TO REPENT HER SINS!!!! There are huge pictures of me being held up along with the slogan 'say no to alcohol' on their T-shirts. Oh My God.

There are film crews everywhere too, which is causing Suse to go into a state of considerable panic because she's only got three pairs of fake eyelashes on. All the earlier cool, calm control has dissipated into the warm African air, and she is now screeching and shaking and generally being absolutely no help to anyone.

'Come on, follow me,' I say, assuming an air of dignity and sophistication that I simply don't have, and attempting to lead us towards an exit sign that I spot gleaming at me in the distance. The sign's not too far away, the only problem is the thousand or so people between us and it.

This whole thing has clearly taken the airport officials by surprise or they'd have rushed me out through a back door like they do Lady Gaga and Madonna. It's taken everyone by surprise: Mich is squealing annoyingly; Suse is giggling unhelpfully and taking pictures on her iPhone; Paskia is horrified and Shiraz, bless her – the girl you'd have thought would be least prepared to cope in circumstances like this and would be inclined to jump into the splits or start fiddling with her third eye – is phoning the police for assistance. The police! What a brilliant idea.

The crowd has reformed itself around us, engulfing us and trapping us. The sound of my own name being screamed by hundreds of people echoes in my ears as we wait for assistance, feeling as vulnerable as if we were bobbing along on a lilo surrounded by sharks.

Then, finally, big men in uniform appear. 'Come on, stand back, stand back,' says a deep, loud voice.

Hoorah! The lifeboats have arrived. A burly South African police officer begins to push back the placard holders. Other police officers follow, and they make a tunnel for us to pass through. Our trolleys are taken off us by security guards, who say they will push them for us (hoorah! I thought they'd never offer) as the police lead us and protect us through the mob to the front of the airport building where our taxis are waiting for us.

'Thank you so much,' I say to one of the officers. 'You're so kind.'

'No problem, ma'am,' he responds. 'My name's Super-intendent Martyn Barnes. Can I ask a favour?'

'Of course.'

He pulls out from his pocket a card with a photo of me on it. I'm lying on the ground dressed in bubblegum pink Lycra in the picture, and you can see the bike in the background. My hair is flying all over the place like I'm a mad witch who got caught in a wind storm. At the top it says 'Tracie Martin gets trashed on YouTube. Oppose alcohol now'.

'Would you sign this for me?' he asks, handing me the card and a black felt-tip pen. 'I'm a fan, but this anti-Tracie card was the only thing I could find with a picture of you on it.'

I scribble my name and he almost squeals with joy. I've never seen a grown man so excited about anything that happens out of the bedroom or off the football pitch.

'My pleasure,' I say to him kindly and he smiles again as I get into the taxi.

'Bye Tracie,' he says, as we start to pull away. 'Bye bye, Tracie, my love. If you have any problems while you are in South Africa, just call me. OK?'

'Come on girls, let's go.'

As we drive away from the airport, the TV cameras and photographers run alongside the taxi like I'm a murderer being driven away from my trial at the Old Bailey or something. The sound of people chanting madly can still be heard. It's clear that this might not be quite as simple as we thought it would when the plan to get me out of Britain was hatched by the brilliant minds at the FA.

Paskia rummages around in her bag and pulls out her phone.

'Can I speak to Oliver, please?' she asks. 'It's urgent, so if he's in a meeting, you're going to have to ask him to leave the meeting and come and talk to me.' Gosh, she can be assertive at times. Not when surrounded by a thousand screaming religious types, but at times she's assertive.

'Oliver, it's Paskia Martin here. I'm sorry to disturb you but we have just arrived in South Africa and it's chaos. There are hundreds of people at the airport, all holding up signs with Mum's name on them and denouncing her for drinking heavily in her video. We're now on the way to the hotel, but I thought I'd better tell you that it's going to be difficult. Some of those guys were mad.'

There's a silence from my daughter while she listens to Oliver's thoughts on the subject. He's clearly not getting it. 'No, Oliver,' she says sternly (too sternly, I'd have thought, for a girl who's falling in love with the boy). 'This couldn't be described as "a few loons gathering at the airport". It was much more serious than that. There must have been at least six TV crews there as well as photographers from newspapers and a whole load of psychos screaming her name.'

'Give me the phone,' says Shiraz, grabbing it off my daughter and addressing Oliver sharply. 'Look, sunshine, it was like the bloody Beatles had arrived back there. There were paparazzi everywhere – it was crazy! We had to go speeding away from them at about a hundred miles an hour. Tracie is like the new Princess Diana. Now, you need to make sure she's safe. We need lots of security at the hotel. Do you understand?'

The phone goes dead and I sit there, my hands cupped in my lap. I look up at everyone gently through the blonde hair that I've allowed to fall across my face in a feminine fashion. The new Princess Diana, huh? I'm liking that.

9 a.m.

Cape Town is truly amazing when you get away from the screaming mad protestors. Have you ever been? You probably haven't, because it's not necessarily the sort of place you'd think of going on a holiday. It's not like Spain or somewhere like that, is it? Spain's great because you know you'll get cheap cocktails, drunk boys, loads of sunshine and guaranteed sex. I think you can ask for a refund if you don't get them. You'd go to Spain or Ibiza way before you thought of somewhere like Cape Town but honestly it's really cool here. Really cool!

There's this huge mountain by it, with a completely flat top. It reminds me of the Christmas trees that Dean buys;

he *loves* Christmas, so every year he goes out and buys a huge, big fat tree that has no way on earth of fitting into our house. I always end up screaming at him, 'How did you think that was going to fit?'

But he just shrugs and says that he completely fell in love with the tree and thought we were bound to be able to get it in somehow. Every year he ends up having to saw the top off so that we can get the tree in to the sitting room. It ends up being this great big fat tree with a completely flat top and Dean ends up in A & E with a saw-related injury.

Once I had bought an angel and customised it by adding a bit of bling to her wings and dressing her all in pink. I'd even cut off the hair of a Barbie doll, and stuck it on to the ends of the angel's hair, giving her hair extensions just like mine. She looked amazing, and so, when I saw the tree with its hacked-off top, I cried out in distress while Dean sat there with a big bandage around his thumb, 'There's nowhere to put the angel! I need a pointy top to put my angel on.'

But then Dean said something inspired. He said, 'Sweetheart, it's not everyone that has a flat top to their tree, allowing them to put loads of Wag angels up there.'

'Oh my God, you're a genius!' I declared. And I did exactly what he suggested. I put a whole football team of Wag angels on the flat surface on top of the Christmas tree, and it became THE talking point amongst the Wags at the club that year. They came from far and wide and all declared that next year they too wanted to have a flat top Christmas tree.

*

The Hotel we're staying in is like something out of a dream. It's as if they looked into my mind, worked out exactly what I might possibly want from a hotel and designed it with all my desires in mind. I don't think I've ever seen a more perfect hotel. Not only can you see flat top mountain (which I've been told is called Table Mountain because it looks a bit like a table top especially when the clouds fall over the side of it like a cloth), but you can also see the ocean and the harbour because the hotel is based at Victoria and Alfred waterfront, which is just about *the* most stylish place on earth. And I speak as one who used to live in Luton, so I know stylish when I see it. It even has a private underground car park so the paparazzi can't get to it. We came up from the car park through the hotel lift and were completely free of the press and TV cameras.

We're now sitting in the super-stylish reception area, flicking through the hotel information booklet and learning that by far THE most important feature of this spectacular hotel is ... drum roll please ... the private Spa Island. Can I just repeat that ... A PRIVATE SPA ISLAND. I know!!!! How cool is that? Even in my most fabulous and elaborate dreams, there are no Spa Islands, for Christ's sake. Just how much fun are Abbey, Coleen and I going to have here? There are hammocks strung on the trees by the gorgeous blue ocean that us Wags will frolic in as we get to know one another. It doesn't get much better than this!

I carry on looking through all the glossy leaflets telling me about the various attractions of the hotel but the truth is that I don't care about any of it. I'm not interested in whether my bedroom has a bed in it, or whether my bathroom has a bath in it. I don't care whether there is a single toilet in the whole damn hotel. I don't care about anything in the whole world ever and probably never will care about anything again because I'm wholly distracted and utterly delighted by the news that there will be a Wag's Spa Island for me to play on. A BLOODY WAG'S BLOODY SPA ISLAND at this fucking hotel!!!! Mr Capello, I salute you. Honestly, I do. I wish him all the best in the football World Cup and all that, but surely his greatest contribution to British cultural life this summer has been to separate the wives from their husbands, and send them all to a Wag's Spa Island. What could be more exciting?

We'll be able to play here all week, then jet off to the games, all freshly tanned and wearing ludicrously priced outfits and frighteningly large sunglasses, then fly back here the following day for more beauty sessions, more drinking, and much more shopping. I'm already breathless with anticipation.

'Look,' says Mich, pointing to the leaflet tucked inside the 'Where to Eat' file. 'The restaurant here in the hotel is one of the new Gordon Ramsay restaurants.'

'Yes,' I say, vaguely remembering Dean talking about it. 'I think Gordon's due to come out during the tournament and cook for us one night.' Now, I never eat, but even I can see that that would be a hell of a night. I wonder if old Gordon likes a drink or two. I'm thinking that he probably does.

The hotel has all the usual things in it, of course, like poncey staff, annoying tinny music being played everywhere, daft art on the walls and stupid sofas in reception that are so big, soft and cushiony that you sit down for five minutes and it takes you three and a half hours and a hydraulic lifting-device to get you up afterwards.

The hotel is perfect, just what we need, but when I look over at Paskia, I see her scowl as she flicks through the brochures on the huge glass tables in reception. She looks desperately miserable.

'What's the matter, hon?' I ask, putting my arm around her shoulders, and giving her a big squeeze. 'You don't seem happy at all. Is everything all right?'

'Sure . . .' she says slowly.

'They have great facilities,' I say. 'I mean, as far as I can see they've got everything here that you could ever possibly want.'

'They've got nothing here that I want to do,' she says. 'It's all pampering and no real sports facilities. There's not even a library for me to work in and I've got loads of studying to catch-up on because I'm missing time off school.'

'Don't worry so much,' I tell her. The school's fine about her breaking up a few weeks earlier than the rest of the class as she's so far ahead and thought that spending time in South Africa would be both interesting and different.

'And I'm worried about you, Mum. What will you do? You'll be stuck in your room all day and not able to have any treatments or anything.'

Er . . . hello? I won't be stuck anywhere. I'll be having treatments 24/7 until every inch of my body has been scrubbed, exfoliated, polished and tanned so many times that I'm screaming for mercy.

'What do you mean, sweetie? There are lots of different treatments that I can have.'

'No, you can't. The spa treatments are all being done on an island, which means that photographers can come out in boats and take pictures of you. It's going to mean you have to avoid Spa Island or risk being photographed.'

Jesus Christ alive . . . I'll be taking the risk of being photographed, thank you. I don't care if the photographers come out on the back of humpback whales to get pictures. Nothing is going to stop me from pampering myself on this island with the other Wags. Does my beautiful daughter not realise that nothing as exciting as this has ever happened to me in my life before?

'We've got to be careful,' joins in Shiraz, picking up the hotel brochure. 'Look at this. "The hotel is set by a lagoon". When I read that all I think it is: oh my God, it's accessible from all sides.'

What? How different she and I are. When I read that all I think is: cue sparkly, ill-fitting bikinis, one-piece swimming costumes with so many cut-outs that you might as well take them off for all the coverage they're giving you, acres of tanned skin, and more tattoos than a building site, and me'n'Abs'n'Col'n'Vics'n'Alex.

'And there's a pool bar,' she announces gravely, shaking her head. 'Think of the potential risk of alcohol and water. Terrible.'

Oh, yeah, dreadful. Or think of the potential for enjoying forty-seven bottles of Cristal, thirty-seven pints of vodka and coke (diet, of course), every Bacardi Breezer on the island and thirty-eight cocktails called something naughty like a 'Sloe Comfortable Screw Against the Wall' or 'Sex On The Beach' before giggling over a bar bill of several hundred thousand pounds. Then there's the standing up and almost breaking your ankles when you attempt to move into the piano bar for a sing song, forgetting that the floor is wet in the poolside bar, and you're wearing Christian Dior, bejewelled, wedge-heeled shoes that you can't walk in at the best of times. Think of me'n'Abs'n'Col'n'Vics'n'Alex cementing our new but deep and increasingly meaningful friendships by going on the piss while wearing bikinis, waterproof make-up and false eyelashes. What's not to like about that?

'Don't worry, Shiraz,' I say. 'It's all going to be just fine.'

'Have you seen this? Beauty treatments are available twenty-four hours a day in the wellness lounge on Spa Island.' This seems to amuse Shiraz greatly. She chuckles like a baby as she declares that she doesn't understand why anyone would want beauty treatments through the night. Doh . . . it's so that nail extensions, waxing, facials and eyebrow-plucking can be taking place on a round-the-clock basis. As soon as a hair on a Wag body so much as pops its head out, it'll be swiftly snatched away by a kindly lady in a white overall clutching a pot of wax and a pair of tweezers.

Coleen will be fine here too because there is a kids' club, so little baby Kai won't get in the way while she's having her eyebrows threaded. The baby can be dressed up in Burberry and sent off to enjoy the resort's children's club, where he can meet up with other children with hellishly silly names and Col can have her skin sprayed ginger.

It's all just about as good as it can be. I don't think it's possible to want for anything in a hotel like this. I share this view with my daughter, who still looks desperately worried about everything.

'I think we need to be careful about where in the hotel

you go,' Paskia mutters, 'and we need to make sure that you are kept away from photographers at all times, even if that means missing out on some of the things you normally like to do.'

I nod on the outside, just to appease her, but on the inside I'm already planning the amount of time I'm going to be spending on Spa Island.

'Come on, let's go up to the rooms,' I say, struggling out of the sofa cushions and strolling towards the lifts with Paskia in hot pursuit. She's on her mobile every five minutes like a bond dealer, heavily involved in discussions with Oliver at the FA over what they are going to do about the fact that there were thousands of people demonstrating at the airport. I'm cool about it all, to be honest. This hotel is totally safe. There are armed guards and a series of alarms down every corridor.

As we get out of the lift and head towards my suite, Paskia's phone rings and I hear her talking to Oliver, and ruminating over what they should do with me. Mark Gower can't work out whether I should do a handful of interviews to get the press off my back, or do as Shiraz suggests and ignore them in the hope that they will eventually go away. At one point he suggests they fly me straight home.

'Is there no one you can talk to who understands this sort of thing?' asks Pask as we walk down a sunshine-filled corridor with wooden floors, pale lemon-coloured walls and plants and flowers everywhere. The door to my suite is large and wooden. We let ourselves in and are confronted by the most astonishing sun-drenched room with soft, cream, voile curtains dancing against the window in the gentle breeze. It's all creams, whites and wood in the room and out of the giant windows nothing but blue . . . blue sky, blue sea and the gorgeous bright blue of the pool directly below and the lagoon on the right. It's heaven. I can't believe this is Autumn. I wish our Autumns were like this.

'I suppose we could send Mum to somewhere in the world where they won't have seen the video,' says Paskia in the background. 'Maybe Poland?' I spin round, hands on hips and scowl at her. 'Although, maybe not,' she says, without stopping for breath. 'I don't think Mum would like that.'

It's agreed that Mark will talk to someone who is used to dealing with situations like these.

'Fine,' I say, opening the patio doors and stepping out on to the balcony. 'As long as it's clear that I'm not going to Poland. I'm staying here. Now let's have a little drink while we're waiting.'

'No way,' she says jumping up and looking quite serious. 'No drinking. We need to be on our toes. No balcony either. The press might get a picture of you. We need to stay in the room with the curtains drawn until Mark calls back.'

Oh, for God's sake.

After much heavy duty negotiating, my daughter relents and says that I can walk around the hotel while I'm waiting, though I mustn't leave it and risk having my photograph taken (this, as you will no doubt agree, is now getting ridiculous. Debating with my daughter demands high-level negotiating skills that would not disgrace Kofi Annan. She's absolutely determined that nothing else relating to me should appear in the newspapers on her watch). I decide that since the spa is temporarily out of bounds, I will head, naturally enough, to the bar.

I troop back down in the lift, check my make-up in the mirror, and decide that another layer of highly glittery, shockingly pink cheekbone enhancer might be the answer to all my concerns in life. I layer it on and step out into reception.

'Are you Tracie Martin?' asks the plump and smiley concierge.

'Why?' I reply nervously. 'Who's asking?'

'My name is Ronald. I was told watch out for you to make sure that you were OK. If you are lonely, why not talk to Jane sitting here?' He points out a middle-aged, very well-kept woman with short blonde, highlighted hair, a light tan and a dusting of freckles across her nose. She looks very fit and healthy as she sits and relaxes with a newspaper and a fruit smoothie. She's wearing cream trousers and a white shirt with expensive-looking dark brown loafers. She looks as if she's fallen out of a Ralph Lauren advert. Most un-Wag-like.

'Why would I talk to her?' I say, wondering whether this Jane character is a spy sent by the tabloid newspapers, and whether this concierge, in turn, is in cahoots with the newspapers and determined to foil my plans to stay out of them.

'That's Jane, the wife of Grimaldi Palladino, one of the England coaches.'

'Oh! Jane Palladino. I was told she'd be here. Fantastic. Thank you very much. Of course I'll go and talk to her straight away.'

I clump over to Jane in my big, chunky heeled white platform boots, scarily short pink dress and arresting make-up and smile warmly. She jumps a little, looks me up and down, looks ever so slightly scared, then looks back down at her newspaper.

'I'm Dean Martin's wife,' I say. 'He's one of the England coaches with your husband. Do you mind if I join you?'

'Join me?' she says with great alarm in her voice. You'd think I'd asked whether I could join her and her husband for a threesome or something. I only want to sit down.

'Yes, if you don't mind. My feet are killing me.'

She looks down at my eight-inch heels and back at my face. Before she can say anything else I have sat down and called over the waiter who takes my order for a triple Bacardi and Diet Coke and a vodka and Red Bull chaser. 'No fruit at all,' I say. 'I'm happy with ice, but no fruit.'

'If you're worried about the water here being dangerous, then you should avoid the ice,' says Jane. 'The fruit is far less of a concern than the ice.'

'No, Christ, I'm not worried about dangerous water at all ... bring it on! I'm worried about the fruit because it has calories in it. No, dodgy water's fine by me. If I get ill, I'll lose weight in time for the first match, which would be great. I'm really worried about my waist measurement. What's your waist measurement?'

'Excuse me?' she says. She's very unfriendly.

'I was just wondering what your waist measurement is, because I can't get mine under twenty inches and I never eat. As you can see I've now started avoiding fruit in drinks in order to make sure that no wayward calories creep into my diet undetected but it still seems that my waist is too big. I might get some ribs removed or something. What do you think? Should I get some ribs removed?'

She's looking at me with sheer terror in her eyes. God

knows why. I'm no harm to anyone. My drink arrives and I lift a glass to clink hers, but she's too absorbed in her newspaper to notice me.

'What are you reading? Is it interesting?' I say, making one final stab at friendly conversation. I've told the woman my goddamn waist measurement, for Christ's sake, so the very least she could do is talk back to me when I'm speaking to her.

'Very interesting,' she replies with a smile. 'Want to see?' She opens the page and shows me a huge feature.

DRUNK WAG FLIES OFF TO SOUTH AFRICA

Tracie Martin, the wife of one of England's defence coaches, who became notorious when a video of her getting drunk on an exercise bike became a YouTube sensation earlier this week, has fled the country in disgrace. According to sources, Martin was asked to leave London by Football Association officials who were acting on behalf of England manager Fabio Capello. They suggested that the Wag get out of the country immediately because her presence in London was too embarrassing and too distracting for the players and team coaches. It is not clear whether her husband Dean will retain his position as one of the lower-ranking coaches in the defence department. A source this morning said, 'It is highly unlikely that Martin will keep his job. There is an expectation from Capello that the coaches' wives should set an example. He is furious about what has happened here.'

The squad, which will be revealed to the public for the first time in a press conference tomorrow, is due to leave for the World Cup in South Africa on Sunday.

The Tracie Martin episode is a huge embarrassment for Capello who has been anxious to avoid the embarrassing scenes witnessed last time England played in the World Cup. Capello has spoken openly about wanting to avoid a 'Baden-Baden situation', and has expressed his eagerness to keep the Wags out of the papers. This significantly failed to happen as Martin became the biggest news story of the week. Google announced that hers is the most searched-for name on their site and YouTube have confirmed that the video of her drinking vodka in a pink catsuit and falling off the exercise bike is, officially, the most frequently downloaded YouTube video of all time.

Capello is thought to be furious about Martin's antics and is embarrassed that he hasn't been able to silence the Wags as he promised. It seems like the Wags might, despite Capello's best efforts, have a negative impact on this World Cup after all.

What are your views on Tracie Martin? Do you think she is a sectionable exhibitionist who should be kept away from the national team? Or do you think she was having harmless fun, and Capello is making too much fuss? Go to wwww.dailymail.com/traciemartin and let us know.

'Oh, that's horrible,' I say, downing my drink and reaching for the chaser while thinking of all the people in England who now have this really terrible impression of me. 'Dean's not going to lose his job. And I'm not like that at all,' I say to Jane, attempting to appeal to her softer side. 'This article makes it sound like I've deliberately set out to upset England's chances. It was just a mistake. It could have happened to anyone.'

She gives me a stern look at this stage and I accept that, OK, it's unlikely to have happened to 'anyone'. I'm sure someone like Jane would never get herself into such an unholy mess.

'Look, I never knew that the video would be made public,' I try. 'If I'd known that, I wouldn't have gone to do the video at all. I only offered to do it to help someone out. Oh, God, this is awful . . .'

Jane stands up from her seat, folds her newspaper, takes her healthy fruit smoothie and looks down at me. 'I have to go now,' she says, then turns and walks away.

My iPhone vibrates in my hand, and I look down to see a text from Shiraz asking me to come back to the room because Paskia has a publicity adviser on the phone who wants to discuss a plan of action with me. I notice that there is also an email from Glitzy Girlz. Oh, goody. Perhaps they have good news for me. Perhaps now that I'm a YouTube sensation, they'll let me design some more jewellery for them.

To: Tracie.Martin@wags.com
From: Carla_Cresta@GlitzyGirlz.com
Dear Tracie,
Thank you very much for the emails that you have been sending to us here at Glitzy Girlz. We have been monitoring the situation with regards to the YouTube video, and whilst we do take your point that you are now famous, and therefore we might consider doing another range of your jewellery, we also have to consider whether the image

you have portrayed is the right image for Glitzy Girlz. We are strong believers in spreading a positive message to our largely young shoppers. Given the circumstances of the video and the popular public opinion of it, we have decided to shelve any plans for a future range of Tracie Martin jewellery, indefinitely. We do appreciate that this may come as a disappointment to you, but we hope you understand that we have to protect the interests of our brand above all else.

Kindest regards and many good wishes for the future.

Yours,

Carla

Oh, joy . . . it just gets better and better, doesn't it?

I let myself back into the room and once again I'm stunned by the brightness and beauty of it. The view down to the pool is amazing. If I go and get myself some binoculars, I'll be able to see every stitch on the clothing of any Wag out there. Paskia is on her feet and pacing around the room like she's in an American legal drama or something. She speaks into the mobile phone with confidence and authority, and for the millionth time I think how proud I am of her.

'Of course. No problem. I totally understand, and I'm very grateful that you are willing to help,' she is saying as she attempts to mouth to me the name of the person she is talking to. As far as I can make out she's talking to a lizard. She tries mouthing the name again and pointing dramatically towards the phone to make sure I don't misunderstand. 'Damn lizard,' she mouths. What is she talking about?

'Right, well, Mum's just come back into the room so I can brief her and call you back after your meeting.' She ends the conversation and turns to me. 'Damien Wild is on the case,' she says.

'Damien Wild? What do you mean "Damien Wild"?' My God, this is now, officially, totally out of control. Damien Wild is the new hotshot PR guru, second only to Max Clifford in his ability to handle the media.

'I mean Damien Wild. His agency has been brought in to oversee the situation in the short term. He thinks it might be better if you do an interview to take the heat out of the story. He says that he simply doesn't think that this is going to calm down if left to its own devices, and that we need to get you in front of the press before they ruin you with their depictions of you as someone deeply flawed and a danger to the credibility of the national football team.'

'Oh, God, is that what he said? Does he think I'm a danger to the image of the national football team? That is so unfair. I doubt they'll find a woman anywhere in the world who is as keen for England to do well in this tournament as I am. I'm the most patriotic person who ever lived. They should see the outfit I've got lined up for the first match . . . I don't want to ruin the surprise for you Paskia, but I've got everything sorted for that match. I even got the Cross of St George picked out in red sequins on the front of my white frilly knickers. Yet *I'm* the one who's threatening to damage the England football team? Oh, Paskia, this is unbearable, sweetheart. Where's the Bacardi?'

'No Bacardi,' she says sternly, unaware of the three I had downstairs. 'We need to be completely sober when Damien's people ring back with their final thoughts on the subject. A guy called Steve Hobbs is due to ring. He's Damien's number two and he sounds like he knows what he's talking about. He's also going to investigate the possibility of talking to a South African newspaper instead of an English one. He says he'll then let all of the English newspapers have the quotes equally distributed between them. If you do an interview with an English paper, then all the rival newspapers will turn on you.'

Oh, great. 'Any more good news?'

'Just one more thing,' says Paskia. 'Shiraz said someone left a message while I was talking to Damien's people.'

'Who?' I ask my daughter, though she seems reluctant to tell me. 'Come on, sweetheart, who called?' It's not as if things can get any worse, is it?

'It was Granny,' says Paskia, with a hint of apology in her voice.

'Great.' My mother. Christ. I feel my heart stop. Things just got a hell of a lot worse.

I probably need to tell you a little bit about my mum at this stage. She's called Angie and she's a terribly glamorous slim blonde with skin that's been sprayed tanned so much I think it's orange through to the bone by now. She has enormous fake boobs, which make her look as if she's about to go toppling forward every time she stands up on her skinny little legs. She also has these permanently pouty lips that are so huge that the term 'fish lips' doesn't even begin to cover them. It's like enormous bright red cushions have been sewn on to the front of her face. Because her lips are so enhanced it's almost like they have turned themselves inside out. She's always heavily made up, whatever time of day you catch her, because she's had her make-up tattooed on. In other words – she looks brilliant. But her lovely figure and face mask a less than appealing personality.

She spent the whole of my childhood bouncing between different lovers, moving on as soon as one man tired of her and quickly winning the affections of another. She selected her men for their ability to buy her diamonds and gave no thought at all as to which of them would be a suitable father figure for me. I grew up hearing I was ugly, unattractive and a real pain. I was always aware that having me there cramped Mum's lifestyle considerably, and since her lifestyle was all she cared about, I knew that having me there was ruining everything that mattered to her. I grew up feeling guilty for my very existence.

Looking back now, I don't see how I was any sort of inhibiting factor. It seemed to me that she went out every night regardless of the fact that she had a little girl at home left alone. My only memories of my mother during my childhood are of seeing her getting all dressed up to go out and shooing me out of the room when she came back with men. Then, one day, she just upped and left the country and decided to go and live in LA where she planned to seek her fortune. I was absolutely crushed when she went, and I realised that I meant absolutely nothing to her. I was just a teenager, still at school, when she decided to flee. It was such a colossal rejection that all the many rejections I have received since mean nothing in comparison.

I had real problems with relationships when Mum left. Don't they say, 'you find the teeth to fit your wounds'? Blimey, did I do that or what! Dating men who would reject me until, entirely by accident, I met my gorgeous, perfect, lovely husband, we fell in love and I realised that until that moment I'd never known what love was. Then we had my beautiful daughter Paskia-Rose (though that's her proper name she likes to be called just Paskia) and I've never been happier.

One thing I'm absolutely determined to be is a better mum to Paskia than my mum was to me. I know I embarrass Paskia sometimes (well, a lot of the time), but I adore her and am determined to be the absolute best mum I can be.

So, that's basically sums me up; I sometimes crave attention because I never had it as a child, but mainly I try to be the best mother and wife I can be, and when people insult me or put me down, like when that Jane dismissed me in the bar just then, I tend to just absorb it and move on. I know that a lot of women would have said something to her, and told her not to be so rude. But to me insults like that just scratch a little and slide off.

So despite what Mum was like, I have a great life. I know I'm incredibly lucky to have found Dean, and to have Paskia and this lovely lifestyle, fantastic friends and Bacardi. Every day I count my blessings, but any talk of my mother still sends me into a mad whirl of upset and pain at the best of times, and since now is significantly not the best of times, I feel particularly concerned that she's called.

Despite my reluctance to speak to Mum, I know I won't be able to relax until I phone her back, so I walk silently over to the hotel phone, and sit down on the leather chair and try to think positive thoughts before I make this phone call.

I can't talk to her here, so I take the phone and walk into the bedroom and over to the window just as two small, bright green birds zoom down and perch on the wall of my balcony. I watch them and they remind me of Dean: they're small and perky and bright and friendly. My mum never understood why I bothered with Dean. The whole concept of love, commitment and the family are as alien to her as flat shoes to a Wag. She doesn't get it. She was appalled at me spending time with him when he was just a junior player. She thought I should be off, finding myself a wealthy banker. It wasn't until Dean made it into the Premier League that she even acknowledged his existence. Imagine that? She ignores my husband for years, and then when she thinks she might get something out of him, she suddenly appears on the scene and decides to befriend him.

I remember when she first started coming round to see Dean after he was selected for Arsenal. I always thought it was odd how she'd appear at the house when I wasn't in, and just thought she'd been unlucky with her timing. It took me bloody months to realise that she wasn't interested in seeing me at all. She'd only come round to flirt out-rageously with Dean and any of his football-playing chums who happened to be there. She'd beg to be introduced to his more famous teammates and because Dean was desperate to get rid of her as soon as he could, he promised her introductions and tickets for matches because it was only then that she would leave.

Dean found mum very uncomfortable company, and would bristle whenever he saw her car pull up, or her name flash up when she phoned, but all the same he never slagged her off. She was my mother so he always treated her with respect. In fact, when Mum really wound me up by using Dean – borrowing money from him and asking him to come round and help in her house – Dean would always tell me not to be so hard on her. He's such a decent guy. I never hear him slagging off anyone . . . not ever! Well, except referees, and Grimaldi Palladino, but no one else. Other footballers slag each other off all the time – they're like a bunch of teenage girls in the playground when they get together in the changing room. Not Dean though. When I'd criticise Mum for the way she behaved, he'd always say, 'She knows no better . . . she had nothing herself. You can't expect too much of her, Tracie.' He was right. She'd been brought up to believe that a woman's only chance of acceptance and success in life was through her most feminine assets. Everything she has, she achieved through the relationships she formed with men. That's just the way she is. I suppose you could say that I am the same . . . everything I have is mine because of the man I married. That's what being a Wag is all about. But the thing is, I married Dean because I loved him, and I continue to love him. I'd even go so far as to say that if Dean lost everything tomorrow, I'd still be with him. Though I must admit I would find that quite difficult. Because I do really like having lots of nice shoes.

I reach over, pick up the phone and dial her number.

'Angie speaking, hello,' she says in a sing song, semi-Californian tone. She left the place about ten years ago, but has managed to cling on to the accent.

'Mum, it's me,' I say, and I brace myself for the crushing sense of disappointment that will be implicit in every word she says.

'What on earth do you want?' she says crisply. 'I'm waiting for an important visitor.'

I swallow the familiar lump in the back of my throat. Why does she have to be so cruel? Does she talk to everyone in this tone of voice, or am I being singled out for special treatment? No one has the power to hurt me like my mother. Her swinging rejection comes like a punch from a heavyweight boxer.

'I thought you called me,' I say. 'I'm just returning the call. How are you? Is everything OK?'

'No, everything is not OK,' she says. 'I'm waiting here for a newspaper journalist to arrive, and he's late. They want to talk about you and this silly YouTube thing you did. The journalist wants to check whether you are in this hotel in South Africa, so I called to check. That's all. There was no need to call me back.'

'Mum, please don't do interviews with journalists. The Football Association are very keen for me to try and keep out of the papers now while they work out a plan for getting through this. It's going to make my life very difficult if you start talking to the media.'

'No, Tracie, what makes your life very difficult is that you do silly things, like get drunk while cycling in a pink Lycra tracksuit on a bicycle. That's what got you into trouble. Now people want to talk to me. I'm about to launch a range of macrobiotic candles so I need the publicity. I can't turn down free press like this, Tracie. If you really don't want to be in the papers then you need to think about how you conduct yourself. Don't start lecturing me.'

Oh, great. This is going as brilliantly as phone calls to my mum always do.

'OK, talk to the newspaper then. But don't tell them what hotel I'm in, please.'

'I'm quite sure that they'll be able to find out,' she says. 'They're not stupid . . . unlike someone I could mention.'

I put the phone down and collapse into tears, sobbing like a baby on my bed. No matter how many times she punches me in the face with words as hard as stone, I still cling on to the hope that one day I'll ring up and she'll have found something within herself that allows her to be pleased I'm calling, and perhaps even say she'd like to see me. The more I cling on, the more bitter the disappointment that clobbers me

'Hey, are you all right, Mum?' says Paskia, walking into the bedroom and running over to me when she sees me crying on the bed. 'Have you been talking to Granny, by any chance? You always look miserable when you have been talking to her.'

'Yes, sweetheart,' I say. 'But don't worry, I'm fine. Just give me a couple of minutes and I'll be back to my usual bouncy self.'

'You should just ignore her . . . everyone else does. It's not like she's important to our lives, is it? As long as you, me and Daddy are OK, then everything is fine.'

I feel tears pricking at the backs of my eyes again. This time they're tears of happiness. 'You know, you're right,' I say, cheering up immeasurably. 'You're absolutely right. Thanks, sweetheart.' I hug her closely and remind myself how incredibly blessed I am.

'Are you ready to talk business?' she says.

'Sure, fire away . . .'

It seems that while I was talking to Mum, Paskia was chatting to Steve Hobbs from Damien Wild's team and they're now convinced that the best thing is for me to do an interview not with a newspaper, but with a South African television station. They've suggested that *Morning Live* on SABC2 would be a good programme.

'They think you should go on there sooner rather than later, Mum. What do you think?'

'I think I'd better take their advice. When does this Steve Hobbs guy suggest?'

'Monday.'

Oh, lord. Monday – the day after tomorrow? The need for a Bacardi is almost overwhelming.

'OK,' I mutter, 'but I'd better talk to him first, so he can tell me what to say, or I might end up making things worse.'

'Here's his number,' says Shiraz, handing me a piece of paper with a London number scrawled on the top and a mobile number beneath it. 'He says he's in the office for the next hour, then after that he'll be on the mobile. If you call him, he'll talk through the whole thing and tell you what subject areas it would be good to avoid, and how to answer some of the questions they might ask you.'

'OK, I'll call him in a minute,' I say. 'Paskia, have you mentioned all this to Oliver at the Football Association? Are he and blazer boy happy?'

'I called him about five minutes ago,' responds Paskia. 'He said that he was very grateful to me for helping to sort all this out, and he said that with someone as intelligent and sophisticated as me in charge he didn't anticipate any more problems.' Pakia blushes to the roots of her naturally brown hair as she speaks, and gives me a big hug. At least someone seems to be having a good time. I hope this Oliver guy doesn't hurt my daughter or I will burn his genitals with hot wax and pick his eyeballs out with tweezers then shoot him with an AK-47.

To: info@theskyatnightltd.com
From: Tracie.Martin@wags.com
Dear sir/madam,
I wonder whether you can help me. I am desperately searching for a very powerful telescope that I can use in my hotel room. I need to rent it for the month of June, and it needs to allow me to see items in great detail at a far distance. For example, it might be the sort of telescope that someone could use to view the swimming pool area of the hotel from a bedroom window. I would need the telescope to be powerful and not only allow me to make out the figures by the pool but also what they're wearing and, if possible, to see the little labels on the back of their outfits indicating where they were purchased. It's also important that I can see details like the jewellery being worn by the people by the pool and the sort of make-up they are wearing. The telescope must also be able to see into handbags lying by the pool. I have attached a diagram of where my room is in connection to the pool; the arrows show distances. I have marked with little crosses where those people I wish to view may be sitting. Also, please note the spa area also marked on the map. It's important that I know whether I can see it from my room, and the level of detail I might be able to see.
Please advise.
Yours in hope,
Tracie Martin
PS I would need to hire the telescope from 23rd May and

will need to keep hold of it until England get knocked out of the World Cup. Please don't be witty and suggest that this is going to be within the first couple of weeks.

PPS I'm not a stalker; this is research. There's a big difference.

Chapter Eight

Monday 17th May: my first international TV appearance

Here we go then ... I'm all dressed up and off to the TV Centre in Cape Town from where they film segments for *Morning Live*.

My daughter is here with me in case things go wrong, and she has Oliver on direct dial on one phone and Steve Hobbs lined up on another. Nothing, I tell you, *nothing* can go wrong!

Shiraz was very insistent this morning that she, Mich and Suse should stay behind at the hotel, for fear that their presence might ruin everything. The disappointment in Mich's gorgeous moss-coloured, slighty slanty eyes was clear for everyone to see. She hadn't been to bed and had spent the time getting herself dressed up until she was a vision of Wag perfection. Honestly, when she walked into my room this morning with legs of vibrant orange and hair as yellow as banana custard I felt a swell of pride. You don't find yourself the colour of tango by accident; it takes a lot of work. As does turning naturally glossy mahogany-coloured hair to a bright canary yellow. You need to put in some serious labour to be a Wag and you can never accuse Mich of being work-shy.

I was particularly pleased to see that Mich had lost the

plot around her ankles in true Wag style, and the contrast between the white patches on her feet and the deep orange of her calves was a sight to see. Her hands were the colour of chocolate HobNobs, which made me smile. Fancy taking the time to do the tanning herself when there's a Spa Island where some kindly lady would have done it for her, and not made her look like a patchwork quilt.

'Love, you should have gone to the spa to get your tan done,' I said.

'I tried, but they wouldn't let me in,' she replied. 'They were moaning on about how I was too drunk, and that they didn't want to treat me while I was singing, burping and falling over.'

Blimey, this hotel is in for a real shock if that is their view. They've got two dozen Wags arriving here in a week's time; drunkenness is something they're simply going to have to get used to.

Anyway, we left Mich in the bar with Suse and Shiraz (my exercise-obsessed assistant, not the drink – though I'm imagining by now there'll be plenty of drink out as well) when we headed for the TV station. Paskia led the way like a general leading troops into battle. Stern and stony-faced she marched us to the reception and announced our arrival.

Now I'm here and preparing to take my place on the sofa. I have been told in no uncertain terms what I can and can't say by Steve. Above all, he has urged me not to be waylaid into talking about the YouTube thing too much. 'They'll ask you about it, of course, and that's fair enough. What you need to do is to shake your head, tell them it was all just a silly thing that went wrong, and move on to other subjects. The more seriously you treat it, the more seriously it will be treated by everyone else. OK?'

'Yes,' I said, though I have to confess that I don't trust myself to be able to remember all this when I get chatting.

'Don't get chatting,' was his simple advice. 'You're not there to get chatting; you're there to try and put this YouTube story to bed and make people realise that you're a desperately nice person. I think for that reason you must avoid talking about alcohol as much as possible. Just talk about Wag fashion and beauty, and if they ask you about the England team don't make contentious comments about the players.'

'I'm never in a million years going to remember all this. It sounds too hard,' I told him.

'If you're worried just remember one thing: the whole point of this interview is to show the world that you're a really nice person. So make sure you do that.'

'OK,' I said meekly.

I'm led on to a set, which is very similar to the *GMTV* studio, and there's a female presenter called Kay Grendig who will be interviewing me. She smiles warmly, and touches my knee gently as I sit down. Her hand slides off my knee and she pulls it away in alarm ... I don't think she expected it to be so greasy. She smiles again and wipes her hand on a tissue. I'm loving the way in which the white tissue is smeared with orange afterwards. The guy beside her is called David and he's just finishing off the news headlines as I sit down. He couldn't be more perfectly designed for breakfast television if he were drawn by an artist.

'Well, that's it from me. Now over to Debbie for the weather,' he says. 'Debbie, tell us, what's in store today?'

The camera switches to a giggling and enthusiastic blonde lady who begins to tell viewers what kind of weather they can expect over the next few days.

'It's unseasonably hot,' she says. 'The hottest Autumn for a decade.' Nice one!

Kay turns to me. 'We won't mention YouTube very much,' she says loyally. 'Only where we have to for the sake of the integrity of the story, so please don't worry.'

Integrity of the story. Who does she think she's interviewing? Nelson Mandela?

'With you in five,' says a guy in jeans. Presumably he's the floor manager. They are such scruffy creatures, these floor managers. Why do they feel the need to dress like carpenters? It's the same with the guy who works on Lorraine Kelly's show. When you are working with someone like LK, the least you expect is that men would come to work in shirts and ties, wouldn't you? I mean, Lorraine Kelly!! But no, even Lady Lorraine is surrounded by floor managers in jeans and T-shirts.

'With you in two.'

'Ready?' asks Kay and I nod. I suddenly feel nervous. I know that there's a lot of interest in this interview from newspapers in Britain, and that if I say anything remotely stupid, it'll be used to attack me under headlines like JUST HOW STUPID CAN ONE WOMAN BE?

'Good morning, and a very warm welcome back to the *Morning Live* sofa where we are thrilled to tell you that we are here today with Tracie Martin. Tracie is the wife of one of the coaches to the England football team, and was all over the newspapers around the world recently when a video that she starred in became the biggest YouTube hit of all time.'

Oh, great. So much for her promises. She's managed to mention the YouTube disaster in the first sentence.

'Tracie, welcome to the morning show, and, indeed, welcome to South Africa.'

'Thank you,' I say. 'You have a very beautiful country.'

'Yes, we do, don't we?' says Kay with that duty-fixed smile that is common to morning television presenters the world over. 'Have you had the chance to see much of the country yet?'

'I've seen a couple of bars, restaurants and shops, and some of the lovely landscape,' I say, now struggling to think of what I've actually seen. I can't remember the name for the mountain with the flat top, so I decide not to mention that. 'Mainly the hotel bar.'

'Ah, yes, because you do like a drink, don't you, Tracie? The England Wags are known for their drinking. Is it something that all Wags do?'

What am I supposed to say to that? I know I'm not supposed to talk about drinking but I can't not answer the question. I'm not a politician! I decide there's no other option but to tell the truth.

'Yes, I love drinking,' I say. 'I love that feeling when you're completely hammered and don't know what on earth you're doing. I'm always looking for people to drink with. One time I got my housekeeper so drunk she thought she was an owl. That was hysterical – she was hooting as she ran around the house.' I'm laughing away to myself, recalling how funny it all was when I look up and see Kay looking at me like I'm nuts.

'OK,' she says, smiling bravely. 'Now, we've all heard about you here in South Africa because of your YouTube hit which became such an international story. You've been on the news, in the newspapers and in the magazines around the world. It's been amazing, hasn't it?'

'Yes, it's been amazing, all right,' I say, 'though I don't quite understand why it took off like it did.'

'Well, let's see, shall we?' she says with a look and a tone that can only be described as smarmy. 'Let's remind the viewers what the YouTube video was all about, and why it became such a tremendous hit.'

They cut to the video of me shrieking and laughing while downing vodka from the bottle, and I'm forced to watch the thing for the first time. I don't look fat at all! I can't believe it . . . the three of us are just three normal girls, having a drink while we chat. I fall off the bike and collapse on to the floor and fall asleep. I can't help howling with laughter. No wonder it's been such a huge hit. It's hysterical!

When the video ends and the camera cuts back to me, I'm laughing so much I can't control myself. Tears are running down my face. God, that was funny. Mich looks hysterical when she cycles, and Suse's hair is all over the place. I wish I'd watched that before – it might be the funniest thing I've ever seen in my life.

'Do you think that was very responsible of you?' asks the presenter.

I'm sorry, and I know I'm supposed to be trying to rebuild my reputation with this TV show, but I can't help but just be honest with her. 'That was hysterical!' I say. 'It was three great friends having fun, having a little drink while chatting to each other. It's harmless. The world is full of people doing really bad things, and hurting one another. There is never a time when there is not a war taking place somewhere in the world. Politicians are behaving badly on a daily basis, there are children starving, suffering and dying. This is just a funny video in which three women drink too much and fall off their bikes. We didn't hurt anyone but ourselves.

'If I've made people around the world laugh and smile through this video then, I'll be honest with you, I'm glad I did it. I know that's not a very politically astute thing to say, and I know I should regret what I did, but come on – that was very funny and a lot of people have laughed a lot after seeing it, so what is it that I'm supposed to be regretting?'

'People are saying that you poured shame on your national football team, and have made them laughing stocks'

'That's absurd,' I say honestly. 'What's it got to do with the England football team if I get drunk? Anyway, I just hope that those who are laughing at the team enjoy their laughter now while they can, because I know how hard the players have worked. There is one thing I can guarantee to everyone watching this show . . . there will be no one laughing when they start playing football.'

'We'll be back after this break with more from Tracie Martin,' says Kay to the camera, as they cut to adverts for nappies. Neither of the two presenters talks to me during the break, which doesn't bother me unduly. I know I'm breaking all the rules, and failing to think about my reputation, but Dean's nan, who I was really close to, once told me that whatever you do in life, you must be true to yourself.

She often used to talk about having belief in yourself. She used to say that as long as you did what you believed to be the right thing, no one could ask any more of you. I'm kind of doing that now, and it's giving me a confidence I never realised I had.

'In five, four, three, two . . .'

Kay puts the smile back on and begins to speak. 'Now, you join us back on the sofa with Tracie Martin and we have been chatting about the YouTube video that caused such a sensation. Tell us, would you Tracie, where this whole Wag thing came from? We didn't have Wags in the past, but now suddenly it seems to be all we're talking about whenever football tournaments are mentioned.'

There's a warm smile and a jolly laugh from David – you know, one of those TV laughs that is designed to encourage you to think of him as your best friend. He's got his hands interlocked and placed on his thigh as he leans in with his head tilted, his hair immaculate, his face flawless and his smile permanent and slightly irritating. I'm not fooled by his false integrity. I suspect that, by night, he's a brutal serial killer who breaks into hospitals and murders babies.

'Oh my God,' I say, and smile at her in a pally fashion, crossing my legs slowly, taking care to make sure that my Barbie-pink Louboutins are seen from every angle by every camera. I love these shoes, and I know that all the women watching will be wondering 'are those Louboutins?' I don't want to leave them guessing, so I leave to one side all fears about how much of myself I expose to the camera in this short skirt, and make sure they can see the giveaway red soles.

'As long as there have been footballers, there have been footballers' wives,' I say. 'Honestly, I know it seems as if the Wags are a very new breed of woman, but the truth is that we have always been around. In the past though, the Wags kept out of the spotlight because football wasn't very big business, and the footballers themselves didn't get that much publicity, unless they were someone like George Best. Footballers are much more famous now, and I guess that because of that, and because they're much richer, there's been more interest in them and in the lives they lead.'

'Yes, very interesting,' says Kay, while David nods and continues to smile. 'Is it true that some people in England don't like the Wags?'

'I find that very hard to believe,' I say with absolute honesty because I do find it very hard to believe that anyone has any sort of objection to the Wags. 'People have accused us of having the spending power of trust-fund babes and the sophistication of teenagers left alone in the house for the first time. What's wrong with that? These are the glory days of the Wag. People who don't adore us for our mindless extravagance with our husbands' wallets and our colossal drinking power are simply jealous.'

Kay claps her hands together in joy, and laughs out loud. 'You know, Tracie Martin, you're an absolute star. I love your confidence and honesty and I know that the people of South Africa are going to love you too. Would you mind coming back on here again soon?'

'Sure,' I say. 'I'd love to.' I'm quite startled by the turn-around. I felt sure that Kay and I were not going to hit it off. She's not the sort of woman that I usually end up becoming friends with. But if she wants to hold out the hand of friendship, then I will shake it. I wonder whether she is angling for a night on the vodka with me.

'Now, we've got some hot news in from London,' Kay continues. 'The England squad and coaches have assembled at the Football Association, where the details of the playing squad and coaching squad is about to be announced to the world. We're trying to see whether we can go over there live now.'

'Tracie, do you have a view on which players you think should be named in the squad today?'

'God, no. No views at all,' I reply, much to their surprise. 'Well, the only thing I'd say is that it would be good if Dio got selected. I honestly don't know anything about football. I used to go and watch Dean playing all the time but I never had a clue what was going on. I have learned how to understand some of the rules of the game ... for example, I know how to explain the offside rule through shoe shopping, and I can explain free kicks through make-up application, but that's where my knowledge of football ends.'

I look up and see that Kay and David are laughing heartily.

'You're a scream,' says Kay. I shrug. Why am I a scream? 'Can you really explain the offside rule through shoe shopping?'

'I can indeed,' I say.

'Oh, hang on, we've managed to connect to London, and we understand that Dio has been selected – a complete surprise selection, so it looks as if you might be more up on football matters than you realised Tracie. Now, apparently there is someone there would like to talk to you.'

I look at the monitor and there, in all its stubbly glory, is my husband's lovely face.

'We have Tracie here on the sofa, Dean. Would you like to talk to her?'

I feel my heart beating furiously just at the sight of my husband. He looks absolutely bloody terrified. It must have taken a lot for him to have been persuaded to do this. I called him last night to tell him that I was going on to *Morning Live*, but I had no idea that he'd be on here too.

'All right, sweetheart,' he says. 'How's it going?'

'It's going well, love,' I say. 'Are you OK? Are you eating properly?'

Dean nods. 'I've got some news for you,' he says. 'I've been promoted.'

There are *oohs* and *ahhs* in the studio, and I just feel this massive relief that things are still going well for my husband. My greatest fear after the YouTube fiasco was that he would be overlooked by the England management because of his difficult wife.

'What are you now, love?' I ask, because I must admit that keeping track of Dean's job title and the various promotions he's had of late is proving beyond me.

'I'm the first-in-command to the assistant defence coach now,' he says. 'They think Richard, the guy who was the first-in-command has got swine flu, so they've had to take him away from the players in case he contaminates them.'

'Hoorah for swine flu!' I say. Prompting a wide-eyed, open-mouthed look from Kay, headshaking from my daughter and continued smiling from dashing David. 'I mean, sad for him, hope he gets better and all but—'

'Well,' Kay interrupts, 'that was Tracie Martin telling us all about her life as a Wag. We look forward to having her back on the sofa with us again soon. Now, have you ever wondered why your pastry is too salty? According to leading chefs and food experts at the University of Johannesburg it could be because you're putting too much salt in it. Here's Jamie with the full story . . .'

While the groundbreaking news stories continue to roll in the newsroom, I'm taken out by the floor manager who congratulates me wildly, and suggests that I come back on to the show next week.

'We'll obviously pay you,' he says, which makes me think that I must look as if I need the money. Did he not see the red soles on my shoes?

'I'll talk to my people and get back to you,' I say, and he hands me his card.

'Thanks again for coming in,' he says. 'You did brilliantly. Well done.'

'Thank God that's over,' says Paskia. 'I was terrified all the way through. I kept thinking that you were going to say something daft, and get yourself into trouble all over again.' She gives me a huge hug.

'Thanks for having so much confidence in me,' I say.

'I don't mean it like that,' she says. 'I just didn't want you all over the papers again, that's all. I can't believe you've told them you'll go back on next week.'

'I've got no intention of going on again,' I say, shoving the floor manager's card deep into my Chanel handbag. 'That's me done now. I'm going focus on the important things in life for the rest of the trip, like having facials, acrylic nail extensions, Hindu abdominal pummeling for weight loss and electro-thermal pore-reduction suction therapy.'

'Sounds painful,' she says. 'Now are you coming back to the hotel? The cab's waiting.'

'No, not yet, love. You take the cab. I'll see you back at the hotel later.'

I want to look around the shops first because you know those gorgeous silver thigh-length, stiletto-heeled boots that I saw in *Heat* magazine and am desperate to buy – no, *need* to buy – to wear when the other Wags arrive. Well, I *have* to have them, and Shiraz reckons I should be able to get them at this store called Apsley in Cape Town.

'Where are you going?' she asks, the alarm ringing through her voice.

'There are a few things I want to buy,' I explain. 'You're more than welcome to come with me, in fact I'd dearly love you to come, but I am going to be shopping, and there are going to be thigh-length boots involved.'

'I'll see you back at the hotel,' she says with a smile. 'I'll go for a swim and read my book by the pool. I might as well make the most of this hot weather while it lasts.'

Pask jumps in the cab and I ask the guys at the television centre to book me another. I sit down in the shiny white reception area to wait for it, perching myself on a bamboo sofa loaded with bright multi-coloured cushions. I hate waiting for things. I always think about the things I could be doing instead . . . like drinking or shopping.

My phone tinkles into life in my handbag, and I reach in and grab it. It's an unknown number.

'Tracie Martin speaking,' I say, in my best sing-songy voice.

'Tracie, it's Damien Wild here.'

'Hi! Damien!' I say. 'I just did the TV show.'

'I know, I saw.'

'Did you? Are you in South Africa then?'

'No, on the web. It was excellent. Well done.'

'Thanks.'

'You came over very well today and now I'm convinced it's going to blow over, OK.'

'Yes,' I say. 'I'm not worried.'

'Your assistant seems to be fraught with worry that if you're spotted by a photographer it will be the end of the world, so I'll have a word with her. It would be best if you kept the lowest profile that you can, but if you do end up in the papers, it's not the end of the world. OK?'

'Yes, thanks for calling,' I say, and he hangs up. Awww . . . what a nice man.

Damien Wild has a reputation for being a complete savage. I thought he ate babies for breakfast and children for lunch. He seems nice though. I wonder whether he's single. Perhaps I could fix him up with Mich or Suse . . .

I look up to see a guy waiting by the doors. Fantastic, my car is here. I can now concentrate on the serious issue of buying silver foil-covered boots. Focus, Tracie, it's shopping time.

'Are you Mrs Martin?' asks the guy. He's a huge man – maybe six foot six with a gorgeous but weathered face and stunning blue eyes. They're small but the most intense blue – like the sky in Spain, when you're lying on a pedalo, looking up on a hot summer's day. They're fringed by pale, sun-bleached lashes. He looks like a windsurfer with his messy blond hair, tanned skin and rippling muscles. He's a beautiful man in a delicious, unkempt sort of way, with heavy stubble all over his chin, but a gentleness about him as he leans down to talk to me, looking ever so slightly nervous.

'Yes, I'm Tracie Martin,' I say with a warm smile. 'Can you take me here please?' I show him the name of the shop I want to go to that I've written down on a scrap of paper. He reaches out for the address and I can't help but notice the strength of his forearms beneath the sun-kissed blond hairs on them. Gosh, this chap is *all* man. I must be missing Dean more that I thought if I'm lusting after random taxi drivers. It's all this sunshine. It plays havoc with a girl's hormones.

'I'll need to go back to my hotel after that, is that OK?' I add, smiling at him girlishly.

The guy looks desperately confused by my request.

'Oh, you think I'm the cab driver, don't you?' he says eventually, all smiles and blushing beneath the dark blond stubble on his strong, manly chin.

'Yes. Are you not a driver? I'm waiting for a cab. That's why I'm sitting here.'

'No, I'm not your driver,' he says. 'I'm here because I need just a minute of your time.'

He reaches out to touch me as he speaks, and I notice how large his hands are. Good God, what is it they say about men with big hands? Or is that men with big feet?

'My name is George Evans,' he says, continuing to speak, sublimely unaware of my fascination with his hands. 'I work for AFFAH, a charity that helps people in South Africa's slums. There are children dying on the streets of South Africa every day. There are children here in Cape Town without homes, parents or anyone to look after them. Our charity desperately needs help in looking after them. I saw you on the television this morning, and you seemed so sweet and kind so I thought I'd approach you.'

Me? Sweet and kind? Shucks. That's so nice.

'But, what can I do?' I ask.

'Did you know that over fifty per cent of the population of South Africa is living below the poverty line?'

'No,' I say. The country doesn't seem poor. They have a Gordon Ramsay restaurant in the hotel. They have a Spa Island, for goodness sake. How can they be poor?

'Well it is. All the city's wealth is owned by very few. There are hundreds and thousands of people who wake up hungry and go to bed hungry. Please let me show you the problems in Cape Town and tell you how you can help. Let me buy you a cup of coffee and explain. I'm not going to do anything to hurt you. I need you to trust me.'

The thing is, as eager as I am to buy my silver boots, and trot off back to the hotel for pampering treatments, I'm touched by his words. I find myself completely trusting this guy. There's something so warm, simple and kind about him. He seems desperate for my help, and I love the idea that I may be able to do something useful for someone else, though quite what he wants me to do is a mystery.

I'm such a soft touch when it comes to charities of any kind. Dean's always telling me off. He played a charity match in Blackpool once and I was so moved by the plight of the donkeys on the beach that I paid hundreds of thousands of pounds for them to be released. It caused chaos of course, as most of my helpful gestures do. When I stood there waving my hands and shouting, 'You are free! Go, be happy, free donkeys! Gallop around all day' they just stood there looking at me with their funny little faces tilted to the side, not going anywhere and masticating slowly.

OK, I thought. I'll take them back to Oxshott with me, but Dean wasn't having any of it. 'You've bought what???' he said when I turned up at the game with four donkeys clip clopping behind me on pieces of string. I couldn't get them into the clubhouse, and was worried about tying them up outside. I'll admit now that I never thought the thing through properly when I said I'd buy them.

'And how do you propose we get them back to Oxshott?' he said.

'Ride them,' I said wisely.

'What? On the fucking motorway?' he replied as I fed sugar lumps to them outside the director's box.

Anyway, I ended up giving them to a donkey sanctuary and we pay a chunk of money every month for the sanctuary to look after them. They send photos of how well they're doing now, which is nice.

I'm like that with any charity-type thing. Those NSPCC adverts on the television leave me in pieces. You know the ones with the gorgeous little boy with huge eyes, staring out sadly and appealingly. 'This is little Timmy; he's scared to go to bed at night because . . .'

Oooooo . . . that's me – done. I've got my credit card in my hand before they've finished the sentence, and I'm phoning up begging them to save Timmy with twenty grand.

As soon as Dean so much as hears a charity advert on the telly he's down those stairs like greased lightning; if only he'd shown such speed as a footballer, he might have had a more impressive career. He races into the room and hurls himself between me and my credit card. He's usually too late though, and that's why I make monthly payments to NSPCC, Save the Badgers, various wildlife sanctuaries, dogs homes, cats homes and bird protection leagues, life boats, army benevolent, the Make-A-Wish Foundation, Cancer Research UK, children's hospitals and charities for every illness known to mankind. Also Wild And Green (don't know what the charity does, but they said they were the WAG charity so I signed the form in seconds).

So, given that I'm involved in around twenty charities, it wouldn't hurt to talk to this guy about what he does, especially since Dean's miles away . . . and this guy has madly large hands and lovely forearms . . .

George leads me down the street in search of a coffee shop, him taking one stride for every six of mine, as I hobble along on my pink high heels next to him. I notice that he has a slight limp but it doesn't seem to affect the speed at which he skits across the pavement. We stop outside a scruffy little cafe and he suggests going inside. I'm not going anywhere near this place. It looks so grubby and not me at all. I'm happy to 'do' charity, but can't we do it in style? Besides, you can't get a drink in there. We walk on a bit until we find another cafe. 'I simply couldn't be seen in there,' I explain when he tries to manoeuvre me into it. We walk past six coffee shops in the end, but they're all, well, not me.

'Can't we go for a drink?' I say. 'I could murder a cocktail.'

'I don't do bars,' he responds sombrely. 'I'm a recovering drug addict and alcoholic.'

'Wow!' I say, open-mouthed. 'Wow, wow, wow! I've never met one of those before.'

'There are lots of us around,' he says with an embarrassed

shrug. 'Coffee's my only drug these days.'

'Well, let's get you some coffee then,' I say, leading him into the coffee shop despite my initial reservations. We order at the counter then head over to an empty table by the window. George sits down opposite me. He's such a big guy that he spills over the sides of the chair, his big shoulders extending way beyond the confines of the wood itself.

'Tell me about being an alcoholic,' I say. 'What was it like?'

'Let me start at the beginning,' he says. He explains that he used to be in the army in South Africa, but that he was forced to leave when half his foot was blown off after he stepped on a land mine. He pauses for a moment when the waitress comes over with our drinks. 'I came out of the army, back to Cape Town, and couldn't work out what to do with my life. I just wasted years drinking and taking drugs because I felt so sorry for myself. I was totally out of control,' he says, stirring sugar into a small black espresso while I work out how on earth to drink my frothy double mocha, chocca whipped latte with vanilla and hazelnut essence. (I don't usually drink milky drinks but I have a sudden craving. I only hope the caffeine will offset any of the calories in there.)

'What happened?' I ask.

'I ended up living on the streets; poor, tired and fed up with life. I got involved with gambling to raise money for drugs, which threw me in with some seriously bad people. I was a mess. If I had carried on living like that, I'd be dead now, but this guy called Robbie came along and helped me. You need help when you've sunk that low, which is what my charity's about now. Robbie and his wife Sarah took me in, gave me food, clothing and put me back together. With their help I went out and found my brothers Ben and Tyler, who I hadn't seen for years, not since leaving the army. The three of us set up the charity. I run it because they both work, but they're very involved. I managed, slowly and painfully, to overcome my addictions and I haven't relapsed since.'

'You what? You haven't had one little drink since? How long ago was that?'

'Six years ago. I'm an alcoholic. I had to stop drinking or I would have died.'

Bloody hell. Six years? 'Sorry, please carry on,' I say.

'Well, that's it, really, except that I'll never forget what Robbie and Sarah did for me. They were from the local church and they ended up being like a mother and father to me. They were killed in a car crash last year, but they made me realise that I could help other people. Now I run a charity called Away From Fear And Hunger (AFFAH). It's about providing food, water and clothing and sometimes shelter, if we can, for the most vulnerable people in the country. There are lots of charities working to integrate the people in shanty towns into mainstream South Africa. I just work to give them whatever we can find, to keep them alive.'

'That's amazing,' I say, genuinely impressed with George. 'But what can I possibly do to help you?'

'I rely on people contributing clothing and money,' he says. 'I can't do anything without peoples' help. I can only attract these contributions by having a public profile. That's where you come in. You're the talk of the town. You're attracting the publicity that we desperately need. Come with me and see how these people live.'

I'm intrigued by the guy's passion; the only time I see feelings running so high is when the new shoes arrive at Pitch and we squeal and jostle for the ones with the highest platforms. But how can I really help him?

'I'm still slightly confused about what I can offer you,' I say.

'Right, come with me. Let me show you what we're dealing with here and you'll soon understand what I'm after.'

George pays for our drinks and leads the way to his scruffy Land Rover. I clamber in inelegantly and buckle myself in safely. I know I'm behaving recklessly and there's a possibility that I'm about to be murdered and/or sold into white slavery, but, to be totally honest with you, what concerns me more, right now, is the fear of the dirty seat belt leaving an ugly mark on my outfit.

'The problem in South Africa is that forty per cent of the income is in the hands of the top ten per cent of the population, whereas the bottom forty per cent hold only ten per cent. So whilst the place may seem to be full of money, very few people actually have any of it.'

'Oh, I see,' I say, as the reality of what he's saying dawns on me.

'Look at this,' he muses as we drive through the city with its modern motorways, skyscrapers, and downtown parliament buildings. There are luxurious shopping complexes (so want to go there), theatres, cinemas and concert halls. We pass the waterfront where our hotel languishes luxuriously.

'This truly is a land of contrasts,' he says. 'You've seen the wealthy side of the city, now I'm going to introduce you to abject poverty. We're off to the Cape Flats.'

I peer through the bushes as we drive along and see tens of thousands of flimsy shacks made of cardboard, wood and paper. Soon the bushes clear and that's all I can see – these simple huts made from rubbish.

Behind the cardboard huts are corrugated iron huts shimmering in the morning sunshine on the sparse landscape. As we get out of the Land Rover, gusts of wind sweep down the hills and across the dusty ground, nudging litter into the air and swirling it around. There are people everywhere, and bony young children so skinny they look almost skeletal. Too skeletal. Who'd have thought that was even possible. These guys have got even tinier waists than Abbey Clancy. The children hunched on the sun-drenched hill jump to their feet when they see the Land Rover arrive. George goes to the boot and pulls out bags and boxes. Despite my overwhelming concern for the well-being of my fingernails, I go to help him, and we unload everything from the boot and start handing it out to these children.

'I didn't think there was poverty like this in South Africa any more,' I say, realising how naive I must sound. 'I thought that when Nelson Mandela was released from prison, that all got sorted.'

George looks at me as if I'm stark staring mad. I'm used to people looking at me like this. I've had a lifetime of people looking at me as if I am insane. But now suddenly I really care that George obviously thinks I'm stupid and for some crazy reason I burst into tears.

'It's moving, isn't it?' he says, as I slump against the vehicle and watch him handing out everything he has to tiny children with fear and desperation in their eyes. He has handed out everything he brought with him within minutes. He brought loads, but it's clear that so much more is needed. 'Children will die tonight because we can't feed them all,' he says.

'Then we must come back,' I say. 'We'll get more food and drink and come back. We have to.'

'Yes, OK, if you will,' he says. 'I come back every day. You're welcome any time.'

George introduces me to a young girl called Zelenza. She's fifteen and has a three-month-old baby called Lilli. 'Her boyfriend was murdered while she was pregnant,' George explains. He tells me that homicide is the most common death for fifteen to forty-year-old men in Cape Town. Zelenza lives in a shack that has a pit-latrine outside. There's no plumbing so she has to beg for water from an overcrowded nearby hostel.

'I want to take her back with me,' I say.

George smiles and touches my arm lightly. 'You can't,' he says. 'It doesn't work like that. You can't rescue these people, but you can help them to rescue themselves by mentioning the charity next time you're on television.'

'I will,' I say. 'Of course I will, but tell me, how has this happened?' I survey the hundreds of thousands of people who appear to be discarded here with nothing to help them.

'They were expelled from the city and dumped into townships during apartheid. These people were the wrong colour so were exposed to legally enforced poverty. They have nothing . . . absolutely nothing.'

Even as he's talking, I can see the modern skyscrapers sparkling in the distance behind the sprawling, impoverished townships of the Cape Flats.

'I'll do everything I can,' I say, as I look out at the sea of troubled faces staring at us. They can't believe that there is no more in the truck for them. I rush over to my gorgeous designer handbag, and start handing out everything I've got. I give them the money, of course, but also the make-up I hold so dear that they may be able to swap for food that will keep them alive, the handbag itself and all the knickknacks that I kept in there that now may help save a child's life. 'I'm going to come back and help you,' I say, and I turn to George. 'Of course I'll help you. I'll do anything I can to help you. Tell me what you need.'

We drive away from the scene and the image of Lilli's hungry little face is burned into my heart and soul.

'I need publicity. We need people to know all about the charity. This is our big moment when the World Cup comes to town. It's a chance for us to bring in real money to help these people.'

I tell George that the TV company has asked me to go back on to the show next week and his eyes light up. I'd had no intention of going back on there, but I don't tell him that.

'Give me a minute,' I say, and I ring Shiraz. 'Take this number down, this is urgent,' I say, giving her the details from the card handed to me by the floor manager. 'I need you to tell them I will come back on next week if they promise to let me talk about a South African charity I'm involved with. If they won't guarantee that I can talk about the charity, I won't be doing the slot on the show. And tell them that my fee will be going directly to the AFFAH charity.'

Shiraz starts asking all sorts of questions about the

charity and where on earth I am. 'I'm in the townships on Cape Flats,' I say, and I swear I hear her scream. 'Just call the TV company straight away and I'll explain everything when I'm back' I say. 'I'll be in the hotel in around three hours.'

In the end it's more like five hours before I get back and I'm exhausted, mentally drained and emotionally frazzled as well as being laden down with more bags than you have ever seen in your life before. Seriously, there is no way you have ever seen more bags than there are lying around my feet at this moment. George's Land Rover is absolutely crammed with shopping as we pull up outside the hotel. It's unbelievable but amazingly – I know you won't believe this but it's true – the shopping is not for me!

I got on the phone and rang up every major store in South Africa, asking them to donate clothes, food or drink. I just rang round and told them that if they donated I would mention them on my television slot. That seemed to do the trick. Anything we were missing, I decided to buy myself. I also took as much money out of a cashpoint as the machine would allow me and gave it to George to help him with his work.

I clamber out of the truck. I have no shoes or jacket because I gave those away to the children in the shanty town, no handbag, cash or make-up. George stays outside in the truck with the rest of the shopping, while I wander inside to tell security that he will be coming in to unload all the stuff I've bought. He says that if he leaves it in the back of the truck, even for the afternoon, it'll be stolen and he doesn't think it'll be safe in the little shack they have (they call it their warehouse but it's just a really ropey old shed) so we'll have to bring it into the hotel before taking it all out again this evening.

I walk in and bump straight into Jane strolling through reception in neat leisurewear. She's carrying a wet towel and it looks like she is coming from an early afternoon swim.

'Hello,' I say, trying to be as friendly as possible.

'Oh, it's you,' she says, regarding me with alarm. 'What have you done to yourself?'

I know I look a dreadful mess: my clothes are all dishevelled, my hair's all over the place and I'm not wearing shoes, but none of that mattered earlier when we were focused on getting as much stuff as possible to help the poor people. Now I find myself squirming uncomfortably under her condemning gaze and smoothing my hair down.

'I've had an incredible day,' I say, and I'm about to start telling her all about the shanty town to try and recruit her to help in any way she can when my phone rings and Dean's number flashes up.

'Excuse me just a moment, would you please?' I say.

'Darling, how are you?' I say to my husband. He's at the altitude training base today, and then he heads for Rustenburg tomorrow.

'I've been trying to call you for the past few hours. Where have you been?' he asks, but before I can answer he says that the bank have called him to tell him that they think that the card's been stolen. 'An absolute fortune's been taken out of the account,' he says.

'No, it was me. I took about quarter of a million rand from cashpoints around Cape Town to spend mainly shopping and on food and drink and stuff,' I say. 'Oh, and there might be some big payments on the account because I must have spent about half that again in the shops today.'

I look up and see Jane staring at me, open-mouthed.

'Mrs Martin, where would you like this man to put all your shopping?' says the concierge, as George appears in the doorway with all my bags. A rugged, handsome man, smiling at me warmly and carrying my shopping.

'Well, it seems as though you've had a wonderful morning,' says Jane, looking me up and down and looking at George in disgust. Behind him the porters are bringing in bags and bags of shopping. The mountain of bags continues to rise, filling the reception area. I suddenly realise how dodgy all this looks . . . I'm here in a state of considerable dishevelment with a young guy who I have clearly just spent the entire morning with, clutching the phone to my husband who is asking me about all the money I've spent.

'Oh, God, Jane, this must look awful!' I say, laughing a little as I speak while Dean is on the other end of the phone chatting about how he doesn't mind me spending money, but this was really quite a lot and it might be an idea for me to set myself a limit when I go shopping.

'No need to explain,' says Jane, walking across the reception towards her room. 'No need for anything, Tracie.' With that, she's gone, and I'm left in the reception with a million shopping bags, one of the kindest men I've ever met, a bunch of very confused hotel staff and a husband who thinks I've gone on the biggest spending spree of our entire marriage.

'Dean, I'll call you later,' I say, hanging up the phone, and turning to the hotel staff. 'Now, is there anywhere we could store these bags until tonight?' I ask. 'We'll need them to be carefully looked after.'

'I'll pick you up at seven o'clock, shall I?' asks George, and I nod warmly.

'Looking forward to it,' I say. 'You're a remarkable person, George Evans, and I'm going to help you all I can.'

I notice the knowing glances between the staff on the hotel reception desk but decide to ignore them. It's time for me to have a well-earned glass of Bacardi. Though for some reason when I get to my room what I end up ordering is a bacon sandwich and a nice pot of tea.

Chapter Nine

10 a.m., Tuesday 18th May

It's bright and early when I begin to rouse from a deep sleep full of colourful images of me on a white stallion (wearing the long silver boots, of course) riding into the shanty towns of Cape Town like a knight in shining Armani. I give out love, money, food and happiness wherever I go. Everyone adores me. Even my mother appears and tells me how proud she is of me. It's amazing. Everyone is chanting my name but it's not like at the airport where they chanted because they thought I was a terrible drunk; they're chanting now because I'm their saviour. I turn to leave but they insist that I stay, they're all reaching up and trying to hold me, they're pulling my hair to try and stop me going because they love me so much, and want me to stay . . .

I wake up in considerable discomfort to find that my gorgeous pink, glittery eyemask has tangled itself up in my hair extensions and bundled itself into a knot, which is pulling on my scalp. Damn thing. I try to go back to sleep to pick up the dream where I left off, but it's no good. It's gone, so instead of dreaming about saving the world from poverty, I'm forced to tackle the rather more mundane job of untangling my hair extensions. I'm not sure whether it's the thin elastic at the back of the eyemask or the plastic nature of the hair extensions themselves, but the whole thing has got itself into the most tremendous mess. Damn thing.

I push back the voile curtains and see Shiraz running round and round the pool in athletic gear while Mich stands there in a gorgeous leopard-skin playsuit and knee-length black boots, clutching a stop watch. What is Shiraz up to? Is she hoping to get picked to play football for England or something? She's obsessed with being as fit as she can be.

Still, the good thing is that if they're all happily entertaining themselves, it means that I can sneak out for the morning and buy those silver boots at last. I grab a couple of miniature bottles of Bacardi and throw them into my bag. I'll have them in the cab. Breakfast's the most important meal of the day, so it's important that I have something, but – weirdly – for once I don't fancy the Bacardi right now.

I slip into the back seat of the cab, hand over the name address of the shop and sit back and relax. The boots are so beautiful, you wouldn't believe it. They're stunning. The nicest boots I've ever seen in my whole life, and I have to have them. I've even worn a short, silver mini dress so that when I get the boots they'll match perfectly. I'm wearing them with long white, plastic boots for the journey, then I'll swap them over once I've bought the shiny new ones. I'm beyond excited. New boots. NEW BOOTS. IN SILVER!! Can you imagine?

1 p.m.

How depressing! The shop's not open because the woman who runs it is ill. Ill? What can she possibly be ill about when she works in a room full of Louboutins all day? For

God's sake, what's wrong with this country? Why's it so hard to get a simple pair of thigh-length, glittery, space-age, shiny, silver designer boots on a Tuesday morning? Why? Can you buy bread? Oh, yes, you can buy bread. Can you buy milk? Oh, yes, plenty of milk. But boots? Nope. You can't buy boots. Well it seems to me that they've got their priorities in life completely muddled up.

I sit back in the cab and think about the hellish predicament I'm in. No boots. Even the thought of Bacardi isn't exciting me all that much. I just don't fancy it when I'm bootless. Bacardi simply doesn't taste the same when you're not wearing Louboutins. And I so wish I hadn't just brought up the subject of food in my mind. Now I'm dying for something to eat. How weird is that. Must remember to leave extra notes for Shiraz when I get back.

1.20 p.m.

Shiraz,
Just to remind you (yes, before you ask, you can put this in the pink file), under no circumstances must I eat while in South Africa. If you see me attempt to eat, please cut off my hands. I mustn't eat. Do you hear me? Food is a joke. A joke. Don't let food anywhere near me.
Tracie x
PS I'm having a hot leaves eyebrow massage in 10 mins. See you later.

Tracie,
Oooo . . . I love jokes. Please leave me a food joke!
Thanks,
Shiraz x

2.45 p.m.

Shiraz,
No, not 'food jokes'. Food is a joke. I don't mean that I had food jokes, I just meant that food itself was a . . . oh, what the hell . . . Which cheese would you use to entice a grizzly down from a mountain? Camembert.
Tracie x
PS I'm going for a cherry blossom cuticle treatment in 15 mins. See you later.

Tracie,
Ha ha ha ha . . . more food jokes please. More food jokes.
Shiraz x

4.10 p.m.

Shiraz,
I'm happy to provide you with food-related humour as long as you are taking on board the most important factor in all this – you must stop me from eating. OK. What cheese would you use for hiding small horses? Mascarpone.
Tracie x
PS I've got a lily and ginger hip-wrap now. Catch you later.

Tracie,
Don't worry, I'll definitely stop you eating but please tell me more jokes. I've met this FAB guy in reception just now. He's gorgeous. He was asking for you. I told him the cheese jokes and he loved them.
Shiraz x

5.30 p.m.

Shiraz, where are you? Can you stay in the room please so I can talk to you when I get back from my butterfly wing eye therapy? See you back in the room at 6.30pm.
Tracie x
PS What do you call cheese that isn't yours? Nacho cheese!!
Final cheese joke of the day: What do you call a cheese factory in the Middle East? Cheeses of Nazareth.

6.45 p.m.

I hope Shiraz is prepared for an almighty shock because I'm returning from my rather elaborate butterfly-wing lower-eyelid therapy with the mashed butterflies still on my eyes (they said they needed a few hours to work their magic so I thought I'd leave it on).

I wander through the hotel's reception area, smiling sweetly and taking in the alarmed faces of all the staff. I look like an extra from a Lady Gaga video or something. I'm tempted to fall into a robotic dance but I opt instead for diving into the lift out of view.

Sadly, and much to the great surprise of both of us, Jane is coming out of the lift in her standard-issue gym wear as I leap into it covered in butterfly wings. She jumps a little, baulks at my alarming appearance and darts through the reception area as if being chased by a swarm of bees. Bless here. I bet she's not one for extreme beauty treatments.

I practically run down the corridor towards the room, having convinced the security guards situated at the end of it that I am indeed Tracie Martin and not a loon, and burst into the suite, relieved to be out of public view. But, my problems aren't over yet. Oh, no. Unbeknownst to me my delightful assistant has invited George into the suite and he leaps up when he sees me, with concern written across his face.

'Have you been attacked?' he says.

'No,' I say, shielding my face.

'You look as if you've been attacked by insects,' he says. 'How could someone be attacked by insects?'

'I haven't been. It's just a beauty treatment. It's nothing. I've just been relaxing. How about you? What are you doing here? Did we arrange to meet up?'

'Nope,' he says, still squinting at my face to get a better look at the dead butterflies lying across it. 'Just wanted to pop in to say thanks very much for yesterday. You were a star. A complete star,' he says.

'Yes, you are, you are,' says Shiraz. 'George has been telling me all about the charity. It's completely amazing. Really brilliant. You're such a super-woman. I didn't realise that's where you were last night. Helping poor people. What an amazing person.'

Gosh.

'Thanks,' I say, as she hugs me tightly. I'm not quite sure how to respond to that. There's nothing amazing about me; I'm just a silly woman with squashed butterflies all over her face. I only did what anyone else would have done. All the praise belongs to George.

'Have you told Dean?' asks Shiraz

'No, he's kind of got his hands full, and there's nothing to tell, not really.'

'Yes, there is,' she retorts. 'You absolutely have to tell him or I will.'

'Why?'

'Because I want him to know how special you are.'

That's so sweet.

'Well, OK then. I'll tell him.' The thing is, far from being impressed, I think Dean will just become concerned. He'll remember the donkey incident and be fearful that I'll arrive at the first match with fifty thousand Cape Town children following me, and that I'll be trying to adopt them and take them back to Oxshott. Wait a minute – could I do that? Could I become the Madonna of South Africa?

Chapter Ten

Wednesday 19ᵗʰ May

South African Daily News

A WAG WITH A HEART OF GOLD

A news report special by Stuart Prentice-Bronks

England's brightest, blondest Wag, who hit headlines around the world when a video of her cycling while drunk became a YouTube hit, proves there's more to her than lip gloss and hairspray. Tracie Martin was famed for her YouTube video sensation, which became the most watched in history, but I can reveal that she has been spending her evenings with the poor and destitute of South Africa. While lesser Wags might be indulging in spa treatments and champagne at the luxury hotel in Victoria and Albert Harbour, Martin has been helping the poor.

Tracie, wife of defence coach Dean Martin, was spotted by our reporter Monday night as he observed her dishing out food and drink to the poor and lonely, offering clothes to the needy, and spending hours talking to the young mothers in Cape Town's Khayelitsha area. The heavily-made-up wife of the England coach was so busy handing out food parcels and clothing to starving children that she said she did not have time to be interviewed when approached by our reporter.

It's been an interesting few weeks for the permanently tanned Wag who conducted her first TV interview on Monday morning and became a real hit with South Africans for her lively personality and complete honesty. This further news of her kindness towards others will serve to further endear her to the people of South Africa.

George Evans, the coordinator of the AFFAH charity based in Cape Town told us: 'Tracie has donated all this food and clothing herself – she has paid for it and she has offered to raise funds for us in the future. She has been extraordinarily generous with her time and her money. She has already done more for the good of this country and its people than many do in a lifetime, and she only arrived a couple of days ago.'

I can't get over that someone has written something so nice about me. A lone tear slides down my face and through my make-up. I peer into the mirror; it's like the blades of a skier have sliced through freshly fallen snow.

'That's nice, that is,' I say to my daughter, snorting back the tears inelegantly. 'Really nice.'

'I think it's time to tell Dad, don't you?' she says, so I pick up my phone and dial my husband's mobile. I'm slightly cautious because I hate to disturb him and I really don't want to worry him. In the end, though, it turns out to be the loveliest thing I've ever done, according to Dean. He says he couldn't be more proud of me, which is a pretty nice thing to hear when the only thing people usually comment on is how short my skirt is and how high my heels are.

Dean also says he's going to suggest that the players all donate some money to George's fund. 'Let's see if we can really make a difference to those children's lives, shall we?' he says and suddenly life seems almost perfect (I say 'almost' because I still don't have the damn boots).

When I've finished talking to Dean, I decide I ought to have a meeting with Shiraz. We seemed to miss each other all day yesterday and without her instruction and guidance, I've no idea what I'm supposed to be doing on a day-to-day basis. I call her into the suite and sit her down. 'OK Shiraz, what's been happening?' I ask.

'Well, I've been emailing George a lot. He's really nice,' she says, her eyes wide, bright and glowing. 'He's been telling me about all their plans for the future and the help they need. It sounds like the main thing they need is food.'

'Yes, dear, but don't mention food,' I retort. I've no idea why I seem to be so bloody hungry all the time. I'm a Wag for Christ's sake. I don't *do* hunger.

'Sorry,' Shiraz apologises. 'I'll call it the "f word", shall I? Now, I have some correspondence for you. Do you want to deal with it now?'

'Sure.'

To: Tracie.Martin@wags.com
From: Carla_Cresta@GlitzyGirlz.com
Hi Tracie,
We hope you're well and enjoying your time in South Africa. This is an email just to say that we at Glitzy Girlz are thrilled at all the work you're doing, and the amazing amount of positive publicity that this seems to be

generating around the world. The newspapers in England have all carried stories today about how hard you've worked for the poverty stricken over there. Well done! What a great tactic for getting good publicity. We're all very pleased to be associated with you.

We should also let you know that since you arrived in South Africa sales of your jewellery currently in Glitzy Girlz have rocketed. It's actually sold out in all shops, and just three bracelets exist in the warehouse.

Now, you mentioned that you might interested in designing a new range of jewellery for us. We all think this would be great! But we think we should get on with doing it as soon as possible so that we can maximise the publicity advantages that presently exist.

Rather than trouble you in South Africa, we have worked to commission a local jewellery designer to come up with some sketched ideas by the end of the day, with the hope of being able to put these into production under your name within the next few days. How does that sound? It would be under the same terms and conditions as the last project, which I hope you will find satisfactory. Kindest regards,

Carla xx

'Oh, that's an interesting development,' I say to Shiraz. 'I can't believe they thought that my being involved in charity was a publicity tactic. Why's everyone so cynical? I give loads of money to charity. It's not just to make me look good ... I genuinely want to help people.'

'I know,' says Shiraz. 'I wanted to write straight back to them and tell them to get lost when I saw that email. First they say they're not interested in you, and then they send this email saying they are full of enthusiasm and bursting with excitement about working on a new range. How dare they, Tracie? How dare they treat you like that?! Just because there was something nice in the newspapers about you they want to ride on the back of you. Makes my blood boil, Tracie, it really does. Shall I email them back and tell them to get lost?'

Now this presents me with a particularly difficult moral dilemma. Obviously I should ask Shiraz to charge back and say: 'no way, how dare you insult Tracie with your email.' But the trouble is I'm really desperate to do another range of jewellery.

'Let's hold on going back to them for now,' I say.

'You're not going to do it, are you?' Shiraz looks horrified. 'They're not even going to let you design it. Oh, please don't, Tracie. You're worth so much more than that. Let me tell them to get lost. Please.'

The trouble is I'm not sure whether I *am* worth more than that. I feel I'm lucky to have been offered this opportunity so I want to grab it with both hands.

I take the email and tuck into my handbag. I'll deal with it later. 'I'll think about that one, Shiraz,' I say. 'Nice to be wanted though, isn't it. Now, what's next?'

To: Tracie.Martin@wags.com
From: Herbe.Schmidt@SABC.com
Hi Tracie,
Just to confirm that we are looking forward to seeing you on Monday 24th of May on *Morning Live*. As requested by your manager, Shiraz, we will denote your fee for the

appearances to the charity of your choice, with an additional 50% of the fee we pay you added on as a gesture from the TV company. We are also happy to allow you a couple of minutes to talk about the charity and the work that is being done. I hope this fulfils our obligations, and we look forward very much to seeing you on 24th May. Kindest regards,

Herbe Schmidt

To: Tracie.Martin@wags.com
From: Dean.Martin@football.com
Hi gorgeous,
I got your email with the details about the charity for the players, so I thought I'd email back. Do you think that Paskia would be interested in spending some time over here with the team? There might be a role for her helping with admin. She might prefer it to spa-ing and gossiping with the ladies

Deany x

To: Tracie.Martin@wags.com
From: Rodney@theskyatnightltd.com
Dear Tracie,
Thank you very much for your email, and the detailed map indicating areas that you would like to view using our telescopes. I fear that we might be the wrong company for you, however, because we only supply telescopes for astronomical usage. It strikes me that a pair of binoculars might better suit your purposes, although I would warn you that peering through hotel windows with binoculars at people who are lounging by the pool in a semi-naked

state may lead to claims of stalking or harassment.
Kindest regards,
Rodney Von Piertsen

Silly man. Of course I'm not going to be done for harassment. Has he been talking to Dean or something? Dean's always mumbling on about stalking claims. Honestly.

'Is that all, Shiraz?' I ask, after I look through the rest of the emails, and she nods. 'Well then, I think I might have a little wander round the hotel and see who's around. What are you going to do?'

'Oh, nothing planned, really. I thought I might call George, you know, just to see how he's getting on, and see whether I can help him at all, with anything.'

'Sure,' I say, noticing the twinkle in her eye. How lovely. I don't blame her. If I were Shiraz's age I'd be in there too. He may not be a footballer, but he has these huge hands. Did I mention his hands?

Chapter Eleven

9.30 a.m., Sunday 23rd May

There is no doubt that today will be one of the best days of my life. It has to be. It's impossible to see how it won't be. It will be a day greater than any other day that anyone has ever lived in the world ever. If things go as well today as I hope they will, this day could be greater even than the time when me, Mich and Suse got really, really drunk and decided to go shopping on Oxford Street. God, that was fun. I don't know which of the many funny moments of the day was the real highlight, but I think that for me, coming home in a police car with two hundred and fourteen carrier bags of clothing, footwear and sparkly hair accessories was the perfect end to a most perfect afternoon.

I'm not sure whether the police officers felt the same way, especially when I couldn't remember my address so we had to go on a diversion to a St Tropez shop to ask them where I lived. The police didn't like that at all, but the girls in the spray tan shop thought it was the funniest thing they had ever seen.

Anyway, sorry, I got distracted there. The reason that today is going to be so fabulous is because the Wags will finally arrive in South Africa. *Yeeessssss*! There was all this talk in the papers that half of them weren't going to come and Capello wanted them to stay away, but that's rubbish. They're all coming, and they're all coming today and all of them – bar Victoria Beckham who's got lots of friends in the US camp as well, so will be mingling with them – will be staying at this hotel. MY hotel. Yep, the England Wags will be enjoying the next four or five weeks (if the players sort themselves out and win all their matches) in this fabulous hotel and spa, enjoying my sparkling company and witty repartee and getting to see my fine collection of swimwear.

Before all that though, first thing this morning I need (not want, you notice, but *need*) to buy the beautiful silver boots that I've been trying to buy for days, but have significantly failed to purchase because of a host of annoying problems.

Yesterday afternoon, I helped George out at the charity HQ. Paskia came too and got really stuck in, helping out one guy whose house was collapsing. I was so proud of her; she's only young and the shanty town is a lot to cope with emotionally. Shiraz was there too, of course; she spends more time on the Cape Town flats these days – mainly smiling at George – than she does at the hotel. Afterwards I decided to go and buy the boots, but realised I had forgotten to bring the name of the shop we were supposed to be going to. Imagine my fury at myself. I ended up telling the taxi driver the name of a shop in completely the wrong area of town where they wouldn't have known a pair of silver foil Louboutins if they jumped up and bit them on the knee.

'This is all wrong!' I declared in horror and disbelief, tugging at the hem of my short dress and stamping my big Prada boots in disgrace.

'But this is the shop you said,' he replied, which was correct. It was the shop I said, but it wasn't the shop I *meant*, so we trundled back up to the hotel empty-handed.

I have to buy them today. HAVE to. If I don't, what will I wear when the Wags arrive later this morning? Imagine having to meet the world's greatest Wags wearing last season's Louboutins? No, no and thrice no.

I'm dressed in a simple white outfit because I think that once I put the silver boots on, I won't want to take them off, so I need to dress in something that will work with them. That something is a pair of white hot pants, a white plunging top, and a short, sleeveless, mini white duster coat that I once saw Cheryl Cole wear. I wear it done up in the taxi because I'm desperately keen to channel Cheryl Cole, on this day more than any other in my life, as a kind of tribute to her. On two occasions already this morning, the taxi driver has asked me whether I'm a nurse. Cheeky bastard!

He'll be sorry when he realises how unbelievably fantastic my outfit looks with the inclusion of the spiky-heeled silver boots. I can just picture myself now looking like a model from the Pitch catalogue, draped across one of the luxury sofas in the reception area as the Wags walk in one by one and gasp in appreciation. They'll wander up to me and someone will immediately say, 'My God, you must be Tracie Martin. Your boots are amazing. You have more Waggish style than anyone I've ever met in my life before. Please be my best friend.'

As you've no doubt grasped by now, becoming best friends with the leading Wags is a long-term goal of mine. I know they're in a separate part of the hotel to the rest of us – the coaches' wives – and I know that Victoria is staying somewhere else entirely, so it's this first chance encounter, in the reception area, with me looking divine, that will be the key to the whole best friends forever thing working for me.

Just in case this daydream scenario doesn't quite work out as I'm planning, I've ordered a telescope from a department store in town so I can spy on them instead.

The telescope is due to arrive today at eleven o'clock, so I must be back by then, especially since the guy said he would bring the telescope up to my suite himself so he could show me how to use it. Apparently they're quite complicated and the last thing I want is to have an enormous telescope in my room and no way of seeing the outfits being worn poolside. So, as you can see, I've got a lot to pack in.

'Are we almost there, driver?'

11.30 a.m.

Well, that was a disaster. The shops aren't open this morning. What is wrong with the people in this country? It's Sunday morning, and apparently they don't open their shops on a Sunday. I know. Weird eh? Something to do with religion, apparently. And you know what the worst thing of all is? I could see the Louboutins in the window. They were there, staring at me, begging me to come in and buy them so that I could look super-cool and bang on-trend for when the Wags came, but I had no way of getting to them without smashing the glass down. I did at one stage contemplate the crash, smash and grab route to the boots, but the taxi driver peeled me off the shop-front window, and dragged me screaming and kicking back to the cab.

Once I'd calmed down, I rang Shiraz and started squealing and shouting about the fact that it wasn't open, and I would be a laughing stock if I didn't have the gorgeous silver boots by the time the Wags arrived. She fully grasped the seriousness of the situation, and agreed that, yes, I probably would look a laughing stock without the right footwear and she quickly went on to the Internet and found other shops in the area that claimed to stock Louboutins, but it was no good – they didn't have the boots that I need.

Now I'm in a dreadful rush to get back to see the guy who is coming with my telescope, before placing myself alluringly in a prominent position in the reception area to catch the eyes of the England Wags when they come trooping in. God, my life's so busy and stressful sometimes; I don't know how I cope. Good that I haven't got a job or anything. How do people ever manage to fit work in around buying sparkly footwear?

I'm sitting in a cab, which must be the world's slowest. 'I have to be in the reception area to bump into the Wags,' I say. 'You understand how important it is for me to get back to that hotel quickly, don't you?'

'I understand but cars in the way,' he says gloomily. 'Busy morning. I do my best.'

Yeah, yeah, yeah . . . well, I just hope that his best is good enough, because if I'm not in the reception area to see the Wags as they arrive I'm worried that I might struggle to get near them after that. It's so bloody disappointing that they've put the players' wives and girlfriends in a separate section of the hotel to the rest of us, with loads of security guards looking after them. It's going to make my efforts to befriend them extra difficult.

'Can we not go any faster?' I plead.

'I am doing my best,' he insists. Any slower and we would be reversing down the street. By the time we get to the hotel, my worst nightmare has been realised, and the Wags have gone to their rooms, leaving me alone in the reception area with the bright and breezy, immaculately groomed reception staff. There is just one girl standing there but she's clearly not a Wag. She's slim and blonde but dressed in jeans and a kind of lightweight anorak thing. She looks about Paskia's age and a little lost.

'Mrs Martin,' says an extraordinarily tall and smart-looking woman, coming up to me and shaking my hand. 'I'm the hotel manager. It's lovely to meet you. I haven't had the chance to introduce myself yet because I've been in Johannesburg for a few days, but I'm back now and I'd just like to say that it's a pleasure to have you staying in our hotel. My name is Nancy Cherrywood and if there's anything you need during your stay, please don't hesitate to ask for me, and I'll do everything I can to help.'

'Thank you,' I say. 'That's very kind of you. Could you tell me something? Who is that girl over there?'

The manager turns to the receptionist and asks her. 'The young lady's name is Rosie Jones,' says the receptionist. 'She must be one of the players' girlfriends because she's marked code red on my computer.'

She can't be the Rosie that Dean was talking about, surely. She looks nothing like a Wag. Hang on, what did she just say?

'Code red?'

'That just means that she's in the top security section of the hotel.'

Oh, God, I *so* want to be a code red guest.

'How do you get to be code red?' I ask.

'It's the term used for the elite players' wives and girlfriends, because they're considered to be under greater risk of security threats than other guests, from the media and fans for example.'

'Can you not to make me code red?' I ask.

'I'm sorry, madam. Code red just describes the England players' wives and girlfriends.'

'Please?'

'Sorry, madam.'

Damn. I need to get myself put into the players' wives and girlfriends section of the hotel, and marked code red then everything will be OK. I'll get Shiraz working on that as soon as I see her.

'Thanks for your help,' I say to the rather confused and frightened-looking receptionist, who's clearly baffled about why I would want to be marked down on their danger list. I decide to head over and say hello to this Rosie girl. Can this young thing really be Dio's girlfriend? If she is, she clearly needs a bit of help from me in the looks department, poor lamb. What is she thinking, turning up in the Wags hotel dressed like that?

She doesn't look like she's enjoying herself at all, as she sits looking forlorn on the huge sofas in the reception area. I'm not surprised, to be honest; she's wearing navy, for Christ's sake. Who ever looked happy in navy?

'Hello, I'm Tracie Martin,' I say, and her sad, limpid little unmade-up eyes look up at me, full of fear and anguish. Gosh, she's pretty: absolutely flawless skin, a sweet heart-shaped face and light-brown eyes with lovely long eyelashes, but no make-up. I mean, no make-up? What's that all about? 'My husband Dean is a coach with the team,' I explain.

'Oh, yes, sorry,' she says, smiling in recognition. 'Dio said that you would look out for me. Thank you for coming to find me. I don't really know anyone. I thought your video was fab by the way! Really funny.'

'Oh, er, yes, thanks.' Let's not dwell on the video. I'm only just managing to put the whole damn thing behind me.

Rosie and I sit down on the squishy sofas in reception, with me crossing my orange tanned, shiny legs and folding my immaculately manicured fingernails over my knees while she curls a denim-covered leg beneath her and picks at the cuticles of her bitten-down nails. It's all wrong. Wags should have long, painted nails, everyone knows that. My nails are kind of light blackberry colour today which, if I'm honest, makes them look a little bit like I've slammed my fingers in the car door. I picked the colour out because it reminded me of summer fruits and berries, but now they just look bruised. I wish I'd gone for peach, like Mich wisely did, because when you've got three coats of it on, it looks a shocking orange colour that matches your legs. Who knew that matching fingernails and legs could look so good? Mich said matching limbs and nail extensions are the latest Wag thing. Am I so completely behind the times? I must get Shiraz to check up on this for me.

But I clearly have more pressing concerns here for the minute. Rosie looks a mess. I hate to be brutal about it but it's true. Her boyfriend's worth millions but she looks as if she buys her clothes in supermarkets. I'm not judging. I'm just saying.

'So, tell me, what do you like doing, Rosie? Do you like dressing up and going out for a drink, and things like that?'

'I'm not really into dressing up,' she says. No shit! 'I much prefer just curling up on the sofa and watching a good DVD, or catching up on the soaps; that's what I really like.'

'I could help you when it comes to fashion,' I say, sweeping my hands down my body to indicate my fabulous outfit as an illustration of my skills in this area.

'That would be great,' she says, wide-eyed. 'I'd probably want something a little bit understated though, because I'm not really a "look at me, look at me" sort of person.'

'I bet Dio would like it if you dressed up every so often though, wouldn't he?'

'I guess,' says Rosie, 'though he doesn't like me to go to nightclubs and pubs and things like that. He doesn't think girls should flaunt themselves in places like that.'

Eh?

'OK, well, leave it to me. I'll dig out some clothes that will make you look really special. Now, tell me a little bit about Dio. What's he like?'

'He's just lovely,' she says, hugging herself as she speaks. 'He's a really nice boy. He's kind and so generous; he buys me the most expensive presents ever but sometimes they're completely over the top and I just get embarrassed.'

'Like what?' I ask. Now we're talking. Now I'm interested. I love over-the-top presents.

She rummages about inside a horrible, nylon duffle bag and pulls out a pile of photos.

'Look!' she holds out a picture of a car that Dio has just bought her, and I don't think I've ever been more impressed by anything, ever. It's a Bentley that has been customised for her. By this I mean that all the normal standards expected of a Bentley have been dropped considerably, and the car has been painted in a gorgeous pale pink, with white trimming.

'It's like a Juicy tracksuit!' she declares, with embarrassment. 'Imagine that. A car designed to look like a fashionable tracksuit.' Actually, she's right. The car does look rather like a giant tracksuit with its pale-pink body and white piping. It is surely the first time in the history of the universe that a Bentley worth quarter of a million pounds has been altered to look like a popular velour leisure suit.

'I'm so lucky to have found him. He's so kind to me,' she continues, 'but I do feel embarrassed driving around in that car. I mean, look at me.'

'Worry no more,' I say. 'With my help, you can look like the sort of girl who drives around the place in a terrifyingly expensive, pale-pink car. Now, let's see that picture again.'

Rosie holds it out, and explains that the winged 'B' logo was taken off and was replaced with her initials – RJ – for Rosie Jones. 'It's got pink seats in it and a love message across the back seats in white. It says, 'To the girl next door. From Dio.' Can you imagine that? It shows how much he loves me, doesn't it. That's how we met, you know, we lived next door to one another when we were growing up.'

'Ah,' I say. 'Childhood sweethearts. How nice.'

'And he's put my initials on the wheels as well, on the bright-pink alloy wheel rim!' she says. 'It's embarrassing, really, but very kind of him. He's always giving me great surprises . . . like sweeping me off to Paris for the weekend, and that time he sent me and three of my girlfriends away for a great girlie weekend in the sun, when he was all tied up with football. He's really great with all his presents. He must really love me. Mustn't he, Tracie? He must.'

'He must, love,' I agree.

'Thank you for being so friendly,' she says, taking my hands in hers (big mistake, she'll never get the orange off her palms). 'I'd love it if you'd help me. Dio's been fantastic and I'd like to look a bit smarter for him. I mean, look at the life I have because of Dio. I'm the luckiest girl in the world. I moved away from all my friends and family to be with him, even though they warned me against it, and I left everything behind for him. Now just look at me! I never thought anything like this would ever happen to me. You should see the house that Dio has bought . . . honestly, it's right next to the Rooneys' house, and it's gorgeous. Dio has spent millions on it . . . it's got an indoor swimming pool and everything. Imagine that! And me and Dio can't even swim a stroke between us. There's also a big area for a children's playroom, with the room for a nanny and everything, and we haven't got children yet!'

'Wow,' I say, thinking that I'd probably not be so excited about a ton of rooms that were of no use to anyone, but each to their own, I guess.

'Do you have a walk-in wardrobe?' I ask.

'No,' she says.

'Shoe room?'

'No, I don't.'

'How about a handbag room?'

Nope, it appears she has none of those. Instead she has a pool that she can't swim in. I can see that I have my work well and truly cut out here.

'Oh, Tracie, thanks for taking the time to come over and talk to me. I find it very difficult to make friends and – if I'm honest – I was dreading coming to this hotel because I thought all the wives and girlfriends would know one another, and would be watching each other carefully and looking at who had the best clothes on and who was wearing designer brands. I was worried that I would never fit in. But you're so nice, Tracie; you seem so down-to-earth and really nice. I hope that we can be the best of friends.'

'Of course we can,' I say. 'You'll never be judged by me. I'm much more interested in the person beneath the clothing. The heart and soul of a person rather than what she's wearing.'

'Mrs Martin, sorry to interrupt,' says the receptionist, coming over to me, clutching a piece of paper. 'There was a message while you were out - a man came from a security company who said you had requested a telescope to be delivered to your room. We weren't sure whether to send him up, but he had emails from you and proof of his identity. In the end, we told him to leave the package at reception and security took it up. That seemed to be the safest thing.'

'Yes, thanks,' I say. 'It's just some astronomical research I'm interested in pursuing.'

'Well. he also left his phone number, and urged you to call him as soon as possible so he can explain it to you. Does that sound OK, madam?'

'Absolutely. Thank you,' I say, as she walks back across the reception area.

'Astronomical research . . . that sounds interesting,' says Rosie. 'Will you tell me a little bit about it?'

But I can hardly hear her. It's as if a bright light has suddenly flooded into the reception area. As if an angel has been beamed down from heaven, illuminated by the light of God's own eyes.

'Fuck me,' I say. 'Have you seen what I've just seen?'

Rosie looks up and follows the direction of my stare, and she sees it too. A vision of loveliness in a turquoise and emerald-green maxi dress, striding through the reception area, the sunshine flickering through her dark-blonde hair, creating a halo effect around her beautiful, famous and perfectly made-up young face. It's as if this lovely creature has been beamed down on a huge force of light.

'Bloody hell. It's Coleen,' I say slowly. 'Oh my God, it's Coleen!'

'Oh my God,' repeats Rosie. 'It's Coleen. I *have* to go to the loo.'

Rosie rushes out of the reception area, heading towards the ladies' toilets while I reach into my handbag to powder my already heavily powdered nose and check whether my lipstick is thick enough (it is – any thicker and my lips will be entering the room a full ten seconds before the rest of me).

This is my moment. Coleen is pushing a small pram containing, one assumes, baby Kai. She's looking around the reception area in a rather agitated fashion. Perhaps I can help? After all I've been here almost two weeks . . . I know where everything is.

'Hello there,' I say, bounding up to her and smiling sweetly. 'It's so nice to meet you Coleen. Amazing.

Wonderful. Just awesome and brilliant and . . . oh my God, Coleen, I can't believe it's you . . . ' I'm rambling now; I know I'm rambling but I don't know how to stop myself. 'How are you? How was your flight? Was it OK?' I'm trying to sound like a normal person who's meeting up with another normal person but I clearly sound nothing like one. I try to push to the back of my mind that I'm meeting one of the world's greatest Wonder-Wags.

'Oh, hi,' she says. 'Great, I'm glad you're here. Are you the woman who my mum spoke to earlier?'

'Yes,' I say, because I don't want to let her down.

'Great. I can't tell you how precious my baby is to me, so I wanted you to look after him because you come very highly recommended.'

'I do?'

'Yes. All the staff were raving about you. I wouldn't trust Kai with just anybody but we need someone to look after him for an hour while we both get our bearings in the hotel, settle in and maybe cool down with a quick swim.'

'Sure, fine,' I say. 'No problem.'

'Great. You will take great care of him, won't you?'

'Of course,' I say. I don't know what's happening but I'm going to keep talking because I seem to be saying all the right things so far.

She hands me a bag with little fluffy toys in it along with sleeping suits and bottles. 'You must call me if he's worried about anything,' she says. 'I'll be on my mobile phone. The number's on the form that I filled in earlier in the nursery. They've got all my details in there and mum's details as well. Is that OK?'

'Sure,' I say, not quite sure what I'm saying OK to. Of

course it's OK if she and her mum go for a swim and get their bearings in the hotel. Does she want me to go for a swim with her? Because, if she does, that would be pretty cool even though I can't swim. It doesn't matter about swimming. Even if I drowned, I'd still like to go swimming with her.

She leans over and kisses her baby on its little head.

'See you later then, bye.' And with that she's gone, but – get this – she has left Baby Kai behind. Fuck. What has she done that for?

It takes a few seconds, but it suddenly occurs to me that Coleen clearly thinks that I am the nursery nurse due to look after her baby. Bollocks, it's the lovely white outfit minus the silver thigh-length boots that have done it.

I look outside where I see her plonking her bag on to one of the sun loungers and I think, hell, it's only an hour. I might as well look after baby Kai. Then, when she discovers that I'm not a nursery nurse at all, but a Wag just like her, she'll think I'm lovely and become my new best friend forever and ever and ever. My God, how we'll laugh and laugh about the misunderstanding that led to us becoming the very, very best of friends. So I push the pram into the lift, and take the baby up to my suite.

Gosh, it's a nice pram, quite old-fashioned-looking but clearly expensive. There are no knick-knacks of Coleen's anywhere in the bottom of the pram for me to nose at, but the baby suit that Kai is wearing is lovely – it's pale blue and he looks so snugly and comfy and cosy in it that it makes my heart leap.

I check the baby's fast asleep and leave the pram to one side while I hastily set up the telescope so I can watch what

Coleen is up to. It's easy enough to assemble – surprisingly easy really. I didn't have high hopes of being able to get it working without at least forty-seven calls to the manu-facturers but in no time I have the best view of the pool that there has ever been. Christ, I can see up close and in astonishing detail. It's quiet by the pool, just a couple of people milling around, then I spot Mel and Alex lying on sun loungers and *ooooo* Coleen's spotted them too and she's heading over there and stripping down to a black and gold bikini. I think it might be Gucci. Hang on, can I focus in a bit on that bikini? I twiddle the small silver knob. Yes. That's definitely Gucci. The baby stirs in its pram, making a kind of gurgling noise and a little baby squeal. I look over but he seems to have gone back to sleep again, thank God. It's a long time since I took care of a baby and I'm way passed remembering how to change a nappy.

I remember when Paskia was little, and I had to change a nappy before going in for a hair appointment. I hated doing those nappies, and I remember running my hands through my hair in relief when I'd finally done it. I walked into the hairdressers and I remember Mario saying, 'what you got in your hair? It looks like chocolate.'

I knew straight away what it was. 'Oh, that's just poo. Don't mind that,' I said.

It was only afterwards when I was back home and enjoying a nice glass with my Dean that I realised that I'd never explained myself. I just said 'it's poo' without telling Mario that I had a baby or anything like that. He probably thought it was my own.

Oooo . . . what's happening now? Coleen is lying back on the sun lounger, and Alex has moved over slightly, so I can see that she is wearing a Juicy bikini. Nice. It's like one of the ones that I nearly bought in Pitch. Damn, I wish I had now. I bought everything else in the shop. I should have just bought it all and been done with it; then I'd know that there was a chance of me being in the same clothing as the Wonder-Wags.

They're chatting and reading a magazine. It's hard to see exactly what they are reading but it looks like *Glamour* magazine. How annoying; I wish I could see more clearly. I should have stipulated when I ordered the telescope that I needed to be able to see articles in magazines that the Wags are reading. I just didn't, for one second, think that the Wags would be caught out reading. It's most unusual behaviour. Perhaps they're looking at the pictures?

Oooo . . . hello, here comes an older woman, rushing to Coleen's side. Oooo . . . drama! Coleen has jumped up and is grabbing her maxi dress and rushing inside with the older woman. Is that Coleen's mum? I think it might be . . . I recognise her from one of the *Hello!* spreads. The two of them go running inside, and the other Wags have jumped up and are talking in an animated fashion. Mmmm . . . that Juicy bikini is great; I really wish I'd bought one of those. Coleen's mum has now dashed back outside, and all the girls go rushing up to talk to her. I wonder what on earth has happened. They've left all their bags and everything by the pool.

Oh, hello, what's this now? Eveyone's rushed inside, and as I look out through the telescope, I see that Rosie has run over to the sunbeds, and is picking up their bags, discarded sunglasses, and the magazines left lying open by the poolside. Perhaps they've spotted the paparazzi and need to make a quick get-away or something. Now Shiraz has gone rushing over to talk to a simply beautiful, slim blonde girl. She looks like a model or a movie star or . . . no . . . It's Abbey. ABBEY?? Oh my God, Abbey Clancy has been spotted by the pool. This is my first sighting of Abbey and I almost drop the telescope in excitement. How has Shiraz managed to befriend Abbey Clancy? How? And just look at Abbey . . . how tiny she is, and how pretty. Oh, no. I'm never going to get into the Wonder-Wags. I need to lose loads of weight really quickly . . . how am I going to do that?

Abbey and Shiraz have collected all the bags, and dash inside. Perhaps they're expecting rain? I don't understand all this activity. I can't believe how lucky Shiraz is to meet the amazing Abbey. I might give her a ring on her mobile. Perhaps I could pop down and meet them for coffee or something. The baby is still fast asleep in its lovely soft, pale-blue sleep suit. If Coleen has changed her mind, and isn't going to go for a swim any more, then she can damn well come and take the baby back. I'm not a bloody nanny or anything.

'Shiraz, it's me. Tracie.'

'Hi, Tracie. It's a nightmare.'

In the background I can hear people shouting, and an air of general confusion pervading.

'What's happened?' I ask, realising too late that I'm talking too loudly, and little Kai has opened his eyes, and is looking around the room and gurgling to himself.

'It's Coleen . . . she's had her baby stolen.'

'What? What do you mean she's had her baby "stolen"?'

'She was supposed to meet one of the nursery nurses at reception and she handed the baby over. But when her mum went down to the nursery to check Kai was settling in OK, the nursery said that the baby had never been dropped off. It turns out that it was a kidnapper masquerading as a nanny and hanging around in reception to steal Kai. Everyone is worried about where the baby is. It's bound to be a kidnapper, don't you think? With all their money, someone probably thought they could make a few quid. What's that sound?'

Little baby Kai is now fully awake and screaming in his pram. I put the dummy gently into his little mouth, and rock the pram, hoping he'll drop off back to sleep. Oh. My. God. Why the hell did Coleen think I was a nursery nurse? I look nothing like a nursery nurse. It's obvious that I'm a Wag.

'What did the person who Coleen gave the baby to look like?' I ask, wondering whether Shiraz is going to suss that it is I who has the precious child.

'Apparently Coleen said it was an older woman with nasty yellowish-coloured hair and a lot of make-up.'

Bitch. How could she? I'm not old. And my hair is sunshine blonde. It's the colour of daffodils in a sunny meadow; it's not a nasty yellowish colour. This is outrageous.

'I bet the person she gave the pram to didn't have horrible hair,' I say, defensively, forgetting that the real problem here might be the fact that I have Coleen's baby in my room, and the entire hotel is on a search to find him, not what Coleen's perception of my hair colour is. As we're talking, I hear the sound of sirens wailing outside. Oh. My. Fucking. God.

'Gotta go,' I say to Shiraz, and I put down the phone. I

really, really don't want to be arrested and charged with kidnap. I don't want Coleen to be worried about the safety of her child either, and I want to give the baby back now, but how? If I leave the room with that child, I'll be in so much trouble it doesn't bear thinking about. I can't work out what to do.

My mobile phone rings, and I think straight away that it's the police who want to talk to me urgently. Perhaps they've got the room surrounded.

'Hello,' I say nervously.

'Hello, love. It's Gladys here.'

Oh, God, not now. Gladys is a ninety-year-old nutcase from an old people's home in Luton who was a friend of Dean's nan before she died. I love the woman to death, but, honestly, not now.

'Can I ring you back in just a bit?' I ask her. 'I'm in an awful mess.'

'I know, I saw the video . . . I don't think I've ever laughed so much,' she says.

'No, something else now – they all think I stole Coleen Rooney's baby. Well, no, that's not true. They don't realise that I have stolen Coleen's baby. They are looking for Coleen's baby without realising that I've stolen it. Except that I haven't really stolen it; I thought I was looking after it, but now the South African police are here, and they carry guns, and they are all looking for the baby, and I've got it.'

'Right you are then,' she says. 'You call me back later, dear.'

There's a knock on the door and I flinch, wondering what I'm going to do now. I feel like I'm in one of those police dramas. I'm the bad guy, and they're closing in on me. There'll be twenty men out there, all armed and dangerous and willing to die in the name of the law.

'Hiya,' comes a sweet, girly voice, ruining my imaginative tale somewhat. It's Shiraz.

I open the door, and she comes in to see the pram sitting there. Mich and Suse follow close behind her, and they all stand open-mouthed staring at the pram where little baby Kai is looking up at them, his beautiful big blue eyes filled with wonder and mystery. The sound of the sirens still wails.

'I'm not sure what to do,' I say, biting my lip and looking around the room in the hope that inspiration will come bursting out of the walls. 'It all seems a bit complicated.'

'You stole a baby!' exclaims Mich, getting to the heart of the problem in her unique fashion.

'I didn't exactly *steal* it. I was standing in reception, trying to work out which of the girls were down by the pool when Coleen came up to me and handed me a baby.'

'What? She just walked right up to you for no reason?'

'Well, no. That's not true. Looking back I can see that she presumed I was the person who was supposed to be looking after her baby for an hour, but I didn't listen properly. I was too excited about the fact that she was there in front of me. I just said "yes" to every question she asked.'

'Right,' says Mich. 'So you took her baby away? I don't understand why you didn't just say to her: there's been a bit of a misunderstanding. I'm not a childminder. My name is Tracie Martin—'

'Urgh . . . have you seen Coleen? She has the most amazing bikini on and she was wearing this perfect maxi dress. She's one of the Wonder-Wags; I can't just go saying

"I'm Tracie". She's like my dream woman, along with Cheryl, Abbey and Vics. I got confused. I don't think I knew what my name was. It's all a bit vague, and I was very thrown by the sight of her, and it's very hard for me when I meet these Wags because I love them so much. I thought that if I looked after her baby, as she asked me to, then she might like me. Is that such a bad thing?'

'No,' says Suse, kindly. You can always rely on Suse to say something kind. 'But what is a bad thing is that at this moment the hotel is being searched for the baby by the South African police, and the paparazzi are collecting at the front of the hotel in great numbers. Security guards are wandering around the hotel stopping and searching everyone they come into contact with. And most importantly poor Coleen is going frantic with worry. You are going to have to tell her that you have her baby.'

'I CAN'T!' I yell so loudly that Kai murmurs, drops his dummy and begins to cry. Fuck. This is all we need. 'I can't tell her,' I continue. 'She will hate me if I tell her that I had her baby all along. We will have to smuggle the baby into the reception area and leave it there.'

'Oh, very clever,' says Mich, standing up and attempting to re-insert the dummy into the baby's mouth with staggering lack of ability. 'And how the bloody hell on earth are we going to do that? The whole damn place is surrounded by the police. Everyone in the hotel is on high alert. You are going to have to give Coleen her baby back yourself. You can't hide because as soon as she sees you walking around the hotel she's going to recognise you as the person she gave her baby to.'

It's hard to dispute the logic being employed here, but

it's also very hard to contemplate handing over baby Kai and admitting my mistake and having the whole world thinking I'm a complete numpty again. I don't want to be the loon from the video nasty YouTube clip, I'm quite enjoying being 'Tracie Martin, saviour of the poor and destitute in South Africa'.

'Let's phone Coleen,' says Shiraz. 'We have to let her know that Kai is safe. She's going out of her mind with worry.'

Shiraz digs out Coleen's number from her cell phone as if it's the most natural thing in the world. How on earth does Shiraz have Coleen's number in her phone? The woman's only been working for me a few weeks, and she seems to be best friends with all the Wags. I, on the other hand, have spent a lifetime trying to befriend them all. I've gone so out of my way to try and befriend Victoria Beckham over the years that it's not even funny. Me and my friend Simon pretended to be pool cleaners when I was living in LA just so we could get a look at her garden. I won't bore you with the details, but suffice to say that my efforts at pool maintenance were as catastrophic as my current efforts at child-care provision and we dyed her garden – grass, flowers and footpath – a bright blue colour.

'Hi Col, it's Shiraz here.' Col? She calls her Col like they're great old friends?

'Listen, I just wanted to tell you that we found Kai and he's safe. He's been well looked after and everything is fine. There's been a complete misunderstanding. I'll tell you all the details when I see you. Now where are you?'

It turns out that Coleen is in her room sobbing her heart out while police attempt to extract information and a description of the woman who disappeared with her baby.

'We'll bring him over now,' says Shiraz, adding, 'Everything is fine, Col. We'll be there with Kai in a few minutes.'

'Now,' she says, looking over at me. 'You just need to work out what your story is, Tracie.'

My mind immediately starts to wander and I start to think of all the fantastical tales I could tell. Perhaps I should say that I rescued baby Kai from the jaws of a lion, or from an evil-looking baddie who was preparing to make away with the young baby, and if I hadn't got there when I did, he would surely have done great harm to the golden child.

'If I were you, I'd just tell the truth,' says Shiraz. 'You haven't done anything wrong; it was just a misunderstanding. If you tell Coleen this, and then explain to the police what happened, I'm sure that everything will be OK.'

So off we go then, heading past the security guards that ring the area reserved for the Wonder-Wags, and into Coleen's luxury suite, pushing the pram bearing the baby. My mind is fizzing with different ideas, and things that I could say to get myself off the hook. Sod what Shiraz thinks, I've got a reputation to protect here. I need to make up a fabulous lie. We walk in to the suite and Coleen and her mum rush over to us. For one magical moment I think Coleen's going to give me a huge hug, but she ignores me completely and goes over to the pram from which she lifts out the baby and makes the most enormous fuss of him.

Once she's contented herself that the baby is OK, she looks at me, and I prepare to tell her a whopping great big lie about how I snatched her baby from the jaws of a runaway shark and saved him from certain death, but she ruins my moment by saying, 'It's you . . . the fake nursery nurse. You're the one I gave my baby to. Why did you take my baby? You're not a nursery nurse at all, are you?'

'No,' I say. 'I'm not. I just got confused when you asked me to look after the baby.'

'How did you get confused? What on earth was confusing?'

'I didn't realise that you thought I was a nursery nurse; I thought you were just asking me to look after your baby. I thought I was doing you a favour. I'm Tracie Martin.'

'Tracie who?'

'Tracie's married to Dean Martin who's one of the coaches,' pipes up Shiraz. 'Tracie was in that YouTube video.'

'Oh, that was you?' says Coleen. 'The falling-off-the-bike one.'

'Yep.'

'But you're dressed just like a nursery nurse. Why would anyone be dressed like that if they weren't a nursery nurse?' says Coleen, now burning with anger. I understand why she's so upset; I'm a mother too. I understand the pain of being separated from your baby, but to insult my style is stooping too low.

'I'm dressed like this because this outfit sets off the lovely long, silver Louboutin boots,' I reply.

Everyone in the room looks down at my feet where I'm clearly not wearing silver thigh-length Louboutin boots. Now they all think I'm mad. I've got myself into one of those ridiculous situations where even telling the truth is making me look insane. Suddenly the idea of me saving baby Kai from the jaws of a shark looks like a much more convincing tale than the one I'm telling. Still, I've got no choice but to battle on with the truth here.

'I don't actually have the silver boots because the shop was shut. But I put this outfit on so that the boots would look good when I bought them.'

'That's true, actually,' says Shiraz. 'Tracie has been trying to buy the boots all week and has had no luck.'

'Could you still not get them, love?' asks Suse, all concerned. 'I was sure you'd be able to get them this morning.'

'No, the shop was closed, and no other shops seemed to stock them.'

'Perhaps Coleen knows where you could get them,' volunteers Mich.

We all turn to face Coleen, but she doesn't seem keen to offer an opinion. She appears quite shocked to be asked.

'*Enough!*' she screams. 'What is wrong with you people? I don't want to hear any more about your shoe shopping. All I care about is my son, and whether he's safe.'

She sits down and cuddles her son closely, absently tickling his little toes. Then she stops her tickling suddenly and looks up, 'Where are his little booties?'

Everyone looks at me. 'I've no idea,' I say truthfully. I certainly didn't remove them and start playing with the baby's toes. What do they think I am? Some sort of bloody loony. 'They might have fallen off when I picked him up in my room and gave him a cuddle,' I say, because it's the only thing that I can think of, and the last thing I need now is for them to start thinking I'm a sock thief as well as a baby snatcher. 'Shall I go and have a look and see if they are there?'

'You can't,' says Coleen. 'The police want to talk to you.'

'Oh, but the baby is safe. I've explained that it was just a simple mix-up.'

'They still need to talk to you,' says Coleen. 'They said they'd wait for me to get my baby back, then have a chat to you.'

'I think they went up to your room, actually,' says Coleen's mum. 'I'm sure that's where they said they would be. Perhaps we should all go up there, collect the booties, and talk to the police.'

So, off we all troop, marching through the hotel with security guards in front of us and behind us. Coleen, her mum pushing Kai, and a friend of hers who keeps staring at me in a really angry fashion as if she might punch me at any moment. We arrive at my door to find three police officers waiting and we all troop into my suite. The men look extremely angry. 'There's another officer coming,' says one of the cops, looking me up and down menacingly.

Coleen wastes no time in the hunt to find the booties, and rushes straight over to the window where they lie on the sun-soaked wooden floor . . . right next to the telescope trained on the sunbeds by the pool being used by the Wags. Oh, shit. I forgot about that.

'What's the telescope for?' she asks.

'I like watching the sky at night,' I lie.

'Really?' she says. 'How odd.'

There's a knock on the door and we all turn to see another police officer arrive in the room to a chorus of 'sir, sir, sir' from those in attendance. The guy looks vaguely familiar.

'Hey, Tracie!' he says. 'It's me, Superintendent Barnes. We met at the airport when you gave me a signed photo.'

Oh, yes. 'Hello,' I say. 'How are you?'

'I'm good. I've been seeing all the good work you've been involved in since you got here. Man, you've done well. You're a heroine.'

'What's this?' asks Coleen, so I tell her briefly about the charity work and show her a copy of the article lying on the table. I sense her mood change as she's reading it. She's clearly moved by what she sees. 'Wow. That's amazing.'

'Thanks,' I say. 'Look, I am genuinely sorry about the baby. I didn't mean any harm. I thought you knew who I was and that you wanted me to take care of him while you went for a swim. I should have said something but I sort of got thrown by events and thought it would be easier if I just looked after the baby. I never expected any of this.'

'Don't worry. It's all OK now. I'm not going to press charges or anything.' She turns to the police officers. 'Can we just forget this?' Then she turns back to me. 'Can I take this?' she asks, indicating the article. 'Perhaps I can help too?'

'Sure, that would be great,' I say. 'Really great. Take it, take anything you want. What's mine is yours.'

'That's fine. I'll just take the article. Come on, Mum.'

Coleen, her mum and her angry friend leave the room and I turn to my new best friend in the whole of the South African Police Force.

'Thanks,' I say. 'I thought I was going to be in all sorts of trouble there. What were you planning to do next if you hadn't found Kai in the hotel?'

'Well, we've got a detailed description of you from Coleen, which is actually a very good description as it turns out,' he says. 'So we would make sure that was sent out to all border controls, police cars and security guards in the area.'

'Out of interest, what was the description?' I ask, unable to help myself. The police officer looks at me, looks at the notepad and says, 'I handed my baby over to a woman who I believed to be a nursery nurse. She was a desperately thin woman, looked very malnourished and with the brightest-orange skin and most incredibly yellow hair imaginable. She was around forty years old and had so much make-up on that it's very difficult for me to describe what she looks like underneath it all. The most noticeable thing about her was just how incredibly thin she was.'

And suddenly life seems worth living again. The kindly police officer hands me his card and tells me to call him if I have any further problems in South Africa, but I'm too distracted by what I've just heard and I take the card in a daze. Barely registering it. Clearly, I'm going to need a facelift urgently because Col thinks I'm forty, and I'm actually six years younger than that, but since I pretend to be thirty, the age she perceives me to be is ten years older than my real imaginary age, which can't be good at all. But the most important thing is that Coleen thinks I'm skinny. She said I looked malnourished. Can there be any greater compliment in the world?

Chapter Twelve

Monday 24th May: TV time for Tracie

Dear Shiraz,

I'm going to be out in the morning at the TV studio, then I DEFINITELY plan to buy the long silver boots and I'll be back in the hotel by midday. I've had a long chat with George and he's desperate for help over the next few weeks so I have said that you can go and work with him in the afternoons as part of my commitment to the charity. I have a feeling that will be OK with you!

I will be spending the afternoon helping another charitable cause: I'll be beginning the process of re-styling Rosie, so could you please book sessions for manicures, pedicures, waxing, eyebrow threading and facials this afternoon so that I can begin her great ascent to Wagdom. Once you have organised the appointments, please leave me a list with them on and notify Rosie. In the meantime, a joke for you: A woman gets on a bus with her baby. The bus driver says, 'That's the ugliest baby that I've ever seen. Ugh!' The woman goes to the rear of the bus and sits down, fuming. She says to a man next to her, 'The driver just insulted me!' The man says, 'You go right up there and tell him off. Go ahead, I'll hold your monkey for you.' Ha!

Catch you later,

Trace x

*

Here I am, back at the TV studio, dressed to the nines and raring to go. I've gone for an even shorter dress today, buoyed on by the lovely comments made by Coleen, and conveyed to me by my favourite police officer yesterday, that I look painfully thin and, indeed, malnourished! It might not be politically correct to delight in such a description when I'm setting myself up as the woman who's going to end starvation in South Africa, but I am truly, truly thrilled beyond words because I've spent my life fighting against the inner demons that tell me I'm madly overweight. The inner demons are wrong; I do not believe there could be a greater feeling. It was almost worth nicking Coleen's baby to hear a description of me like that.

Today, apparently, I'm going to be answering lots of questions about my life as a Wag. They've promised me that they'll keep the questions very general, and not attempt to delve too deeply into my personal life. We'll see!

'Tell us first, Tracie, about the charity work you've been doing. I think we've all read about your involvement with the poor and homeless in South Africa. Would you mind telling us a little bit more about it?'

Oooo ... good start to the interview! I thought I might have to shoe-horn a mention of the charity into the interview there. I'm delighted that they have brought it up of their own account.

'I was humbled by what I saw,' I say, patting down my pink and white stripy minidress and thinking for about the fiftieth time in my life how much happier I would be if I was wearing this outfit with the long silver boots. 'What makes me feel angry is that the whole problem could be sorted because what they need is money and there is plenty of money in Cape Town and there is a lot of money in the world. I'll tell you what . . . if everybody who watched my YouTube video gave one pound to the charity, or two dollars, or ten rand, or whatever the equivalent is, or whatever they can afford, they would be able to solve all of the problems that currently exist and build a better and brighter future for these people. If you can find it within yourself to donate, please do. It will make the most enormous difference to these people. Just a pound will save a life tonight. Please go on to the SA TV website and look at the many ways in which you can donate money.'

There, that was all my own idea. I asked George to send an email through to the floor manager last night with a list of ways in which people could donate money to the charity. We asked the floor manager to make sure that the list was put on their website. I'm intrigued to see what will happen. Will loads of people donate money? I don't know. I've never done anything like this before.

'Well done, Tracie,' Kay is saying. 'We do appreciate how important this charity has become to you, and I think I speak for all of South Africa when I say a big thank you. Now then, we have had several emails this morning from members of the public who have questions they would like us to put to you. Would that be OK?'

I smile nervously. What on earth am I going to be asked? 'Fire away,' I tell her, and she looks down at her notes.

'OK, the first question today has come in from Sandra from Port Elizabeth and she says that she thought the YouTube video was great fun, and she has become a big fan of yours since reading about your involvements with the charity. She asks whether you were embarrassed when you first realised that the video had been put on YouTube.'

'Yes!' I reply. 'I was completely shocked, humiliated and embarrassed. I was promised that we were just messing around in the studio, and nothing would ever be broadcast. This was the last thing that I expected to happen.'

'And Sandra has another question for you, Tracie. She asks what was the most embarrassing thing that had ever happened to you before the YouTube video?'

'It's so hard to say,' I answer slowly. 'To be honest, lots of very embarrassing things have happened to me over the years. I don't know what it is about me, but I do seem to be forever embarrassing myself. There was the time when I got my hair extensions caught in the car door just after I had them done – the car drove off with my hair stuck in the door and swinging along beside it as it disappeared into the distance. Then there was the time I went for a spray tan and fell out of the cubicle, through the open door, and arrived in the reception area wearing paper knickers, with half my limbs sprayed orange, and the other half still white. That was quite embarrassing. There are loads of others . . . shall I go on?'

'That's probably enough, thanks Tracie,' she says, looking down at the card in her hands. 'Now, a guy called Martyn from here in Cape Town has a question for you. He wants to know whether you get lonely with your husband being so far away, and would you like company sometimes. He says he's available if you want someone to talk to occasionally. He's obviously being funny, Tracie, but in all seriousness, do you get lonely when your husband is away so much? Obviously it's something that all foot-ballers' wives have to deal with. Are you quite a loner, would you say, Tracie?'

'No! I'm not a loner at all. I always surround myself with people. I travelled out here with my daughter Paskia and with my two best friends, Mich and Suse, who I simply couldn't do without. As long as those three people are with me, I never feel alone. I also asked Shiraz, my lovely assistant, to come along, so I had four people there for the journey. Good job there were four of them actually; it needed that many of them to drag me out of the duty-free shops at Heathrow Airport. Honestly, I'm a nightmare in them. This time I bought make-up in such large quantities that I could have opened an in-air beauty parlour.'

'OK, Tracie, let's move now to Melissa Young from Johannesburg who says she is from England originally, and wonders whether you might have any views on how England will do in the World Cup. Do you think England will win?'

'I always used to think that the World Cup was a bit like the national lottery,' I hear myself saying. 'You enter it but you know you're not going to win.'

'OK …'

'I mean you absolutely know in your brain that you haven't got a chance but still your heart pumps when you see the numbers, still your emotions run riot as you plan how you'll spend your new vast wealth, but still you do know that you won't win. This is what it's been like supporting England in every World Cup competition. But the reason I say that I always *used to* think it was like the national lottery is because I do think that this year it is very different, and I think that England have a very good chance of winning the tournament. So, in answer to the question how will England do in the World Cup, the answer is that I think that they will win it.'

'I know you didn't want to be asked questions about the football, Tracie, but obviously because you've arrived in South Africa as part of the England squad, some of the questions are inevitably going to be about the sport. And we've got one here from someone who is asking about the structure of the tournament. He is saying that the World Cup takes place over a month, but the first round is over quite quickly. Am I right in saying that?'

'Yes,' I reply, trying to think of something funny to say. 'I guess it's in tribute to George Best.'

'Oh,' she says. 'Why is that?'

'You know ... get the first round in as quickly as possible! Ha, ha, ha, ha ...' Oh, dear, I'm laughing at my own jokes now. Never a good sign!

Kay is smiling while I talk and looking over at the weather presenter who prepares to come on for her slot. I've come to quite dislike the weather presenter. She's a children's TV presenter trapped in an adult presenter's career. Why doesn't she just tell people what the weather is going to be like? Why does she have to say things like 'oooo, time for me to get my sweet little shorts out ...' She is also young and very pretty, which annoys me.

'Well, that's all from Tracie Martin, I'm sorry to say. You've entertained us majestically, my dear. Can I ask you, are you enjoying being in front of the screen?

'In front of the screen? Don't you mean in front of the

camera? If I were in front of everyone's screen that would be really annoying for them and slightly odd for me because I would have to be in their houses.'

'Right, well, as we say goodbye to Tracie, it's time for us to reveal news just in that gardening experts have revealed that people who worry that their grass is too short probably mow it too much. We'll be back after the break with more on that breaking news.'

Midday

I go rushing back into the hotel in something of a temper after another failed attempt to buy myself the beautiful long silver boots that I am lusting after with increasing passion as the days go by. I stamp into the lobby, dismal and dejected. How can I keep going on like this without them? The only thing that can cheer me up now is the sight of Wags lounging around in reception, drinking Bacardi. Ooo . . . no, not Bacardi. I don't fancy Bacardi at all, maybe sparkling water for now and chips. Mmmm, what I'd give for a plate of chips with sugar to dip them into. Yum. Bizarre, admittedly, but yum. Sadly, there are no Wags, no chips and no sugar when I arrive in the reception area, just three Chinese men in dark suits poring over a laptop with some sort of presentation on it.

They barely look up as I walk in. It's funny, when you've been on TV you imagine that people will recognise you afterwards, but apparently that's not the case. Does no one round here ever watch TV? I grab myself a sparkling water (DO NOT TELL ANYONE! If they ask, tell them you saw me put vodka in it or something) and head out of the reception area and up to my room. I throw off my fabulous pink and white creation and begin looking through the collection of swimwear that I brought with me. I've got time to stroll down to the pool before I begin my magnificent transformation of Rosie because the appointment isn't until seven o'clock (Shiraz has booked a mega-appointment so the waxing, pedicure, manicure, facial and eyebrow threading will be done at the same time).

So, the main question is: what swimwear to opt for today? There is the particularly adorable costume, the one I bought because I'd seen Cheryl Cole in it, that has so many cutaways it looks like a spider's web with a gusset. I hold it up against myself. There's nothing to it and it's barely decent. In other words, it's perfect! I peer through the binoculars to see who I can spot lounging by the swimming pool. There's Shiraz practising some sort of Tai Chi or yoga or Pilates or something before she goes off to help the poor. My God, that girl needs her legs waxed. I see someone wandering over to talk to her, so she unwraps her legs from around her neck and stands up. Perhaps it's someone from the hair police, come to arrest her for having limbs like a chimp (actually they're not that bad – I'm just very fussy about these things).

OH MY GOD!!! OH MY GOD!! It's not someone from the hair police, it's only bloody Victoria Beckham. I'd heard that she and Becks were still going to come and see some matches and support the lads, despite the tragedy of Becks not being able to play. She must have come to the hotel to say hello to people because I know they're not staying here. Oh My God, Oh My God, Oh My God. This is serious. She's gone up and started talking to Shiraz. Fuck,

fuck, fuck. Shiraz is just my assistant!! What the bollocks in hell is she doing suddenly becoming best friends with all the Wonder-Wags? One minute it's Coleen, the next it's Vics. I grab the complicated cutaway swimsuit and attempt to climb into it at high speed, desperately draping the tiny slips of material across my body in the hope of creating a costume that looks vaguely decent. How the hell are you supposed to put this thing on?

Whatever I do, my gigantic, unnaturally inflated breasts seem to pop out from between the strips of fabric. Bollocks. I need to get down there as soon as possible. It'll have to do. I grab my sunglasses, and the large sun hat that makes me feel as if I'm Sophia Loren on the set of a 1950s Italian movie, and slip on a pair of white cowboy boots that make me feel as if I'm Jordan on the pull in Ibiza.

I grab my keycard and go bursting out of the hotel room and hurl myself into the lift. I see the looks of unbridled horror on the faces of everyone in there as soon as the doors close. What the hell is their problem? I look into the mirror at the back of the lift and see that I look adorable. I'm still wearing the very heavy TV make-up from this morning, and my hair is magnificently blonde. I look down a little further at my swimming costume. Aha! That'll be why everyone is staring . . . my swimming costume is plainly not doing what is required of a swimming costume. One breast has burst completely free and is sticking out in front of me. 'Sorry,' I mouth as I wriggle my way to the back of the lift so I'm staring straight at the mirror. Behind me is a lift full of men who are desperately trying not to show that they are watching me.

The men look as if they're dressed for some sort of

dull marketing conference. This is clearly going to be the highlight of their day. I set about trying to adjust the swimming costume to cover the escaped right boob. Easier said than done. As soon as I start moving the strips of material around in order to cover my right breast, the left breast pops out. I try to rearrange things back again, covering the left breast and pulling over the material to make sure that my left nipple is not on show, but all that happens is that the right breast pops back out again. Before long, my efforts to cover myself are being watched intently and quite openly by everyone in the lift, and pretty soon I'm being accompanied by the sound of grown men saying 'ooohh' and 'aahhhh' every time I cover one up, and the next one pops out. There are whispered comments like, 'ooo . . . I thought she'd got it then' as the next breast escapes against my wishes.

The simple fact here is that the swimming costume's too small for me, but I'm determined to make it work somehow because I'm buggered if I'm going back up to the room to change. Then a thought strikes me – the keycard – that might work. Before too long I have employed the use of my keycard and strategically placed it across my left nipple, allowing me to pull over the material to the right side to cover my right breast. I stand up straight, look into the mirror, and realise that both breasts are now properly covered. There's a ripple of applause from the assembled guys in the lift, and were I not so concerned about my breasts bursting back out again, I'd be inclined to do a small bow. As it is, I just exit the lift with a smile, and stomp my way out to the swimming pool area.

*

By the time I get there, Vics is nowhere to be seen. Shiraz is still on her mat doing her ridiculous posing but she's all alone. 'WHERE IS SHE?' I shriek. 'WHAT HAVE YOU DONE WITH HER?'

Shiraz removes her ankle from its position somewhere behind her neck, and pulls herself round into a normal shape.

'What are you talking about, Trace?' she asks. 'I don't know what you're talking about.'

'Victoria Beckham,' I say. I'm out of breath and gabbling. 'Vics, Vics, Vics . . . you know, Vics.'

'Oh, yes. She was here just a minute ago.'

'I KNOW! I SAW HER THROUGH THE TELE-SCOPE.' I'm shouting now, but I can't help myself. I just need to know where Victoria is. 'WHERE IS SHE NOW?'

'She's gone to a Pilates class,' says Shiraz. 'She was asking me about classes this morning, and I told her that the Pilates class was particularly good. I did the class early this morning with Alex and it was excellent.'

'You were what? Doing classes with Alex? Talking to Vics? To *Vics*? How could you be talking to her? She's Victoria Beckham, for God's sake.'

'She came up to me when I was outside this morning during my salutations to the sun, and asked whether she could join in. I'd just got back from Pilates so I started telling her all about it.'

This is beyond belief now. I sat at the bar all night in the hope that one of the Wags would come down and I could get to know her and bloody Shiraz is out there at the crack of dawn saluting the sunshine or some other daft thing, and suddenly she's best mates with the greatest Wag that the world of Wags has ever known.

'I'm going to join Pilates,' I shout, rushing off in the direction of the gym area. 'If anyone else comes to talk to you, tell them you can't speak until I'm back. I don't want you making any more Wag friends. These Wonder-Wags only have a certain amount of friendship to give out, and the last thing I want is then wasting it on you.'

'Right,' she says. 'But I don't think the Pilates is in that gym, I think it's . . . .'

Whatever. I'm not listening any more. I need to find my new best friend Victoria Beckham.

5 p.m.

'Anywhere else?' asks Paskia.

'Everywhere,' I say bitterly. I feel as if this is all Shiraz's fault, though clearly it isn't. It's not like she *made* me go to Pilates. 'Ah! There!' I say, as she massages my shoulders and upper back. The problem was not Pilates in the end anyway, because I went into the wrong bloody studio, and ended up doing a boxercise class.

There are lots of reasons why this was a bad idea, but let me just run through a few of them with you. First of all, there was the fact that I was only doing a class in the first place because I wanted to meet Victoria Beckham, and Victoria Beckham wasn't in boxercise; she was in Pilates. Then, there was the fact that I have absolutely no interest at all in punching a little bag very fast and holding my hands up while some overweight businessman from Durban aims little rabbit punches at my hands. Third, was that they played 'Fight For This Love' and I almost cried. It's so sad that Cheryl's not here. I really feel that she and I could be the best of friends. Whenever I hear that song these days I can't help myself from wailing, 'Why? Why?' Finally, and probably the most compelling reason why I shouldn't have been in the class, was that I was wearing a teeny-weeny swimming costume made out of a couple of strands of flimsy material. The whole thing doesn't stay together and cover my considerable assets when I'm standing still, so can you imagine what sort of impact I made in boxercise when every movement resulted in my keycard popping out followed swiftly by a mound of breast and a loose nipple. They also didn't like the fact that I was doing boxercise in cowboy boots. It was all a fiasco. I didn't do very much, but what I did do really hurt.

'Ah, well, it could have been worse,' says Paskia.

'Could it? I never got to see Vics and got punched many times in the process. It's hard to see how it could have got any worse. I feel so depressed today.'

'Me too,' she says. 'I feel so fed up out here, Mum. There's no football anywhere. Dad says I can go and join him in the players' hotel after the first match. Can I? Can I, Mum?'

Oh, no, I should have never mentioned feeling depressed. I don't want her to go.

I always feel really torn in moments like these. I desperately want my daughter to be happy, but I also want to make sure I'm doing what's genuinely right for her rather than simply acceding to her every wish.

'I'll talk to your father tonight and we'll make a plan,' I say. 'I'm not promising anything but I know how much you like your football, so I'll see what he says.'

'Thanks, Mum. Thanks,' she says, hugging me close to her. Dean has already said she's welcome to go over there because he knows how much she'd love to be talking football, but I'll miss her if she goes. I just like having her round.

7 p.m.

Rosie has been stripped down to her knickers (big ones . . . can you imagine? Has she never heard of a thong?). She's wrapped in a big, fluffy white dressing gown and looks adorable. When she took her hair down from its dreadful ponytail, and when I saw what an incredible figure she has, hidden away beneath layers of man-made fabric, I became more convinced than ever of my role as the fairy godmother to this poor darling.

'Just relax. You're in my hands. Everything's going to be OK,' I tell her, though the look of terror flashing through her eyes is a clear indication that she doesn't believe me one little bit.

'OK, ladies, let's go.'

On my command, the beauticians step forward and begin their assault upon the skin and nails of this delicious young Wag-in-waiting. There's a bit of screaming, to be honest. The poor girl had no idea that the bikini wax came with the leg wax, and we fought a little about the colour for the nails. I was determined that she should have the peach (orange), she wanted nude. I won, and Rosie emerged from the salon with not a hair below her waist, the narrowest eye brows imaginable and toenails and fingernails the colour of satsumas.

'My work here is done . . . for today,' I tell her, as we saunter back to the main hotel. 'We need to look at clothes next, get your hair and a spray tan sorted before the first match, then all you'll need after that is a face full of make-up and Dio will be thrilled to the bottom of his goal-scoring feet with the way you look. Excited?'

'Kind of,' she says wearily.

'Well, you should be,' I say excitedly.

Chapter Thirteen

Tuesday 25^h May

I am up at the crack of dawn again (i.e. 10 a.m – I've gone mad with these crazily early mornings since I got to South Africa) and I'm down to that poolside before you can say, 'salute to the sun in the shape of a frog or howl at the moon in the shape of a fox' or whatever else it is that they say in yoga. There's no sign of the Wonder-Wags, annoyingly, but Rosie is here with towels wrapped around her legs. 'You're not cold, are you?' I ask. It's lovely and warm (like a gorgeous British summer's day).

'No,' she says, peeling back the towels to reveal that her legs are still scarlet and sore from the waxing yesterday.

Jane is here too, and she gives a sharp intake of breath when she sees the red raw flesh.

'What have you done to yourself?' she says.

'I had my legs waxed,' says Rosie, pitifully.

'It's fine,' I say. 'It'll be all cleared up soon, and then we can get you spray tanned and into some fancy clothing and you'll look unbelievably fantastic.'

'I hope so,' says Rosie, while Jane just shakes her head.

I'm quite glad to bump into Jane, to be honest, because I think the two of us just got off to a bad start. I haven't seen her since the incident in reception with George and all the shopping I wonder whether she saw the article in which they talked about the great charity work I'd been doing, and how I was an asset to South Africa. I do hope so, and I hope she realises that everything I bought that day was for the poor people of South Africa, and not for myself. I'd like to be friends with her. After all, we are both coaching Wags. It is only right and proper that we should socialise together when I'm not out shopping, partying and drinking with the Wonder-Wags (who I just know I'm going to end up becoming best friends with, any day now. It just seems to be taking much longer than planned).

'How are you, Jane?' I ask, turning to face her as she lies back on her sunbed.

'I'm very well, Tracie. How are you?'

'I'm very well too,' I reply. 'Managing to keep myself busy.'

'So I hear. I read the article about you in the *South African Daily News*.'

'Oh, good,' I exclaim, 'because I hope you realise that all those shopping bags I had in reception last time I saw you, and all that money I took out – it was all for the poor people, not for me. And that guy – his name was George and he runs the charity.'

'Of course,' she says. 'I realise that. I never thought badly of you.'

Like bollocks.

'No, I've been extremely impressed with all the charity work you've been doing. You really have done very well.'

'Thank you,' I say, though I must say that I've gone off her a bit; there's something a little smarmy and discomforting about her. I find myself annoyed that she only likes me now that I've been officially endorsed by the nation's media. Perhaps I was a nice person before, but she never hung around long enough to find out; I'm longing to tell her that I stole Coleen's baby, then stalked Vics into the wrong fitness class before flashing at everyone and running out, just to upset her. I won't though. I think that would be a case of cutting your nose off to spite your face. (I *love* that saying!)

'Have you done much television before?' Jane asks. 'I always think that I would be very good on television. You know, I'm sure I'd be a natural in front of the camera. I'm used to talking in front of large groups of children, because I'm a headmistress. I think television would be easy after talking in front of hundreds of children every day.'

Blah, blah, blah . . . I so don't like this woman now. I don't know why I ever cared whether she liked me or not.

'Are you still a headmistress?' I ask, out of politeness more than anything.

'I worked all the way through the early part of Grimaldi's career. We'd travel all over the country, and I'd get a job in a school near whichever club he was playing for but it started to get very difficult. Sometimes they're only based at the club for a couple of years. I've spent a year trying to get a job, done six months in that job, then had to give in my notice so many times I've lost count. It got a bit ridiculous and I was letting people down all of the time. So I decided I'd better put my career on hold. I was very sad, though, because I loved being a teacher, and the last thing I wanted was to become a vacuous blonde Wag who spent the whole time worrying about hair, clothes, and how far up the greasy football pole her husband was going to climb. Gosh – sorry, Tracie. No offence meant at all.'

'None taken,' I say, adjusting myself on the fabulously comfortable sun lounge, and sipping a (Virgin) cocktail. I signal to the waiter who comes over from the beach bar, and he takes my glass away to replenish it.

The woman's a bore, but I know what she means about moving around the country all the time for football. There are lots of bad times as a Wag as well as the obvious good ones. I think back to the many times I've got myself a spray tan, piled on the make-up, and come staggering out on searingly high-heeled shoes to support my husband in some godforsaken football match in some godforsaken place, only to spend the whole time watching him sit looking forlorn and unloved on the bench. He'd spend entire matches on his bottom on a bench, chewing gum and jumping up every so often when an event on the pitch moved him to do so. I remember when Paskia was asked to describe what her daddy did for a living for a school project; she said he was a footballer. Then they had to draw pictures of their daddies doing their jobs in art. Paskia drew a picture of a sad man sitting on a bench. That was her entire childhood understanding of football. Amazing that he's come so far, and that we as a family have remained so close.

'Could you not do that thing where you go into schools to help out if the teacher's away? I can't remember what the name of it is, but we used to have them all the time at school.'

'Peripatetic,' she says.

'Oh, are they? Well you don't want to be one of those then, do you.'

'Sorry?' she says, as the waiter returns with another fruit cocktail.

'I was saying that you don't want to be one of those teachers that comes in when another teacher's ill if they're very pathetic.'

'No, peripatetic,' she repeats, saying the words slowly, as if that will help.

'I did think about doing something like that just to keep my hand in while Grimaldi's career was taking off in the early days. But the trouble with working like that is that a lot of the jobs you get offered are in some schools that are – how do you say it politely – very trying!'

'Oh, I can imagine,' I reply, making like I might have some sort of clue about the problems faced by a school headmistress. I imagine that I was one of the kids that she is now categorising as 'trying'.

'The children are all from broken homes. It's far from ideal,' she says.

'I'm from a broken home,' I say. 'Lots of people are.'

'Oh, right,' says Jane. 'Well, I'll be honest with you; it can cause difficulties for children—' She stops talking suddenly and looks up. 'Who on earth is this?' she asks.

Coming towards us is Mich, who's dressed up beautifully in a lurid-green bikini with a huge green sun hat that has a black band around it (a bit like a Liquorice Allsort, but in a nice way). She has piles of bangles up both arms (I mean *piles*. She must have forty on each arm, and I bet she can't lift her hands), and quite terrifyingly high clog-heeled shoes that lace up to her knees.

The clumpy shoes are in an almost-translucent white colour so they really set off the outfit. Jane and I both shield our eyes as she approaches, protecting them from the glare of the stunning whiteness. I make a mental note to congratulate Mich on such a stunning outfit, and to implore Rosie to take in all the finer details of the styling because that's the sort of look that I long to create for her.

'Mind if I join you?' Mich asks.

'Of course not,' I say, answering on Jane's behalf, because Jane is too busy lying there open-mouthed and incredulous while tending to her eyes, which are now watering quite a lot. The shoes really are a terrifyingly white colour – it's worse than being in my kitchen. My eyes are throbbing too. All credit to Mich.

I introduce the ladies to one another, and call the barman over to provide Mich with a morning drink.

'Are you sure I can't get you something?' I ask Jane. She said no before, but it's only polite to ask again.

'I'll have two,' says Mich, but Jane insists on fresh orange juice.

'I'll get you another one as well, shall I, love?' she says to me. The thought of drinking a proper cocktail makes me feel quite sick for some reason, but I'm reluctant to say no because Mich will think the world has ended. I never knowingly refuse alcohol but right now I just don't fancy any at all.

'Sure,' I say. 'Get me another one will you.'

All three of us sit, looking out over the glistening blue water in silence, enjoying the peace, until suddenly there's an angry shriek as a heavily toasted skinny woman with incredibly yellow hair screams at a young child and drags him off by his ear.

'Sorry to ask, Trace, but have you spoken to your mum recently?' asks Mich, throwing in the world's biggest mood-killer. Seeing an angry mother abuse a young child has clearly reminded her of Angie.

'I spoke to her but it was a waste of time,' I say. 'It turns out that she's been doing interviews with the journalists in London about me, when I specifically asked her not to. I asked Shiraz to check whether any were published and there's been no sign of any yet, so I'm hoping no one prints them.'

'Tracie's mum is a complete nightmare,' says Mich, turning to face Jane. 'Really, she's a total bitch. She never loved Tracie; never loved anyone but herself. Tracie never knew what love was till she met Dean. Isn't that right, love?'

Mich is right; Dean and Paskia were the two first great loves of my life. Then Dean introduced me to the Wags and that's when I found love for the third time. The Wags seemed like this impossibly beautiful group of feminine women who understood what their role was in life. When I met the Wags at first I thought they were amazing and I really wanted to be like them. There was something so magical and fairytale-like about them. It seemed they lived in a world devoid of problems and pressures. I worked hard to look like and behave like the perfect Wag, and started idolising all the Wags I met and heard about.

I'd never had a clue what my own role was previously. I didn't know how to fit in or what was expected of me. There were no rules until I became a Wag. I was the one who put Mum to bed when she came in drunk, I was the one who phoned up when bills arrived that we couldn't pay. I was the one who took time off school to look after Mum. I never minded one little bit; it just meant that I never got to be a child. That's something that I have fought so hard for for

Paskia. Sometimes when she was young I treated her like she was a real baby and gave her no responsibility at all because I wanted her to have the fun that I didn't.

When I was young we would move house all the time, which used to really get me down. I never settled anywhere and didn't have a proper group of friends until I met Mich and Suse down at Luton. When I was young I used to think I must be in the witness protection programme or something because we seem to move house so much. I didn't realise it was because Mum was bouncing from lover to lover. Every time a relationship ended, I'd be packed up and shipped off to stay with a friend somewhere, until she had found another lover to look after us. It wasn't until she decided to start flirting with rich men, and therefore ended up with a house and some diamonds at the end of every relationship, that I found myself living in a home that I could call my own for any length of time.

Jane is looking at me with concern in her eyes. 'Did you have a very difficult childhood?' she asks. Mich guffaws loudly.

'Just a bit!' she says on my behalf.

'It wasn't good,' I confirm.

'And how did that affect you in school, Tracie?' asks Jane. 'Did you find your work suffered if your home life wasn't very good?'

'I guess so,' I say but the truth is that I've never really thought about it like that. I always assumed that I never did very well at school because I was stupid. Mum always said I was really dense so I suppose I've always grown up thinking that was the case. It never really occurred to me that I was always bound to fail at school, and thus confirm the views of many that I was worthless and stupid, because Mum created such an atrocious home life for me.

I tell Jane a little bit about my school life, and how I never really bothered turning up to the classes, and thought it was all a bit of a waste of time.

'The teachers never really seemed to care whether I turned up or not,' I say. I don't know whether this is true, but I don't ever remember being in trouble when I didn't turn up so it must be true to a certain extent. They can't have cared all that much.

'We had such big classes in our school, so the teachers were very busy with the other pupils and just didn't seem to notice whether I was there. With forty other people in the class, the teachers had their hands full anyway.'

'Forty in a class? Are you sure? That seems a lot,' says Jane. 'It must have been quite a rough school.'

Why am I bothering. What does she care?

'Yes,' I answer, assuming she'll be happier if I conform to every stereotype she has about me. 'A rough school, Jane – that's right.'

6 p.m.

It's quite late by the time I speak to Dean. We seem to have missed each other all day, with him leaving messages for me, and me leaving messages back for him, without us getting to actually talk to one another. I hate it when I go through a whole day without chatting to my husband. Back in England we talk all the time. I mean, I know I've got my great mates Mich and Suse, but I would say that Dean is definitely my best friend. He's my soul mate and the person

I want to talk to more than anyone else. Not being able to chat to him every few hours is horrible.

When he calls, he tells me that the place the players are staying in is amazing. I've told him all about our hotel, obviously, and explained about Spa Island and the fabulous pool. His hotel doesn't sound anywhere near as luxurious as ours, but I guess it fits the purpose for them. He keeps trying to remind me that they're not there to get drunk in the bar, or sing songs on the terrace at night; they're in South Africa to win a World Cup, and he wants the hotel to have all the facilities needed to get the players in the best possible shape to do that.

While he chats on about the amazing facilities, I regale him with details of the amazing pool here, and the fact that the spa is unbelievable. 'You know they have facials on Spa Island in which they use the buds from roses grown in a bath of milk and pumpkin seeds.'

'Sounds lovely,' he replies. 'I hope you're having fun.'

'I am,' I tell him. 'Shiraz has been getting really involved in AFFAH. She goes there most afternoons to help George. She's my contribution to the charity.'

'Yeah, and the three hundred grand you spent on it when you first met George.'

'Yes, I guess there was that as well.'

'You're such a soft touch, aren't you? What have I always told you – you're the softest touch in the world when it comes to charities. You'll be pleased to know, though, that I've spoken to the players and some of the team sponsors about the charity and they're all going to contribute something,' he says. 'I wasn't going to tell you till I saw you at the match but I'm hopeless at keeping secrets, as you know.'

'That's brilliant!!' I say. 'George will be so pleased. When will we know how much? When can I tell him?'

'I think each player will contribute twenty thousand pounds and that will be matched by the sponsors who'll pool together. We should be talking about a one million pound contribution – perhaps more, but don't tell George yet. Not till it's all sorted.'

'Don't tell him? Oh, Dean, you know what I'm like about having information that I can't share. I'm dying to tell him. You have to let me.'

'No, love. Now, changing the conversation – what about Paskia? I've got a whole pile of messages from her saying that she loves you dearly but is dying to see what a World Cup is really all about. She wants to come and stay at the players' hotel. What do you think?'

'I don't like the sound of it,' I admit. 'I don't want to be a big party pooper but I'm not sure that it's the right place for a sixteen-year-old girl to be.'

'Come on! She's the most sensible teenager ever and she'll be well looked after here,' says Dean. 'There'd be a role for her in organising the press conferences with Oliver. We could look at paying her a small salary. I think she'd like it and I know it would be good for her. She has her head stuck in books all day, and I think it would be handy for her to have an idea about the real world of work.'

I agree with him there. I think it would be very valuable experience.

'OK, but when?' I ask, reluctantly.

'Well, it makes sense for her to stay there with you for now. Then how about when you come over for the match, Paskia can stay here with me. You'll see her every week at the matches and if she gets fed up, or it's not working out, she can fly straight back to you.'

'OK.'

'It'll be fine, love. Do you think I'm going to let anything bad happen to her? Do you? I'd rather die than see her hurt in any way.'

'I know, love, I know,' I say. 'You're right.'

'Good. Now, is Rosie OK?' he asks. 'Have you been out with her much?'

'We've had treatments together,' I reassure him. 'I'm going to take her shopping. Why are you so worried about her? She seems fine. Very happy.'

'That's a relief. Dio's a very important player. He's struggling a bit with a knee injury and is knocked a bit low by it. He's young, and he's quite an aggressive little kid. He's a bit out of sorts at the moment. He's not used to playing at this level so we want everything around him to be a settled as possible. The happier she is, and the more she leaves him alone to play football and doesn't ring up to moan at him, the happier we'll be.'

'OK, love. Well, I'll go check on her later then,' I say, 'but she doesn't strike me as high maintenance at all. She seems to adore Dio.'

'That's a relief to hear. Now, a bit of gossip for you. Don't mention it to anyone else but Coleen had her baby snatched. Apparently she left her in the care of a mad woman in the hotel who was wandering around pretending to be a nursery nurse. Imagine if it got in the press!'

'Imagine indeed,' I say with a nervous chortle. 'Just imagine ...'

Chapter Fourteen

Thursday 27th May

I wake up to a familiar feeling in my stomach. There's a churning sensation, like my intestines have broken free and are banging on the inside of my stomach trying to get out. Oh, I feel so sick; it's horrible. I haven't had a hangover for ages. I feel terrible. I bet that's because I ate bread last night. Yes – you read that properly – I ate bread last night. I don't know what's wrong with me at the moment. Eating's bad enough but to knowingly eat carbohydrates? And bread at that? Bread is evil. I feel flushed with shame.

They should have a confession box for Wags, like they do in Catholic Churches. 'Forgive me, Victoria, for I have sinned.'

The truth is that if they did have something like that, I really wouldn't be in there that often because I stick to the laws of Wagdom like newly spray-tanned thighs stick to a plastic bar stool. I do. I'm very good. I drink, always wear terrifying amounts of make-up, don't own flat shoes . . . I do it all. But on this holiday (erm, I mean trip to support the players in the World Cup), I've completely fallen apart. I have. I think about food all the time. I don't want Bacardi and, actually, come to think of it, I didn't drink last night. I haven't drunk anything alcoholic for a few days if truth be told, which for me is just plain weird. It *must* be the bread that's made me feel like this. I'm going to go and see a doctor. Things simply aren't right.

I rush off to the loo and whilst I don't want to burden you with too many of the gory details, I am as hideously and violently sick as it's possible for a woman to be. I don't hold my long and luscious hair extensions back out of the way so there's a whole story there I won't tell you about cleaning them, but – happily – I do feel better afterwards. As I stand up from the floor, lightheaded but relieved that it's all over, I hear my phone ringing in the bedroom. Hell's bells, do people have some sort of sixth sense about the worst time to ring?

'Tracie Martin speaking,'

'Hello, love. It's me.'

'Dean! Your number didn't come up. How are you, sweetheart?'

'Promoted,' he says, and I can hear the smugness in his familiar voice.

'You've been promoted *again*?'

This is now taking on farcical proportions. He'll be prime minister by the end of the tour.

'One of the guys has broken his leg quite badly, so had to go back to England for surgery. It means I'm now the assistant defence coach. Isn't that great news?'

'It's brilliant news!' I say. 'Just brilliant news. Assistant defence coach!' That's actually starting to sound like a proper job now. 'Hoorah!'

'I've been given total control of goalkeeping as well as being second-in-charge of all the defence for the team. Can you believe that?'

'I actually can, love. What I can't believe is that they took so bloody long to realise how fantastic you are.'

2 p.m.

There's a knock on the door and in comes Rosie, a picture of youthful beauty and peachiness with Paskia, my gorgeous but unkempt daughter, in hot pursuit. They're like a couple of fashion dropouts – Paskia in her trademark khaki trousers and plain green shirt with bits of string tied around her wrist like she's a hippy or something (I've asked her about them but can't find out why on earth she chooses to adorn herself in this manner). Then there's Rosie, wearing navy-blue school shorts which go down to her knees, and a plain white T-shirt. They're the girls who style forgot. But, not to worry. It's the second of my 'turn Rosie into a Wag' days today. This is my opportunity to focus all my considerable sartorial skills on turning Rosie into a proper footballer's girlfriend. When Paskia heard what I was up to she became so alarmed that I might 'over-style' Rosie (apparently there is such a thing) that she insisted on attending personally.

'Dad's keen for Rosie to feel happy and relaxed so that Dio's happy and relaxed. If you make Rosie look stupid and upset her, it's going to upset Dio, which will upset Dad. So all I'm saying is no crotchless knickers or nine-inch heels or anything like that. OK?'

Right. OK then. So they have very little faith in my ability to make someone look better do they? I'll show them.

Paskia and Rosie take a seat on the pale-blue banquette

that used to lie by the window (before the telescope took pride of place there and I was forced to push the banquette thing to the far side of the room). They look at me eagerly, awaiting my words of wisdom.

I stand up in the centre of the room.

'Rosie, today I'm going to make you look wonderful. I plan to transform you from this natural beauty we see before us into a gorgeous and lovely creature in time for the first match. I want Dio to take one look at you and be swept off his feet. You'll have perfect hair, nails and clothing and be spray tanned to a beautiful shade of deep, dark orange. You will look simply amazing. People will stop in the street and stare at you – I promise. Today we're going to look at Wag clothing that you should wear. Does that sound OK?'

'Oh, Tracie, that sounds amazing!' says Rosie, jumping up from the banquette rather too quickly, and causing the whole thing to up-end like a see-saw, causing poor Paskia to tip off the other end. Rosie apologises and rushes over to give me a hug. 'Thanks for all your help,' she says. 'I really, really appreciate it.'

'It's my pleasure,' I tell her, which it is really. 'OK, the first thing we're going to look at is colour. Everything I've seen you wearing since you've been in South Africa has been navy blue. How do you respond to that accusation?'

'Well, yes, you're right. I wear navy because it's smart. I think it's nice to look smart, isn't it?'

'Er, no . . . not unless you're a policeman, a security guard or about to start a new job in a bank. The navy needs to go. But don't worry, you can put the clothes aside and come back to them when you're ninety-four. You never know, they might be in fashion by then.'

Rosie has pulled out a small notebook and is writing down everything I say, bless her! Paskia smiles at me while Rosie scribbles away. It's lovely that this pretty teenage girl is taking my style advice so seriously.

'OK, and so, let's look at colour . . .'

On my instruction, Mich comes sauntering out from the bedroom wearing a lime-green minidress that is so astonishingly bright it's almost neon. It skims her knickers and perfectly matches the thigh-length green socks. She's wearing the super-white, laced-to-the-knee shoes that she was wearing by the pool and has big gold earrings, a bag big enough to live in and tons of bangles up both arms. She has about a grand's worth of make-up on her face. It's a lovely look.

I glance at Paskia and Rosie to see them both staring open-mouthed at Mich, as my dear friend struts and preens around the room like she's Naomi Campbell.

'Rosie, you'd look perfect in this dress,' I say. 'I think you should wear it to the first game against the US. What do you think?'

It takes a while before Rosie manages to regain the power of speech but then, finally, she gives her verdict. 'Um. It's a bit short and – what's the word – loud. I think Dio would have a fit if I turned up dressed like this. Even though it's very lovely, Tracie, and I can see you've gone to a lot of trouble, and I'm very, very grateful to you. It's just that I am not comfortable in bright colours especially because my skin tone is very pale.'

'Rosie, Rosie, Rosie. Did you listen to nothing I said? We'll be spray painting you with three coats of fake tan the night before the game. I can assure you that whatever else you look like when you go to the match, it certainly won't be "pale".'

'Oh. Well, perhaps that's OK then. I guess if I'm not pale that won't be so bad.'

'It won't. It'll be lovely. Now, Suse, where are you?'

Suse comes out of the bedroom in a raspberry-coloured, skin-tight, Lycra dress and minces across the room so slowly it looks like she's got both legs down the same leg hole in her knickers. The dress is way too tight for her but that's the way it's supposed to be. Her mighty mincing is accompanied by a considerable amount of stumbling as she struggles to cope on eight-inch heels. That girl needs to sort herself out. She says she never normally goes above five inches (we're talking shoe heels here; in every other respect she's a 'bigger is better' kind of girl). She's wearing the dress with long white, PVC, platform-heeled boots with matching earrings, jewellery and handbag the size of a suitcase. When she turns round (this takes a bit of time, what with the heels and everything) you can see the word 'Wag' picked out in white beads across her bum. The dress itself is backless. She looks radiant. Truly radiant. And I know that Rosie likes this one because she audibly gasps when Suse turns round.

'There,' I say. 'Two outfits that I have bought especially for you to wear to the first game and to the evening party after the first game. You'll need huge bug-eye sunglasses and I've bought you a huge, big, shaggy fake fur coat in case it gets cold in the evenings. It's beautiful – pure Katie Price. Now, what do you think?'

'I'm very grateful, Tracie,' she says. 'But I'm not sure what Dio will say. He'll be so shocked.'

'The whole point is to surprise him, isn't it? What would be the fun of walking in and him saying, "Oh, it's you, looking the same as ever"? You want to blow him away, don't you? You want to stun and amaze him. Well, I think you'll do that if you follow my advice.'

'Yep, you'll certainly do that,' says Pask.

'OK, let's leave the lesson here today then, Rosie. You've now got two beautiful outfits to wear and all we need to do closer to the match is to sort out tanning, hair and make-up. I'll have some interim treatments for you to do to make sure we keep you properly groomed and styled around the hotel. I've also got these for you.' I hand her a large fluffy bag containing a range of itsy-bitsy clothing she can wear around the hotel to attract the admiring glances of the other Wags. She takes it from me, along with the outfits handed over by Mich and Suse and prepares to leave the room. As she gets to the door, she spins round. 'Tracie, I really am very grateful,' she says. 'Truly. This is all such a change for me but I trust you and I do want to be different. I want to be a proper Wag . . . for Dio.'

That went well. I think. Paskia can't speak after the redesigning of Rosie. She soon perks up when I sit her down and tell her she's going to spend time with the players though. She races out of the room like a rocket, muttering about the need to pack and get herself ready. As she bursts from the room, I'm treated to the phone ringing and the dulcet tones of a ninety-year-old from Luton with her hearing aid not turned up properly.

'It's me,' she screams so loudly she doesn't actually need a phone. 'Gladys. Remember me?'

As if I could forget. I try to look after Gladys whenever

I can, and she's become a good friend in many ways. She's wise, like Dean's nan was. My friend Simon, who used to work as a journalist on the *Guardian*, then moved to study Russian Literature at Moscow University, is really super bright and whenever I took him to see the ladies at the old people's home, he'd listen to them talk and mutter, 'ah, the wisdom of the elderly' over and over again. God bless him. I must go over and see him when I'm back. Take Paskia. She and Simon get on like a house on fire, as you can imagine.

'Of course I can hear you, Gladys,' I say.

'Stolen any babies recently, have you, love?' she asks. Cheeky cow.

'I didn't steal it,' I say. 'It was a complete misunderstanding.'

'I'm only kidding you,' she replies. 'Now, where are you, love? Still abroad, are you?'

I explain that I am and that's pretty much it. Old people are a bit like children. Once they've finished talking to you it's 'goodbye' and they're off. None of this getting into a horrible tangle of etiquette and reluctance to go in case you appear offensive in some way. 'Bye love,' she says, and she's gone.

8 p.m.

I decide to wander down to the bar to see if I can force myself to drink alcohol. There must be a way in which I can rekindle my love affair with Bacardi Breezer. BB and I have been through so much together – we can't give up on the relationship now. I'm just thinking about why we fell out of love in the first place when the most amazing thing happens... Abbey Clancy comes up to me and introduces herself. *She introduces herself. She* comes up to *me*. I don't have to stalk her or follow her or frighten her or break any laws. The woman just charges up to me like it's the most natural thing in the world and says, 'Hi, you're Tracie, aren't you? I'm Abbey.'

Then we shake hands. She has tiny hands, by the way. Lovely nails and soft skin but tiny and narrow.

I am breathing really heavily as well, which I think might frighten her a bit, but I just can't help it. She says that Coleen told her about the charity work I'm doing and they are going to get in touch with George to offer their help too. 'It's an amazing thing, isn't it?' she says. 'Urrrrrrrrrr . . .' I reply. I've lost all control over my ability to speak now. I hate it when this happens.

'Well, nice to meet you any way,' she says. 'You should come with us next time we all go out for a drink. If you want to.'

'URRRRRR . . .' I say, leaning into her a bit too closely, and sounding a bit too eager, though still quite mad, and she backs off and looks ever so slightly scared.

'Right, well, I'll make sure you know next time,' she says.

She is really very thin and captivatingly beautiful. She is so much thinner than I am. I'm going to have to have my ribs removed or something. Perhaps my lungs, or my kidneys . . . something non-vital like that. She's definitely way thinner than I am.

'By the way, my Pete loves working with your husband,' she says. 'He's always saying what a great coach he is, and how he should be right at the top, running the team with

Capello.' With that, she's gone. A vision of pink loveliness, with perfect golden hair and enormous big blue eyes that take up half her face, walking slowly away from me after what might be the best moment of my life to date.

I turn to walk back up to the room when my phone rings. It's *Morning Live* calling to ask me whether I'll go on to the show tomorrow morning. There's been a ton of emails sent in to the station asking questions and they wonder whether I'll go and answer them.

I don't want to, I hate very early mornings and I don't want to leave the hotel now that I'm great friends with Abbey. Yet, for some reason – probably because I feel pathetically flattered by their attentions – I decide that I will go on to the programme.

Chapter Fifteen

Monday 31st May

'Hi, we're back with everyone's favourite English Wag, Tracie Martin. How have you been, Tracie?'

'Great,' I say.

'And we've got lots of questions for you today and next week. There's one here from a lovely lady called Melody who's about to have her first baby. Congratulations, Melody. She wants your advice on baby names because she says the Wags have such great names for their babies. Any thoughts?'

'Lots of thoughts. Obviously you want to keep the name as daft as possible or constructed in such a way that it appears daft when spoken; for example, Nicole Kidman called her firstborn Sunday Rose. Now anyone remotely sane can see that that sounds exactly like Sunday Roast: a name that you probably wouldn't want to call your daughter. Perhaps she was postnatally hormonal when she thought of it – or had one too many celebratory Barcadi Breezers. One particularly ridiculous thing to do is to call your child exactly the same thing as you, or even rearrange the letters in your own name to make another. Confused? Let me offer you an example from the world of popular music. Lee Ryan of Blue named his daughter Rayn Lee. Perhaps he was under the impression that the only letters that exist in the world are the ones in his name.

'I have to say though that my favourite name of the minute is the name of my lovely assistant, Shiraz. Calling a child after your favourite drink – considering that the excessive consumption of it most likely contributed to the child being brought into the world in the first place – is a truly lovely idea. If I were to have a child now I'd call him Bacardi . . . no question. If he was a boy, of course. Silly name for a girl.'

'OK, thank you, Tracie. The next question here is from Dillon, and he wants to know who is your favourite celebrity, not counting the Wags.'

'Mmmmm . . . that's a difficult question. I spend most of my life looking at Wags. Who else is there out there? I do like Lady Gaga. She's thin, blonde, wears unfeasibly high shoes and tons of jewellery. She has the heart and soul of a Wag, there's no doubt about that. She's completely amazing. Some of her outfits look like they've been put together in order to be able to survive a nuclear explosion, and when she said she used to have a portable fog machine in her handbag "so I could fog myself", I nearly died from excitement. A self-fogging diva! I *so* want one of those fog machines.'

'Goodness,' says Kay with a smile. 'How unique. Next question is from Stephen of Cape Town, who wants to ask you whether you would ever consider going on *I'm A Celebrity Get Me Out Of Here?* Would going on something like that ever interest you?'

'The truth is that I'm really not interested in being a celebrity,' I say, and I see the look of surprise in her eyes, but I'm being honest. 'I just want to be a Wag. I like pretty clothes, high shoes and being around footballers. Why would I go on to a show on television that takes me away from fancy clothing, high heels and footballers and brings me into contact, instead, with eels and kangaroo testicles? It's just not me. Celebrity's not all it's cracked up to be. I mean . . . look at Jordan. She has roughly eighty-two point six-five per cent of the available British famousness and she never even smiles. Anyway, I'd miss my Dean too much.'

Chapter Sixteen

Wednesday 2nd June

Another day where I have awoken to a massive hangover despite not drinking, been sick everywhere, and have then spent most of the rest of the day engaged in unsuccessfully peering through my telescope in the hope of seeing one of the Wonder-Wags. I toyed with the idea of turning up at Coleen's room earlier to apologise once again about what happened with Kai, just in case I could rescue some sort of friendship from that little misunderstanding, but I just can't get past the security guards at the end of the corridor. No matter how eagerly I chat them up, giggle with them, and offer to get them one of my special Tracie cocktails, they insist that they are not allowed to let anyone who doesn't have a room in the corridor go down the corridor, and since my face is familiar to them as the woman who took Coleen's baby, they are particularly reluctant to allow me to go wandering down there.

I considered trying to reach Abbey too – after all we're great mates after yesterday's encounter – but there's no sign of her either. I left a note with reception but when they said she hadn't been past to pick it up I took it back. She's probably not interested in wasting her valuable time with someone like me anyway.

The day is brightened immeasurably by a call from Dean to say that he has been promoted once again. It seems that with every day that passes, my dear, darling husband rises to become a yet more impressive and influential coach in the England set-up. This time it is a sickness bug that is to blame (perhaps that's what I've got). The poor guy was struck down by a bug and when he went to hospital they discovered massive infection in his blood and he needs to be kept in, meaning Dean's been promoted again. He is now *the* team's defence coach. It sounds serious so I managed not to say 'hoorah!' when Dean told me. Still, I'm delighted that Dean has been promoted to his rightful position. Hoorah!

'I'm completely in charge of all the team's defensive strategies,' he says proudly, which seems only fair really since he's the defence coach, but I don't want to pour water on his fiery enthusiasm, so I just squeal a lot and tell him how happy and proud I am, and I think of how close me and Abbey are going to get now.

Chapter Seventeen

Thursday 3ʳᵈ June

I am sitting in the spa with my nail extensions being lengthened and my elbows being purified with dried grapefruit and lavender seeds that have been crushed and rolled on the thighs of virgins in Israel, when Rosie comes bursting in to see me. She's still wearing navy shorts and a terrible, cheap blue cotton shirt. Not for the first time, I wonder whether I'm wasting my time here.

'Can I talk to you?' she asks. She looks prettier than ever this morning – all youthful with her lovely plump cheeks and flawless skin. If only we could sort out the 'American tourist in London' clothing situation, her look would be hugely improved.

'Of course you can,' I say, removing the mouth exerciser from my teeth (it gives you a better jawline and more pronounced cheekbones apparently, though I've seen no sign of that yet).

'What are you here for?' she asks.

'Well, I'm having my nails and elbows done at the moment and I'm waiting for my lemon and peppermint heel massage with dandelion head rub.'

'Oh,' she says. 'Should I be having things like that?'

'Let's take it one step at a time, shall we?' I say. 'We'll

leave the heels and elbows till we've got the face right. I've booked you in for a hair session and tanning session so everything will be perfect for the match on Saturday.'

'Thanks,' she says. 'Listen, I just wanted to tell you I've got amazing news. Dio has sent me the most gorgeous bright-green silk scarf from Chanel.' She pulls it out of her terrible cheap hand bag – all silky and the most spectacular green colour. It's divine; the boy clearly has great taste.

'That's astonishing,' I say. 'Wow. It's going to go beautifully with your new outfit.'

'I know,' she twirls it between her beautiful (but pale) fingers, and squeals with delight. 'You know, Tracie, I was really worried about whether I was doing the right thing by getting all Wagged up for the match on Saturday, but it's like this scarf is a message from Dio to say that's a good idea.'

'That's exactly what it is,' I reassure her. 'A message from your man telling you that you can cast off the navy and begin a new technicolor, bright and spangly, sparkly life as a Wag.'

'He's so amazingly thoughtful, isn't he?' she says. 'You know he's always buying me little trinkets and gifts and things to say how much he loves me.'

'I know. You said before, sweetheart,' I say. 'He does sound lovely. I'm glad it's all going so well for you two. He sounds like a great man and Dean says he's a very talented footballer too, so it looks as if you – my love – might have hit the jackpot with that one.'

'I have. He's just perfect.'

'Sorry to interrupt,' says a Thai lady, walking up to us. 'I need to give Mrs Martin a Yak Shak Tang massage on her middle toe, to help the grapefruit seed work.'

'OK,' says Rosie. 'I'll see you later, Tracie.'

The massage takes a couple of minutes and seems to involve a great deal of chanting and waving of hot towels. 'Chai Yaven Aiiiiiiiiiiiiiii . . .' says the therapist before throwing her towel at the window and leaving the room. 'Be at peace. I'll be back in twenty minutes to restore your inner chi,' she says as she walks away. Christ. What was that all about?

The thought of being at peace for any length of time doesn't excite me in the least, so I decide to use the time to call Dean to drop a few heavy hints about the importance of buying gorgeous silk scarves for your loved one. It's OK me helping Rosie to great Wagginess in order that her relationship may continue to flourish, but what about mine? I could do with a few surprise presents arriving.

'Hello, love,' I say. 'It's only me. How are you doing?'

'OK,' he says, but he couldn't sound more miserable. He sounds just dreadful. It might be the wrong time to request a series of terrifyingly expensive gifts from him. Who'd have believed there was a 'wrong time' to do that?

'What on earth is the matter?'

'Nothing,' he replies in a petulant voice. 'Nothing at all is the matter.'

There's a silence on the end of the phone and I know that something is seriously wrong. Dean never goes suddenly quiet for no reason.

'Sorry, Trace,' he says eventually. 'I've just had a horrible day with the assistant manager – you know, Grimaldi Palladino – who is trying to undermine me constantly. He's such a bloody prick. He doesn't understand about defensive play at all. He keeps sauntering along and trying to influence the defence patterns I'm creating. All the changes he's making are just going to make England weaker. It's no good at all. He's going to really damage all of our chances unless he backs off and lets me get on with this. Sorry, sweetheart, I know you don't like listening to me going on about football, but he's making my life miserable. I don't know what to do. It's like he's been employed by the US team to make us as crap in defence as possible. We play them on Saturday and he wants to change all the plans I've laid down.'

"Oh, Dean, he can't be that bad, surely.'

'He is, love. I'm not joking. The man is dangerous. I don't think he knows anything about football at all.'

'Then you have to go and talk to Fabio, Dean. You have to.'

'But that's not such an easy thing to do. I can't start slagging off the assistant manager when I'm just some measly low-level defence coach.'

'Yes, you can!' I shout. 'Dean, stop putting yourself down. You are the guy that they have chosen to lead their defence coaching. You've been promoted about forty times in the past week alone, so when it comes to defence coaching they must believe that you know what you're talking about. Anyway, I forgot to tell you Abbey said that Peter Crouch thinks you're great.'

'Well, as long as Abbey approves, then everything should be OK. It's a shame that Abbey isn't in charge of coaching the England football team.'

'There's no need to be sarcastic,' I say. 'I'm only trying to help.'

I look up and the Thai lady is back, standing in the door

to the treatment room clutching a cauliflower, a stapler and a candle. Oh, God, what now? I think I'd better start reading the small print when I book these treatments.

Chapter Eighteen

Friday 4ᵗʰ June

For the first time in about fifteen years I'm going to see a doctor today who isn't going to give me botox, a boob job or a cheek lift. He's one of those plain ordinary doctors that you go to when you're ill. I wasn't sure they still existed but they do!

I'm going to see him because I think I must be allergic to something in the water here because I keep being sick and I'm not drinking at all (in fact, that's one thing I really need to check with him: could it be that I'm barfing all over the place because I'm *not* drinking? I know that sounds odd but I do normally drink a lot and now I'm not drinking perhaps my body can't cope with the change?).

3 p.m.

Nice waiting room for a doctor's surgery. It's all wood-panelled and expensive looking, with lots of lovely magazines all over the place. There are articles about the Wags in all of them, which is quite funny. I feel like shouting at the top of my voice, 'I know all these girls. They're my friends,' but that would be completely mad because I'm the only person in the waiting room. Instead I decide to flick, quietly and sedately, through the pages of magazines called things like *Fair Lady*, *Food & Home* and *WeighLess*. The only one that really appeals is *WeighLess*. *Fair Lady* sounds like a magazine for people who can't afford spray tanning and *Food & Home* sounds like a terrible magazine that just encourages women to eat. I'm having enough trouble curbing my appetite at the moment, thank you. I need no assistance from a magazine.

'Mrs Martin, Dr Bence will see you now.'

I stand up and adjust myself on the platform heels that I've chosen to wear for this visit. I wanted to get dressed up and look nice so that the doctor wouldn't think I was ill.

'Follow me.'

I scoot along behind the receptionist (dressed in navy. What is it with navy at the moment; why's everyone obsessed with it?) and she opens the door to the surgery. A very beautiful doctor is standing in the room, dressed in a cream dress with surprisingly (and pleasingly) high beige stilettos. She must be around fifty but she holds herself like a model and exudes sex appeal and sophistication in equal measures. I take the seat she offers and fight to stop myself laughing when my pink plastic skirt makes a farting sound against the plastic of the chair as I sit down.

'I wanted to talk to you because a very strange thing has happened. I've gone right off alcohol, I'm hungry all the time and I feel a bit sick, sort of nauseous.'

'Could you be pregnant?' she asks, just like that.

I thought she'd give me pills to make me feel better, and then send me on my way.

'No. My husband's in Rustenberg. I haven't been near him for weeks.'

'But you could still be pregnant.'

'How? Are you calling me a slapper?' Is she suggesting that I sleep with other men?

'Well, you can be two or three months pregnant before you start feeling different. It's very possible that you are pregnant. Would you like to do a test?'

'OK. Is it hard?'

'No, I'm mean a pregnancy test.'

'Oh, I see. Ummm, but I can't be pregnant. I've already got a daughter. Dean might not like another child. And he's very busy right now, you know; he's the defence coach of the England team.'

'I didn't know that,' she says, handing me a pregnancy-testing kit and explaining how it works. It's weird to listen to a terribly smart and sophisticated lady in cream silk telling you to go pee on a stick and bring it back to her. I wonder whether there are times when she feels that the world of high finance would have been better suited to her intellect.

'Here you go,' I say, handing it over after I've done the deed. She glances down at the stick, looks at me and smiles.

'Congratulations,' she says. 'You're pregnant.'

Holy fucking mother of Christ.

8 p.m.

'You went to the doctor today?' says Paskia. 'Why, Mum? I didn't know you were ill. Are you all right?'

'Of course I'm OK, sweetheart. I've just been feeling under the weather, that's all. Nothing serious. Just thought I'd go and get myself checked out.'

'Good. What did the doctor say?'

'Well, it was quite interesting actually. There's a reason why I've been feeling a bit odd and it's not what I expected at all.'

'What is it?'

'Are you sure you don't want a drink first?' I say. 'Pour yourself a sneaky little vodka and I'll tell you.'

'No, I'm fine, Mum. Please don't say you're really ill. You're not, are you, Mum? I couldn't bear it if you were. Please say you're not ill.'

'Pask. I'm pregnant.'

'Whaaaaaaatt?!!' Paskia's voice echoes through the suite, through the window and across to Spa Island where it ricochets off all the trees and swirls off into the distance.

'I'm pregnant,' I repeat. 'Isn't that wonderful?' Now that I've had a chance to get used to the idea I'm beyond thrilled. Dean and I always wanted another child but when it didn't happen we just thought it was one of those things and counted our blessings.'

'Yes,' she says simply, a little tear rolling down her pretty face. 'It's totally wonderful. I'm going to have a brother or sister. Do you mind if I tell Shiraz? I'll swear her to secrecy.'

'OK,' I say. 'But make sure the news doesn't get to your father until I've had chance to sit down and talk to him. I don't want to tell him over the phone.'

Chapter Nineteen

Sunday 6th June

The damn TV company have done it again. It's Sunday night, and I'm sitting in the suite with Paskia and Shiraz massaging my feet and hands and feeding me chocolate (before you say a word, it's for the baby, not me), debating what's the best way to tell Dean (or Daddy Dean as Shiraz keeps saying) that he's going to be a father once again, when the phone rings. It's *Morning Live* ringing at the last minute again to book me on for tomorrow's show.

'Why me again? There must be other people who you want to get on the sofa.'

'You're so popular. People love you. You should see the number of emails we get. You must be the most popular guest we've ever had on here . . .' and on, and on, and on until I'm flattered into submission.

'OK,' I say eventually. 'I'll come on.'

We make the plans and I put the phone down.

'I'm not going on next week,' I say. 'I'm not. This is it now.'

'Yeah, right,' says my daughter. 'Whatever you say. Now, back to the fun . . . how are you going to tell Dad?'

'I'm definitely not telling him on the phone so I guess

I'll have to tell him when I see him for the USA game on Saturday. What do you think?'

'Good idea,' says Pask. She agrees that it would be a really bad idea to tell Dean that his life's about to be turned upside down with the patter of tiny feet while I'm in a different part of South Africa. We even talk about whether I should tell him at all when he's in the middle of a major tournament. The thing is, I know Dean will want to know so I don't want to keep the news from him. No, the USA game represents by far the best opportunity to share the good news with my husband.

Chapter Twenty

Monday 7ᵗʰ June

This is my last live TV appearance ever – definitely. These early mornings are hard enough when you're just a normal person, but when you're with child, they're excruciating. Utterly unbearable. In the few days since I've found out I was pregnant I've been playing the whole thing to maximum effect and making Shiraz and Paskia run around in circles after me. I don't want anyone else to know that I have a child growing within me in case they let slip to Dean. I can't tell Suse and Mich for the obvious reason that they'll never be able to keep the secret, so Paskia and Shiraz are having to do the work of dozens.

I arrive at the studios just as Dangerous Dave comes mincing down the corridor towards me, looking like he's just wet himself.

'Morning, Tracie,' he says, as if we're the best of buddies.

'Morning, Dave.'

'What are you going to talk about today then? For your last broadcast to the nation?'

'Football!' I say, much to his amazement. 'I'm going to explain how the off-side rule works.'

'Good God, Tracie, are you feeling quite all right?' he asks, backing away a little and holding his clipboard in front of him in what can only be described as a highly defensive fashion.

'Na! Only messing with you. I've been asked to come on and answer viewer questions about hair, make-up and life as a Wag.'

'Great,' he says, with all the conviction of a man who really doesn't give a toss. 'Lovely and great.'

Chapter Twenty-one

10 a.m., Saturday 12th June

It's the day of England's first World Cup game against the USA. We're off to Rustenburg but Mich has such a bad headache that she can't get out of bed and Suse is being sick. Me? Oh, I'm fine because I'm so used to being horribly sick all the time so it simply doesn't bother me any more.

We're all looking as if we're off to a hen weekend at Aintree Racecourse in our finest collections of bright and girly coloured clothing and footwear that is entirely inappropriate for a football match. Our exposed, tanned thighs are gleaming in the morning sunshine causing a glare that requires us to wear sunglasses so large that our noses threaten to break beneath the weight of them. None of us has fingernails shorter than the requisite three inches in length nor eyelashes shorter than four inches in length. We look divine . . . even if we do say so ourselves.

In fact, there are only two things wrong with today. The first is that I still haven't got my luscious and delightful thigh-length silver boots because they didn't have them in my size. Not in my size? Stupid, stupid shop. Grrrr . . . . I *SO* wanted them for today more than any other because they'd be perfect to wear when I'm telling Dean that he's

278 • *Alison Kervin*

going to be a father again.

The other major problem with today is that the Wonder-Wags have gone off on a plane specially chartered by one of the team's sponsors, heading for some glitzy, glamorous lunch, and they aren't travelling with the rest of us. This is obviously of intense disappointment to me because I long to see what they're all wearing, how they've done their hair, make-up, eyelashes, accessorising and what level they've reached on the spray-tan front. I just want to travel with them and be part of their little entourage, to see them and touch them (but not in a lezzy way). The nice thing is that Rosie has decided to come with us on our plane, instead of travelling with the first XI Wags, even though Dio is in the team, because she wants to be near me as her style adviser. 'I just feel more at home with you guys,' she said when I called her last night to see how the spray tanning had gone. 'Would you mind if I came in your plane?'

'No,' I said quickly. And I almost said, 'Would you mind if I took your place in yours?' But that wouldn't really have worked because Rosie wanted to be near me, bless her. It's sweet and it's nice that she's done that, but I tell you, if they came in here and said they wanted to put me on a private plane with Abs'n'Coll'n'Alex'n'Vics you wouldn't see me for dust and nothing in the world would drag me off it.

Our flight to Rustenburg this afternoon is at half past two, so the general consensus is that we really do need to get some drinking done double quick this morning or we won't have enough time to get hammered before we get on the flight. This poses some serious problems for me because I can't drink now that I know I'm pregnant, and don't even want to. But I've never been on a flight while sober before.

Do they even let you on a flight if you're sober? It's been so long since I was pregnant with Paskia that I simply can't remember the rules of sobriety any more. I also don't want anyone to know that I'm not drinking because they'll ask me why.

We've got our overnight bags with us, because we going to stay with the guys in their hotel tonight, which should be fun (I think, unless Dean reacts with horror to the news that he's going to be a father again). I've got fifteen bags.

We decide to meet in my suite for drinks before we go. Shiraz arrives looking like she's about to take a PE class. I don't know why I expected anything different really. I presented her with a lovely, frilly, baby doll-style cream dress and pink cowboy boots for today but she said they made her look like Little Bo Peep so she wouldn't wear them. 'Please don't think I'm being awkward,' she told me. 'I'd do anything to make you happy but I'll hate the whole day if I'm dressed like a sexy milk maid.'

'OK,' I said, in a rare moment of compromise. 'If you promise to keep helping the charity like you have been, then I'll tolerate you dressing like a naval PT instructor for the day.'

Shiraz sits down next to me and I ask, 'How's George, by the way?'

'Gosh, he's amazing,' she says. 'I was talking about him on my early morning jog along the beach with Abbey today. You know, I think he really likes me. I don't know for sure but – well – I *think* he might.'

I've got no doubt that he likes her. He'd be mad not to.

'Abbey was saying how nice you are.'

Now we're talking!!!

'Abbey was saying what? About me? She likes me?'

'Yes, we were chatting about the charity. They're all putting some money in, you know. They're all eager to get involved. She said she thought you were really nice.'

Awwww . . .

'She's so fit, you know,' says Shiraz, and she stretches and limbers up as she talks to me. I watch her, feeling fleetingly quite envious. It's bizarre how her devotion to health and fitness and her determination to attend every fitness class ever run is what is bringing her close to the Wags. It shows how much things have changed over the years. When I first started out my long and illustrious career as a Wag, you'd never have found us anywhere near anything fitness-related . . . unless the gym had a bar heavily stocked with Bacardi, but I guess much has changed about the world of the Wags since I first got involved. Some of them have jobs and everything now, which seems to rather defeat the whole point of being a Wag. Some of them are more famous than their husbands! If the access to handbags and expensive champagne can be earned by a woman in her own right, then why on God's earth would she endure a relationship with a footballer?

While the girls stand around and chat, I go into the bedroom area and finish getting ready. I decided earlier that the best way to avoid drinking alcohol would be to spend the time they're drinking getting myself ready. Once I've spent three hours doing hair, make-up and styling my outfit to perfection, they'll be through the worst of the drinking and we can head off for the airport.

'You look AMAZING!!' says Shiraz as I walk out into the room. She's open-mouthed as she stares at me. I have pulled out *all* the stops today. First of all, I have spray tanned myself to such a degree that my ethnic origin could be questioned. My skin resembles a newly fallen conker, or a recently varnished coffee table. My extensions look a perfect lemon colour in this lovely African sunshine and my eyelashes are especially arresting thanks to these great eyelash extensions made from feathers. I can hardly open my eyes without straining my upper eyelids and I do feel as if I might take flight when I flutter them but – what the hell – they look divine.

I'm wearing a fabulous outfit featuring a skin-tight sleeveless white T-shirt with the Cross of St George on it, a white miniskirt that fails to cover my England knickers, and long white boots on to which I've painted a pretty pink cross (it's me supporting England, the Wag way). I've decided to place my hair in child-like bunches on the side of my head, while my nails are fixed with the Cross of St George on them. I also have fake England-flag tattoos sitting on top of the four inches of make-up on my face.

Mich and Suse are also looking special. Mich in a banana-yellow bandeau top and a green frilly short and bright-pink shoes, and with the orange skin she looks exactly like a lovely fruit salad. Suse's gone for skin tight, pale-blue leggings that are about three sizes too small for her. She's a bit bigger than the rest of us, is Suse, and the nice thing is you can see the slight bulge of fat above her knickerline and the orange-peel thighs through the material. She's going to get loads of attention when the boys see her today. On top she's wearing a startlingly bright-purple PVC halter-neck top with a white belt, white earrings and really high white, patent leather, platform boots that she must have borrowed from one of the girls out of ABBA.

The only person we're waiting for now is Rosie.

'Have you spoken to her at all?' I ask Paskia who is, perhaps understandably, beyond excited at the fact that she is going to be spending the rest of her time in South Africa in the players' hotel with her father and a bunch of footballers who she adores, respects and admires as much as I do the Wags. Paskia was a great footballer when she was younger. I mean properly good. If you don't think women play football, like I didn't until a few years ago, then you'd be in for a real shock if you saw what skills some of them have. Paskia was headhunted to play for an LA football academy and everything. In the end, she gave it up because she wanted to concentrate on her studies. (I know, I know, she doesn't get that from my side of the family and she certainly doesn't get it from Dean's – it's a mystery to us too). Now she's really settled in school and happy just to play occasionally when the mood takes her.

'*Waaaaaaaaa . . .*'

I'm blasted out of my thoughts by Suse screaming like a banshee and clutching her chubby hands to her face (she's not fat, really – just size ten chubby).

'Oh my *God*!!!'

'*Wow*!'

Rosie has walked into the room looking like she's just arrived from planet Wag. She. Looks. Amazing. Truly beautiful. Great wedges of yellow hair extensions have been weaved into her dark mousy hair. When the hairdresser suggested this, I did think, 'Oooo . . . too tiger-like?' but then Mich reminded me that animal prints on fabric are all the rage this year, so why not in hair? Why not think outside of the box for a change and have animal print hair?

What is most captivating about Rosie, though, is her make-up. I arranged for two of the ladies from the spa to come and do it, under strict instruction from me, and they've done a blinding job. She looks like a heady cross between the joker and a drag queen but totally in a good way. The make-up is amazing and arresting and Rosie is truly transformed. She looks good orange; much better than the delicate, pale, understated waif I first discovered in reception. There you go – just shows what a bit of Tracie-ing can do for a girl.

'You look divine,' I tell her. 'Truly divine.'

The flight leaves on time despite the fact that we are hideously late. It wasn't my fault . . . well, OK, it was, if we being truthful, my fault, but I was thinking of all the other girls when I loaded twelve bottles of Bacardi into my hand luggage. Just because I'm not drinking doesn't mean they have to stop. I'm living vicariously through them.

'Are you all right, love?' I ask Rosie, as she plays with the hem of her dress. She looks incredibly worried as we take our seats on the plane; either that or it's the way they've done her make-up. She looks like a slightly sinister clown with the enormous mouth, incredible eyelashes and apple cheeks. The transformation of her is quite, quite stunning. She looks like Barbie's ultra-plastic younger first cousin. It's beautiful. I just feel proud to have been part of it.

Rosie knits her hands together in her lap nervously but assures me that she's not scared of flying or anything; she's just worried for Dio. 'I want him to do well. I know how nervous he gets, and I'm just hoping that he's OK,' she says. She picks up her handbags and starts fiddling with the green scarf, pulling it out and absently wrapping it round her head before tying it in a bow. She looks odd . . . like she was in an accident and they'd run out of white bandages or something.

It's a lovely scarf, though, with the Chanel logo dotted all over it in black. I've never seen one like it before; Dio must have really gone out of his way to find something special and unique for her, which is lovely of him.

We're met from the plane and taken to a reception at the club by a very glamorous young woman.

'Welcome to Rustenburg, my name is Emily,' says the girl. 'I have been based with the England team this week, acting as their liaison officer for the South African football association. The players have had a great week, and have all been working very hard, and I know that they are looking forward to the match today so let's hope the right team wins.' With that, she raises her glass and toasts the England team. 'Cheers,' we all say. Emily is wearing a gorgeous, but plain, cream dress and matching shoes. Bizarrely – get this – she is wearing exactly the same green scarf as Rosie.

'What are the chances of that?' says Rosie. 'I mean really, Tracie, don't you think it's completely amazing that we have exactly the same scarf on? What an unbelievable coincidence. I take that as a sign that England are going to do really well today. Don't you think?'

'Sure,' I say, though I can't imagine that two girls with matching scarves amounts to anything more than a complete coincidence.

'Now, when you've finished your drinks, ladies, I wonder whether you'd mind following me through to the reception room just through these doors where there is a small buffet for you to enjoy before we collect you and take you down to your seats to watch the match.'

There is still no sign of the Wonder-Wags but presumably they will go straight to their seats from their extravagant lunch, which is annoying. I spot some of the American Wags, though, and I'm desperately disappointed. I thought they'd be like cheer leaders but they're dressed in simple linen clothing and nowhere near enough lip liner to be taken seriously. 'I feel let down,' I tell Mich. 'Look at them. You'd think Baden-Baden never happened. Have they never seen pictures of Jordan?'

I always thought that the World Cup would be a glorious Wag festival in which no outfit was too tight and no tan too bright, but some of the girls here are plainly devoid of artificial colourant. When I think of the ideal World Cup Wag, I think of Barbie soaked in tango overnight. I mean, look at my skin. Just look at the outfit I'm sporting today 'Why couldn't they make as much effort as I clearly have?'

9 p.m.

The match is over and the England team has won! It's a great victory in the opening game of the tournament but I can't give you any more information on the match than that because I spent very little time actually watching what was happening on the pitch.

Want to know why?

I'll tell you ... because I was wholly distracted by the sight of Victoria Beckham and Christine Bleakley giggling away together in the seats in front of me. Bloody hell. What an amazing vision of celebrity Waggishness. I was palpitating so much that I thought my heart might stop, and I'd have to send Shiraz off to find a doctor with one of those fibrillating machines. And I'd go into labour early and have the world's teeniest tiniest baby, so tiny I could keep him in a locket around my neck. Luckily I got through without needing an oxygen mask, and Christine even smiled at me and said she thought my YouTube video was great fun.

I'm told that England won the game 3–2, and I know that Dean will be disappointed with that because two goals were scored by the opposition, which means that England's defence was not very good. You learn to understand these things when you're married to the England defence coach. Dean has been saying for months that England's ability to win the World Cup will depend on them stopping the opposition from scoring. He's a big believer in defence and he gets very, very upset down at Chelsea when they let goals in. He says it counts as a defeat in his book. Now I can't begin to tell you how much I hate it when Dean comes home and says he's had a defeat. I feel traumatised at the thought of his little face and the desperation in his sad brown eyes. Horrible. I had so many years of it at Luton that I feel like a Vietnam vet of football defeats. The fact that the side has let in two goals in the first game today will be a matter of horror and embarrassment to him.

Talking of embarrassment, you won't believe what happened to me. I was sitting in the stand when I noticed that the lady a few seats along was wearing exactly the same beret as me. I smiled at her warmly, pointing to my beret with great enthusiasm, and sticking my thumbs up. She looked at me as if I was completely mad, smiling nervously as she looked away. Next time I managed to catch her eye, I pointed at the beret again, this time really jabbing my finger at it, so she knew I was indicating my hat to her. This time, she simply turned to the guy sitting next to her whispered to him, and then the two of them turned round. Ah, he'll understand what I'm getting at, I thought, and I started pointing madly at my hat again. The two of them just looked at each other in horror and turned back away from me.

What is it with the South Africans? I'm only being friendly and pointing out the embarrassment of us turning up at the same match in the same hat.

I turned to look at Mich who was staring at me open-mouthed.

'What are you doing, Tracie?' she asked.

'Pointing out that we are wearing the same beret.'

'You're not wearing your beret, love,' she says kindly. 'You've just been madly pointing to your head like a loon for the past twenty minutes and everyone in the stadium now thinks you're clinically insane.'

'Come on, let's go and get some food . . . I mean drinks', I say, dragging Mich and Suse behind me.

Finally, the players troop out of the dressing rooms, led by a woman with a badge that says: Mary Cooper, England team communications official. She's wearing a blue blazer, a blue skirt and sensible shoes (navy again – not good). Around her neck she has a beautiful green Chanel scarf.

'This is just weird,' says Rosie. 'I mean it is, Tracie, isn't it? You must admit it's very weird.'

It is. I can't understand it at all.

'Hi, doll,' Dean appears by my side, and looks me up and down. 'You look gorgeous. Look at this outfit. It's amazing, love. If the players had been as well prepared for this match as you are, doll face, we wouldn't have conceded two goals.'

I smile at him affectionately and cuddle in towards his chest, making sure I don't smudge my lipstick on his shirt.

Paskia comes over to join us and I feel this enormous pull in my chest. How am I going to cope without her? What am I going to do when she stays here and I go back to the hotel without her?

'You will be OK here, won't you, love?' I say.

'Mum, I'll be fine. It's going to be great to be able to talk football. I'm looking forward to it.'

'She'll be fine,' says Dean. 'I'll look after her and so will the others. We might even put her on the pitch. She's got to be a better defender than those muppets today. Two goals,' he mutters. 'Two goals!' He's shouting now. 'TWO FUCKING GOALS!' I rush to put my hands over my teenage daughter's ears.

'Let's talk about something else,' I suggest.

Next to us I see Dio appear, a vision of pin-up-style boy-band beauty, with his deep caramel-coloured skin (I think it's natural, though if he got it from a spray tanners, I want to know which one because he looks amazing). He has these show-stopping dimples and the cutest smile in the world. There's no way of disguising it: he's an incredibly good-looking boy. I bet he has girls hurling themselves at him all the time. Newspapers have described him as being football's answer to Lewis Hamilton and I can totally see why they've made the comparison.

I watch him saunter through the room, knowing all eyes are on him. He has one hand in his pocket and all the confidence of George Clooney as he swaggers, stops to chat to people, and swaggers on. Then, he sees her. He stops in his tracks and stares at Rosie. See. I knew he'd love the new look.

'What the *fuck* have you done to yourself?' he asks. 'Is this some kind of sick fucking joke?'

Rosie looks over at me and I look over at Dio, waiting for him to burst out laughing and say, 'Only joking! You look great, really. What a transformation!'

'Doesn't she look lovely,' I say encouragingly. 'She looks spectacular. Don't you think?' Rosie and I have been chatting about this moment for days but it really wasn't supposed to go like this. He was supposed to have swept her into his manly arms and kissed her by now. He should have been planning how to propose to her by now.

Dio's not planning anything though. He just stares. 'You looking fucking awful,' he says, and with that he turns and walks out of the room.

'Go after him,' I say to Dean. 'Go check he's all right. I'll sort out Rosie.'

I watch as my lovely Dean runs along behind him – half running, half skipping in an embarrassed way, trying to catch up with one of the fastest men in world football without making it obvious that he can't.

I, meanwhile, look round for Rosie but she's disappeared completely. Oh, for heaven's sake. Where's she gone now?

It's a good twenty minutes before I find her, and by the time I do things are good and bad; good because she's back in Dio's arms and is smiling, and bad because she's taken off her beautiful, gorgeous outfit and has put on a stupid plain navy jumper and trousers. Her face has been scrubbed clean too.

'What's this all about?' I ask Dean. 'She clearly looked better when I styled her.'

'Yes, love,' he says. 'But I think Dio's a little insecure. He doesn't like Rosie hogging the limelight. He prefers her to look, well, plain.'

'Hmmmm . . .' He may look like a pop star but he's acting like a prick. Even as Rosie sits on his lap in her horrid jumper and hair scraped back into a ponytail, I see how Dio's eyes continually roam around the room. She looks directly at him, while he looks hungrily at all the girls dotted around, handing out drinks. I see that another of them has a flash of a now-familiar green scarf around her neck.

'Dean, you have to tell me what it is with the Chanel scarf. Why do so many girls seem to have the same green scarf on today?'

'You talking about Dio?' he says, leading me over to the far corner of the room.

'Yes, I am.'

'He's a complete handful,' says Dean, with a shake of his head. His spiky hair doesn't move an inch with the head shake, which puts my mind at rest . . . at least, with all the pressure of the lead up to this opening game, Dean has not let his hairdressing standards slip. 'Someone told me yesterday he's got this thing about buying girls presents when he sleeps with them. I think he saw some old film in which there was a gigolo who gave away gifts to the girls he slept with. Dio does the same, and then he compensates for letting down his girlfriend by buying her a present too. And he's got no imagination so it's always the same present. Maybe he gets a discount for bulk buying or something ...'

'Compensates for letting his girlfriend down? Dean, he's going to break her heart. She adores him. Doesn't he realise what he's doing? She's given up everything for him. She's just a shy, nervous girl who worships the ground he walks on. Now he's even telling her how she can and can't dress. You can't let him treat her like this.' I ignore my slight reservation that I've also been telling Rosie how she should dress.

'There's nothing I can do,' he says, bubbling with defensiveness. 'My job is to make sure he plays the best football he can. And he's a striker so I don't do all that much work with him on the pitch. I certainly can't start meddling in his private life off the pitch, Tracie. I've got enough on my hands as it is. Did you see those goals they let in? Did you? Bloody appalling. We've got so much work to do if we're going to get ourselves through the qualifying rounds.'

I'm standing there fuming as I hear a woman's voice come over the loud speaker system. 'Ladies and gentlemen, my name's Lisa Weyton and I work for Calibre Systems, one of the World Cup sponsors. Thank you for coming along to our reception today. And if you wouldn't mind, could you spare us just another couple of minutes of your valuable time for me to introduce Phil Southons, the CEO of Calibre, and the man behind our decision to sponsor the World Cup? Thank you.'

The CEO reaches the microphone and the lady walks out from behind the small podium that has been erected in the corner of the room. I see straight away that she is wearing a simple navy-blue suit. Around her neck there is a scarf rather extravagantly tied, and coloured a gorgeous lime green with a distinctive Chanel logo dotted all over it.

'This is unbelievable!' squeals Rosie, jumping off her boyfriend's lap and joining me. 'I can't believe how many women are wearing exactly the same scarf as me. It's unreal!'

Chapter Twenty-two

Monday 14th June

'Can't you just ask me the questions, and I'll say my answer and you type it in?' I say to Shiraz. We're sitting in the back of George's Land Rover on the way to help George, Ben and Tyler order a load of clothing and food for the coming months with the money donated by the England football players. The million pound cheque from the players has been added to the hundreds of thousands of pounds since my appeal went out on TV a few weeks ago, leaving George almost orgasmic with delight. I'd love to join in with the feeling of happiness and joy but I'm quite prepossessed by what's going to become of Rosie, the fact that her boyfriend is stopping her from dressing like a Wag, and the fact that I never got to tell my husband that I was pregnant last night. I just never got the chance to talk to him properly on our own, and then we flew back early this morning. Now here I am in a scruffy old truck having volunteered to do a 'lighthearted Q & A' with a Wags website.

At least I'm dressed properly for the occasion, in a rather gorgeous pink, plastic jacket and miniskirt. 'OK, Shiraz . . . what questions do you have for me today. I want to have as much fun with this as possible . . .'

'Right. I'll just start reading the questions out, shall I?'

she says. 'First one: "Obviously, I realise that it is important to wear lots of make-up while watching football, but foundation can be tricky to apply. How do I know whether I've got too much on?" That's from Kelly in Mossel Bay.'

'Mmmm . . .' I say, thinking about the madness inherent in the question. 'This is a difficult one to answer because it is so utterly ludicrous. There's no address printed on your letter, Kelly, so I don't know exactly where you're from in Mossel Bay but I can only imagine it's a mental institution of some sort. Too much on? What on earth is wrong with you? There's no such thing as too much make-up. Have you never taken a look at a WAG's face? Any Wag? Have you not seen Abbey Clancy's lipstick? Katie Price's eye make-up? Or her eyelashes? Christ, when she was going out with Dwight Yorke those spidery lovelies would enter the room roughly two and a half hours before the rest of her. And that's before we even get to the foundation.

'Let me be straight with you – there is nothing that screams "I'm a Wag" quite like four and a half tons of tan-coloured foundation. Wear it everywhere. Wear it always. Wear it in the gym, in the shower, in the swimming pool and in the sun. The foundation should be applied thickly on to very heavily moisturised skin. It must stop traffic, demand a double glance, and have doctors heading for their textbooks. Young children should cry when they see you, and ringmasters should try to recruit you for the clown section of the circus. I repeat, there is no such thing as too much make-up. Now, no more silly questions, Shiraz, please.'

'Right,' says Shiraz. 'Seems a bit harsh, but if you're sure.'

'I am. Next question.'

'OK. "I feel embarrassed when I have spray-on tans. Is it really essential for me to be spray tanned when I'm watching the World Cup?" That's from Petra in Durban.'

'Just write yes,' I say. 'Next question.'

'"My spray tanner says that she recommends two coats of spray tan. But this gets expensive. Do I need two coats?" That's from Melissa, Jo'burg.'

'Yes, you do, sweetheart. If it is getting too expensive for you, is there something you could do? Perhaps get rid of your boyfriend and get yourself one who earns decent money? Or do you have something you could sell? Life is about prioritising. Perhaps you have a granny lurking around who could be sold into slavery, or a small child who could be sent up chimneys to fund your obsession with orangeness. There's no way you can get the right colour without several coats of spray tan – only a foolish Wag would leave the house without being the sort of shade of tangerine that makes her look as if she has been living unhealthily close to a nuclear plant, drinking too much Tango or eating too many cheesy Wotsits.'

'Next. "I think my partner may be having an affair while he's away at the World Cup. What should I do?" From Jean in East London.'

'Oh, dear, I can't imagine how utterly devastating this must feel,' I say, thinking of the lovely Rosie. 'Sit down, take a deep breath, think about all the good times you had together – the real special times – then screw him for every penny he's got, embarrass him, expose him, bring him down. Do a naked *FHM* cover underneath the headline SERIOUSLY, WOULD YOU CHEAT ON THIS GIRL? and let nothing stand in the way of ruining his life. If he has found another girlfriend, remember that it is your duty to ruin her life too. Stop at nothing. Call the papers, smash his car up, lie about him, humiliate him, keep all the jewellery, sell all your keepsakes, do a revenge book. Be as bitter, nasty and demanding as any human being ever in the world could be.'

'Woooah,' says Shiraz. 'That's a bit over the top, isn't it?'

'Over the top? *Moi*? Of course not. Next question, please.'

'Philippa from Newcastle asks, "Where should I socialise to meet Wags and, hopefully, meet a footballer so I can turn into a Wag myself?"'

'Clearly most socialising for Wags is done in über-trendy nightclubs, bars and football matches,' I answer. 'There's little need to go anywhere else. Many social occasions are a trial at the best of times . . . like Opera. What's all that about? Who needs to sit around and watch very overweight women screaming at each other in Italian when there are no footballers in sight?

'Theatres are clearly a complete waste of time when it comes to hunting for footballers, as are most "middle class" venues. The only place you might have a bit of luck is the horse-racing track, which does sometimes attract foot-ballers, and has gambling, drinking and the opportunity to dress up associated with it.

'If you do decide to head down the races with a couple of wannabe-Wag friends, do make sure your clothing is absolutely right. Picking the right size for your outfit is crucial. It's most inappropriate to turn up in clothes that fit properly . . . always dress in clothing at least a size too small, making sure that as much flesh as possible is on display at all times. This strategy works particularly well with bigger girls. Obviously you need to make sure that your skin has been heavily spray tanned until it is a remarkable colour that can safely be described as "unknown in nature". Never wear any sun protection cream so that's your skin turns a bright lobster-pink during the course of the day. Right, any more questions, Shiraz?'

'Nope, that's it,' she says, as she types in my answers.

'Good, then I can call Paskia and see how she's settling in.'

Chapter Twenty-three

Tuesday 15th June

I am having my legs de-haired today with wax made
from organic and ecologically sound whalebone (retrieved
from the ocean bed so don't be alarmed; no animal has been
hurt in any way during the removal of these hairs) mixed
with rice powder and purified squid ink. My phone rings.
It's Dean.

'Owwwwwww!' I say. Shit, this wax may be ecologically
sound but when it's applied to your skin at nuclear
temperatures then torn off at lacerating speed, it bloody
hurts.

'Are you all right?' he asks.

'I'm fine,' I lie. I'm already panicking about the bikini
wax that's supposed to follow this torture. It doesn't usually
hurt so much. Perhaps I'm more sensitive now I'm pregnant. Do you think I should have mentioned that before
she started? Oh, sod it, it's too late now. 'How about you?'

'Not great,' he says miserably.

'Is it Paskia? Is something wrong with her?'

'No, no. She's fine, love. Absolutely fine. She's in her
element chatting about football all day. She loves it.'

No, it turns out that it's the fact that the USA scored two
goals against England that's continuing to eat him up.

He has just come back from having a long chat to Capello, during which he repeated his concerns that Grimaldi Palladino, the assistant coach, had a negative effect on his ability to build a good defensive strategy for the first game.

'I had to say something, doll face,' Dean explains. 'I hate the idea of getting anyone into trouble, but I would have been letting the team down if I hadn't spoken out.'

It turned out that he was absolutely right to have taken such a stance. Capello agreed that Grimaldi should be kept away from the training ground in the days leading up to crucial matches, allowing the individual coaches to work on specific areas of play. Capello also hinted that he too was concerned about the motivation of his number two, and thanked Dean for being so honest and straightforward with him.

Despite this ringing endorsement of all that he's doing for the team, Dean is shattered that he has had to go behind the assistant coach's back to talk to Capello. 'It's just not me,' he keeps saying. 'I am not the sort of guy who complains about other coaches. I'm much more comfortable in a team in which everyone gets on, and supports one another. I'm really not good at dealing with people when they start cocking things up.'

'Dean, stop being so hard on yourself. I think you have acted brilliantly, and done exactly the right thing by telling Capello when you thought things were starting to go wrong. Stop beating yourself up. You're my hero!'

'Awwww, thanks, love,' he says. 'I don't know what I'd do without you. Love you.'

'Love you too,' I reply. 'Love you madly. And tell Pask I love her too.'

I put the phone away and look round at the beautician. 'Ready?' she asks.

Fuck. Next time I'm going to shave my bloody legs.

Chapter Twenty-four

Wednesday 16th June

I go down to breakfast to find Rosie sitting there, her pretty face aglow with delight. She looks as if she is lit from within. She's certainly not lit by make-up as she's fresh-faced again. What can I do? I can lead a Wag to make-up but I can't make her paint it on.

'Hey, you look well,' I say, trying to play down the obvious snub at my transformation attempts. I join her and order a decaf black coffee.

'I am more than well,' she says. 'I'm super-well. I'm, like, the wellest person in the world. I'm more well than the wellest person ever. I'm so well, in fact, that I—'

'Yes, OK, love, I get the picture. Things are going well. What I want to know is what happened to make you like this?' How can anyone be 'well' without lipstick? It's beyond me.

Rosie fiddles about under the table and pulls out a gorgeous, glossy pair of lipstick-coloured leather gloves. They are by Chanel, like the scarf that came last week. Rosie is clearly rippling with excitement about them. I'm hoping that we're not going to get to the match on Friday night and discover that everyone is wearing them. I suddenly have a terrifying glimpse into the future in which the entire Algeria team comes running out in red gloves, along with the referee, everyone in the commentary box, the ball boys and even the guys manning the hot dog stands.

'They're gorgeous, aren't they?' she says.

'They are,' I reply honestly. They are gorgeous, there's no doubt about that.

Chapter Twenty-five

Thursday 17th June

I can safely say that I'm making the most of the facilities on Spa Island during my stay here. I've now had just about every different beauty treatment they do there. Today Rosie and I had treatments together, which was lovely once I'd convinced her that it wasn't in any way going to change the way she looked on the outside (which, you'll agree, kind of defeats the whole bloody point of bloody treatments in the first place). We both had the chocolate body wrap, which is supposed to rejuvenate your skin. I read the small print on this one so know it's fine for me to have while pregnant. Though I'm terrified that I might have absorbed some sugary calories via osmosis or something. Can the calories get through the skin's surface? If they can, I'm suing; I've been eating so much recently and I really don't want any more calories inside me (I had a spoonful of boiled egg and half a bite of toast this morning. I'm going to be so large I'll need my own postcode).

While I try to calculate the number of calories in a bite of bread, Rosie chats away about Dio and how much she loves him. 'I know he was a bit mean about the way I looked but he only says these things for my own good. He's a lovely man, Trace, and I'm dying for you to get to know him better. I'm hoping we'll be able to have a baby soon,' she says, forcing me to sit up suddenly from the treatment bed, splattering the lovely beautician with warm chocolate-scented gunk.

'Why don't you wait until you're both a bit older? Having a baby is a lot of hard work. The two of you should just enjoy life while you're young. You can do the whole baby thing when you've had a bit more time together.'

'Oh, no. I want one straight away,' says Rosie. 'I'll be a good mum, honest I will. I'm ever so patient and caring.'

Oh, God. I have no doubt that Rosie will make a fabulous mum. It's whether Dio is quite cut out to be a fabulous dad at this stage in his life, given that he appears to be sleeping with, and offering expensive gifts to, any woman who comes within a foot of him. I wish I could tell her what Dio's really like but I can't – it would be disloyal to Dean.

Chapter Twenty-six

Friday 18th June

OK, first thing to say about today is that I'm *dying* to see Paskia. I hate being away from her. We've talked about three times a day since she left but that's just not the same as seeing someone every day, is it? I can't wait to spend the evening with her after the match.

The next thing to say is that I think we need a quick recap, don't you? So . . . here we go . . . I'm pregnant, but haven't been able to tell my husband Dean yet and, until I tell him, I can't tell the girls, which means I have to spend my whole time pretending to drink and, more embarrassingly, pretending to be a bit drunk so they don't get suspicious and start asking questions .

Then, there's my husband who's involved in such a rift with the assistant manager that on the morning of England's second game of the World Cup the two of them aren't speaking to one another. Fabio Capello has wisely sided with my husband, which means that the manager and the assistant manager aren't talking to one another either. I don't know much about team sport, but I'm thinking this can't be a good thing.

Then there's Rosie, who is blithely unaware that her boyfriend is shagging every woman in South Africa and I can't tell her the truth because I'd be letting Dean down.

There's Shiraz who's hopelessly in love with George, who thinks the world of Shiraz but doesn't seem to think of her romantically.

Then there's Mich and Suse who've not really been sober since they got here (and – unlike me – they haven't been pretending). They've flirted with every man they've seen, spent a fortune on lipstick and genuinely had as much fun as it's humanly possible to have. I applaud them and adore them – I really do. They take a little bit of Luton with them wherever they go and I love that about them.

Despite the slight hitches I mentioned earlier, I think things have gone well on this trip so far. Certainly it could have been worse; at least I wasn't arrested for kidnapping Col's baby, or for stalking Abbey by watching her through the telescope, indecent behaviour after flashing in the lift, by the pool and in boxercise, or banned from travelling with the team altogether after the YouTube fiasco.

Anyway, everything's going to go well in the match today because Dean is completely in charge of defence and I am dressed head to foot in gold. It's hard to imagine how anything can go wrong for England when I'm so fabulously attired. I'll bring the Tracie Factor to this damn tournament if it's the last thing I do.

Today England play Algeria and I have no prior information on what the Algerian Wags look like (as Shiraz is too busy saluting the sun and putting her feet round her neck and up her nostrils in the morning, and flirting with George in the afternoons, to research it properly). However, I imagine I'm safe in assuming that they won't be as devilishly well dressed as I am. The combination of long white boots with gold toes and gold heels on them and gold braiding up the front (don't even ask about the silver boots. They *still* don't have them in my size . . . madness!), with a gold microskirt, white-and-gold-striped jacket and *huge* gold earrings has me looking like a Hollywood diva. I've put a ton of gold necklace around my neck, giving me the gangster look. I reckon that if the manager of the Black Eyed Peas walked past now he'd recruit me before you could say, 'Watsup, innit.'

I sit next to Jane on the flight to the match, and feel a little awkward. I'm not at all keen on her, and my husband hates her husband, so we're probably not going to be the bestest of friends. I don't foresee any cosy dinner parties when we get back. As I'm sitting there, applying more and more make-up to my heavily-laden face, I look over at Jane, reading a book (I *know*!).

I wonder what she knows of the problems between Dean and her husband. Is she aware that they have been caught up in a tremendous power struggle? If so, does she realise that my husband won that struggle hands down? Half of me's tempted to point this out to her, but the other half thinks that it's a conversation I don't need to have, so I opt instead for annoying her and interrupting her reading with increasingly daft and pointless questions about her hair and where she gets it highlighted.

9 p.m.

Dean and Paskia are leaping around and clapping their hands together like children at a birthday party who've just seen the clown arrive. 'If they continue to play like that in defence they will win the World Cup,' Dean says definitively. 'No one will score against them when they're playing like that. No one at all.'

'No one,' echoes Paskia.

His clear delight at the way the team's defensive strategy worked on the pitch appears to be confirmed time and time again, as players come up, pat him on the back, and say things like, 'Yes, yes, yes! No gaps. No room. No score. 2–0. *Yeeeees*! Bring it on.'

Even Capello comes up and pats Dean on the back in a manly fashion, telling him that he's turned out to be one of the greatest assets that the team has. I'm thrilled to hear this compliment, of course, but feel it does rather ignore the huge asset that the Wags are to the side.

'Well done again,' he repeats, whacking him with such intensity that I fear poor Dean might be winded and have to be airlifted to hospital and miss the rest of the tournament. Luckily he regains his composure just as a girl called Georgina takes to the podium and introduces her boss, the CEO of an airline company that sponsors the team.

She walks back down the stairs and I see that she is carrying a pair of gorgeous, shiny, lipstick-red gloves. My heart falls. She joins her friend while they wait for their CEO to make his speech. I look over at her friend and she too is wearing cherry-red Chanel gloves. Christ almighty, it's getting beyond a joke. Dio must be getting a thrill out of the very public display his affections are creating.

'Thanks,' says my husband humbly, as yet another player offers heartfelt praise and thanks to him. I notice that behind Dean stands a big, rough-looking guy with jet-black hair and bad skin. He looks like a cross between a Bond villain and a pizza. There's something dark and sinister about him. Who on earth is he? He's making me feel very uneasy and I don't know why. I'm sure he must be something to do with the Algeria team. Perhaps he's going to poison Dean for his role in their downfall!

'Who's that?' I ask Dean, pointing to him.

'Oh, him. That's Grimaldi Palladino,' says Dean. 'He's the one I upset.'

Good choice! Upset the one who looks like he'd kill you if he got within an inch of you.

Chapter Twenty-seven

Monday 21ˢᵗ June

Another day, another Wag website that wants to interview me about my life as a Wag. This one's called Wags At The World Cup; it's the main Wags website out there, so I've paid tribute by putting my hair in bunches secured by pink roses, and dressing up in a tiny white leather dress and long pink boots (no, in case you were wondering, I haven't got the silver boots yet. They're still waiting for new stock. They have it in a UK size two. WTF use is that?).

'Fire away, Shiraz,' I say.

'The first question just asks "What does Tracie Martin think a Wag is?"'

'Oh, great. Well, this is clearly a deep philosophical question masquerading as a simple one. Technically, any fool knows that the official term "Wag" is a straightforward acronym for Wives And Girlfriends of footballers, but equally any fool knows that to be a Wag is a lifestyle choice, a clone-like existence of fake tans, long and loud hair, extraordinarily large sunglasses, a permanent pout, boutique bags and a compulsion to live life in the public eye.'

'What are your rules for looking like a Wag?' asks Shiraz.

'Well, I'd say that a Wag should never be seen in the same outfit twice, nor should a Wag be seen alone. Friends, mums and dogs are important Wag-cessories. Wags are not measured in terms of their husbands' footballing stature, although England's most high-profile Wags (McLoughlin, Curran, Beckham) do belong to the country's most celebrated footballers (Rooney, Gerrard, Beckham); a Wag is judged on hair (long), tan (bright and orange), clothes (designer) and car (eye wateringly expensive).

'The final question is "Why do people love Wags? What is it about them that makes them so special?"'

'Gosh, that's a toughie,' I answer. 'I suppose people love us Wags because we're quite brazen, uncomplicated and orange. We love that life is so simple when your perception of quality is entirely dependent on price. If it's expensive, it must be good. We love that there's never "too high" when it comes to heels, and "too low" when it comes to body weight. There's never "too much" when it comes to alcohol, and never "too big" when it comes to handbags, sunglasses and houses. There are rules and there is "a look". To be a Wag you don't have to be a natural stunner and there is no correlation between attractiveness of a Wag and attractiveness of a player: Abbey Clancy is truly beautiful and she's going out with Peter Crouch. Indeed, if you are not naturally attractive, no one will be any the wiser by the time you have covered yourself in five inches of make-up. The only "asset" that you need is to be thin. The rest can be faked. If your hair is not long, get extensions; if your nails aren't long, get extensions; if your breasts aren't the right shape, get them uplifted, boosted and fixed. To possess any natural beauty is altogether unnecessary. It's an accessible world full of people having loads of fun and drinking hideous amounts.

That's why people love us, I think, though I don't suppose people love me all that much because I'm nowhere near as pretty as say Col or Vics or especially not Abbey.'

Chapter Twenty-eight

Tuesday 22nd June

I'm lying on my sun lounger without a care in the world, flicking through the list of beauty treatments offered at the spa and double-checking I've had them all, when along comes Rosie, smiling from ear to ear. She's clutching a gorgeous shiny, lipstick-red, Chanel bowling bag that matches her gloves exactly. Oh, no.

'Guess what?' she says, swinging her bag so I can get a good look at it.

'Dio?' I say.

'Yes!!!!' she exclaims. 'It shows how much he loves me, doesn't it?'

Oh, God, how I wish I could tell her. I feel so incredibly disloyal to her if I don't say anything, but incredibly disloyal to Dean if I do say something. The Chanel division of South Africa must think it's Christmas.

'Doesn't it?' she repeats. 'I mean, why would he buy me such gorgeous presents if he wasn't in love with me? The presents definitely show how much he loves me.'

'As long as everything else in the relationship is going well, then, yes, presents are great,' I say with uncharacteristic common sense.

'Does Dean buy you as many presents as Dio buys me?' she asks.

'No, not as many but we've been married for a long time.'

And he's not trying to make up for the fact that he's sleeping with a host of other women at the same time.

Once Rosie leaves I think about the situation with Rosie and Dio. I'm so terribly concerned about Rosie's emotional state and worried that this fragile girl will be broken by Dio if she finds out what he's been up to that I'm moved to tears by it all. I wonder whether Paskia knows anything about this. She might be able to help.

'Darling, it's me,' I say to Pask, when she's answers her phone. 'Can I ask, do you know what's happening with Dio?'

'Yes,' she says. 'It's a nightmare, a complete nightmare. We're trying to disguise it here but I'm terrified people will find out.'

'They will find out if he doesn't stop being such a slag,' I say.

'Who, Mum?'

'Dio. Who are you talking about?'

'I *am* talking about Dio. He's injured and we're hoping none of the opposition sides finds out or they'll target his weak knee. We're having a real drama here about whether to bandage the knee. We kind of need to because it's badly hurt but, at the same time, if we bandage it, the injury will be obvious. It's a tough one, Mum. We can't work out how to disguise it.'

Chapter Twenty-nine

Wednesday 23rd June: Slovenia v England

I became so distracted this morning by the fact that Dio is behaving like a complete shit towards Rosie that I never even made an effort to go and get the silver thigh-high boots. I just kept mulling over the facts: this lovely girl might get pregnant and settle down with him, and all the time he'll be off buying random gifts for random women. It's no good. But if I tell her, she'll call Dio, scream at him, his game will be affected and England might find themselves out of the World Cup. What's more important: one girl's happiness or the joy of a nation? Fucking hell, this is tough. This responsibility's killing me. I'm pregnant, you know. I shouldn't be put under these levels of stress. I'm definitely going to have a long chat to Dean after the game and see whether there's anything we can do to curb Dio's behavior.

Now I'm sitting on the coach next to Shiraz as we wait for someone to take us inside for a 'ladies lunch' (hey, get me! I'm a lady who lunches!). Finally a lady gets on to the coach and welcomes us to the ground. 'We are most genuinely pleased that you are here,' she says in a strong South African accent. By her side she swings a beautiful, shiny red handbag.

Marvellous.

*

A couple of hours later, we take our seats for the match with Rosie sitting next to me. She squeezes my arm in excitement whenever her boyfriend touches the ball. I see that both his knees are bandaged so the opposition won't know which one he's injured and thus won't be able to target him. Good thinking from the England camp! Dio runs, darts, scores and lift his arms into the air like a great hero. Rosie cheers his every move. England are on fire in this final group game. Slovenia cannot touch them. In the second half, Dio has the ball when a defender storms in for a tackle, slamming his boot into Dio's right knee. The crowd rises in horror as Dio is felled. He lies there, motionless, while chaos ensues all around. Dean's anger-filled face fills the giant screen in the stadium. Rosie screams. The whistle blows and men with stretchers run on to the pitch. Still he doesn't get up. He rolls around on the floor, clutching his leg in agony. Rosie is frantically shaking her shiny red handbag in the air and screaming 'Noooooo . . .'

Chapter Thirty

Sunday 27th June

Well, what with the injury to Dio, the hysteria from Rosie and the sheer bloody fury from Dean, I still haven't had the chance to tell my husband about the fact that I'm pregnant. He's asked several times, 'What are you drinking, love?' but I've been telling him I have vodka in my orange juice and that seems to silence him. Luckily he got so drunk Wednesday night that he lost track of whether I was sober or not, so in the morning I blamed the alcohol when I was duly sick. That's obviously why you have morning sickness, so you can pretend you were drinking the night before and get away with it.

I've had a call from Dean this morning. He's desperately worried about what's happened to Dio and he's convinced that somehow the Slovenian players knew about Dio's injured right knee. 'They targeted him through the game. You must have seen that. Every bloody defender charged in and aimed for his right knee. They knew. They *definitely* knew. I need to find out how.'

He's also still moaning about Grimaldi. Even though the assistant manager is not supposed to be working with the team on the days leading up to important matches, Dean says he keeps coming down to training sessions, and keeps trying to get himself involved. It's clearly driving my Dean loopy.

'What shall I do if he's there at training this morning?' says Dean.

I want to say, 'Tell him to piss off!' I know that sounds harsh, but with some people you have to be harsh to get anywhere. Dean would never do that though; he's the world's nicest man. Instead I suggest that he just reminds Grimaldi that Fabio has told him not to come to training.

'But what if he won't go?' Dean asks.

'Then you have to talk to Fabio. Come on, Dean, you're through to the next round of the World Cup. You have to get tough with this guy. You have to shut him out somehow or he'll mess everything up for you. You're in the top sixteen match against Serbia, then after that it's France. Come on Dean, you know you can do it.'

You see, sometimes I go way and above the traditional role of a Wag.

Chapter Thirty-one

Friday 2nd July: World Cup Quarter-final – England v France

This is where the World Cup gets serious: when England are playing against a team that I've actually heard of in a round of the competition that means something. England versus France in the quarter-final . . . even I can relate to that!

It's been a tough week this week. I've missed Rosie enormously and without her around to keep me company, I've felt Paskia's absence all the more acutely. Rosie and Dio headed back home after an emergency operation on his knee, so he can have further reconstructive work in England. I've promised to keep in touch with her and I have, sending her daily texts from the poolside with funny gossipy bits and pieces about what I'm up to. I almost told her that I was pregnant but thought better of it. I really should talk to Dean first about that. But I haven't really had the chance and part of me doesn't want to distract him at this time. But it's only right that he's the next person I tell about the baby. I sent Rosie a picture on my iPhone of the tight shiny pink catsuit I'm wearing today, and she replied, 'Beaut.' That was sweet of her. I'll call her as soon as we get back to England and by then I'll be able to tell her that I'm with child.

I feel less worried about her now that Dio's injured and out of the tournament. I think the setback that Dio's suffered from getting injured and having to leave the World Cup just as it gets interesting might be a reminder to him that there are other things in life besides football and shagging random strangers. He might realise that he's got a real treasure in Rosie, and that she'll be there when the others have all gone walkabout to find new footballers to buy them shiny red handbags and pretty designer scarves. Well, I can only hope.

Anyway, Rosie will be OK. She's very beautiful and we've all seen what she can look like when she puts her mind to it and wears tiny skirts that show her knickers, so there'll be more footballers after Dio has done a runner, and with a bit of luck one day there'll be a footballer who doesn't shag every other woman who wanders into his field of view. If she's really lucky, one day she might meet a man as wonderful and perfect as my Dean (but only if she's extremely lucky).

Dean has been on the phone non-stop this week, sounding more and more grave as the days leading up to the match have passed. He's more excited than I've ever heard him before but the thrill of being in the quarter-final is tempered by an absolute conviction that someone 'grassed' the Dio injury details.

'This, Tracie, is a special time for Englishmen,' he told me in a voice I was sure had dropped three octaves since we last spoke. I've never heard him sound so deep and manly. It was quite a turn-on actually. Part of me wanted to suggest phone sex, but I kind of knew he wouldn't be in the mood. 'Englishmen should rise up in harmony, look each other in the eye and declare, "We are Englishmen and we will triumph". There is greatness in this team, Tracie. *Greatness*. There are men in this team who can win this World Cup and change the face of English football, English sport and England's very understanding of itself and what England means. This, Tracie, is a great day.'

There's no doubt that today is a huge day, and that hugeness should be properly reflected in my choice of earrings. I do like to wear knock-'em-dead earrings on days like these. So what should I go for? My white earrings with the Cross of St George on them? Or this pair of earrings in the shape of enormous footballs? They are obviously very classy but are they special enough for today?

Also worth throwing into the mix are my earrings with a little football-playing man hanging from them. Actually, when I say 'little', there's nothing little about these earrings at all. They practically come down to my shoulders. Another couple of inches and the men would be life-size. I have to be careful with these earrings because they are so large and heavy. I loaned them to my friend Ellie once and she turned round too suddenly and the little earring man swung out and broke the cheekbone of the guy sitting next to her. Very nasty, it was, and even though a man with a facial deformity is a small price to pay for beautiful earrings, it's still better if you don't take out half the crowd when you turn round.

Chapter Thirty-two

Saturday 3rd July

Oh. My. Fucking. God. England are in the World Cup semi-final! Hello? Shall I just repeat that for the hard of reading? *England are in the semi-finals of the World Cup!* They won with a massive 4–0 victory over France yesterday; apparently all the players were determined to give France a good kicking after a handball incident in a match against Ireland. Does that make any sense to you?

My darling husband is the main driving force behind the team's ascent to glory of course (slight exaggeration but only slight). He and Capello have masterminded the entire coaching strategy in late-night coffee sessions and early-morning gym sessions (I would be a rubbish England coach).

The unbelievable news is that Dean has been made coach of the England team as a result of all this. COACH! Please, no need to stand and bow. No, but seriously – he actually has. Capello is manager and my Dean is coach. It's funny, but if you'd told me at the beginning of the tournament that Dean was going to become the coach of England, I'd have been incredibly thrilled and delighted and rushed out and bought some very, very expensive shoes and announced the news on banners across London as well as taking out TV ads and newspaper spreads to announced the news. Now though, all I can think is that I don't care what he's called as long as he has the control to do what he needs to do with the team to make them good enough to win because I know how much that means to him. How weird is that? It's like I'm saying I don't care what the designer label says as long as the clothes look good and keep me warm. Except it's not exactly like saying that because I never would!

'Fabio says I'm the finest football brain that he has ever worked with. He wants me at the top of the England tree!' says Dean, and all I can think about are Christmas trees with space for the Waggy angels. Awww . . . Fabio thinks of Dean as a Waggy angel. Nice.

However, Dean is very concerned. He says he's deeply flattered by everything that Capello is saying, but that he has huge reservations about the work involved. 'What if I'm no good? I'm just not experienced at this level,' he confides. 'Perhaps I shouldn't take the job on.'

'*Noooo!*' I shriek in a mad, blind panic. OK, OK, I was wrong. I *do* relish these titles. It's easy not to be bothered about them when your husband's got one, but now I can see it vanishing in front of my eyes I am very bothered.

I can see my new role as über-Wag popping and disappearing before me. 'You'd be perfect, brilliant, awesome, amazing. You have to do it!' I tell him. 'Seriously, you *have* to. You'll be great.'

After much persuasion, Dean agrees with me. 'You're right, love . . . I will make this country great again,' he says. 'Under me, England will win the World Cup. We will bring back England's hope and glory. We will restore this nation's greatness. Let there be joy and dancing on the streets of England for we shall be a great nation once again!'

Marvellous. Now, what earrings shall I wear to the press conference?

'Mich, Suse. What are you up to tonight? We're going out celebrating. Dean's only gone and become the bloody England coach.'

9 p.m.

The bar is practically empty, which is a blessing. I normally love packed bars and loud music but tonight, since I'm not drinking, and since I've been getting madly tired by 9 p.m., I'm delighted that we've got the place almost to ourselves. It's quite a trendy bar this, so I bet it's packed at the weekends. The strobe lighting pulses round the place, bouncing pathetically off empty seats.

'Bacardi?' I ask, and the girls look at me as if I've asked them whether they wear high-heeled shoes.

'Er, of course,' says Mich. 'What's that sound?'

'Ahhh . . . that sound, my dear, is my new ringtone. It's the national anthem. We should stand up really but we'll fall over and that wouldn't be patriotic in the least so let's stay sitting.'

'Hello,' I shout over the music. 'Tracie Martin speaking. How can I help you?'

'Hey, it's George. How are you?'

'It's George,' I mouth to the girls. They haven't met him but they've heard all about him.

He tells me that he has something very important to tell

me and needs to see me straight away. 'Come to the Lazy Lounge,' I say. 'We're near the bar. All three of us are bright orange with bright blonde hair and wearing pink and white. You can't miss us.'

'I'll be there in ten,' he says, 'but can we move on after that? You know I'm not big on bars.'

Actually, it's more like half an hour before George arrives and we've used that time to good effect, with the girls knocking back large glasses of Bacardi and me hiding them and making like I'm really drunk.

'OK, he's here,' I say as soon as I spot him arrive. 'Down the drink you've got in your hand and let's all head into the restaurant next door, shall we?'

The girls look understandably horrified by the prospect but to their credit they down their drinks as instructed. I look over at my friends. I wonder what they'll make of George?

'Mich, your tit's escaped,' I observe. 'Wanna tuck it back inside your boob tube, love?'

George comes sauntering across the bar to us and I introduce him to the girls. They just stare at him all glassy-eyed as we leave and I'm not sure whether that's because he's so big, hunky and good looking or because they're so drunk that they're incapable of seeing in any other way. Alternatively it could be because he's come from the charity and is dressed like a tramp. I hope there's no dress code at this restaurant.

We wander through and take a table. We order three bottles of wine and a plate of chips. I'm guessing they've had more stylish dinner guests in the past.

'Listen, I don't want to hang around and ruin your whole evening but I've got something important to tell you,' he says. 'You know how I said I used to be involved with some dodgy people . . . drugs and gambling and things like that?'

'Yes!' we say, all three of us moving forward a little at the first hint of scandal. Mich and Suse sway gently in their seats.

'Well, one of my old mates, a guy called Joe, has been in touch about something. He's been offered in on a huge World Cup betting scam and wanted to know whether I wanted in too.'

'Oh,' we all say, and you can sense the disappointment rippling in the air between us. We were expecting something a little more dramatic than that. What the hell is a betting scam anyway?

'A very dodgy betting scam based in the Far East is offering bets on England defeats. Do you realise what I'm getting at here?'

Nope.

'Sorry, George. No idea,' I confess. And I'm the only one who's sober so I'm damn sure the other two don't understand what he's talking about.

'OK. Well, what happens is that groups of businessmen in the Far East want to bet vast amounts of money on sport, but they want to guarantee winning.'

'But you can't do that,' says Suse. 'Nothing's guaranteed in sport, is it, Trace?'

Certainly not, I think, pondering on the many, many times that Dean has told me the team's definitely going to win, only for them to lose 4–0, or the number of times he's bet on a horse because 'it can't lose' only for him to come home all dejected, dragging his heels behind him, and declaring the world a miserable, evil place.

'Well, it is possible to guarantee a victory in sport as long as you fix the result,' George tells us.

'And how do you do that?' I ask.

'You need to pay someone on the inside to influence the game so that you get the result you want. Many times that involves getting to an influential member of the team, like a captain, and getting him to offer bungs to players in return for them "throwing" games, or it can involve getting to a key member of the coaching staff. Sometimes you just need the team to concede goals, so getting to a defender, the goalkeeper or a key defence coach is enough. Sometimes you want information, like the fact that a player has an injury that you can exploit but that the team management is keeping secret.'

'Ah!' I say. 'That's what Dean said happened to England. So what exactly are you saying?'

'It means is that a key member of the England coaching staff is trying to fix results so that syndicate members who place bets against England winning can make themselves a lot of money.'

'There's no way that this is my Dean,' I say, defensively, suddenly concerned that George is implying that Dean is to blame.

'No, I know that. There's no question of that, Tracie. The guy they've got on the pay roll is a guy called Grimaldi Palladino. Does that name ring a bell? He was the assistant manager at the start of the tournament, but it's not clear what his role is now.'

'I'm not sure. All I know is that Dean was promoted. I don't know what happened to the Grim Reaper.'

George laughs when I say Grim Reaper. 'Is that what you call him?' he asks.

'Yes, because Dean never liked him. Actually ... come to think of it, he always said that Grimaldi was trying to undermine the team and he didn't rate him as a coach. Shit! This all makes perfect sense, doesn't it?'

'Yep,' says George. 'There's no doubt that Grimaldi is involved with the betting syndicate in some way and there's real pressure on him to make sure that England don't do well in key matches. He's failed to deliver in one key match and now there's extraordinary pressure on him to produce the goods in the next targeted match. If my information is correct, they're keeping Grimaldi on the books through the next game then will be throwing everything at the final. There's a huge amount of money at stake and there will be a colossal amount of pressure of Grimaldi to give them the result they want.'

'An England defeat?'

'That's exactly it.'

'Fuck.'

'Yep, "fuck" definitely covers it,' says George.

'Well, I'll have to go and tell Grimaldi that I know what he's up to. I'll tell him that he has to stop behaving in this way.'

'No, Tracie, you absolutely must not! You have to promise me that you won't breathe a word of this. I *mean* it.'

'Why? If we don't talk to him, how are we going to stop him?'

'We'll find a way. If you approach him directly your life is at risk. Grimaldi has got himself tied up with extremely dangerous people out of pure greed. I'm telling you because

I want to help, but you *must not* interfere. Understand?'

'Yes,' I reply dejectedly.

'What should we do then?' Mich looks all concerned.

George shakes his head. 'I've been racking my brain. If I knew someone trustworthy in the police, that would be a good place to start but I don't. I've been on the wrong side of the law too many times to count. They wouldn't take a call from me seriously.'

'They would from me!' I declare, fishing in my handbag and pulling out a card.

'Who are you going to call?' asks Suse.

'Remember the police officer who saved me from the mad religious zealots at the airport, then helped me again when I accidentally kidnapped Coleen's baby?'

George looks slightly taken aback by this announcement but has the good grace to shrug it off and not ask me for further details.

'Oh, yes!' The girls shout, when they remember who I'm talking about.

'I'm sure this guy will come through for us because, unless I'm mistaken, I think he had a bit of a soft spot for me.'

'He fancied the arse off you,' says Mich, putting it rather more crudely.

'Yeah,' agrees Suse. 'He just stared at your tits the whole time.'

While the girls carry on talking about the police officer and his apparent love for me, I take out my mobile and type in the number on the card. 'Hello, can I speak to Superintendent Barnes, please? My name's Tracie Martin.'

I'm put straight through to him.

'Please, call me Martyn,' he insists. 'Now, how are you doing this fine evening?' He continues in his flirty manner but I don't care. As long as he comes down here and tells us how to stop Grimaldi in his tracks, he can flirt all he wants.

We arrange for him to meet us the next morning at ten o'clock. 'You can be there too, can't you?' I say to George.

'Of course. Anything I can do to help I will. The England football team have been incredibly generous to the charity. They're good guys and I think the world of you after what you've done, Tracie, so count me in for anything I can do. If Grimaldi can't be stopped and exposed, the England team's chances of winning the World Cup are compromised,' he says sombrely. 'It's vitally important that we stop him. I'll head off now and let you ladies finish your evening. See you tomorrow.' He smiles softly at me as he leaves and I think to myself that if these were the days pre-Dean he wouldn't be going anywhere . . .

Chapter Thirty-three

10.30 a.m., Sunday 4th July

Mich, Suse and I are sitting with Superintendent Barnes near the ocean hammocks behind the dance studios on Spa Island, still waiting for the arrival of George. We're lazing in the sun in our bikinis while we wait (well, Barnes isn't, but we three girls are). I'm amazed that George is late ... more amazed still that he hasn't made any effort to contact us to explain his absence. It seems most unlike him and, to be honest, I'm starting to worry as each time I ring his mobile it goes straight to voicemail.

'We'd better get started without him,' says Barnes. 'What did he say to you last night?'

I begin to explain the conversation of the night before, and how George had warned me not to approach Grimaldi myself. 'I hope George is all right,' I say. 'It does seem incredibly odd that he just hasn't shown up.'

'He'll be fine,' says Suse with confidence, but I can't shake this nagging feeling in the pit of my stomach.

I've gotten to know George fairly well over the past few weeks and he never lets anyone down, not ever. He works hard to help people and looks after everyone and ... I'm worried.

'No, I don't think it's fine,' I say. 'I'm really worried now.

I think we need to try and find him and check he's OK. When we were talking last night about Grimaldi he was very clear that we shouldn't approach him. He looked . . . scared, don't you think?'

Suse shrugs unhelpfully but Mich finally speaks up. 'Yes, Tracie's right. The last time we saw him he was talking about the betting syndicate as if they were terrorists who would go bonkers if they knew we knew about them, and now – the day after he tells us – he doesn't show up when he says he will and his phone is off. I think we should do something.'

'Tracie, do you know where he lives?'

'No,' I say. 'I've no idea. I only ever saw him at the charity's base. But I do know someone who might know.' I dial Shiraz's number.

So, now Mich, Suse, a random friendly police officer, Shiraz and I are trundling through the Cape Town countryside in a police car.

Shiraz is in such a horrible panic since we told her about George that she just can't think straight. She says she's been to his place a couple of times (remind me to quiz her about that at a more appropriate time later) but can't remember where it is. 'It's not far from where he goes to distribute food and clothing,' she says. 'It's around there somewhere.'

It's generally agreed that, in the absence of a better lead, the only place to start looking for George is in the shanty town itself and at the small rickety warehouse used to store clothing and food before distribution. I try my best to direct Barnes towards the small shanty town that I've visited so many times before. Shiraz is shaking as she sits quietly, dressed in a pair of navy (*grrr*) tracksuit bottoms and an Adidas T-shirt.

'It's left here!' I scream, then, 'no, right! Sorry, I don't know! I can't remember!'

'Look!' Mich screams and points out of the window and there, running across a rough plain, is George, waving madly at the police car. Shiraz screams so loud I think my eardrum is going to explode into a million tiny pieces, then begins sobbing hysterically and muttering things like, 'I thought I'd lost him, I thought I'd lost him.' Barnes slows down and George starts screaming, 'You have to take me to Riverside Casino quickly. My friend Tracie is being tortured!'

'Hey, I'm here,' I say. George glances at the four of us, sitting in the back of the car (three of us wearing bikinis), and almost collapses with relief. 'Shiraz, sweetheart, I'm so glad to see you're safe too.'

'I was so worried,' she says. 'I'd hate it if anything happened to you. I love you, George.'

'Oh, God, Shiraz, I love you too. I love you so—'

'OK, OK, just get in,' says Barnes, before radioing for reinforcements to meet us at the Riverside Casino. He turns to George. 'Tell us what happened. You two love birds can do all the mushy stuff later.'

'Er, yes, of course,' he says. 'Well, I woke up this morning to find a note had been slipped under my front door. It said that I had to be at the charity warehouse by ten o'clock or Tracie would be murdered. It also said that if I called the police or attempted to contact anyone, she would be slowly tortured and killed.'

'Eughhhh . . .' I find myself saying.

'Well, I obviously didn't want that to happen, so I planned to get down to the warehouse as quickly as possible. It's very near where I live, but when I got outside my truck was gone. I supidly left my wallet and phone in the truck last night so I had no option but to run down there. But when I arrived, there was a note saying "We've started torturing her. Go to Riverside Casino now to stop it." That's where I was going when I saw the police car.'

'OK, let's go,' says Barnes, and speeds off. He takes the details about George's truck and radios over again, this time requesting unmarked cars and giving them the details of George's missing vehicle. 'Let's move guys, move, move, move' he says, like he's in *The Bill* or something. George looks shyly over at Shiraz while Mich, Suse and I sit in our bikinis, wishing – for the first time in our lives – that we were wearing something a little more demure. I can't begin to imagine how this drama is going to end.

12 p.m.

We're at the big brick building that houses the Waterside Casino, along with four other police cars and a bunch of tough-looking police officers with guns. We've descended on the place like a swarm of bees – a mixture of bikini-clad girls and uniform-clad officers buzzing around, wondering what to do next. Three guys recognise me from the Coleen kidnap day, which is a little embarrassing, but since nothing could be as embarrassing as being a newly pregnant woman in a bright pink, sparkly bikini on a major fraud and corruption bust in one of the most dangerous cities in the world, I don't let it bother me too much.

'Hey, we're like Charlie's Angels,' says Mich, pulling an imaginary gun from her fancy turquoise bikini bottoms (they're made from amazing material that's like fish scales).

'Yeah,' says Suse. She's been looking very bloody scared all the way through this thing so far, so it's nice to see her high kick in her far-too-tight leopard-skin bikini.

'OK, we're go. We're go, go, go,' says a deep male voice to the side of us and they all storm into the warehouse, breaking down the doors despite the fact there's a door on the far side that is plainly ajar. It's all so thrilling; exactly like they're on a really impressive film set.

'We're go. We're go,' repeats the man, as a second wave of officers piles through the door. It's so exciting I can hardly breathe. The girls and I look at one another and I think, what the hell, let's go and see what's going on. So, equipped with nothing more than a fine range of designer bikini wear, pretend guns and a rather weak high kick from Suse, we storm too.

Inside the building is soulless. It houses the various machines and stations one would expect to see in such a place – blackjack, roulette, one-armed bandits, poker – all looking dismal and forlorn when lit by the harsh morning light. There are four angry looking guys at the far end. They jump up menacingly when they see the gun-wielding police officers coming towards them and scream, 'We've got the girl! We've got Tracie Martin!'

There are police marksmen with guns trained on the men all around the room.

'She'll be killed if you don't back off!' one of the men shouts.

'No, I won't be killed, because you haven't got me,' I say,

standing up and pushing my way to the front of the room. 'You haven't got me at all.'

'*Back in the car!*' screams a furious voice. 'Why didn't someone keep these girls back?' And we're surrounded and moved quickly back outside while all around I can hear police officers muttering things like, 'Yeah, yeah, the one from the TV – that's right. YouTube. That's the one. Nicked the baby then gave it back.' How nice to have made such an incredible impression in such a short time.

We're escorted outside and told in no uncertain terms to Get In The Car. The police officer looming over us has a huge gun that looks much better than my two-fingered one, so I decide to do as I'm told. When we get in the car, George and Shiraz are still there, looking into one another's eyes and smiling warmly. It's a lovely sight.

'Where the hell have you been?' asks George, pulling his gaze away from Shiraz for a second.

'In the Casino.'

'What?!'

'We went in to see what was happening but we weren't really wanted so we came back out again.'

'You went running in there with twenty armed officers and some seriously dangerous armed criminals?'

'Yes,' I say defensively. 'It's fine. I know about these things. When Dean was coaching in LA, I became great friends with America's most wanted criminals. They were really nice to me.'

'That's right, she did,' choruses Mich. 'Did you ever stay in touch with them?'

'I would have loved to but it was too hard to contact them because of where they were staying.'

'Where were they staying?' George asks. 'In some remote part of the country or something?'

'No. A maximum security prison.'

'Bloody hell, Tracie! You need to be more careful,' says Shiraz. 'It was OK when you were in LA but you have to watch yourself now. George was just telling me that apparently the police want these guys on a number of extortion and violence charges. They're seriously bad news. There's no way you should be running around in there, especially in your condition. Think of the baby.'

'Baby?' asks George.

'What baby?' ask Mich and Suse.

'Oh, shit,' says Shiraz.

4 p.m.

What a day. It turns out that the betting syndicate hoodlums had George followed when they realised that he didn't want to be involved in the betting scam. 'I was a loose cannon as far as they were concerned, and when they worked out Tracie's connection to the England team they grew deeply suspicious and started to get heavy.'

They thought they could panic George into coming to the Casino without telling anyone where he was going, and they did! If he hadn't bumped into us in the police car he'd have gone there on his own. Then they were planning to try and pay him off and get him onside by offering him a suitcase of money for his charity. They thought that he'd take the money, keep quiet and they could carry on with their plans. If he didn't, God knows what they would have done to him. It doesn't bear thinking about.

'What happens now then?' I ask.

'The guys have been taken in for questioning, but they're obviously trying to get to the root of the betting syndicate so I think they'll all be offered lenient sentences for speaking out.'

'And what about Grimaldi?'

'Well, technically, he's not done anything illegal because no one can prove, at the moment, whether he's taken any money but obviously there's no question that he was trying to influence the team and planned to take money for doing so. I think other members of the coaching staff were involved too.'

'That's right!' I say, in a sudden lightbulb moment. 'There were two guys early on who were sacked because of links to a betting syndicate. That's how Dean ended up being promoted so quickly. So that's all connected, is it?'

'I don't know,' he says. 'But if I were a betting man I'd say so.'

'It seems as if Grimaldi's going to get away fairly lightly from all of this,' I say.

'Not really. He's out of the England management team just as it looks like they're about to win the World Cup. If any further information comes to light, he'll be prosecuted. His career's in tatters. The police need to find the organisers of the syndicate; they're the ones who need to be behind bars.'

'I still don't know why they picked on the England team in the first place. Why us?'

'Well it seems from what the police have said that the betting syndicate has its roots in the Far East and was eager to bet against England in the early stages of the tournament because they had a relatively easy draw for the first few matches.'

'That doesn't make sense,' I say. 'Why bet against them winning if they're likely to win?'

'Because that's how you make a lot of money. If the odds are stacked against your team winning, and you win, you make more money. Simple.'

'Right,' I say. 'So all they had to do was influence the England team so that they lost matches they were expecting to win.'

'Exactly, my dear,' says George.

'But England won all their early games,' says Mich. 'They haven't lost a single game in the whole World Cup because Dean is such a brilliant coach.'

'Yes,' George says. 'But in the USA game, the syndicate members were betting on USA scoring goals, so they won a load of money then and all was well. But, from what the police have said, it seems that after that Grimaldi was becoming increasingly obvious and reckless in his efforts to influence things behind the scenes and was thus being alienated from decision-making meetings, making him less able to have the influence he needed to have as the tournament went on. The police think that there was extraordinary pressure put on him, especially as the syndicate guys really wanted to put big bets on the final because lots of people around the world bet then, so the huge bets from syndicates would get lost and wouldn't attract attention.'

'Oh, God! Imagine if England had got to the World Cup final then lost because of him!'

'Yes, so when he couldn't influence the team as directly as

he wanted to, he started leaking information out so that the other teams knew information about what the England team's plans were, and what injuries they were carrying.'

'Dio! I bet it was Grimaldi who leaked the information about his injury.'

'Yep,' says George. 'I'm sure it was.'

6 p.m.

I've just come through the door when the phone rings in the hotel suite. Mich is with me and she lurches across to get it. 'It's Pask.'

I take the phone from Mich and my daughter screams hysterically. 'Is it true, Mum? Is it true that you single-handedly stopped these guys from ruining England's World Cup chances?'

'Well, I don't know about that,' I say. 'I mean, I was involved in helping to bring them down, but it was George who did all the hard work. He told me all about them and then, when they turned nasty and had him followed, we brought the police in. I called Barnes, that guy from the airport. Remember him?'

'Yeah, I remember him,' she says. 'Well, Mum, everyone's talking about it here. They're saying it was you who saved the day. Hang on, Dad wants to talk to you.'

Dean comes on the line and I tell him everything (except the bit about me being pregnant. I still think I need to wait for a face-to-face moment for that).

He's laughs when I tell him me, Mich and Suse were in our bikinis during the whole thing.

'Ha, I bet you guys were like Charlie's Angels, weren't

you? You're Cameron Diaz, Suse's Drew Barrymore and Mich is Lucy Liu.'

'Yeah,' I say. 'Charlie's Angels is exactly what we were like. Suse was doing high kicks and me and Mich had pretend guns when we ran in to confront the armed men with the police.'

'What do you mean you ran in to confront the armed men? I thought you said you were wearing a sparkly bikini and high heels?'

'I was,' I say, and I sense that the silence on the other end of the line is an indication that I have said too much.

'Can you keep away from chasing after armed and dangerous men,' he asks patiently. 'That's what the police are for.'

Chapter Thirty-four

Monday 5th July

South African Daily News

STUNNING BLONDE SUPER-WAG IN TERRIFYING GAMBLING SYNDICATE HEIST

A news report special by Stuart Prentice-Bronks

She was clad in nothing but a sparkly pink bikini and high-heeled shoes, but Tracie Martin, wife of the England-team coach Dean Martin, single-handedly foiled a gambling syndicate yesterday and saved England's World Cup campaign.

The Wag managed to track down the member of staff who was leaking team secrets to the syndicate, put all concern for her own personal safety to one side to track down the syndicate members themselves, then, finally, she led the police to them in what is being hailed by officers today as an act of 'sheer, unadulterated bravery'.

Police cannot reveal who in the England camp was leaking information about the team's strengths, weaknesses and playing plans in advance of their semi-final against Brazil, but a statement from the team is expected shortly.

> Meanwhile, Martin is playing down her role and insisting that charity worker George Evans is the real hero of the hour.

We're in for a special treat today, because Gordon Ramsay is coming out to South Africa to prepare brunch for the Wags. There are even rumours that Victoria Beckham will come along to eat with us, because she's great friends with Ramsay. I'm not sure whether I speak for the others or not, but the thought of seeing Victoria Beckham is way more exciting than the thought of eating the food prepared by Gordon Ramsay. We all have to meet in this fabulous small restaurant that I was in once before when I first arrived in South Africa and was terrified that they'd end up sending me straight back because of the 'anti-Tracie' demonstration at the airport. Gosh, those days seem a long time ago now, though I remember the restaurant well, with its chandeliers, gorgeous green tablecloths, white crockery and amazing bright gold cutlery. It's just fabulous, and the gold cutlery would look lovely in my kitchen in Oxshott. I'm determined to leave with a knife, fork and spoon in my handbag so I can see what they look like at home, and try and buy some more just like it. You see, you can take the girl out of Luton, but you can never take Luton out of the girl.

I walk into the restaurant and everyone applauds. Abbey is cheering madly and comes rushing over and gives me a hug. 'We heard what you did,' she says. 'You and that charity guy . . . you manage to expose Grimaldi for what he was. Thank you so much.' Gosh, she's so pretty. I wish I looked like her. The others are equally gushing in their praise for me, and their enthusiasm for what I did and how brave I was goes way beyond the reality of what happened yesterday. They keep asking me to go back through what happened and how I found out what Grimaldi was up to. I tell them about Mich and Suse coming with me, and about Shiraz and how important she was in all this. 'But mainly it was George,' I keep saying, but they won't listen. They're convinced that I was the one who single-handedly exposed the affair.

'Why don't you invite the other girls to the lunch?' says Abbey kindly. 'It would be nice for us all to thank them.'

'Yes,' chorus the other Wags. Coleen comes over with a phone and says, 'Phone them now. Tell them they're more than welcome.'

There's a warm feeling of sisterly love and affection in the room and I'm almost swooning as I bask in it. All these women . . . all these tiny waists, designer handbags and false eyelashes in one room. It's almost too much to handle. I take Col's phone and smile at her warmly.

'Mich, Suse and Shiraz will be down in ten minutes,' I say. 'They're very grateful for the offer, girls.'

It takes about two minutes for the girls to appear. They peer round the door and I stand up to usher them in. Alex is the first to see them, and she stands up and begins the applauding. Everyone cheers loudly as they come into the room and sit down next to me. I can't believe the reception from the girls. It's fantastic. I've always wanted to be welcomed and respected by these Wonder-Wags and it turned out that all it took was for me to catch dangerous syndicate members and save England's chances of success in the World Cup!

Chapter Thirty-four

Tuesday 6ᵗʰ July: World Cup semi-final – England v Brazil
Manager: Fabio Capello. Coach: Dean Martin. Get in there!!!!

OK, the match today is in Cape Town, which is brilliant. It means the wives don't have to travel early in the morning, so I can lounge by the pool saying:

'Hi, Abbey. How are you?'

'Hey, Alex, gorgeous maxi dress. Really suits you! Catch you later.'

'Beautiful earrings, Col. You look fab . . .'

And stuff like that. All the sorts of things that I normally say in my head, or to the bedroom window as I peer through the telescope, I can now say to their faces. I can't tell you how much nicer it is.

Shiraz is lying next to me and we're chatting about George. She's saying she's going to really miss him when we have to go back to England.

'You know, he's asked me to stay,' she says.

'And will you?'

'I can't really, can I? How would you cope without someone to look after you?'

'Well, I wouldn't like it very much without you because I've grown to like you very much Shiraz, but if you've fallen in love with George and you want to stay here with him then I promise you that there is no one in the world who would be happier for you than I.'

'Gosh, thanks Tracie.'

'You and he must visit though. Come and stay in the house and play with the baby when he's born. Promise you'll do that. I'll send money for the flights and you have to come and see new Dean Junior.'

'Of course, I promise,' she says. 'Hey, how do you know it's a boy?'

'I just know.'

Chapter Thirty-five

Saturday 10th July

South African Daily News

FIRST PICTURES OF SUPER-WAG TRACIE MARTIN SINCE THE BLONDE BOMBSHELL CAUGHT CRIMINALS PLANNING THE WORLD'S BIGGEST MATCH-FIXING SCAM

A photo special by Stuart Prentice-Bronks and our award-winning photographer Gareth Cross-Lea from the Antlers News Agency

Here are the first pictures of Tracie Martin since the blonde saved the day for the England football team when she discovered that a member of the coaching staff was selling information and secrets about the team to a betting syndicate.

She is pictured here with Peter Crouch, the scorer in England's 1–0 victory over Brazil on Tuesday that has taken them to the World Cup final against Germany tomorrow.

Police revealed yesterday that Grimaldi Palladino, the former assistant manager of the team was the man responsible for the leaks that could have ruined the team's chances of success. He has been sacked by the Football Association and is helping police with their enquiries.

Chapter Thirty-six

Sunday 11th July: World Cup Final Day – England v Germany. Soccer City, Johannesburg

We arrive in Johannesburg to a festival of colour, sounds, and smells as the pungent odour of barbecued meat drifts on the warm midday air. There are signs everywhere reminding people that this is the day of the World Cup final – the greatest sporting occasion the world has ever seen. I'm so proud of Dean and so excited for him that he's part of this. The coach that takes us from the airport to the ground is marked 'England players' wives' and is greeted with cheers or derision at every turn. Some people just stand and stare as we wind our way slowly through the heavy traffic; others cheer and raise their beer bottles.

I call Paskia to see how she is and she tells me that Dean is walking around misquoting Shakespeare. While he informs his players that they have the choice 'to score, or not to score' I'm keeping myself busy with final last-minute decisions on the accessorising front. In the end I opt for bringing the large white football-shaped earrings off the bench for the final match. Yes, let's do it. I take them out of my handbag and fix them in place. If I change my mind I can always make a tactical substitution for the Wag earrings at half-time. I'm wearing an England shirt, cowboy boots, the huge football earrings and more make-up than a drag artist. It's a simple look but it works a treat.

I'm desperately excited about the match, but, as you may have guessed, I don't know anything about football and don't even like the spectacle of twenty-two blokes running about trying to kick a ball. The only thing I like about it is the dressing up and the drinking afterwards (the fact I can't do the drinking afterwards bit nowadays is horribly depressing).

Still, it's impossible not to get excited at a World Cup final. It's like everyone in the crowd is charged with electricity that pulsates through us. I've got Col one side of me and an empty seat the other side, which is bloody insane considering these tickets are selling for thousands of pounds on the black market. Why would someone take a ticket and not turn up? Weird. Alex is just in front of me and I managed to get tickets for George, Shiraz, Mich and Suse. They're in the row in front of Alex. I laugh to myself as I watch them pouring vodka down their throats every two seconds. I don't think either of the girls realises they're at a football match. I'm looking forward to getting back to all that myself. Just nine months and I'll have a beautiful baby on my hands and be able to drink again. Perhaps I should call the baby Bacardi? It really is a nice name but I need to think about it. George thinks it's a mistake to call a baby after a bottle of high-strength alcohol. Is he right? I'm hoping a name will just present itself to me over the course of the coming months.

Shit! Germany's scored. That wasn't in the plan! England can't lose this match. Not now. Not when they've come so far and Dean has worked so bloody hard. They can't, please God, let them equalise soon.

'Goal!!!'

Blimey, have England equalised? How has my plea to God been answered so quickly? The guy three rows in front is celebrating wildly with Mich and Suse. The girls are jumping up and down but that doesn't necessarily mean that England have scored; they know as much about football as I do.

The whistle for half-time goes and I look up at the giant scoreboard. Germany 2, England 0. Oh, no. Oh, no. All around me people are talking about how the team misses Dio and what a catastrophe it was that he got injured when he did. 'Not a catastrophe,' I feel like screaming. 'He was targeted and taken out of the game. It was Grimaldi's fault for leaking information.'

Christ, it all makes me angry. Now I really, really want our boys to win, just to show those vile men that there is nothing they can do to stop England.

The second half starts and I'm in something of a trance. I try so hard to concentrate and to watch carefully but it's impossible when during half-time the empty seat next to you has been taken by . . . Abbey Clancy. Yeeees! I know!!!!

'Hi, Tracie,' she said to me. 'Are you OK?'

Am I? I don't know. I've lost my mind. I might be but I'm really not sure any more.

She smiles warmly whenever I look over at her (which is quite a lot, to be fair).

'I think Peter's doing well,' I tell her, which might, or might not, be true but seems like a nice thing to say all the same.

'Oh, good,' she whispers. She has the tiniest doll-like face ever. She's so pretty close up.

'There are ten minutes to go,' she says, while I sit staring at her boots. They're the gorgeous silver, sparkly, thigh-length boots by Louboutin that I have been trying to buy almost *every day* since I first arrived in Cape Town. I'm so cross that I never got them. If I had, then Abs and I could be sitting here in matching boots now. Damn, damn, damn.

'Wayne's scored!' Coleen screams. 'Well done, babe!'

Hoorah! It's Germany 2, England 1 with five minutes to go.

'Come on, England!' the cry reverberates around the fabulous stadium. God, those boots look even better than I ever thought they would. They're lovely.

'Yeeeeeeeessssss!' Abbey is on her feet (the ones wearing the silver boots), hands aloft now, screaming for joy. Peter Crouch has scored in the final minute of the game and is celebrating with his famous robotic dance. It's 2–2. The World Cup final is going into extra time. I can't stand it any more. I can't.

'It's the end of extra time,' says Abbey (she has to tell me what's happening because all I can do is look at her boots). 'You know what happens now, don't you? It's down to penalties.'

'Your boots are nice,' I say. I'm so much more interested in her footwear than I'll ever be in penalties.

'Oh, thanks,' she says with a smile.

'I think they're lovely. Really lovely,' I say. 'I was trying to get them but the shop was shut, then they'd sold out, then they didn't have my size. It was a nightmare.'

I'm chatting on while the teams are trading penalties. Germany 1, England 1. Well done, Rooney. Col sighs with relief. Germany 2, England 2. Well done, Gerrard. Good lad. Germany 3, England 3, Good work, Gareth

Barry. Germany 4, England 4. Nice one, Frank Lampard. Good lad.

'Oh, man!!!' screams Abs.

What? What's happened now? Are her boots too tight? I'll have them if they are.

Germany have *missed*! It's Germany 4, England 4, with one kick to take. The Jules Rimet trophy and World Cup glory rests on this moment. God, I want them to win, I so want England to win.

Peter Crouch walks slowly to the penalty spot and prepares himself to kick the goal that could launch this team into the history books. He seems to stand there forever, looking at the ball and at the German goalkeeper, who's standing there tensely. Then he goes, he runs, he blasts the ball. The keeper dives. THE WRONG WAY. The ball has gone into the net. Crouchy's on his knees. The players are all rushing round him. There are crowds on the pitch. Everyone's jumping up and down and cheering. Fireworks burst into the Johannesburg sky as tiny petal-like pieces of paper fall from the sky and rest on the grass, like snow has fallen on the sun-dappled pitch.

As the players jump up and down hugging each other, we – the Wags – jump up and down hugging each other too. I pull Abs and Col close to me when the photographers appear, and neither girl pulls away. It's the greatest moment of my life. They don't pull away!! They stay there, happy to be photographed with me. With ME . . . Tracie Martin! England have won the World Cup and my transformation from stalker to Wonder-Wag is complete. Oh my God. I think I might die of happiness.

Six months later . . .

Chapter Thirty-seven

Tuesday 4th January 2011

It's cold, sitting here, though at least I'm sitting down. The others are standing as they wait to go in. I'm madly pregnant so I was given a seat (due next week, in case you were wondering and, yes, I did finally manage to tell Dean! If I hadn't, I guess he'd have worked it out by now!). I've been OK all the way through the pregnancy. I wasn't sick after the first three or four months and have felt fine since then. No, the main reason for me having to have a chair to sit in today instead of standing is these boots . . . the silver sparkly ones! Yes, I got them in the end! You'll never guess what happened – the Wags bought them for me! How unbelievable is that? After the Grimaldi episode they asked Mich and Suse what I'd like most in the world as a gift from them to thank me for what I did, and without pausing for breath the two of them said 'silver, sparkly, thigh-length Louboutin boots.'

The day after the match, just after I'd said goodbye to Shiraz and George, the Wags called me into Col's room and they presented me to them. I burst into tears (pregnant equals *very* emotional) and today I'm thrilled to be wearing them to Buckingham Palace.

Oh, didn't I mention that's where I am? Oh, God, there's so much to catch up on before I tell you why we're here.

First of all, Shiraz and George are engaged and getting married in the summer. I'm just thrilled! I never got a new assistant after Shiraz because in a few weeks time I'm going to be getting a nanny to come and help me, so I think that'll be enough staff for now.

Grimaldi was found to be right at the heart of the criminal operation so he was charged and his case is due to go to court soon. He and his horrid wife were pictured in the paper and I didn't feel an ounce of sympathy for them. Then there's Paskia and Oliver who are pen pals now he's back at uni and they've been meeting up every time he comes home. They are the world's sweetest couple. He's here with her today, actually, which is lovely. I've grown to really like him.

Who else do I need to tell you about? Oh yes – when I got back to England I decided to have a heart to heart with Rosie about Dio but she'd already found out for herself what a scumbag he was! So she left him! She's now going out with a young gardener called Manny Cooper and she couldn't be happier. Dio begged her not to go, of course, but it was too late. She's stayed in touch and I think she'll always be part of my life now.

Who else? Oh yes! Mich and Suse are Wags again!!! Can you believe that? They ended up meeting these two guys at the party after the World Cup final and they turned out to be in the reserve squad! They couldn't be happier. I'm so thrilled. They're really brilliant, brilliant friends and even better friends now we're Wags again.

Yep, life's good for me right now. In fact, the only pressing concern is what to call the baby. It's a boy, as I knew it would be, so I'm thinking of calling him Crouchy-

Roons-Lamps-Gerrard-Ferdinand-Barry-Capello Martin. What do you think? It has a certain ring to it, doesn't it? But he'll be called Dean Junior for short. Because that's only fair. I don't want people to laugh at him, do I?

'I have to go in now,' says Dean, as I stand, hug my daughter, and follow my husband towards the queen.

I watch him kneel and think that those trousers are way too tight for kneeling but they don't rip, thankfully – they just stretch right across his buttocks and give me a complete thrill (that's the other thing about being pregnant – I can't get enough of it!). I watch the queen lay the sword on his shoulder, skimming his earrings as she does.

'Arise, Sir Martin,' he is told, and he stands up and winks at me and Paskia.

'Awright, Lady Martin,' he says, as we saunter out of there – me Lady Barrage Balloon in silver shiny boots and him a bloody sir in skin-tight trousers and earrings. Who'd have thought it?